# THE LOST OASIS

BOOKS BY PATRICK ROSCOE

*Beneath the Western Slopes* (1987)
*Birthmarks* (1990)
*God's Peculiar Care* (1991)
*Love Is Starving for Itself* (1994)
*The Lost Oasis* (1995)

# PATRICK ROSCOE

# THE LOST OASIS

A NOVEL

**M&S**

**Canadian Cataloguing in Publication Data**

Roscoe, Patrick, 1962–
The lost oasis

ISBN 0-7710-7579-0

I. Title.

PS8585.0736L6 1995   C813'.54   C95-930344-8
PR9199.3.R67L67 1995

The publishers acknowledge the support of the Canada Council and the Ontario Arts Council for their publishing program.

Song lyrics on pages 60, 61, 64, 66, and 68 are from "I Don't Know Enough About You." Words and music by Peggy Lee and Dave Barbour. Copyright © 1946 Duchess Music Corporation. Copyright renewed. Duchess Music Corporation is an MCA Company. All rights reserved. Used by permission. International copyright secured.

The excerpt on page 205 is from Wallace Stevens' "Of Mere Being" from *Opus Posthumous*, copyright © 1957 by Elsie Stevens and Holly Stevens. Reprinted by permission of Alfred A. Knopf Inc.

Typesetting by M&S, Toronto
Printed and bound in Canada on acid-free paper

McClelland & Stewart Inc.
*The Canadian Publishers*
481 University Avenue
Toronto, Ontario
M5G 2E9


1 2 3 4 5   99 98 97 96 95

For my parents

# Acknowledgements

Portions of this novel were originally published, sometimes in different forms, in the following publications: *Blood & Aphorisms*, *Books in Canada*, *Grain*, *The Little Magazine*, *The Malahat Review*, *Prism International*, and *What!*.

One extract was originally broadcast by CBC Radio, with the title "Peggy Lee in Africa," upon receiving first prize in the CBC Literary Competition in 1990; another extract, with the title "Wild Dogs," received second prize in 1992. A section of this novel, with the title "The Last Postcard From My Father," was reprinted in *94: Best Canadian Stories* (Oberon Press). A further section received an Honourable Mention in *Best American Stories 1994*.

This novel was written with financial assistance from the Canada Council, the Ontario Arts Council, and the British Columbia Ministry of Culture & Tourism.

This is a work of fiction, and any resemblance between its contents and actual people, places, and events might be called coincidental, except that every journey through love and loss is the same, and similarly real.

# Contents

# Prologue

It was in 1971, while we were travelling by boat between Athens and Ios, that Mitch told me about the lost oasis. We? Mitch, my father. MJ and Lily, my older brother and sister. Myself.

Once again, minus our mother.

At that time the voyage from Athens to Ios was much more of an adventure than today, when ferries crisscross the Aegean like so many sleek commuter vessels; or perhaps it is the false memory of any childhood journey in the dark that has turned my recollection of our midnight departure from Piraeus into a bewildering swirl of blinding light and pitch black and too many indefinable shadows. Beside the dock's slap of waves and stink of oil, our ship loomed like an enormous, ancient beast upon the water; it promised, sullenly, another disturbing voyage. A further troubling chapter of a journey that had already lasted too long and showed no sign of ending soon. All at once, amid rough cries and piercing whistles, a panic of bodies pushed me across the gangplank, while somewhere in the confusion, unseen, Mitch called, "Hold on, crew. All aboard, troops. We're off and away."

Finding ourselves, Mitch and MJ and I, on deck without Lily, we feared that perhaps she had been left behind, or had tumbled into the dark water that now churned white below. Then, as the ship pulled from the swarming dock, to an accompaniment of the whistle's deep bass boom that made me jump, Lily came around the corner of the deck with the white valise that she would allow no one to see inside. "Oh, there you are," said my sister in her voice that was always unsurprised except, sometimes lately, in the middle of the night, when MJ and I woke to hear her talking very quickly to herself in a language we could not understand. "There you are," she said, apparently unperturbed that she had lost us, not especially relieved that she had found us. After all these years I still see Lily in one of Preema's discarded sweaters and a skirt donated by the Morogoro nuns, her sharp face framed by a misshapen bowl of brown hair, with thin, scratched legs, and socks falling down around old Mary Janes.

Mitch had decided that it would be much more exciting to spend the night on deck than inside the salon or cabins, where The Sticks in the Mud, our father assured us, were missing half the fun. We were like Jason and the Argonauts in search of the Golden Fleece, Mitch explained, and the sea was full of calling sirens, sort of like mermaids, could we hear them?

While we commenced to huddle upon the cold deck, shivering beside our untidy heap of luggage (for this was autumn), Mitch regaled us with stories of Ancient Greece, of course. He told us, that night, how Icarus had fallen from the sky above this very sea because he had flown too high towards the sun; its heat melted the wax that held his wings together, you see. He didn't listen to his father, Mitch pointed out with special emphasis, striding before the railing with the night spread behind him, and in the distance a shimmer of lights on the land we were leaving. You could see the lights tremble, though they didn't really move at all, I knew; it was distance that made them seem to shake, the same distance that later would cause my memory of this and

2

other ancient moments to quiver continually with movement, always alive.

The feathers of Icarus's wings are still floating on this water, Mitch swore; and even a year earlier we would have rushed to the railing to look for evidence of something white swirling in the sea. But already, by now, MJ and Lily and I were beginning to doubt the truthfulness of our father's stories, though we still couldn't challenge, for example, his famous view of history as metaphor. Aware of our growing suspicion, our father worked, I think, with added effort to inspire us with his vision of how we were, at that very moment, sailing like Jason and the Argonauts through some ancient but eternal Greece.

Lily and MJ and I looked through the window behind us and saw the other passengers installed safely within the shabby salon where uniformed waiters served glasses of foaming chocolate amid warm, smoky air, away from the sound of our father's voice and from the continuous wash of waves, the cries of sirens, the creaking of the ship. And then Mitch called our attention to the night above us where, he pointed, the hundred starry eyes of Argus were spread across the peacock sky.

By this point we had been travelling for several months on our first extended trip back through Europe since settling in a Tanzanian town in 1968; there had been, during those three Morogoro years, at least half a dozen leaps out of Africa, but they were impulsive, abbreviated, over before they began: five days in Istanbul, a long weekend of *siestas* on the Costa Brava, several *midis* in Marseilles. This longer trip was especially different from the others because our ill and usually absent mother, Ardis, had joined us for a puzzling month in Germany to illustrate to us how completely she had become an *auslander*. In the front seat of rented cars she sat silently beside Mitch, who gripped the steering wheel with whitened knuckles and attempted to engage us in rounds of song. *Michael row the boat ashore*, his voice wavered in uncertain solo, in pitch and tone and volume entirely unlike the heartily confident baritone we were accustomed to. Between Heidelberg and Munich and Hamburg and Berlin we fled with increasing swiftness as the month wore on and our mother's silence grew more lasting, more ominous. During the final ten days in Germany we didn't stop to sleep, but over *autobahns* raced through both light and darkness; once, outside Düsseldorf, sometime before dawn, Ardis said, "This is science fiction." Becoming pale and haggard behind the wheel, Mitch instructed us about Beethoven and Schubert, Nietzsche and Kant, all great men, yes, we must not forget the great men. By this point he was hoarse, red-eyed, frantic; in the back seat MJ and Lily and I wore expressions of distaste, wrinkled noses as our father sweated fear. As if suffering temporary amnesia, we had no idea that this mad flight was nothing, or that soon Mitch would take us from Tanzania to travel without stopping for years. Ignorant of both the past and the future, we were relieved if not blissful when that month ended and it was time to say goodbye once more to Ardis, who would return to the clinic in Canada across the world. In the Frankfurt airport our medicated mother looked down at us, bit her lip, and saw a python, a cobra and a viper; twisting on Mitch's arm, she turned jaggedly to the departure gate. I remembered then how, two years before, during an equally disastrous reunion with the family, she had looked towards the Indian Ocean and told me that I must not forget her, not deny her, not ask her for a thing.

And Ios, Mitch now said in a raised voice that after Germany had taken all of Italy to regain its usual enthusiasm, Ios was an island not yet polluted by godawful Americans or crappy cocktail lounges or damned hippies running around everywhere. Ios, he declaimed, was the ancient island home of several gods and heroes; then he must have told us of the battles of Hercules and of the Trojan Wars, and about the oracle at Delphi, perhaps. We knew not to ask our father when we were returning home to Morogoro, for questions concerning time, always tricky for

Mitch, would in this circumstance have produced answers involving at least centuries or, more likely, millenniums.

I suppose we fell asleep the way we often did, with the sound of our father's voice rushing eagerly forward, drawing us towards places we could not see, leading us, in this case, into dreams of flight from an imprisoning island. And when I woke sometime later only MJ and Lily were curled beside me, with travelling bags for pillows. At first I thought, though I was nine and too old for such a fancy, that Mitch had flown away. I went to the railing to see if white feathers from his wings floated on the dark water: for the moon, perhaps, burned as dangerously as the sun. Then I remembered that in Mitch's story the father did not fall into the water, the father reached safe land.

The sleepless ship shuddered and splashed through waves. Again looking through the window behind me, I saw that the passengers inside were now curled in salon chairs, or dreaming straight up, their heads fallen back, mouths open wide. I knew my father could not be inside with The Sticks in the Mud who were missing half the fun, no, he was somewhere on the decks; and I went to look for him as in an early, rough rehearsal for the day when I would search for Mitch half against my will, almost reluctantly, fearful, alone. No one stood by the railings or clambered up or down the narrow stairways that appeared at the most unexpected moments. Only several sailors in dark coats and caps, with lengths of thick rope coiled around their arms, lumbered silently past, like stolid ghosts.

Then I saw my father. He stood at the prow of the ship, on the upper deck, where the cold spray flew like white stardust. Looking directly into the night, he faced a wind that flapped flags above our heads. Without turning, he began to speak as I approached, as if he could hear my steps though I thought they made no sound.

But how did he begin? Why is it that I can't remember clearly how Mitch came to speak, that single time, about the lost oasis? I suspect he approached the matter indirectly, as if it were not his true destination; beginning, perhaps, with a brief account of the brave Spartans and Alexander and the other great men who must not be forgotten, then threading his way like Theseus in the labyrinth through a dozen dark passages of thought until I became entranced by the sound of his voice in the night, how it swept with the wind against my face.

"She's not going to get better, is she?" I interrupted my father in a way I never had; for I knew that, as a rule, he could not hear my voice while his own described what glimmered in his mind. But on this night I interrupted my father because I think I sensed that even all of Italy had not been enough to seal the cracks that had opened in his armour somewhere between Düsseldorf and Köln. It was not what my father was saying at that moment, nor the situation itself, that made me ask the kind of question which children know not to ask. No, it was something in the way he spoke, more to himself than ever, musing just audibly above the waves.

At once my father fell silent, and at last turned to me, as with a great effort of will, as if he had to force his eyes to abandon, for a moment, the horizon before us.

"Richard," he said, surprisingly, for my father never spoke our names; we were always the gang or the troops or the team, Lily and MJ and I. And in fact I was never certain that Mitch even knew our names, just as I was never sure he could see us as separate beings and know, for instance, that MJ was the one who suffered headaches in the Morogoro heat and that Lily was the one who was fearless in a way that frightened me and that I was the one who claimed he couldn't remember the house on Columbia Avenue, couldn't remember Canada, couldn't remember anything before Africa at all.

"Richard," he said, stunningly. "I don't know."

I knew he understood that I was asking about Ardis, not Lily – though I might as well have wondered about my sister, as things turned out. I know, recalling this moment later, I was always surprised that Mitch responded to my question at all – instead of launching into one of his myths that made our mother into the homebody who, like Penelope, was happy to keep the home fires burning while we, the brave adventurers, had the time of our lives searching and exploring, though for longer than Ulysses, longer than ten scant years, longer than any odyssey, and never finding.

It was then my father told me, that single time, about the lost oasis.

# I

## The Foreign Country of the Past

"There is no pleasure in travelling, and I look
upon it more as an occasion for spiritual
testing. . . . Pleasure takes us away from ourselves
in the same way as distraction, in Pascal's use of
the word, takes us away from God. Travel, which
is like a greater and a graver science, brings us
back to ourselves."

– Albert Camus

# i.

"He finally did it."

The voice cuts through the telephone line, slices across the world. From its jagged edge I know my mother hasn't taken her day's medication. Sometimes she forgets. Sometimes she flushes the gaily coloured pills down the toilet and struggles grimly to get through a week without them. When the old hallucinations begin again – distortions of sight and sound others experience only in dreams and dismiss in daylight – she gives up and has the prescription refilled. Before the bathroom sink she holds the glass of water in one hand, the capsule in the palm of the other. Her lips press tightly together. She hates the pills, she needs them. If she is to stay out of the psychiatric wing of the Brale Regional Hospital.

"*¿Que estas diciendo?*"

The receiver in my left hand is cold, my lover's sleeping body beside me warm. Jose always sleeps more soundly than I do, slipping into unconsciousness with a speed and an ease I envy and remaining there despite shrieks of cats and sirens outside the window. Reaching into darkness, I fumble for clock on the floor beside our mattress. It tips over, falls silent for a beat, continues ticking.

"Don't pretend you've forgotten English," warns Ardis. "Don't play that game with me."

"I was sleeping," I explain. "It must be four in the morning here. What's wrong? Is it Lily?"

"Why don't you listen? I just told you. It's your father."

I remove the arm Jose drapes over me while we sleep and sit up. Cold air presses against my bare skin. I start to shiver. It is nearly winter in Sevilla. No, despite three years in Spain I have not forgotten English, but never speak it except during the language lessons I give and during calls like this from Canada.

"First there was a phone call, then a letter."

Ardis's voice fades out and in; perhaps it is the connection, or she is fighting to hold onto what she has to say. Her sentences are short, their rhythm jerky. Something is wrong besides a lack of medication.

"Both said the same thing. Both were from a Mr. Hurd at the Vancouver consulate. Your father has disappeared. It looks like the real thing this time. Not just another of his stunts. He was last seen definitely nine months ago in a town named El Jadida. South of Casablanca, in Morocco. The Canadian consulate in Rabat reports that his passport was found seven weeks ago, not in El Jadida, but somewhere south of Agadir. Near some café in the middle of nowhere, near some godforsaken desert town. So far the Moroccan police have turned up only that lead. Only a passport, not a body. 'Death not verifiable' is how they put it. Just a minute. I have the name of the place in the letter."

"Does the name matter?" I wrap myself in a corner of the blanket. I've expected a version of this phone call for as long as I remember.

This second call, I amend. Remembering MJ.

"I don't know what matters and what doesn't. Here it is.

Smara. You have to call it something. I don't know. Why don't you ask your father what matters? Why don't you ask him that? He's the man with all the answers."

"I thought he was in Nepal. I'm sure I received a postcard from Nepal a month or so ago. He wrote that he was keeping up the fight – whatever that means. Wait. There was another card, a few weeks ago. Yes. From Morocco. It didn't say anything in particular. Just another of Mitch's fine phrases. A flourish. You know how he is."

"No, I don't. I never did."

"He always turns up in the end, doesn't he? Just when and where you least expect." The damned Spanish phone line echoes, throws my words back at me mockingly, doubtfully.

*Expect. Expect.*

"Listen to me. Your father has disappeared. I thought you'd want to know. I don't know what I thought. They say they're doing everything they can to find him. 'Every possible effort.' That's so you don't think they're making only a halfhearted one. 'A serious situation. We will keep you fully informed. Very concerned –'"

"Does Lily know?"

"Lily's in the hospital again. Lily can't know anything now."

Ardis begins to weep softly, helplessly – until she chokes, as if someone has suddenly strangled her.

Except for a faint, high-pitched whine, the line is silent.

"It's funny," continues Ardis. Now her speech is rapid, driven by panic. "I dug up the other letter. The one about MJ. They're almost identical, except for names and dates and places. They must have a form letter they use in these situations. I suppose it saves time and trouble. It's probably best that way. You start to worry when the bureaucrats get creative. Anyway. I'm hanging up. I have to call Mitch's precious sisters. They'll blame me. As usual."

"All right. I don't know what I can do from here. Send me a copy of the consulate's letter and let me know as soon as you hear anything. Jose would say hello, except he's snoring."

I hear Ardis sigh. "Pinch his nostrils shut, force him to breathe through his mouth."

A click. A series of rapid beeps. I hang up.

*Don't ask me.*

*Ask your father.*

*He's the man with all the answers.*

Jose groans, stirs, mumbles in his dreams. I lean towards him and try to hear what he says. He often wakes me, talking in his sleep. Sometimes I am able to distinguish a single word or cryptic phrase, and make a mental note to remember it. My lover doesn't tell me nearly everything: I need to gather as many clues as I can, any way I can. *Everything you need to know is always right in front of you*, my father used to tell us. *All the pieces of the puzzle. You only have to learn to recognize them, learn to fit them together.* Maybe I am a slow learner. By morning I have invariably forgotten what Jose said in sleep. Maybe I am learning slowly to live with an incomplete puzzle.

I light the candle beside me on the floor and reach for scattered clothes. We came home late last night, undressed each other between yawns. In the kitchen I put on water for linden-flower tea; the blue butane flame trembles beneath the pot. Back in bed I sit cross-legged, my back touching Jose, my hand around the mug. Warmth. Beyond Jose's breathing and the ticking clock stretches silence. The throngs of Saturday night Sevillanos who roam the streets, singing and clapping until late, have gone to bed at last. I flick my lighter and inhale smoke; the candle spits, throws off the glow Jose and I made love within. A golden halo shudders around me. I stare into the flame until my vision blurs, wavers, shifts.

## ii.

My mother still lives in Brale, a small town in the interior of British Columbia, where my father brought her as a bride in 1957. They were married in a double wedding (Ardis's younger sister, Beverly, was the other bride) at her father's place in Cedar, on the Island. A month after Ardis graduated from nursing school in Victoria they drove through the Fraser Canyon on their honeymoon, spending nights in motel cabins along the way. They stopped frequently beside the road for Mitch to photograph Ardis, with a scenic view as background. Ardis posed tensely at the canyon's edge, the world dropping away behind her, beside a roadsign warning of deer or falling rock. In May the evenings were still cold among the trees, beneath the mountains; during the day the air was crisp as an apple. Along the narrow, twisting road they encountered little traffic on their way to Brale, where they moved into the house on Columbia Avenue after a year in his parents' basement, across the river in West Brale. They couldn't afford their own place right away, not on a teacher's starting salary and what a nurse was paid. Mitch taught history and physical education at the small high school in Salmo, out past Fruitvale, and Ardis worked shifts in the hospital on the hill until first MJ, then Lily and then I were born there. We lived in the Columbia Avenue house together until 1965, when Ardis entered the hospital as a patient; Mitch took us children away from Brale the following year. I was four, and Lily and MJ two and three years older respectively.

In Brale, Ardis had from the beginning proved more than just a stiff woman with an ability to make a room's emotional climate uncomfortable. Mitch's four sisters, who all lived in the town, did not grow more at ease with Ardis over time. They read conde-scension in her silence, and, among themselves, said Mitch had probably made a mistake. He could have married a local girl; Shirley Hamilton had given him more than a fair chance. Even early on there were disturbing signs and awkward incidents; they owed to Ardis being from the Coast, Mitch explained. "She's my Island Girl," he would say with a blend of unease and pride. At this time Ardis was perhaps the only woman in Brale with hair dyed platinum blond, a dislike of curling, bowling and canasta, and a subscription to *The New Yorker*.

One afternoon Ardis said she had to go to Safeway to buy milk. They found her five days later in a Seattle hotel, registered under her mother's maiden name. The man who had accompanied Ardis upstairs from the hotel bar telephoned the front desk in alarm when she went into the bathroom with the bottle of vodka and locked the door behind her. *There were worms in her veins, she could feel them wriggling through her blood, she had to get them out, she wanted me to help, we required a special kind of knife.* They needed to break down the bathroom door; then Ardis wouldn't release the pipe beneath the sink where she was kneeling. When Mitch arrived six hours later with his brother-in-law, Ivan, Ardis sprang at him, not with affection. In the front seat, between Ivan and her husband, she hissed softly during the drive back to Brale.

People did not break down in Brale in 1967, not so anyone

noticed, not in public. They appeared fine until the day they waded into the Columbia River or took a hunting rifle up into the hills. That Ardis chose to appear not fine in Seattle, a city in a foreign country, was the worst part for Mitch's sisters. They were still sensitive about the States after what had happened, seventeen years before, with Aunt Annie and the American. You crossed the border for shopping trips when the Canadian dollar was high or for orthodontic appointments to fix the crooked teeth of Brale children.

Ardis was diagnosed, tentatively, as schizophrenic; they weren't sure, they had to call it something. Joining Doukhobor women with tendencies to set themselves on fire, she entered the psychiatric wing of the hospital where she had worked and given birth. Ardis didn't request to see her husband or children during the remainder of 1965, and her doctors said they couldn't advise such contact if she had. A year later, while Ardis was still isolated in the hospital, Mitch and the children left Brale; the timing would always look bad, whatever angle you saw it from. The irony was that the idea to try the family's fortune overseas had originated with Ardis more than a year before her hospitalization. She hated the small town from the moment she had set foot in it. Blind as Brale was a simile she invented.

She was the only one, of all of us, to remain permanently there.

SNAPSHOT: BRALE, 1963

In the photograph it is always summer. The grass at Gyro Park hasn't dried brown; probably this is July, when sprinklers that tick like crickets during the night can still keep Brale green. The light indicates late afternoon, any time between four and seven, with the shadow of an oak to the extreme right (only half its trunk is in the frame) falling partly across the spread blanket, which is blue wool, with a narrow yellow stripe. This is called the car blanket: it usually remains folded in the trunk, nearly forgotten beside the

17

spare tire and jack, ready for some obscurely envisioned emergency. At the left of the blanket, in sunlight, stands a partly open wicker basket, its contents dim, only to be divined. Nearby is a large red thermos that held Kool-Aid, flavoured lemon, strawberry or lime, for the children. A dozen children, siblings or cousins, are not in view. The older ones must be swinging or climbing or sliding in the playground behind the bandstand, where on the third Monday of each May the high-school band performs at Victoria Day festivities; the younger children (some are still babies in 1963) climb over or stagger around three sisters who, in madras shorts and halter tops, sit beyond the camera's eye, on folding lawn chairs with aluminum frames and striped webbing made from a hard, shiny material that feels like plastic. The sisters' names, in order of descending age, are Madeleine, Kay and Dorothy. Absentmindedly, expertly, they swat and pat and throw babies between each other. They have dark hair worn in short curls, and complexions whose duskiness does not owe entirely to summer. The eldest, Madeleine, has peculiarly slanted eyes that suggest a secret strain within the family blood, from somewhere east of dark Romanian forests. The fourth and youngest sister, Jeanette, is taking the snapshot with a box camera she received as a wedding gift six years ago. She squints downward. Her marriage was celebrated in the backyard of the old West Brale house two years before a Christmas fire took their father and their youngest brother, Donald, only twelve, into the cemetery sloping beside the mountain road where the mother already lay, and two months after the bride graduated, as an RN, from St. Joseph's Hospital in Victoria, where her roommate was a girl from a hundred miles up the Island. Jeanette's older brother, next to her in age, would visit from Vancouver, while at university there. He met the roommate; that started. Madeleine, Dorothy and Kay call advice and instruction as Jeanette prepares to photograph them. From their chairs they warn her not to move; at the same time, they try to make her laugh. The husbands of these sisters are at the other side of the park, tossing horseshoes through the air, which arc upward then land with a soft grunt in the sand, or ring against the iron pin. Several cases of beer also lie outside the frame; Madeleine, the sensible sister, has pointed out that they wouldn't make a wise addition to the scene, not with the family's history so far as drinking goes, not after what happened to Aunt Fan and Aunt Lena.

The subjects of the photo, posed nearly in the centre of the blanket, are a young man and woman. He is dark-haired and dark-complected, obviously brother to the sisters, and wears brown swimming trunks. He has drawn his legs into an inverted V with feet planted a yard before him and knees pointing into the air. His elbows drape loosely around his knees and his hands meet, lightly clasped, in front. The man is named Mitch. His black eyes are narrowed against the sun, his mouth widened into a smile. In streaming light he leans slightly towards the camera. It is almost possible to see drops of water clinging to his shoulders, and his hair looks wet to the touch; he has been swimming the Columbia River despite the current, reaching and then returning from the flat rocks in midstream. In the background, beyond a low stone wall, lies a glimpse of the water. It appears benign, blue, a half tone deeper than the sky.

The woman beside Mitch, separated by several inches, not quite touching, is named Ardis. She and Mitch have been married for six years. Her hair is platinum blond around a pale face turned to the left, away from Mitch and the camera. She wears bright-red lipstick and sunglasses with coral-coloured frames shaped in the current cat's-eye fashion. Her limbs escape from a light summer dress of white cotton patterned with small blue flowers. Her legs are drawn under her from the side and one elbow rests on her knees, one hand supports her chin. A cigarette extends from two fingers of the other hand, half-smoked, beneath the faintest smudge of grey. The oak's shadow divides Ardis into light and dark; this effect is uncalculated by Jeanette.

Ardis stopped working in the hospital on the hill when her first child was born, four years ago. Now there are three; she stays at home; the house on Columbia Avenue shrinks. It is fourteen years since Davidson, Saskatchewan, and the silent father in the night. It is fourteen years before her husband and her eldest son, at separate times and in separate directions, take peculiar leave of Brale, of her, for good. In three-quarter profile Ardis's face gleams like stone. Shadow moves farther across her in the time Jeanette peers through the lens. The group around the blanket falls silent as the shutter whirs. In the distance twine voices of children.

So Ardis stayed.

In 1966 we left her in Brale, Mitch and MJ and Lily and myself, to spend the next two years in Europe. Getting our feet wet, Mitch called it. There was a winter of wet feet in Paris, where my father worked at American Express, in charge of client mail, and he was with the Rome bureau of the *International Herald Tribune* for five equally damp months the following year. In between we wandered north during summer and south in winter, until Mitch secured a teaching job, through CIDA, in East Africa.

My memories of those years before Africa are vague to the point of non-existence – I was only four and five – and I had later to rely on MJ and Lily for an account of them. I suppose Mitch began then to develop the tactics for survival on the road that he would employ with greater refinement when we later found ourselves moving from place to place again in the early seventies. Except for several snapshots, I am left with no clear images and have, over the years, created my own history of that time. This version of the past has served me well enough – at least until now.

I know that Ardis's doctors kept Mitch informed of her condition through reports sent to Paris, Rome and poste restante addresses. I have copies of these documents; they form part of the papers I take care not to lose no matter how often I move. Reading them over, it appears that Ardis's mental health improved then worsened in roughly six-month cycles. The doctors repeatedly assured Mitch that our presence in Brale would not serve Ardis any useful purpose – perhaps the opposite, in fact – and they couldn't think of allowing her to join us, in Brale or anywhere else, for the time being. Through the years the doctors steadfastly insisted that it was contact with her family, rather than its unsettled existence, which resulted in Ardis always returning to the Brale hospital, from the visits she made with us, starting in 1969, in a severely deteriorated state. They would remind Mitch that they never advised these visits in the first place.

Much later, I learned that Ardis had been subjected to an extended course of electro-shock therapy. Though this form of therapy is never mentioned or even hinted at in the hospital reports, it is possible to estimate, from description of her general condition, when it was most heavily administered. And while Ardis had managed, by 1974, to leave the hospital and to stay out of it afterwards, and to live fairly functionally from then on, there is no reversal of certain procedures. Not all kinds of damage can be repaired. I have only to look to Lily to see further proof of this. And to myself.

"I had no way of knowing," Mitch would later say, if I brought up this subject he preferred not to acknowledge. "Even if we had stayed in Brale, damn it, I couldn't have known what was going on up on the hill."

Yes and no. Mitch's sisters told me afterwards that everyone in town knew something of the situation all along. The nurses talked. And certainly it was possible to see, when Ardis staggered off airplanes on the arms of nervous flight attendants, with a page of detailed, dubious instructions from her doctors, that something was seriously amiss upon her visits to us in Morogoro or Munich. It might have occurred to Mitch that the psychiatric wing of the Brale Regional Hospital was not the most advanced centre for treating mental illness; more enlightened care might, one would think, have been available in, for instance, Vancouver.

"Son," Mitch would sadly shake his head. "It's just a crying shame."

To MJ, Lily and me, our mother was simply frightening. She remained a stranger we didn't want to know. The deterioration which occurred during her alarming visits may well have been the emergence, upon a numbed mind that was slowly thawing, of symptoms of disturbance only suppressed, not treated. It's hard to say. In the end, it was never established that legal permission necessary to administer the electric shock was ever given in Ardis's case. Mitch denied signing any papers.

What I don't know and can't know is how much it cost my mother not to speak, not to respond, and not to touch her children when she realized, somehow, that the only communication of which she was capable could do them no good.

How much it cost her to see them, after long absence, and to know the best she could do for them was nothing at all.

Ardis slips from the white Peugeot and past the beggars before the greengrocer's. There are always five or six of them there, squatting on cardboard islands in the dust, wrapped in rough brown cloth, eternal victims of flies. They reach out hands, they whimper and moan to me; though we speak a separate language, and they have moved beyond words anyway, I understand what they want: we need the same thing. Their limbs melt in the Tanzanian sun, shrink before my sight: shortened fingers, toeless feet, bare rounded bones like handles of old walking-sticks smoothed by constant touch. They could be male or female, young or old. *Leprosy*, Ardis has told me. I hear her firm, clear voice – this is one of her good days – inside the store, requesting oranges and mangos, rejecting imperfect produce. The main street of Morogoro is empty in the middle of afternoon; there are only the beggars and me. Once a month police with clubs herd them out of town; through the night they shuffle or limp or crawl back to their place before the store to wait for me again: they will always return, I know. Lily and MJ say that if a beggar touches you lightly, even once, you will catch what it has, and no medicine will ever cure you. The features of your face will crumble into dust, blow away across sisal fields, scatter upon the four corners of the earth – until even your own mother and father would not recognize you. Then you too will squat in the dirt, moan eagerly when anyone comes along to spit at you, accept anything as alms. *Don't touch*, Ardis says when I reach towards the red ring on the stove, the red ring around her mouth. I kneel beside the beggars: they fumble at my empty pockets, then stroke my ordinary limbs. I close my eyes and feel the unique imprint of their touch, hands shaped like no other hands in the world. A lipless mouth kisses the centre of my forehead. I am blessed; all outcasts are holy, says the Koran. Ardis emerges from the store, her string bag filled with brilliant tomatoes, perfect papaya. We stretch out hands to her, we whimper and moan. All we want is a single coin, small and round and flawless, to hide within our rags. We have learned not to ask for much; give us only a token of pity, please. Now I am missing one ear, a nose; this is only the beginning: one day my soul's straitjacket may disintegrate with divine disease, my heart lose its cage of bone. Ardis glances indifferently down, her cool summer dress is just beyond my reach, the white Peugeot pulls away. Then the street is very silent, very empty.

They had let her out of the clinic too soon or she returns to us too late. In 1969, four years after she unwillingly enters the cold white rooms in Canada, Ardis flies with one light suitcase to where we have ceased waiting for her on the Ngondo hills of Morogoro. Mitch explains to Lily, MJ and me that she will seem different after having been apart from us so long; he does not prepare us for muscles twisting like taut ropes beneath dead white skin, for eyes looking a little beyond whatever falls before them, for her head constantly turning to see if someone stands behind her. "Did you get the presents?" she asks in a voice roughened and deepened by all the medication. Sometimes in Occupational Therapy Ardis fashioned gifts for us: on her eighth birthday Lily received a clay ashtray painted with anguished faces of flowers; for my sixth Christmas I was sent a papier-mâché paperweight supported by more wiry legs than any spider has. In the airport Ardis looks at us evenly, taking in who we are and what we might ask of her. Then she looks away, and she will not see us again, except as another feature of the landscape, like the bent baobab at the end of Mitch's garden. During the drive home from Dar es Salaam Lily and MJ and I hang over the front seat and watch her bite her lip, silent. Perhaps she is struggling to find appropriate words, suitable sentences. "Judy Garland died," she finally remarks, flatly. "She died to save us all." Mitch's hands tighten on the steering wheel; Ardis looks beyond what is ahead of us. Apparently this continent that she has never seen is familiar to her nonetheless. Schizophrenia has shown her everything already, nothing can surprise her now.

I believe, mistakenly, that the beggars before the greengrocer's suffer so I will not. Their sickness is my health; their want, my wealth: we are that closely connected. Later, I come to think that the beggars are blessed with wisdom which increases in direct proportion to the gravity of their disease and need. As compensation they are endowed with magical powers, like wizards and witches who with waves of wands can alter flowers into foetuses, sticks into snakes. Now, as in the year before they took her away, Ardis cannot touch me or her other children: despite the doctors, her hands are still poisoned. They would leave a pale patch upon my skin, the first sign of sickness that spreads and erodes and eats at bone, tissue, cartilage. When I fall and scrape my knee, her

24

mouth twists, her hands clench each other tightly in her lap. I stare at her entwined fingers which are stained with nicotine. I would like to tell her that I am already contaminated by need, that it is too late to worry about contagion now. Ardis is infected with the power to transform terrain into symbols which speak its truth. The baobab beyond the wall, the armies of ants which file relentlessly through the garden, the mica glinting upon the road: what do these things mean beyond themselves? Ardis has learned to hoard knowledge which they call madness. This is all that is left to her, she will not speak. Or possibly each of her visions is the product of a biochemical disturbance of the brain, the tendency towards which may or may not be hereditary. I do not know then that I will spend my life fearing Ardis's secrets, which I am convinced are the same secrets guarded by all the indigent and infirm, and in denying that they are only distortion. I am persistent as any unwanted thing: if you drive me out of town with your blunt, heavy clubs, I will always crawl or limp or shuffle back.

At the beginning she is always careful, like a paroled prisoner who dreads being returned behind bars. After her most casual comment she will glance towards Mitch to read his reaction; he has become the doctor with the drugs, the warden with the keys. This is only a conditional release, she knows. In the afternoon her limbs flail the Morogoro Country Club pool, churn enough laps of murky water to equal the width of any ocean, pull her finally out to pant in a puddle on burning cement, short blond hair darkened with wet, dreaming. Lily and MJ and I are supposed to play healthy childish games in the distance. Instead, concealed by fences and shrubs and camouflage, we stalk Ardis like spies, watch her stride back and forth across the roughly stubbled golf course, swinging her club at the ball, sending it out of sight, playing one round after another until sunset, when, with burned skin, she drives us home. There she sits on the verandah and looks down into the valley. Her cigarette's smoke winds through the air like the steam from the train snaking through sisal fields below. Mitch straightens his back from his gardens, shades his eyes with one hand, watches her sink into her private shadows. This is more than he bargained for; perhaps already he is planning his famous disappearance into the desert, twenty years in the future, far from the acrid taste of medicated kisses. Inside, the houseboy fixes food, makes sure our clothes are changed, our faces washed. Sometimes I separate myself from Lily and MJ who dance rings around the lemon tree and in weak voices sing the song about the circle game. Stealing up on Ardis from behind, I whisper into her neck, then watch her back stiffen, the cigarette fall from her fingers. *Mother*, I say into her shelled ear. A moment later she rises to walk swiftly to her room, where behind a closed door she whimpers and moans, pleading for Mitch to pity her with a pill.

Sometimes for long periods the heavens are clear and calm. Ardis makes careful lists in handwriting that does not waver, composes intricate menus with many courses for the houseboy, at the market requests perfect produce in firm tones. Then clouds return, and she dozes on pills in the afternoon, wanders from her room to ask me what time it is. Her face is puffy, her short blond hair uncombed, a trail of fallen ash follows wherever she roams the cement-block house. Halfway through the rainy season she no longer makes an effort to keep up appearances, doesn't hastily comb her hair and put on lipstick when she hears Mitch whistling home from work. She stops making casual comments that might meet with anyone's approval. With one finger she pokes at the wire-mesh screens that keep out snakes, makes minute openings which Mitch will not notice. Escape is always on her mind.

Before sleep I chant my prayers to Judy Garland and Jesus, then in dreams lipless mouths open to impart essential information into my waiting ear. The surrounding world requires interpretation;

five senses are not enough. From the eroded ovals, however, emerges only moaning. I waken to realize this is really the painful sound Ardis and Mitch make together in the dark.

Later she begins to vanish. When Lily and MJ are at school and Mitch is at work, Ardis will put on lipstick, tie a scarf around her head, drive off in the white Peugeot. The grey house beats with silence. The houseboy will only answer yes or no; he pushes me away, gently but firmly, when I try to touch his smooth black skin. The dirt road to the village beyond the college is wide, and shaded by ancient trees. Huts are grass and tin, flowers of coloured clothes hang to dry in shrubs, children as small as I am flee at my approach. Ardis's voice emerges from a hut, garbled and incomprehensible as a foreign language, though the white Peugeot is not in sight. When I knock on the door, her voice falls silent; birds still whistle about over the rainbow and way up high. The door won't open, there are no windows, it must be black inside. Ardis must be feeling the darkness with her hands, it must be dissolving her form, rendering her invisible for another four years. I crouch in the dirt before the hut while shadow lengthens and the hills above turn deeper green. Now Lily and MJ will be home from school, colouring pictures and playing crazy eights in our room. Then Mitch will also return, change out of his good teaching clothes, work in his gardens that bloom with the speed and brilliance of hallucination. The supper will be silent except for the screams of crickets outside in the dark. Later we will lie in bed and listen for the white Peugeot to crunch the gravel drive. The car door slams, the kitchen door opens, Mitch begins to beg in their room at the other end of the house. Lily and MJ hold breath in beds near mine. Years later I will study their photographed features, faces thinned and hardened by the effort required not to ask for anything.

Once she takes me with her. When the white Peugeot has passed the edge of town, she stops to kick off her sandals and to open all the windows. Then we are flying faster and faster along the narrow road that winds all the way to Dar es Salaam. Her bare foot presses hard against the pedal; wind whips her scarf and tears my eyes. I blink to see soldiers chew sugar cane beside the road, spit pulp at our swift passing. Her eyes are fixed straight ahead; she doesn't glance or talk to me. When her foot presses right to the floor the engine begins to whine, the metal body shudders. Sometimes, hitting a rough place, the car seems to lift into the air for a mad moment as timeless as a skipped heartbeat. We rise and fall across the hills until the sky is red and clouds are bloody and the Indian Ocean stretches beyond a foamed shore before us. I ask Ardis what is on the other side of the water. She bites her lip; a fleck of red sticks to a tooth. Now the palms are disappearing and *dhows* drown in darkness. We sit in the car and watch waves turn silver as the moon, the stars. There is a great gulf between us, as much salty space as separates this shore from Zanzibar. I can't see what is across the water and I can't see her face when at last she speaks. "Don't ask me for anything again," implores Ardis in the dark, before she vanishes back into the clinic at the other side of the world. "Please," she says, before she turns the key and takes us slowly home.

In 1974 we returned to Brale and the house on Columbia Avenue, in which Ardis's younger sister had been living while we were away. Her doctors had emphasized all along the importance of Ardis knowing that she had this house below the hospital, that she always had the choice of living there with Beverly. Ardis had elected that option more and more in the early seventies. By the time we returned to Brale, she had been out of the hospital nearly a year.

She never entered it again.

A new course of medication stabilized her to a certain degree. Sometimes she was withdrawn and frightened, haggard with the effort required to keep distortion at bay. Sometimes she retreated to her room for several days and emerged especially shaky, uncertain. At thirty-nine her face was etched with deep lines; her hair was mostly white. She would always move and speak with caution. My brother, sister and I learned to avoid sudden motions and abrupt or unconsidered conversation around Ardis. We already knew not to make demands of her. Later, when she was able to discuss these years with me, Ardis said she would have done whatever it took to remain permanently out of the hospital.

When I like to remember now, what I need to remember about my mother when the mirage of her Morogoro visit looms before my eyes, are the two visits I made to Brale in the eighties. She lives quietly in the Columbia Avenue house, not seeming aware that Mitch and MJ left years ago, not seeming to notice that they have never come back. She looks after Lily when my sister is able to leave the hospital on the hill where she also ended up. "I can take care of her better than anyone," Ardis says, mouth twisting into her version of a smile. "I know what it's like." The mortgage is paid off and a monthly government cheque covers Ardis's modest expenses. My mother's needs are not many, it seems. Her brother-in-law, Ivan, puts up the storm windows in autumn and shovels the sidewalks during winter and clears the gutters beneath the eaves each spring. The house itself is unassuming on the outside and painfully neat inside, with little indication of the personality that inhabits it; much is unchanged since I left in 1978. Now, Ardis says, she no longer fears returning to the hospital, and remaining outside is not so taxing on her.

"You can learn to live with anything," she says during my last visit to Brale.

More and more I understand the subtext of those words, how they apply to me also.

And now I think of the drives we made out to the lakes and up into the mountains in a rented Ford. Ardis doesn't have the chance to get out of Brale often; she doesn't own a car, and is no longer able to drive, though once, I know, she drove swiftly, expertly, daringly. I notice how intently she observes the scenery. We both watch leaves turning on the maples and smoke rise from burning leaves in backyard fires. Often we are silent together in the house; conversation is difficult because she has forgotten so much even about yesterday. It is necessary to navigate carefully around the large holes burnt out of her memory. And we don't mention Mitch. Sometime between my two visits she stopped wearing her wedding band. Or maybe she lost it.

When Ardis proposes, one midnight, that we have chicken for dinner, though we had chicken for dinner three hours ago, I say that's a great idea. "Let's make chicken with mushrooms and onions and white wine," I say. When she wonders worriedly why MJ is late for dinner, though MJ hasn't been home for dinner in eleven years, I suggest we wrap some of the food in foil for his return. "He'll be back soon," I say, though none of us have heard from my brother in all these years and he has, apparently, disappeared for good. The coffee Ardis makes after our midnight dinner is only water; she forgot to put anything in the filter.

"I forgot," she cries, in the alarmed voice of a small child.

Suddenly I understand the meaning of a mixed blessing: I am presented, at this moment, with the thorny gift of knowing my mother as a girl of six, fifteen years before my birth. I experience her voice, manner and reactions as a child at the same time that I look, with awe, at someone who has survived the furnace, the holocaust, the white-hot current. Time bends, twists, knots around me.

"No, you didn't forget," I say. Looking at her, I smile and raise my mug. "Cheers. This is the best coffee I've ever had."

And it is.

All around the house are deposited notes Ardis writes to her-self. They remind her to pay the phone bill by Tuesday and to take out the garbage on Friday and to mail Beverly a birthday card next Wednesday. She forgets where she leaves the notes and writes others, that will also become misplaced, reminding herself to look for them. Though Brale is a small town, she is unable to leave the area right around Columbia Avenue or she will become lost. She can find her way to and from the nearest bank, postal outlet and Safeway. If she is to venture further, say across the bridge to downtown, someone must go with her.

Yet she refuses the suggestions, made by Beverly on the Coast and her inlaws in Brale, that someone live with her. Beverly would move back to Brale; her second husband has died, her chil-dren have left home. When the subject is gingerly raised, Ardis quickly leaves the room, shuts her bedroom door behind her, closes the topic. She will not consider, either, weekly visits by a home-care worker.

"I do all right," she says.

Once, I wake to feel something is not as usual: the hall light is on. The empty house throws me into panic. I have been told that several times, before she learned she couldn't go far on her own, Ardis was found weeping in West Brale, unable to remember where she lived.

"I'm out here," she calls from the back porch.

She stands, arms folded in front of her, looking above the line of rooftops and trees behind her house, to where the hospital hovers on the hill. Lights always burn up there, open eyes shining down, watching. Is Lily watching?

"It's nice out," says Ardis at three a.m. "You can still feel the summer."

She's right.

It is nice out and you can still feel the summer.

Back home, in Sevilla, I know that my mother sometimes

forgets to eat and sometimes forgets to take her medication. I know that often she sleeps during the day and passes the night sitting on the living-room couch, an afghan she made in the hospital around her shoulders. She touches the arm of the couch and feels the rough knit of its thread. She knows that it is really there, that she is really there. Sometimes, on those nights, she calls long distance to ask me something, in the indirect way she has developed to discover information she realizes she shouldn't have to ask for. She wants to know what day or year it is. She wants to know how old she is. She wants to know her middle name.

"Joan," I say, and I remember Mitch calling her Ardy-Joan, how he sang the name.

Yet she is able to speak easily, and in detail, about when she was a girl, before marrying Mitch, a wild Island girl who hitchhiked up and down the Island highway in 1953. Her hair was still long and dark then. It flew around her when she jitterbugged in Qualicum, when she ran laughing with Swedish loggers along the Parksville beach, drunk beneath the moon. It was beautiful in Cedar, in the big house right on the water. The trees, she says. I'll never forget the trees.

My mother and memory.

I try to imagine what it must be like not to remember your middle name or what you wore on your wedding day or when your first child was born. Jose calls me *elefante* because I never forget. For years I have lived inside memory, within a house constructed of photographs and letters, doctors' reports and airline schedules. What if the walls and roof of this house vanished – I know my home is as flimsy and fragile as a house of Japanese rice paper beneath a hurricane – and like my mother I were exposed to the elements of sky, weather, landscape, and the kind of trees, cedar and arbutus, you can never forget? Would that mean a sort of freedom as well as fear and loss? Should I envy the dark patches of my mother's memory, her bitterly mixed blessing? For having only the present moment to touch to prove you are here. To be stripped of nearly everything that has come before, all the occurrences that combined to make you an uncertain, ageing being, alone and lost.

Mitch would say: There is no such thing as being lost.

I say: There is no such thing as being either lost or found if you are unable to remember the place you have come from, the place where you belong.

Sometimes, lying awake beside Jose in the dark, I can't help but remember that over a decade ago MJ said he was going to Montreal to look for work and was never heard from again. Six months later Mitch also vanished from Brale, to return only in the form of postcards mailed from places like Afghanistan and Irkutsk. Ten months after that Lily slipped like a snake from the skin of sanity, curled hidden beneath a flat stone in the hospital on the hill, more mad than our mother. What happened to us all? I ask incessantly of Judy Garland and Jesus. I think both Lily and MJ tried to follow our parents in the only way they knew how, as if it were possible to arrive where they dream in the distance and to discover their private places.

Then, as Jose sleeps beside me, I remember Ardis placing her hand over mine as we sat with coffee that was only water, at the kitchen table or before the living-room radio, in Brale, in 1988. She left her hand there for a moment that seems now to lengthen until it lasts as long as all the years that have gone before. A light weight. A warm touch. A hand nearly the same size and shape as mine, with long, slender fingers, their knuckles swollen, ending in nails bitten to the quick. With veins rising high upon the surface, faint purple, faint blue. I watch blood pulse through them. A slow throb, a visible beat. The rhythm of life. Of love.

*Does the name matter?*

*You have to call it something.*

*Ask your father what matters.*
*He's the man with all the answers.*

Grey light of dawn enters the window and birds begin to sing outside. Jose still sleeps beside me. The scent of wax hangs heavy in the air. The candle has burned low; I pinch it out. I am cold and stiff. I should get up and hunt for my father's last postcard. Check to see if there is special significance in its message. A final goodbye before he disappears one more time, apparently the last time, into the desert.

Instead, I shake Jose's shoulder.

He groans, sighs, opens his eyes.

"*¿Que te ocurre?*" he mumbles.

"Wake up. Something has happened."

October 25, 1992.

# iii.

"You have to find your father."

The terrace on the south bank of the Guadalquivir is nearly empty, and illuminated only by stray lights from cafés in the Calle Betis above. The evening is chilly. In a week this terrace will close for winter; most of the summer *chiringuitas* along the river have already been dismantled, left to August ghosts who speak among the orange trees. Upon the water below waver blue and red reflections, the neon signs of bars, and the *Lola* floats downstream on one of the season's last excursions. From it spills frantic music and laughter of South American tourists who raucously drink and dance on board. Suddenly, nearer the bank, as silent and swift as a bird, appearing to skim above the surface, though its oars shatter gold and silver river light, dipping in rhythm, six on each side, shoots a canoe rowed by twelve boys, shapes and faces indistinct, made delicate by darkness.

"You're the only one in your family who can find him." Jose takes a long, slow sip of beer. His grey eyes regard me evenly. Like his hands, they always calm me.

"I know. I fucking know."

It is not a question of suddenly leaving Jose to search for my father; we must probably separate anyway, at least for the time being. Jose has to finish the year-long military service he began two months ago. While enduring basic training in Cáceres, to the north, he was allowed home on weekends, and would return from camp with the smell of dust from the journey. His body vibrated a long time in my arms. The *mili* is infamously unpleasant; young men go to extreme lengths to obtain medical exemption. Some break down during the course of the year and most require months to adjust to civilian life once it is over. Battle-scarred, shell-shocked, hardened: something is different. Outwardly, Jose has changed already. I am still not used to the extreme shortness of his hair, how it makes his face appear younger, more vulnerable. He is deeply tanned from outdoor training and his hardened muscles hold me more tightly when we make love.

Because he is tall, strong and athletic, and has received excellent scores in target practice and field manoeuvres, Jose has been one of a few selected to serve the remainder of his year as general's bodyguard, in Madrid. There is a dangerous element to the assignment – high-ranking military are targets for ETA terrorists – but he will enjoy greater freedom and better living conditions than ordinary *soldados*. After completing a month of further, specialized training, stationed in Madrid, it will be difficult, because of time and distance, for Jose to see me in Sevilla regularly. There is nothing to prevent my joining him in the capital, except it is not an easy place to live unless you have money. Other considerations must be weighed as well. Jose has a week's leave for us to decide what to do.

"I've already spent enough of my life following my father to places I didn't particularly want to see," I say bitterly. "Why has he done this? Why Africa? Why now? I bet this is another of his damned panning for fool's gold. I bet I find him in some place like Algeria, working as guide for parties of trusting tourists, leading

36

them into the desert without a map or compass, feeding them inaccurate information about every single thing with sweeping certainty. Charming the socks off them, accumulating invitations to visit Lausanne and Bordeaux. Breaking hearts."

"We can be together for good by next summer."

"*Why son*, he'll exclaim. *Great that you stopped by to pow-wow with the old man.* Surprised as hell that consulates are faxing his vital statistics across oceans. Getting a big kick out of the whole thing. Amused to death that anyone would think he could ever get lost. What a laugh. He has the worst sense of direction of any-one I know."

"You can store your things in a back room of my mother's store," says Jose. "I'll tell her you're a friend. I think she knows about us anyway. I think Reyna visited the store and had a long talk with my mother in April. You know how Reyna is."

"My dear friend Reyna should stick to belly dancing. I can just see it. He'd love to catch up on old times, but he has a party to take out at sunrise. Nothing he'd like better than to have a few beers with his boy, if there weren't important preparations to make. *I'll tell you what*, he'll say, inspired. What he'll tell me is that, hell, he'll be in San Sebastián by spring, he's got an offer there too sweet to turn down, enough wampum in it to set himself up in Monte Carlo, put his feet up at last. We'll hook up in San Sebastián in April, he might just be able to use me there, San Sebastián is only a skip and a jump from Sevilla. Right?"

"Summer's not so far away." Jose lights a new Ducado. His foot touches mine beneath the table. A secret signal. A promise that in an hour we'll be making love.

When I met Jose two years ago I was as thirsty as a man who has been travelling by foot across the desert for ten years without water. For ten years mirages shimmered before me with promise of water and shade. I discovered repeatedly, during ten long years, that expectation of thirst's imminent slaking in fact causes thirst to increase until you are unable to think of anything except the water you need and lack. Until you are unable to weep or sweat or urinate. Mitch, there is nothing you could tell me about the desert I don't already know. I know the blackened tongue and the burned retina and the eternal scratch of grit in mouth and eyes. I know the desperate visions of Allah's outcasts. There is nothing I don't know about hope dashed a thousand times inside you but still lodged there as heavy and unyielding as the heart of stone. And when by the power of miracle you finally do find water it is nearly too late; you are almost dead, certainly weakened, dazed, dried to the core. Not all kinds of damage can be repaired. Disbelieving, you deny the fact of water even as wet kisses repeat its real presence again and again: it is true, Reyna, this miracle of slaked thirst is true. These green palms and orange sand-roses are not hallucination, I incredulously wrote two years ago to the belly dancer in Manhattan, who knew, herself, about unrelenting, unremitting sand.

Jose has spent two years patiently, repeatedly proving he is true. No matter how close I come to him, apparently he will not vanish into only air.

"You're lucky to have a father to find," Jose says.

His own lives on Gran Canaria, self-exiled on that island, still talking the extremist politics that drove him from Sevilla a dozen years ago. After a certain point following Franco's death, democracy took hold in Spain and the new king, Juan Carlos, was no longer mockingly nicknamed "The Brief"; by then it was not wise or even safe to occupy the position of assistant secretary of the Partido Nueva Fuerza de Andalucia. Skimming the writing on the wall, Victor Manuel fled to Peru, where his political convictions might find a more sympathetic audience and where he married, though not divorced from Jose's mother, an ageing heiress whose money dematerialized with the groom shortly aftet the honeymoon. Victor Manuel eventually surfaced in the Canaries and currently imports construction materials, with

20 per cent taken off the top, for tourist complexes springing up on Lanzarote.

Jose has told me childhood stories of pasting propaganda posters in Sevilla streets at two in the morning. The bucket of glue overturns in sudden brawls with dissenting passersby. The telephone transmits anonymous threats at all hours of day and night. Rude graffiti appears on the family's apartment building. Jose sings me the song about the new light and the old fight he marched to, wearing a pale-blue uniform with golden buttons, silver piping and green bandana, at December 16 Fascist youth rallies.

The family fortunes took a difficult turn with Victor Manuel's flight in 1981: whatever toehold that had been achieved was lost. Jose's mother was forced to give up her Los Remedios dress shop and begin to sell cheap calculators and clock radios in the small gift bazaar where she still stands behind the counter. She had to move her children into cramped quarters on the wrong side of Sevilla. They had to leave school early to work. A dozen years without seeing or hearing from Victor Manuel has not made Carmen's or her children's hearts grow fonder for him. They would turn the man away if he showed up at the door. He is dead.

"*Hijo de puta,*" says Jose, spitting to his left.

I imagine that our fathers are in many ways not dissimilar, though they would probably despise each other on sight. There is a common capacity for embracing experience with enthusiasm and without regard for consequences, and a shared flair for the broad gesture at the expense of significant detail. Look at the big picture, Mitch was fond of saying. Late at night, in bed, Jose and I compare notes on fathers, top each other with increasingly outlandish stories of how our fathers entered the arms of geography and history in ways that excluded their loved ones. Sometimes we have been able to laugh at our fathers' fierce, foolish belief in the other side of the mountain, the greener pastures, the far horizon.

Now the Triana terrace is deserted except for ourselves, and our glasses of beer are empty. The *Lola* nears its dock on the other side of the river, below the new opera house, and the music on board is winding down. The South American tourists are quieter; Jose and I have fallen silent.

"We never went on the *Lola*," I say at last. "I always wanted for us to sail on the *Lola* once."

"Let's go home to bed," says Jose.

Go, whispers Reyna, the belly dancer, swaying invisibly among the orange trees.


Jose kisses my eyes and I see pink flamingos take flight above Lake Nakuru, scatter across Kenyan sky. They have lifted into the air through desire or alarm; it's difficult to know why the atmosphere is filled with beating wings, and no less easy to discern the pattern of this flock, how it hangs together to form one shape, an entity, more than a confused collection of separate forms too numerous, swooping, dazzling. Eyes turned heavenward, silent, a man and three children hover around a white Peugeot parked beside an empty, badly paved road, with brush stretching in all directions. The flamingos vanish to the north, not migrating, moving for a more mysterious reason as Jose's lips move to kiss my throat.

I have explored but never completely understood the path that took me from Lake Nakuru (for example) to these rooms three floors above Virgen de la Antigua, the street where I live, beside this lover who now strokes my back almost as if I were a lucky lamp capable of offering three wishes. I have never figured out fully the twisting of that path or the landscape through which it ran. Reyna, has the possibility been raised by a disappeared father that I cannot really inhabit this safe harbour – Jose's arms – until I know more thoroughly the voyage that brought me here? There is still more travelling to do, Mitch and the desert demand, more of that curious motion, backward and forward simultaneously, that lies beyond chronology, outside itinerary.

We make love silently, Jose and I, concentrating intently upon how our bodies move together, looking fixedly into each other's eyes. A drop of sweat falls from his forehead onto mine.

The clock ticks beside the mattress.

Five more nights together.

iv.

*The curious motion, backward and forward simultaneously, that lies beyond chronology, outside itinerary.*

It would be a fairly simple matter for me to stitch together the names of the places Mitch took his children after permanently departing the Morogoro Teachers' Training College in 1972. I could match the appropriate cities with the appropriate months of 1973 and 1974, line them up one after the other, create the illusion of an itinerary not entirely divorced from the laws of cause and effect. I could trace paths on a map with variously coloured pencils. Employ visual aids to suggest a reasonable approximation of a pattern. Give the big picture.

For instance.

Jakarta came after Ankara but before Bogata. In Jakarta there was always wind from the bay lifting dust and chewing-gum wrappers and shreds of dead palm fronds, and in Bangkok (Bangkok was after Bogata, Bangkok was before Manila) a blue cloud of automobile exhaust crawled among the beggars and shoeshine boys and soldiers staggering between strip bars on three-day passes. In Bangkok neon flashed *Girls!* and *Live!* along the main drag, but there was no electricity in the slums, constructed out of Third World garbage, visible from the palace.

I leave the big picture to Mitch.

I am interested in detail.

I am compelled by the fact that the Royal Hotel in Manila was financed two-thirds with piastres and one-third deutschmarks, and owned by a consortium whose interest was controlled, until 1977, by a trio of Iranian brothers with a Cayman Islands letterhead.

It interests me that in 1973 the Royal Hotel offered twenty-four-hour room service (except, puzzlingly, on Wednesday) with a menu printed in French but priced in American dollars.

A *salade niçoise* costs three U.S. dollars from the Royal's room service in 1973.

In Manila.

As opposed to Bogata.

The room-service menu of the Hotel de la Paz in Bogata did not offer *salade niçoise* in 1973.

I know how much *salade niçoise* costs at the Royal Hotel in 1973 and I know that the ice machines in the Athens Sheraton are on even-numbered floors and I know that in 1973 the Aeropuerto de Libertad in Bogata was not equipped to handle anything larger than a DC-9, but I don't know what Mitch's occupation was during the two years between leaving Morogoro and returning to Brale.

He was involved in an operation.

He had a little business to take care of.

An iron in the fire.

It is difficult to imagine what business could be competently taken care of in Manila or Bogata or Bangkok by a Canadian citizen with a bachelor of arts (major in history, minor in geography) and a teaching certificate from the University of British Columbia.

The operation that could be efficiently handled by a man whose international work experience consisted, officially, of four months at the client mail window of American Express in Paris, five months at the Rome bureau of the *International Herald Tribune*, and four years with the Morogoro Teachers' Training College in Tanzania, East Africa, where he was head of the history department as well as its only member.

I am speaking about a man with a lamentable lack of talent for languages and a man for whom the fluctuating rate of exchange between, say, sterling and lira was never less than baffling and a man with the poorest sense of direction of anyone I've known.

It is worth noting that Mitch did not attempt to operate in Geneva or Frankfurt or New York. In the early seventies systems of international communication were not as widely existent or extensively used, outside these centres, as even five years later; economic and political procedures still possessed a strong local eccentricity, especially in the remains of colonies, especially upon their fringes, beneath the table, on the edge of what was legal. There a man's white skin carried a certain built-in power, more so if he were handsome, and radiated confidence, a sort of lunatic charm.

Mitch understood, I think, that to a point the currency of charm and confidence does not fluctuate.

I have my own kind of chronology.

My own way of keeping track.

I remember where we were during 1973 and 1974 by, among other things, birthdays and movies and the Muzak in hotel elevators.

The Muzak is least useful in pinning a specific time to a specific place; everywhere sounding the same vaguely wistful note, it seemed designed to deny the differences between places or at least to dim them into a comforting blur, smoothing the edges between, say, Singapore and Spain, in Bombay as in Bonn murmuring familiarly into your ear, like the voice of an unimpressive acquaintance you believed, without regret, had been left behind for good.

Any place we went, during 1973 and 1974, was likely to feature, in the elevator, an identical rendition, cheerful, joyously subdued, of "Raindrops Keep Falling on My Head," which revealed versatility by providing ironic commentary upon either an unusually forceful monsoon or a dry season extending to worrisome length.

"Raindrops Keep Falling on My Head" played when Lily turned thirteen in Manila and when I became twelve in the penthouse of the Hotel Carlotta in Mexico City and when MJ's fourteenth birthday occurred in Cairo.

To celebrate MJ's birthday, Mitch took us to see the pyramids and the Sphinx. The expedition was itself a gift, for Mitch did not usually have the opportunity, or perhaps inclination, to take us to view tourist attractions of places we visited; despite stays of some duration in both Paris and Athens, we never ascended the Eiffel Tower or explored the Parthenon. To this day I find myself dismissing a place's principal point of interest, which has proven itself worth visiting to many people over many years, as lying outside the sphere of my concern and having no part in my purpose at all; for example, during three years in Sevilla I have not climbed the Giralda, to enjoy the panorama afforded by its pinnacle, though I probably pass the site a dozen times a week.

And so it was memorable to stand with Mitch before the great joining of lion to man that crouched, still ready to spring, upon the desert floor. "They don't have anything like this in Brale," he informed us, then lamented again that, less fortunate than us, he hadn't begun to see the world until leaving home at eighteen. With our head start, we had the chance to travel farther than he would ever go. We had more time. Strolling between the ancient monuments, among his children, Mitch turned pensive and his black eyes glowed. In the lengthening afternoon great spans of time stretched behind and before him, and at the farthest limit of his vision uninterrupted desert still reached forward, unfolding beyond his sight, unseen by his eyes. Mitch's gaze slowly slipped out of focus. He mentioned the past and future in abstract ways, and hinted that one day he would be old. Later we became used to hearing our father bewail his fate as a decrepit old man, cry over his wasted limbs while they were still strong, remonstrate against the ravages of time before they began to appear in his face; but on this day his sorrow for his future decaying self was new and moving, not yet cause for impatience in MJ, Lily and myself. We walked nearer beside Mitch, protectively closing the flank against invisible enemies; none were in sight, only two parties of Japanese tourists, and one of German, at a distance. Mitch seemed to become, beside the disintegrating symbols of a past civilization, aware of his mortality for the first time. Gravely pacing the desert, hands clasped behind his back, Mitch called us the fruit of his loins and with quickened interest peered at us sidelong, all at once curious to see what he would leave behind. What remains of his image would crumble beneath wind and light and heat, scatter in all directions, far and wide, add slightly to the enormous, dry expanse? My father seemed to become aware of his children in a newly attentive way that day upon the desert. Perhaps he realized we would always reflect, as long as we lived, what kind of man he had been; people who had never known him would form an opinion of his character by what they saw in us. For a moment we shifted into sharp focus for Mitch; his regard was shy, tentative, tender. He snapped a photo of us astride a camel – MJ in front, Lily in the middle, myself clinging on at the rear – with the Sphinx as background. Suddenly solicitous of our comfort, he bought Coca-Colas and twice asked Lily if she didn't need his coat against the gathering chill of desert evening. He inquired of MJ how it felt to be fourteen and wondered if I still wished to be an astronaut when I grew up. Was that, in fact, my true destiny?

46

We were confused beneath the unfamiliar weight of our father's full attention, perplexed into silence, self-conscious as strangers he scrutinized for the first time while receiving an initial, lasting impression. Happening upon a wooden pole, Mitch grasped it firmly in one hand and with it pierced the ground at each step, as though making holes in which seeds could be planted, or leaving hints of our path, hieroglyphics in the sand, for anyone who might wish to follow. Later, as we walked away from the arrangements of stone and the lights that flooded them, for now it was nearly dusk, the steadiness of Mitch's gait indicated he was prepared to walk, purposefully, a great distance, and his eyes left us to fix on the horizon. Lagging behind our father, we glanced back.

As light drained from the landscape Mitch seemed to tire from his visions. He leaned heavily upon the pole; now it transformed into a walking-stick. His step grew slower, more ruminative, until he paused. Before our eyes he seemed, standing there, to age and shrink, in fact to disintegrate as the carefully preserved objects in rooms sealed deep inside the pyramids – now only black shapes without precise size or shape or definition in the distance – fly into dust the moment they are confronted with unfamiliar light and air. I imagined my father disappearing before me: he dissolved into particles of darkness, a million disconnected atoms trembling like risen dust, that pressed around me and separated me from MJ and Lily, until with a question I sought the sound of their voices, proof of their presence nearby still. For we were again several details in the corner of Mitch's eye, only distraction flitting beyond the main focus of his vision; in this case, stone pointing into sky, time and death, human effort. And as we faded from our father's view, it seemed to me, we dimmed in each other's eyes also, MJ and Lily and I, becoming less distinct even to ourselves, not only because light was lacking. Then Mitch began to speak, as darkness curved around the earth and the pyramids loomed larger, about the pharaohs and the slaves. Over a million lives were spent to build one pyramid, he said, waving to where

Cheops waited resurrection as a higher being. Later, said Mitch, a similar number of Chinese died in constructing the railroads in North America. It's the same story, he told us, drawing a hasty, imprecise map in the sand, with arrows pointing out connections we had not made and could not easily discern even with faces bent near the ground, in darkness. It was equally unclear, from my father's words and tone of voice, whether he identified with the slaves or with the masters. But Mitch wished to say something else – not to us exactly, more to the air itself; his voice strained as he tried to express further ideas, still unformed inside him, lurking latently in that inner darkness, about the desert and the pyramids and the slaves. He wanted, perhaps, to discuss his span of time upon the planet and how this time could best be used. He tried again to tell us, but his voice failed him, now becoming the harsh croak of a parched throat that has not swallowed water during a dozen days of dust and heat. Mitch fell silent, and then we heard only the cries of vendors with the day's last bottled drinks and ice cream. Mitch's thoughts drew away from us, as we neared light and people, like a train that rushes from the station, unable to linger once the conductor has rung his bell, hurtling forward across dark plains, its whistle entering dreams forgotten by morning. Throwing back his head to search for the first star, throat curved like a sickle moon, Mitch stumbled on a stone. On either side – MJ to the left, Lily and I to the right – we increased slightly the distance between our father and ourselves.

We were quiet on the journey back into Cairo, and appeared strange to each other beneath the harsh light inside the city bus. The doors and windows were left open to let in the night air; though it had cooled, we could still smell heat and dust and diesel fumes. Something was always rotting, fruit or meat, nearby. MJ, newly fourteen, stood near the driver, at the front. A bat flew through the doorway and immediately wheeled back outside, a claw nicking MJ's right nostril in the turn. A thin stream of blood ran from my brother's nose into his mouth. He didn't try to wipe or lick it away; he wasn't yet sure what had happened. The Egyptian passengers, descendants of desert slaves, drew back in alarm. For the remainder of the ride into the city, whispering anxiously, they stared at MJ while Mitch turned out pockets in search of the handkerchief he didn't have.

September 10, 1973.

Perhaps we didn't visit the pyramids and the Sphinx that day.

Perhaps Mitch rowed us upon the Nile to celebrate MJ's fourteenth birthday.

Lily curls at the prow of the small boat, her hand lingering in salute above her eyes to shade them. The craft is made of wood, painted pale blue, that has peeled and scratched, with three narrow benches for passengers. Mitch is in the centre, at the oars, explaining the importance of drawing them through water neither too shallow nor too deep, and of exerting even effort with both arms to ensure a straight course. Beginning to sweat in the hot sun, he tells us that the Nile is not really green or any other colour; the blue or green or purple of the water is in fact only the reflected colour of surrounding land and sky. When I am about to trail a hand in the water, to see if it is as cold as it looks, Mitch cautions that the Nile is the most poisonous water in the world. The slightest contact with the skin, he warns, would mean an infection that spreads like leprosy. Allowed to take the oars because it is his birthday, MJ proves less skilful than our father; accidentally he sends the Nile into the air, sprinkling Lily at the front. She flinches, cries out, waits for her flesh to dissolve like that of the lepers before the greengrocer's in Morogoro.

September 10, 1973.

I possess a photograph of three children astride a camel, in front of the Sphinx.

I possess another photograph of the same children, apparently at the same age and certainly in clothes identical to those of the first photo, sitting in a small rowboat moored to a dock in what I believe is the Nile, though the water is not green or any other colour, for that matter, appearing more a muddy mixture of several tones, or a combination of tones that cancel each other out.

I assume Mitch took both photographs.

In both photographs the tallest child, a boy, wears a white cowboy hat, probably brand new, tied beneath his chin.

Several things occur to me.

First I wonder if Mitch took us upon the Nile and to the pyramids both on my brother's fourteenth birthday. That seems unlikely: my memories of these places involve a whole day, not enough time for pyramids and Nile both. I am quite certain we were only once in Cairo. There is no easy explanation for how two photographs could exist.

I wonder, second, if a white cowboy hat is an appropriate present for a boy's fourteenth birthday, regardless if celebrated on the Nile or beside pyramids, or somewhere else altogether.

In the kind of chronology that I have over the years created to give shape, however unlinear, to 1973 and 1974, it is possible for us to be present at the Royal Hotel in Manila and the Tunis Imperial Yacht Club at the exact same moment. In my system of chronology it is possible for us to grace at one time several places separated by great distance, as if during 1973 and 1974 each of us inhabited a number of identical bodies and lived a number of distinct, simultaneous lives, though always together, father and three children. In my system time unfolds on various planes at once and I find nothing startling in a photograph of those days that depicts, for instance, the Alhambra in Granada rising next to Bangkok's Temple of the Golden Dawn.

If Muzak is least useful and birthdays problematical, then movies are the most helpful and uncomplicated element of my system.

My system of history, my method of chronology.

It is easy to know for certain that *Cabaret* occurred in Bogata and that *The Sting* was in Jakarta and that *The Way We Were* unfolded before us in Mexico City.

(Mexico City came at the end; everything finished in Mexico City.)

These films were usually dubbed into a language we understood scarcely or not at all, and we followed them through intent observation and sheer willpower and a burning desire to know. Our senses heightened to compensate for our incomprehension of language; like the blind we developed sharper hearing and like the deaf keener vision. In time MJ, Lily and I became expert at piecing together plot and interpreting action without dialogue to explain them for us. We grew adept at making the most of every clue – the indifferent tone of voice, the hand's dismissive gesture, that burning look in her eye – to give reason to what took place before us, on and off the screen. In several cases our strained attention (we watched in deadly silence, absolutely mute, not once acknowledging each other or unknown spectators) was not enough. We never understood, despite extensive, heated discussion, why Barbra Streisand did not live happily ever after with Robert Redford in *The Way We Were* (Did the reason centre around Streisand's choice of hairstyle, as I staunchly proposed?) and why Liza Minelli and Michael York also separated, in Berlin.

In Bogata and in Berlin.

We never understood, not really, why Mitch didn't live with Ardis ever after, happily or not.

*All the pieces of the puzzle are right before you,* Mitch would say. *You only have to know how to recognize them and how to fit them together.*

Mitch didn't like the movies. He said that he was too busy living to waste time watching others live and that life was large enough in itself and that movies softened the brain; furthermore, he didn't enjoy sitting among strangers in the dark, trapped next to people he probably wouldn't sit near in the light, unable to see their faces to know if they were cruel or kind, enemy or friend. We remembered the times Mitch accompanied us to the movies in Dar es Salaam, when we were younger and lived in Morogoro; how he fidgeted in his seat, twisted constantly to peer at people behind us, whistled and muttered under his breath, and finally impatiently paced the lobby beyond the theatre where *Mary Poppins* or *The Sound of Music* wove magic for MJ and Lily and I, enchanting us with the notion that all the world except where we breathed was a cinematic land, enthralling us in the darkness, making us reluctant to leave our seats for the long, night drive back to Morogoro.

But Mitch allowed us our pleasure, in 1973 and 1974, parting from us beneath a marquee in the same way he would have left us before a Pentecostal tabernacle, not willing to give up his own soul to the strange religion of Hollywood and not wholly approving of this cult for ourselves, but unprepared to stand in our way. In front of theatres that were called, wherever we went, The Strand or The Starlight, The Bijou or The Lux, we watched Mitch move away from us, hands in pockets and eyes raised to the sky, strolling down the sidewalk more quickly than when he was with us, until other, unfamiliar faces got in the way and we could no longer see him. Beneath coloured neon lights we glimpsed how our father might have travelled more swiftly without us, perhaps discovering much sooner the place that shone, in brilliant Technicolor, inside his head.

Then we turned inside the movie theatre and forgot Mitch at once.

In the movies we saw during those years, my brother, sister and I watched wrenching separations occur in larger-than-life dimensions before our eyes, without understanding clearly why these final partings took place, or what chain of circumstances and events could divide people from each other.

I remember Mitch waving, in the Athens Sheraton, what I now know was a report concerning our mother's mental health.

"Another love note from Ardis," he informed us, reading what he pretended were extracts from a breezy epistle meant for all of us; he was sharing the good parts with us now, we could read the whole thing later ourselves. "She's happy as can be keeping the home fires burning. We shouldn't hurry back. We'd just get in the way."

When we asked later to see the letter, it had always vanished in a way that offered Mitch the chance to impart another piece of wisdom about the travelling life. "You can't keep everything when you move around like we do," he would confide. "You have to learn what won't fit into your bags, what must be left behind."

"Travel light, travel right," our father said.

If I think carefully, I don't recall Mitch ever admitting his wife was not well. (Later, if confronted, our father might refer obliquely to "the hospital" or "your mother's difficulties" or "the crying shame of it all.") He didn't like sickness. It frightened him; blood terrified him. During our childhood maladies he always pressed into service one of the sympathetic women who pursued him without (I think) success. "I'm no doc," he would confess, rocking on the balls of his feet in the doorway, making a quick escape, leaving us in the moist hands of an expatriate Anglo, single, married or divorced, whose already watery eyes brimmed at the sight of a brave man doing his best with three children far from home. Violet or Elizabeth held teaspoons of medicine to our lips and subtly grilled us for information my father withheld. They were never clear if our mother was divorced from Mitch or dead or about to join us next week. In their ignorance these women were kept off balance and eagerly helpful, expectant and excited before unstated possibilities which were insinuated by a glance or word from Mitch but never materialized into anything concrete, only dissolved with us one morning into thin air.

Like his charm and looks and children, Mitch's wedding band served its purpose.

He had a way of allowing the clear features of his face to cloud with unspoken suffering during certain key moments (at passport controls when the visa situation was sticky, before hotel reception desks when the credit had run out); then his normally strong, erect shoulders slumped visibly beneath the burden of caring for three motherless children in a foreign land. "Yes, it's hard," he would murmur, gazing towards us tenderly, painfully. "But they're good children and I'll do whatever I can to keep us together." His arms went around our shoulders, his hands cradled our heads. Gathering us close, he presented the necessary picture. Nearly always the passport was stamped, the hotel key relinquished.

As we grew older, this picture lost much of its poignancy. During 1973 and 1974 MJ, Lily and I ranged anywhere from eleven to fifteen in age; we were gangling, awkward children, apparently incapable of entering adolescence, strangely clothed in bargains Mitch picked up at flea markets here and there. No longer so young as to be endearingly innocent or touchingly helpless, we were rigidly silent, especially around strangers, in a way that appeared obstinate or stony but was really the silence of the sleeper who, though incapable of speech, is occupied with complex dreams which throng his darkness. Eventually, towards the end, Mitch had to strain hard to present us convincingly as lost lambs, and it became uncomfortable to watch him struggle to achieve this effect, like a skilled actor made impotent by bad material.

If I remember 1973 and 1974 through the movies we saw then, it is no wonder I often see that time itself a movie, with Mitch, of course, the star, and we children hovering in the background, extras without lines, and Ardis on the cutting-room floor.

Sometimes my peculiar chronology fails me, whatever system I employ.

✧

For a surprisingly long time, though, everything worked.

"All right, troops," Mitch commanded in any new hotel room, snapping his fingers and inspecting the amenities. "Let's get cracking. Remember, we're in this together."

There was a system for settling into a new hotel (or, if we were lucky, a furnished apartment rented by the week) as there was a system for clearing airports quickly and packing bags efficiently and locating restaurants with the best balance between economy and luxury.

I went down to re-inspect the hotel lobby, restaurant and (from the doorway) bar, and, supposedly, to ingratiate myself to porters and bellhops, desk clerks and housekeepers. Lily unpacked the bags, arranging Mitch's clothes in the top bureau drawer and ours, in order of descending age, below. MJ entered expenses incurred in transit between this place and the last into the log. Mitch took off his shoes and began work on the telephone, calling first the cultural events department of the Canadian embassy and the office of the local English-language newspaper (but not the *International Herald Tribune*, not after what had happened with the expense account vouchers in Rome in 1967), then moving on to the American Centre and the Friends of Britain Abroad. Later he would perform stretching exercises and push-ups in the centre of the room, while with books and cards and drawings we settled at its edges. We tried to ignore our father counting off repetitions in a hearty, satisfied voice and didn't respond to his invitations to join in. Mitch headed for the showers, then slapped aftershave upon his face and neck; turning this way and that before the mirror, he admired his reflection from various angles. By evening he would be striding out the door, clean and glowing, in his one good suit and pair of shoes, to attend an embassy function or a press party. "Contacts," he reminded us. "We can't do anything without good contacts."

Mitch instructed us, unnecessarily, to call housekeeping to take care of laundry, then room service for dinner. "And don't forget," he added over his shoulder. "Write a postcard to The Homebody."

The Homebody was Ardis.

She was also The Keeper of the Flame and The Stick in the Mud.

"Your mother has many fine qualities," Mitch frequently told us. "But she lacks our spirit of adventure."

*Wish you were here*, I dutifully wrote on the back of a postcard depicting the Temple of the Golden Dawn, in Bangkok.

*Everything is fine*, MJ wrote on the reverse of a view of the Tunis Imperial Yacht Club.

*Manila (or Paris or Vienna) is nice*, Lily printed neatly.

We were obedient children. I think we learned early on that we had to band together and that there was no point in questioning Mitch's hidden agenda. After he told us enough times that we were in this together, we believed it true. When our spirit of adventure was continually lauded, we were unable to doubt it existed. Mitch reminded us how lucky we were until we knew it for a fact, despite constant clouds of unease hovering over our heads and disturbingly shaped shadows trailing after us even at high noon; they suggested that nothing about our situation, eating *salade niçoise* from room service in the Royal Hotel in Manila, could be described in terms as simple as luck. But what could we have done? Written to Mitch's sisters in Brale, whom we envisioned as endlessly practical and easygoing, asking them to intervene somehow? Approached a policeman, while our father's back was turned, requesting political asylum from a dictatorship we deplored? Mitch discouraged us from forming acquaintances, however brief, with children and adults who crossed our path; he strongly suggested that we would find them a waste of time. They were not "good contacts," as anyone could see from a glance. They did not share our spirit of adventure or live upon our heightened plane of existence or have the luck to experience the wonders of the world with a father who was teacher, philosopher and adventurer in one. Mitch reminded us – constantly, sadly, pointedly – that he had not left Brale until age eighteen and that they definitely didn't have this, that or the other wonderful thing in Brale.

I don't recall even covert rebellion against Mitch's plans, as first MJ and then Lily entered tentative adolescence. In fact, to me the most remarkable aspect of this time was how little we seemed to have changed except to have become increasingly silent and withdrawn, as though we conceded without battle that puberty's storms had no place in Mitch's itinerary. The private games we played with cards and dice to keep ourselves amused grew more intricate, with complex rules evolving into a labyrinth of what was and was not allowed, so twisting that it would have been impossible to guide a stranger through its dark maze. Pretending to ignore our father, we secretly watched him more closely, out of the corner of one eye always observing him if he were in the room, as you know to keep a dangerously unpredictable animal in constant view. When he was not present we allowed ourselves to criticize him vehemently but in small ways. Lily scorned how Mitch parted his hair and MJ thought ridiculous Mitch's manner of shaking hands so energetically and I believed my father foolish to engage every taxi driver we rode with in political discussion.

And we spoke about Brale. Our memories (or, in my case, fantasies) had evolved into the surreal by 1974. We would often talk about Brale when the lights were out and Mitch was still somewhere with a contact; in darkness it was easier to create a place without resemblance to where we really were. In Brale every house contained three children and two parents. In Brale a single maple tree grew in every backyard and with an affection-ate dog three children gambolled around it always. Taxis and airports and hotels did not exist in Brale and in Brale nothing rotted, nothing changed. Brale was a place where everyone knew everyone else, and no unfamiliar face ever appeared on its tidy, clean main street. For years I believed the B.C. after Brale stood for Before Confusion.

We knew our mother had not remained in Brale exactly to keep the home fires burning. Until roughly 1970 we sometimes received in the mail odd notes and small gifts from her which left us disturbed for days; then these stopped, and Mitch began to read us the cheerful extracts from letters we never laid eyes on ourselves. We regarded Ardis carefully and cautiously during the six months she visited Morogoro in 1969, and, later, during a month in Germany, a month in Rio de Janeiro, and a few months in a few other places. Something was clearly missing in her besides a spirit of adventure. But we could not ask her what it was when obviously she did not know herself. We watched Ardis silently bite her lip, her body arranged in awkward angles in the chair, her eyes numb and puzzled. She always hesitated, cautiously, before she spoke. She looked apprehensively at Mitch, who vowed she would feel tip-top once she got back her walking legs.

As soon as we got moving, we would all feel A-OK.

When from time to time Mitch left us in a hotel or furnished apartment, to keep an appointment that would take him away for several days, we spent the money he gave us carefully, deliberately weighing the price of pleasures – a movie, ice cream, a book – against the amount of enjoyment they would bring. We never answered the telephone. (I still think nothing of letting mine ring, here in Sevilla, as if it had nothing to do with me at all or were a summons as distant as the bells in the Plaza de Encarnación, three blocks away.) We never spoke with strangers and we never went anywhere alone. Even after Mitch had been gone for three days we behaved exactly as if he were still there, as if he watched us always, like an invisible secret police, or god.

There are some negative images, never developed, too fragile for exposure to light, that I keep safe inside my mind. They show three children in a room on the twentieth floor of a hotel. After calling housekeeping and room service, after eating *salade niçoise* while the sky darkens, the children lean out the window (this one opens, others don't) and watch the lights of the city below switch on, not all at once, first a swath over here, then a swath over there, in mysterious succession. Voices spiral upward from the street, blurred beneath the sound of honking horns, sirens and taxi radios. There rises the scent of something rotting, of automobile exhaust, perhaps the ocean. Superimposed upon this image, as in a film's slow dissolve, occurring just after it, is another of three children sprawled silently on the floor around an arrangement of cards they move from place to place, in patterns an invisible spectator like myself would be hard pressed to figure out. There is the soft slap of king on queen, the air-conditioner's hum, a voice out in the hall. At midnight the children flip a coin for the smaller of the room's two beds; the losers settle for extra cots the porter has wheeled in. With the lights out they begin to speak. They discuss what their father's plan might be for this particular city. They place bets on how long they will inhabit this hotel and what the next hotel might be like. They fall asleep on pillowcases smelling faintly of chlorine bleach after speculating again upon the reasons why Barbra Streisand left Robert Redford, why they had to separate in the end.

By 1974 MJ and I grew used to waking to hear Lily's voice from behind the closed bathroom door. She spoke very quickly, so rapidly we couldn't make out the words or even know if they were English.

"She misses Africa," said MJ. "Do you?"

"I miss everything," I said.

In the morning Mitch is a misshapen lump beneath his blankets. His good clothes are scattered on the floor. On his bedside table lie six small coins, a half-package of chewing-gum, and a book of matches imprinted with the name Flamingo Lounge. Lily, always up first, bends over her notebook in the farthest corner of the room. Seeing that MJ and I are awake, she quickly closes the book and locks it in a small white valise Mitch had given her on her twelfth birthday. "Sophisticated women always need something private," Mitch explained of this gift. "For makeup and love letters and so on." The valise locks with a miniature silver key Lily wears on a red ribbon around her neck.

Mitch doesn't seem aware that Lily possesses no makeup and receives no love letters to store in her valise.

I never knew what Lily wrote in her notebooks during 1973 and 1974. She filled at least several, I think. I have an impression of one with a yellow cover and another with a green. As far as I know they disappeared or were destroyed at some point along the way.

*Write it for me*, Lily said the last time I saw her in the Brale hospital, in 1988, before she discovered God. The words were muffled, as if reaching through a thick layer of cotton. The white bandage was wrapped tightly around my sister's left wrist again. Her face was puffy, bloated. She opened her mouth and twice tried to manoeuvre her tongue to form more words. She stared at me and swallowed with difficulty. She tried to speak again.

*Write it for all of us*, she slurred.

At night three children float in bed and listen to their father play Peggy Lee records in his room at the other end of the new house. This one is built of cement block, and has a tin roof; instead of glass windows, there are wire-mesh screens to let in breeze and keep out snakes. Her cool voice slips out into the hot darkness, *I know a little bit about a lot of things*, silencing crickets, even hushing cicadas. For a moment she is mute: perhaps the father has finally stopped circling his room, ceased sitting on the edge of his bed, large hands curved over knees, head bowed. Maybe he has turned off the light to join the children who now drown in darkness. But then she begins again, over and over incanting the same spell upon a man who is fearful of snakes and who won't ride roller coasters and who feels faint at the sight of his own blood. The tangled jungle pours scent down the Ngondo hills, poisoned perfume wraps around the house.

Sometimes during the day, when only the houseboy is home with him, Richard enters the father's room. On the record covers the woman's face is pale and smooth beneath short waved hair that is more white than blond. Her lips are painted deep red. The last time Richard saw his mother was during a June picnic in the yard behind a relative's house, two years ago in Canada. Cousins and aunts and uncles balance paper plates of cold fried chicken and potato salad, ride coloured blankets that like magic carpets hover just above the grass. Look! someone cries, pointing upward. Behind the fenced yard rises the hill with the hospital on top. A woman in white stands on a balcony high up there, she waves to the people down below. Richard believes he can see her short blond hair, her deeply red mouth; it will be years before he learns how distance can distort or damage vision, transforming any coiled length of rope into an asp. Someone also wearing white comes from behind the woman and leads her slowly back inside. The people at the picnic begin to play croquet, they send bright balls spinning across the lawn, there is the dull, hollow sound of wood knocking wood.

Soon Lily and MJ are sleeping. Richard can hear them breathing nearby, he still hears Peggy Lee sending messages through the Morogoro night. *I know a little bit about biology*, she confides. She's not here, the father once replied to Richard, running one hand through short black hair, squinting at the sisal fields in the valley below the grey house. Lily squirms in her sleep, something is always trying to get her. The father steps from the kitchen door, flashlight in hand; a weak beam plays upon the darkness, searches for danger undulating nearer on its belly. Tentative, the man takes

61

several more steps forward, retreats back inside. Peggy Lee sings on until dawn.

That old snake in the grass, Lily will write Richard nearly twenty years later from somewhere inside her visions of vipers. Honey, what does Peggy Lee have to do with anything? he once asked me. Apparently, he still thinks MJ will be found, he says he's doing everything in his power to make sure his boy is brought back home, writes Lily from the hospital, poised high above Brale, that Richard pictures having innumerable balconies from which hosts of mothers and sisters wave to people playing summer games below. If you're smart, you won't set foot back upon our native soil, adds Lily in 1985. Don't come back, it's not safe, venom abounds.

During daylight the father is clear-eyed and energetic. After work he changes out of his good trousers, white shirt and thin tie; in a pair of old shorts he throws a basketball at a hoop he has fixed on the side of the house. The children sit in the shaded doorway and watch his skin darken to the colour of an African's. He dribbles and dodges past an invisible opposition, scores two more points. How many does that make? he calls. Inside, the houseboy is fixing dinner. When it is ready, he will set it on the table and go home to the village for the night. One moment after there is bright sun-light, it is nearly dark. Supper cools and hardens on the table, unpacked crates from Canada loom in the dimming rooms. The father goes for one more layup. The children can no longer see him leaping towards the hoop, dropping back to earth. They no longer see him spinning something round between his palms.

While the evening is still early, and MJ and Lily still play the Canada game, the father often listens to Frank Sinatra or Ella Fitzgerald. He hums around the house, practises new Swahili words aloud, interrupts the children's games to tell stories of when he was a boy. I was the only boy in town who swam the Columbia River, he brags, everyone else was afraid of the currents, the rocks, the undertow. In detail he describes certain especially perilous swims, while the children's eyes become heavy in their nodding heads. Later, if they waken to Peggy Lee's voice, they will know that in the morning the father will be silent over his coffee, with puffy skin beneath eyes which do not turn even towards children who squabble or bicker or cry.

The father is teaching; Lily and MJ are at school in the ancient nunnery at the top of the college, where the jungle begins and colobus monkeys make the palm fronds sway. Richard becomes weary of following the silent houseboy from room to room: he walks up the hill, among the buildings of the calm college. The father's voice is suddenly near, clear. Through the window Richard sees rows of young men and women with dark skin and white teeth; they gaze raptly at the father, who sits on the edge of a desk and swings his legs back and forth, then springs up to write white on the blackboard. If we know what occurred before, we may understand what happens now, the father explains. His eyes travel around the classroom, across the window; he continues to speak smoothly about an impersonal past, as though he doesn't see Richard at the window, as though Richard were not there. The boy crouches between freshly watered shrubs and digs hands into damp dirt. He paints his face brown with tribal markings, reels at the rich odour of this earth.

One night Lily finds a snake curled in a corner of the children's room. The father's face pales; he grips the machete, and from a distance of several feet stares at the intruder. You can sleep in my bed, he finally tells the children, closing the door of their room tightly, leaving the snake undisturbed, alone, coiled around itself for warmth. The children crowd into the father's big bed; he and the record player have moved into the living room for the night.

63

*I know a little more about psychology*, her voice winds away, charming the snake into lifting its head, extending its length into the air, swaying in sinuous circles. Peggy Lee performs magic until morning, when the houseboy opens the door of the children's room to find the snake not there. The father carefully inspects the window screens, fails to find flaws.

If I could get back to Africa, I'd be OK, Lily writes Richard from the clinic they won't let her leave. There at least the snakes are real, you can close the door against them, Peggy Lee makes them vanish in a puff of smoke. Do you remember the time he suddenly decided we had to learn to swim, packed us into the white Peugeot, drove all morning until we reached the ocean? Anyone can learn to swim in the Indian Ocean, he said, the water's so salty it holds you up even when you don't know how to float. You couldn't drown if you tried. He shouted instructions from shore, he wouldn't even get his toes wet, he already knew how to swim, he said. Float! he called. And we did, didn't we? We floated all afternoon in that water as warm as blood, while on land he turned over rocks in search of shells. I won't always be around to save you from drowning, he said when we were allowed out of the water at last, to wobble on legs that had forgotten how to navigate solid ground. I can't always save you from this or from that, he frowned, holding a shell to his ear, listening intently. What faint music did he hear? I no longer hear Peggy Lee in the night. Do you? Does MJ, wherever he is? MJ would get me out of here if he were still alive. I keep thinking he drowned, though that's not what really happened, I know. MJ is still with Peggy Lee in Africa, together they disappeared into the jungle, searching for the source of the river, somewhere at the top of the Ngondo hills, that we could never find. *Missing*, is the official word. Not *dead*. Did you know Mitch has started collecting stamps? Honey, I have to have a hobby to keep me busy now that my babies have abandoned me, he explained in a postcard from Thailand. Apparently he's left Tibet; I take it the wise Buddhists wouldn't have him. Stay away, little brother. Remain in Italy or Greece. The snakes have briefly vanished, which only means they'll soon be back in greater number. Everything would be all right if I could smell the frangipani by the river one more time, writes Lily in another of the letters Richard will not answer, not wanting his messages to her to be read first by the people in white with clean pink skin, with cold Canadian eyes.

MJ says she's in a hospital, Lily insists she's dead. Who? asks Richard. Both MJ and Lily say she didn't really have short waved hair that was more white than blond. She didn't use deep-red lipstick, she didn't sing the same song over and over until you fell asleep. You can't remember, they tell Richard. He remembers riding with her on a roller coaster, Lily and MJ in the car behind, the father watching anxiously from the ground. Climbing slowly, then falling fast, snaking swiftly all the way to the end. The children lurch off the ride, join the father on the ground, watch the mother ride again, without them this time. Her head is thrown back, her short hair whips; they can hear her laughter above other passengers' screams. She rides a dozen more times, laughing like she will laugh when they take her away. (Then Richard stays with an aunt during the day, the old house on Columbia Avenue is quiet at night, the father plays Peggy Lee and prepares to take the children across the world, away from everything.) After finally descending from danger, the mother is silent in her summer dress; her red lips press tightly together as the children and father make cotton candy melt in their mouths, throw rings at gaudy prizes. Lily wins a big stuffed snake she calls Honey.

At first nothing grows in the dirt around the cement-block house. It is red and cracked from lack of water and too much heat, or a field of mud during the rains. It would be a waste of time to start a garden, says the father after one year, since we're only here temporarily. The Peggy Lee records become worn and scratched; a constant hissing beneath her voice threatens to drown her out. Richard grows old enough for school in the nunnery up where the butterflies are brilliant, but even Lily and MJ do not go there now. Sometimes the father gathers his children around the atlas or dictionary for an hour in evening; more often he goes into his bedroom right after supper. When are we going home? MJ asks him once. Why, son, this is our home, the father replies, kneading his left bicep slowly – then says he has work to do, shuts his door behind him, makes Peggy Lee sing once more. Slowly the children's hair blanches beneath the African sun, until it is more white than blond. They follow the river that rushes down through the jungle, searching for its source somewhere at the top of the Ngondo hills. They eat green mangos until their stomachs are sore. They file, oldest to youngest, along a narrow path with grass higher than their heads on either side. When they meet the snake, Lily will be the unfortunate one: it will be too startled by MJ, in front, to bite him; it will have already had its fill by the time Richard comes along, at the rear. Unlucky Lily, forever in the middle, sees serpents in the clinic. They are always long and thick, tattooed with intricate designs, patterned by the kind of brilliant colours seen only in jungle or in dreams. Don't bother, Lily replies to the father's last long-distance wish to visit her bare white room. You can't save me from the poisoned fangs, that never was your strong point.

The father cries for help. The children find him at the kitchen sink, a knife fallen at his feet, deep-red blood flowing from his thumb. He leans against MJ, Lily runs for bandages and tape, Richard watches the father's legs tremble. *I'm a little gem in geology*, boasts Peggy Lee, knowing nearly everything. I'm bleeding and it won't stop, Lily tells MJ one day, I don't know what to do. Neither do I, says MJ.

Dear Lily, Richard could write, Peggy Lee is still alive and kicking, though I've heard she no longer resides in Tanzania. The climate, she murmurs, stroking her velvet throat, was not good for my voice. Now the notes are no longer perfectly pitched, now she is old and ill. They prop her on stage in a blond wig and dark glasses, she snaps her fingers through "Fever" for the millionth time. He wrote me you refused his offer to fly across the world to see you, he said it breaks his heart that he can no longer save his children from this thing or the other thing. I always thought everything would be all right as long as Peggy Lee kept singing. She could save us from anything, I believed, Richard might write Lily, who finally coils around herself for warmth: the clinic and Canada are always cold. Sometimes she unwinds her length and flicks her tongue. A slow hiss is her only language now.

Fireflies float through the screen window, drift through the children's bedroom. The colours blink like lights of an airplane searching for a safe place to return to earth. One day we will fly away from all this, MJ has told Richard. Lately the children have begun picking through the father's things; careful detectives, they leave all the Peggy Lee records exactly as they are. They hunt for photographs of the mother, find only a letter from an aunt in Canada. You must do something with those children, read MJ and Lily – while Richard, who hasn't learned letters, stares at the smooth pale face, remembers Peggy Lee laughing all afternoon behind her locked door, in the old house on Columbia Avenue. She wouldn't open it, finally they had to break it down, the wood splintered. Before it's too late, adds the aunt. It's late, fireflies bumble sleepily around the room, Richard hears MJ ask Lily if she's awake. I think so, she says. I don't know, she says a moment later. The father sets the needle back down on the black circle; it will trace a million revolutions before dawn. *But I don't know enough about you*, Peggy Lee finally admits. Her voice is playful, light, certain that tomorrow she will know everything about the ones who pray to her at night.

We are left with the things our fathers teach us.

Mitch taught us to read and write, to add and subtract.

Mitch taught his children names of countries and capital cities, dates of battles and treaties.

He instructed us to stay always in the best hotels. (Inexpensive ones are trouble, nickel-and-dime operations with no potential for leeway.)

Leeway is another word for leaving a hotel with the bill unpaid.

Leeway means wearing, when the time comes, as many layers of clothes as you can without drawing attention to their bulk.

Leeway is carrying passport, money, photographs and papers in an innocently sized bag, such as a small white valise, and strolling out the hotel door with the bright, expectant air of one anticipating an hour's visit to the city's principal point of interest, say the Eiffel Tower or the Parthenon.

Whatever you must leave behind in the hotel can always be repurchased for a fraction of a two-week bill with room service and housekeeping.

My father taught me also that when you are lost in an unfamiliar city, you must stop where you are, close your eyes, and count to one hundred. Open your eyes, move without thinking, and you will always end up headed in the right direction.

In fact, instructed Mitch, there is no such thing as being lost, per se.

*Wish you were here.*
*Everything is fine.*
*Manila is nice.*

Among all our other blessings, which were bounteous and without number, Lily, MJ and I were fortunate indeed to escape the brainwashing of school, Mitch pointed out. Four years at the Morogoro Teachers' Training College had soured him on formal education. His own particular take on history did not conform with the socialist theories of Neyere's Tanzania; Mitch waged a constant and ultimately unsuccessful battle to teach his African students that history is primarily an exercise of the imagination. History is the invention of what has been forgotten. The shape of such invention is entirely flexible and subject to change, peculiar to the particular time and place and circumstance. History is man's feeble attempt to impose design on what is essentially a patternless universe.

Obviously I have absorbed my father's philosophy of history well.

Consider what he left me:

A black daybook containing references in Mitch's handwriting to uranium and Uzis and non-clearance flights.

A room-service menu from the Royal Hotel in Manila.

A schedule of flights between Rio de Janeiro and Quito on Aereas Argentina.

A printout of currency exchange rates from the Banque Nacional de Lyons on October 26, 1973.

I observe that today the Australian dollar is worth considerably less, in relation to the French franc, than it was on October 26, 1973.

What he gave me.

But I am a dreamy teacher, a pedagogue less inspired than Mitch – as the English students who pay my rent in Sevilla know.

Roberto's or Consuelo's tongue clumsily attempts to make the

69

unfamiliar, difficult movements necessary to form English sounds and I remember Lily struggling to speak to me in the Brale hospital in 1988.

Vaguely illustrating once again the challenging *th* sound, I think that after a certain point during 1973 and 1974 we were simply on the run. The bad guys were after us; if they didn't get us, the good guys would.

I am still on the run.

Still unable to distinguish the bad guys from the good guys, despite the clear indication offered by their black or white hats.

Contemplating why Mitch finally brought us back to Brale, B.C., in September 1974, it seems obvious that there are only so many hotels which can offer leeway and only so many contacts which can prove disappointing and only so many operations which can end badly before a faint odour of failure, similar to that of chlorine or lemon, clings to clothes until it can't be washed out despite the best efforts of housekeeping. I see that our stays in cities became increasingly brief and that the flights between them grew longer, and that, finally, in Mexico City, Mitch did not put on his one good suit and pair of shoes to stride out the door, clean and glowing, to meet a promising contact.

And I remember once, in Mexico City, waking to see Mitch sitting on the edge of his bed, the bathroom light falling partly over his face as he looked at the wall in front of him. He sensed me watching and turned his eyes my way. I couldn't recognize their expression. I thought by then I had seen all my father's guises, all his expressive effects, every trick of performance in his book. But I was wrong. I hadn't seen him look like this, and the strangest part of all, what especially amazed me, was that Mitch's face did not alter when he knew I watched him: for once he neglected to pick up the cue, to telegraph his reaction, to respond correctly to the given of the scene. His eyes returned to the wall, their expression unchanged. For a moment I sensed the burden of Mitch's constant role-playing and the strain that must have resulted from keeping alive the nearly flawless performance that commanded the illusion that Ardis was The Keeper of the Flame and that unpaid bills were Leeway and that indifferent strangers were Promising Contacts and that The Big Payoff awaited us in Bogata or Bangkok or Jakarta.

Later, I thought that this face, revealed to me briefly in Mexico City, was the face my father owned when he was alone. His secret face. I imagined he must have looked this way when, six years before, in Africa, he listened to Peggy Lee records late at night in his room. I thought that this must have been his face when he noticed that MJ looked more like him every year and that Lily was becoming too quiet. I don't know what Mitch's secret face told me, that night in Mexico City, about how he thought of me. I fell asleep as my father watched the wall. He didn't speak then, and never told me afterwards what I wanted to know.

What I do know:

We stayed seven weeks in the penthouse of the Hotel Carlotta in Mexico City before Mitch booked first-class tickets on the midweek Japan Airlines flight (one stopover in LAX) to Vancouver.

We touched down in Canada on September 19, 1974.

## V.

"Take a deep breath," says Jose.

The last October morning in Sevilla is cold, and the light still grey. The Estación de San Bernardo is nearly empty. At 7:15 a.m. only a few other passengers wait with us for the Madrid train. They huddle inside coats and stamp feet and wonder if there is enough time for a *solo* in the station's café.

On the platform, between Jose and me, rests his army bag. It is a shapeless bulk of sturdy olive-green cloth and contains the clothes we packed together. Some are mine – shirts that fit him too. In one hand Jose holds the ticket he obtained without charge, by means of a letter from the military, inside the station. The fare to and from home is part of the gift of this weeklong leave, now over.

I must look as tired and as pale beneath my tan as Jose. We have been up all night. Packing, making love, drinking wine, repeating words we don't want each other to forget. Then we made love again, put on coffee, and, just before dawn, made love one last time. At least for now.

My apartment already looks bare, forlorn, stripped of all the pleasant touches Reyna added to it on her last visit. I have been preparing for my own departure from Sevilla, in the opposite direction, later this week. I gave my plants to the *portero's* wife downstairs. Jose and I carried a dozen boxes of books and clothes to the store where his mother works, five blocks away, for storage in a back room. For the first time I was introduced, as a friend, to my lover's mother, though I had seen her a number of times before.

"You know how people here think," Jose would say, when I suggested we invite Carmen for a drink at my apartment, where he spends most of his days and nights while in Sevilla. "If I told my mother I had a boyfriend, she'd expect me to appear in a dress and high heels the next thing she knew. Don't laugh," he warned when I smiled. He is muscular and tall, with a deep, gruff voice that gentles only when we are alone together. He wouldn't look at all good in a dress.

Occasionally, during the last two years, I would enter the Bazar Asunción and pretend to study alarm clocks and telephone answering machines while secretly watching Carmen from the corner of my eye. I would buy something small – batteries, light-bulbs – to have the chance to speak a few words with her. She would handle the transaction indifferently; it was not a big sale.

While unknown to her, only an anonymous foreigner, I know nearly as much about Carmen as Jose does. I have seen her face on a cover of *Cine* magazine, dated twenty years ago, when Carmen Bueso was presented as the new ingénue of Spanish cinema, in the film *Los Chicos*. (It is, I gather, a sort of Spanish *West Side Story*; Carmen plays a gang-leader's girlfriend.) I know that when this film plays on television Carmen cries. I know how Jose's father, apparently a promising architect at the time, came backstage after a performance of the play in which she was featured, as one of Madrid's rising stars, and swept her off her feet, persuading her to abandon her career as actress to marry him. I know Carmen is forgetful, not domestic, a good time when she goes out. She chain-smokes behind the counter of the Bazar Asunción and conducts an unsatisfactory affair with an older, established doctor whose grown children won't permit his marriage to Carmen. Or, at least, that's what he says.

When she gave me my change, in the store, Carmen's hand would graze mine. I would try to feel if there was, in that slight touch, any resemblance to Jose's touch, just as I would search for similarities between the colour of their eyes, the shape of their mouths.

I look back into Jose's eyes as the train approaches in the distance. The ground trembles beneath my feet, as though a minor earthquake were occurring.

Jose asks again if I have the address of his Madrid *cuartel*.

I ask again if he has the telephone number of my mother, in Canada, in case anything should happen, in case we lose track of each other.

"Remember. You can always find out where I am through her. Or through Reyna."

We fall silent. For now, everything has been said.

These train station farewells are familiar. On this same platform I have seen Jose off to camp a dozen times in the last several months. (Never able to remember the time of her son's departures, Carmen hasn't stood with us here.) With mothers and wives and girlfriends of other *soldados* I would remind mine to call, to write, to take care of himself. Many of them appear painfully young, boys of only seventeen, too young to be trained for battle. Their mothers sob and press against them again and again. Then they wave blue and red scarves in the air and with small, awkward steps run alongside the train as it accelerates, then draws from the station.

"It's time to say goodbye," says Jose, as the train hums beside us.

He reaches behind his neck and feels for the clasp of the silver

74

chain he always wears, the one Carmen gave him for communion. It holds a silver cross. Jose lifts it over his head and the silver shines as it swings through grey light towards me. I feel warm metal, and the warmer touch of Jose's fingers, on the back of my neck. They linger a moment after he fastens the clasp, pausing at the place he knows is one of the best places to touch me.

I look down at the silver cross. Sometimes the chain would get in the way while we made love. I finger the cross, rub it, feel its weight and shape and texture.

"Wait," says Jose.

While examining the cross, I have shifted the clasp from behind my neck to near my throat. Jose reaches towards me again.

"Close your eyes and make a wish," he says, sliding the clasp back behind my neck, to its proper place.

I open my eyes.

"I'll give it back when we see each other again."

"*Vale*," he says.

Jose leans down, hoists his army bag onto his shoulder, turns, and quickly enters the nearest open door of the train just as the conductor blows the whistle. The train departs immediately. It glides from the station before Jose has found his seat and reappeared in a window.

All the parts of me that he has never seen crumble inside me, silently, like the speeded-up erosion of a desert city beneath wind and light and time.

I close my eyes again, count slowly to one hundred, then open them again. I begin walking without thought to my direction. I hope that for once one of my father's old laws will prove true and I will find myself headed in the right direction.

All right, Mitch. You win, damn you.

The lover is gone, the apartment is empty, the bag is packed. I am freshly horrified by the speed and ease with which the structure of a life may be levelled, though surely I should be used to such demolition by now. I have promised Jose that I will join him in Madrid by Christmas; really, I have no idea of how long I will be in North Africa, or what I will or will not discover there. I may not be travelling light and I may not be travelling right. But the southbound bus leaves in an hour and I will be on it. Headed in your misguided direction, daddy. Besides my papers, I have a change of clothes and a toothbrush. I have sixty thousand pesetas saved for a rainy day from Roberto's and Consuelo's English lessons. I have two oranges and a box of crackers and a litre of Font Bella water.

Is that enough to get me from here to there?

# II

## *The Sixty Lessons of the Koran*

"Arriving at each new city, the traveller finds
again a past of his that he did not know he had:
the foreignness of what you no longer are or no
longer possess lies in wait for you in foreign,
unpossessed places."

– Italo Calvino

# i.

How did I get here?

Usually this is the question that presents itself when I find myself in a new place without recollection of a journey. I still have the habit, even after three fixed years in Sevilla, of opening my eyes cautiously at morning and regarding with suspicion the room around me. I am always prepared to find it entirely different and perhaps miles distant from the room in which I fell asleep, as though in dreams we are capable of travelling not only in imagination but also, like adventurous sleepwalkers, of packing bags and boarding trains and setting out beneath cold stars towards an unknown destination. And sometimes, when I waken in a strange place, my memories of the journey that brought me there resemble, in fact, the vaguely incredible, often unbelievable memories of a dream.

Where am I?

I am in the bed of a room that is dimly lit, though I can see, through the cracks of closed curtains, that it is daytime, perhaps late afternoon. The light is sufficient to allow me to know that this is a spacious, simple room. Tiles fit together to form a pattern on a floor covered here and there with scattered rugs of faintly oriental design. My clothes are heaped between the bed and my unpacked bag. To my left, through an open door, lies a bathroom. I hear a tap drip and realize I am thirsty. I see an armoire, a low dressing-table before an oval mirror, and a small table covered by checked cloth, with a plain chair before it. The windows make up the upper half of French doors which lead, I presume, onto a balcony.

Another room. A hotel room. I compare it to all the previous rooms, calculate what it offers against what it lacks, process the data according to a formula developed by experience, end up with the answer that this is a good room.

Where am I? How did I get here?

My formula does not answer these questions.

But this time I remember my journey as clearly as if a voice, speaking from as nearby as the mirror six feet away, said to me: Remember.

I remember. This journey was different. This time I had a companion – of sorts.

I didn't notice her at first.

Around me, in the Algeciras ferry terminal, a confusion of hooded, scarved and veiled Moroccans, as well as a dozen apparently disoriented backpackers, waited to cross the Strait of Gibraltar to Tangier. Our departure, delayed more than an hour without explanation, did not appear any nearer still. Outside, the port spread through a chill, damp afternoon. The air inside the terminal was oppressive with stale smoke and sour bodies, coldly accented by salt. Fluorescent lighting seemed harsh and dim at once. A buzz of boredom and restlessness mixed with louder sounds bouncing abruptly off bare tiles and cement. The space was smeared with muddy footprints and puddles, orange peels and cigarette butts, spittle. A child urinated in a far corner; nearer, a one-armed man's stump leaked a colourless fluid. Bodies strewn across the floor – the terminal had no seats – resembled victims of a slaughter or a plague.

A shabby Spanish woman attempted to mop the floor: from a bucket of dirty water she slowly swished grey suds from one area to another. Her face, creased by exhaustion, tightened further when Moroccans wouldn't volunteer to shift their sprawling luggage – large boxes tied with string, bulky garbage bags, mysteriously shapeless bundles – so she could mop beneath it.

A tense transitional zone between the relative order behind in Spain and the greater confusion ahead.

An uneasy no-man's land between two hostile territories: as a rule, the Spanish detest Moroccans, call them filthy dogs, think them scarcely human; the feeling, not surprisingly, is mutual.

Perhaps I didn't notice her at once – not the cleaning woman, the blonde – because I was somewhat dazed from my morning journey by bus from Sevilla. From the previous sleepless night when the space beside me, empty of Jose, became a dark vacuum through which I plummeted until thudding into a grim dawn and discovering the barren Virgen de la Antigua rooms to be apparently abandoned already by myself, not yet inhabited by hungry, homeless ghosts. And beneath the resulting daze of weariness and loss now nudged a fear of my journey's probable futility – doubt enhanced by the cleaning woman, the waiting passengers, the dreary scene. Below that ran a thin vein of anxiety: the longer the boat was delayed, the less likely I would catch the day's last southbound train from Tangier to Casablanca. Where I would change onto a local train to El Jadida. Where I would begin, in the last place he was seen, to search for my father.

Turning from an unclear schedule of boats and trains stencilled crudely on the wall, I wondered at once why I hadn't noticed the blond woman before. She was a singular presence and stood slightly apart from the group. Mid-thirties, neatly groomed and dressed, just a slim leather folder beneath one arm for luggage. Suit jacket, blouse, skirt, low heels, no jewellery. Pale, poised, precise.

From about fifteen feet she stared at me. She didn't glance away when I noticed her. The gaze was coolly intent. I suspected, suddenly and strongly, that it had been fixed on me for some time.

German, perhaps? A Bonn stockbroker? A public relations consultant from Munich? An investment banker out of Frankfurt?

Certainly an anomalous figure in this setting.

But there was something more than that.

Something besides the uncomfortable suspicion that I had been unaware of being watched.

Something else woke me like a slap of cold water.

A small Moroccan child tugged the woman's sleeve. He probably wanted something – a cigarette, five pesetas, one dirham. Without turning her eyes from me, the blond woman spoke a single short word from the corner of her mouth. At once the child moved quickly away, glancing back twice.

A fearful glance?

An odd reaction, anyway. In this situation, the child would tend to tug the sleeve several more times whatever the response, wander unconcernedly away whatever its harshness.

The cleaning woman fumbled with her mop towards the blonde. She spoke, then gestured for the blonde to move. Ignoring her, the blonde continued to stare at me. Grimy water splashed – accidentally? on purpose? – on the blonde's obviously expensive shoes. Something flashed in the blonde's left hand, the hand darted towards the cleaning woman; moaning through a shocked mouth, the latter stumbled over the bucket, dropped her mop, then fled towards a doorway at the far end of the space.

Did the blond woman make a small, tight smile for my benefit?

Her left hand nestled in her jacket pocket.

From the upset bucket water crawled slowly across the floor.

82

The loading gate opened. The crowd muttered, gathered itself, pushed forward as if this were the last boat in the world. Something quite odd just happened, I thought in the confusion at the gangway. Bodies pressed against me from all sides. I struggled to hold onto my travelling bag and to remain on my feet. I lost sight of the blond woman.

On board I methodically searched the public areas – passenger salons, outer decks, bar – several times. Apparently, the blond woman had remained behind in Algeciras. Well, all right. My puzzlement turned to annoyance. What the hell had she been staring at, anyway. I looked presentable, quite ordinary, one more anonymous traveller, no? I settled into a window seat and dismissed the incident.

Something in the air had altered. Though Spain was still visible through low cloud and rain behind, and Africa remained indistinct ahead, the air already smelled different. It was the smell of Africa, more than anything, that I remembered most vividly from my childhood. It was the smell that lingered insistently – after I had forgotten the shape of a baobab and the pattern of sisal fields during harvest and the face of our old Morogoro gardener which I once believed was a face I would never forget. More than the taste of sugar cane, or of mangos from the tree below the garden, it was the scent, not unpleasant yet pervasive, that remained with me: for in Africa smells are not just more pungent than in other places; they possess more weight and density somehow.

From time to time over the years, in Mexico especially, I would catch a hint of Africa's aroma, an intimation of its ingredients in the air around me, and at those moments I would think that if my sense of smell was more acute, or if I paid it greater attention, the scent of Africa would blossom fully around me again; then I would no longer have to lie awake at night seeking in vain to recreate the recipe of that scent in my mind – trying to distinguish its components and to separate them into their essences, puzzling whether this scent were more smoke than dust, more live growth than rot – and hoping that, once correctly analyzed, I would be free of this scent, no longer afraid of its power to haunt me.

As soon as I learned of Mitch's disappearance, I knew that to search for him in Africa would be more difficult, and painful, than to search anywhere else. I had scrupulously and successfully avoided returning to that dark continent during my adult travels; the ghosts of MJ, Lily and myself, slight shadows still haunting the Ngondo hills, waited to be rescued, and I knew I was not strong enough for that task. Why Africa? I asked Jose again and again in the days following Ardis's telephone call.

And especially why the desert, when I had been dreaming fearfully of sand and dunes for so long, so often imagining in sleep their difficult demands that perhaps the force of my unconscious field influenced Mitch, without his knowing, to seek the Sahara and to slip from the globe there.

Why Africa and why the desert and why El Jadida?

All I knew of El Jadida was a piece of trivia picked up somewhere – from a book? a magazine? – in the past: Orson Welles had once filmed there. He shot scenes for one of his unfinished films inside a certain El Jadida structure remarkable for its light. The light! exclaimed Orson Welles. You can never forget the light in El Jadida.

I peered suspiciously at the passengers around me. Both Moroccans and tourists appeared anxious and withdrawn, as if brooding upon the purpose of their journey: where they had come from, where they were going. The low coast of Africa loomed through the rain and mist. It neared like an ancient dreamscape where everything feared and everything dreaded might come true. As the boat touched the dock, a recent memory stirred in my mind.

Four hours before, half-asleep on the bus from Sevilla, I had opened my eyes when we stopped to take on new passengers half an hour before Algeciras, in Tarifa. Through the window I saw drizzle fall onto a nearly empty street that ran between low white-washed houses. In a doorway across the street someone watched the idling bus. As we pulled away, I glimpsed a pale face, blond hair, intent eyes.

Our paths had crossed prior to Algeciras? In Tarifa – and before Tarifa? She had watched me step onto the Sevilla bus as well? She would be there to see me step from the train at El Jadida tomorrow morning? She would hover nearby or stand in plain sight wherever I went on this journey?

The passengers disembarked in another slow-motion crush. I had my passport stamped and money changed. Outside the terminal Tangier boys waited to meet vulnerable tourists. They were determined to carry bags, to guide, to speak whatever language was known by a visitor sized up with one glance: what kind of traveller was this, how much money might he have, how could he be parted from some of it? A little hash, a little sex, a little tour of the medina? Brushing past insistent boys and crooning taxi drivers, I moved towards the southbound train that still waited, luckily, beyond the ferry terminal. Dusk was falling.

A conductor sold me a ticket and directed me to a car. It was dim and quiet and cold. Black shapes, inert and silent, already filled most of the seats. As I settled into an empty space, footsteps tapped down the aisle from behind.

The blond woman sat down in the facing seat, glanced towards me, looked out the window. The train shuddered and clanked into motion, then crawled through the lights of Tangier. Picking up speed, it rocked through the growing darkness beyond the city.

The long car was illuminated only by a single light at each end. The other passengers soon appeared to sleep – hoods drawn over heads, as obscure and seemingly lifeless as the contents of the large bundles around them. At the far end of the car a voice began to wail softly in Arabic; it moaned up and down a scale unfamiliar to my ears. A plaintive prayer. Uncertain of being heard, unhopeful of being answered. I sat wide awake, stiff and hungry, cold.

"It's uncomfortable, isn't it?" The blond woman turned from the window and spoke in uninflected, slightly accented English. "Do you have a long journey?"

"Not really."

A harmless question. A polite remark. Nothing more.

"It's not wise to travel too far into the south."

A lightly offered helpful hint. With a subtle emphasis. A carefully concealed undertone of urgency and weight.

The low wailing at the end of the car stopped – suddenly, unexpectedly – on a rising note that seemed to be reaching towards a higher, conclusive one. The unreached note hung in the air as something unfinished, suspended, waiting. The sky outside lost the last of its light; the interior of the train grew darker.

The blond woman remained silent across from me; without stretching, I could have touched her. Her pale face shone in the darkness; though only three feet away, I couldn't see her expression. Was she sleeping now? I listened for her breathing. Frozen and still, she assumed the presence of a gleaming marble statue, or of a waxy icon of warning. If I did reach to touch her hand, it would feel smooth and cold and hard. I waited for her to clear her throat, scratch her shoulder, shift on the seat, cough.

Several times the train slowed then stopped in what seemed the middle of nowhere. Though no passengers appeared to leave or enter, the train idled silently and indefinitely each time. Then, without a warning shout or whistle, apparently at its own volition, it creaked back into motion and continued through the night.

We passed a skeleton of steel glaring in the darkness. For a moment light from the power station slanted over the woman. Her face resembled a mask of white plaster. Now I could see that she was watching me with the same intentness as at Algeciras. Her

86

pupils looked slightly dilated, her eyes slightly widened. Minutes passed before she blinked, it seemed. Then the light outside fell behind and the car returned to darkness. The woman's eyes continued to glow. Two tunnels, faintly illuminated at the far end, bore through the night before me. Two circles merged into one mouth that grew larger as I rushed towards it, then swallowed me and hurtled me into greater darkness.

*Don't look for your father. You've already found him. Go back.*

The train jerked into motion, my head banged the wall behind my seat, the space across from me was empty.

*Don't look for your father. You've already found him. Go back.*

Were those the last words of a dream – words which in fact woke me – or were they words spoken by a woman as she rose, stood before me, then turned into the shadows?

*Go back.*

I touched the hard surface of the facing seat and felt warmth. Someone had been there moments before. If I used my sense of sight fully, perhaps I could still see her. I rubbed a clear patch in the condensation which now covered the window. Once more the train picked up speed upon a dark, flat landscape, leaving only a few scattered lights behind. No town of any size.

"Where are we?" I asked the man across the aisle. When he didn't respond to Spanish, I tried French.

"Nowhere," he finally said, in muffled French, after a long pause.

"The woman across from me?"

A longer pause. "She got off."

I looked out the window again. Now no lights at all were visible. Without a watch, I guessed this was sometime around midnight. Somewhere between Tangier and Casablanca. Consulting the atlas always floating in my head, I flipped to the appropriate map, saw no large town in this area between Tangier and Casablanca. Only small villages of little obvious interest for the tourist, the holiday-maker, the German businesswoman.

*Go back.*

When you return to Africa, you discover that you have never been away. The years you spent in other places didn't occur. They were a hallucination.

For years I was afraid to return.

*Go back.*

For the rest of the night I pressed my face against the cold window and watched the stars above the dark plain shrink until, just before dawn, the black door of the sky closed.

*You've already found him.*

Said a blond woman on a southbound train in the North African night.

Call her Dagmar or Anke. From Frankfurt or Munich or Bonn.

Does the name matter?

Does it matter what name is given to this town where I now waken, on the following day, in Africa once more?

You have to call it something.

Welcome to El Jadida, says the room.

I know exactly how I got here.

For the thousandth time, I unpack my bags.

# ii.

*Welcome to the Hotel de Provence.*

*Godfrey Bridgeport, Owner. Hisham Latima, Director.*

The card propped upon the bedside table does not include housekeeping among its list of proffered services. I will have to scrub clothes soiled by the trip from Sevilla in the sink, by hand. Washed that old way, they never become quite clean, only less dirty. A faint odour of something like failure or fear clings to them. Certain animals with especially keen noses can sense this odour. Wild dogs, for instance.

Housekeeping or not, this hotel probably costs more than I can afford – I don't remember asking the price upon arriving this morning, and, with something less than the equivalent of sixty thousand pesetas in dirham notes, I will have to change to a less expensive hotel soon. At least here there is running water, at least it's hot. The next hotel will have no hot water, the one after that no water at all. If this bloody search lasts long, I will eventually have to sleep, wrapped in a filthy blanket, on a piece of cardboard in the shelter of a doorway, with the other lepers and beggars.

Excuse me, Reyna, I'm tired.

In my blue bag is a change of clothes resembling the soiled ones. I put on Levis, T-shirt, runners, a denim jacket with a red hood. Along with my documents, I have brought a number of small jars and bottles containing expensive creams. They are supposed to delay signs of ageing in the face; like the beauty secrets of the belly dancer, and despite their lavish promises, they probably don't work. Still. You must believe. I rub cream carefully into my skin, paying special attention to the area around my eyes, where a web of fine lines has formed from living in the sun. I study myself critically in the mirror. Although there should be no one in El Jadida to give a damn about my appearance, I spend several more minutes fixing my hair. If you must walk around alone, and perhaps slightly mad in a strange place, it's wise to look your best. People find you less disturbing; they are assured that you're still making an effort to look like them, that you haven't let go completely – at least, not yet.

Every mirror is different. Someone once wrote about the mystery of kind and unkind mirrors. Perhaps it is the quality of the glass, or the particular amount of light to enter the glass, or the physical objects around it, that bears responsibility for the inconsistent images offered one object by various mirrors. The full-length mirror on the armoire's door in my room at the Hotel de Provence reveals something new to me. These are the clothes of a teenaged boy, not of a thirty-year-old man.

I finger the silver cross that rests below my throat. I lean towards the mirror. There is something of Mitch in the shape of my eyes, the line of my nose, my colouring. But really it was MJ who resembled him most. Darker hair, darker eyes. Several hairs, as silver as the cross, shine just above my ears. From force of habit I reach to pluck them, then drop my hands. Let them stay.

Downstairs, a Moroccan in a wine-coloured coat identical to this morning's young clerk, sits behind the reception desk. An older man, perhaps the European owner, leans towards him from the other side. They appear startled by me. Is this a hotel or am I intruding in someone's private home? Did I fail to prepare myself correctly for the street after all? When I leave my key at the desk, with a bland greeting, the young Moroccan bares his teeth and the older European looks away.

Evening has fallen and the moon is in its first quarter. The rue Fquith Mohammed Errafi is lined with trees too young to assert themselves against two-storey concrete buildings typical of anywhere. Among the leaves streetlamps shine upon a littered sidewalk which leads to an intersection and then a large square closed to traffic. Facing upon it are small stores offering postcards and candy, newspapers and magazines, cigarettes and Kodak film. *Rambo IV* is playing at the Cinema Le Paris. In the streets off the square wait the Hotel de Lyons, the Hotel de Bordeaux, the Hotel de Marseilles. In these names, and in the architecture of the older, more impressive buildings, sound echoes of a former colony's mother, plaintive attempts to summon near a parent sometimes disinterested, always distant. Hooded men hulk before cafés or, inside, beneath ubiquitous portraits of Hassan II, one more despised king. Women with *lathams* over their lower face drift with me towards narrow, congested streets leading off the square's further side. There France fades away. Open stalls, garishly lit with naked bulbs, display fruit and vegetables and spices. There are things for sale everywhere. Whatever you need is spread out on sidewalks, at street edge, between stalls: brightly coloured household items made of tin or plastic, flashy polyester clothes, imitation Levis and fake Seikos, all the cheap goods of the Third World. Cars jerk slowly forward through the crowd, their blasting horns ignored. Arabic enters my ears from all sides and music wails unfamiliar keys. I don't notice tourists among the people pressed around me. They don't regard me with curiosity or interest, as if they've seen me before.

Excuse me, Reyna. I am still tired from my journey and when tired I can't see anything new in even the most startling of unknown places. Now I may only be reminded of what I have experienced before; strangers appear to bear only greater or less likeness, discounting colour of skin and other racial differences, to people already known. That man has the Arabic version of the eyes of a man I used to notice in Paris, the mouth of a boy once glimpsed in Rome, the nose of someone I saw on Spring Street, in Los Angeles. Perhaps there is only limited variety to the human form and character, then only repetition, sameness. Perhaps God is a lazy creator who has became bored with his task. Originally a brilliant artist, without compare, apparently capable of conjuring anything and everything out of darkness, he has degenerated into indifference for his talent, content to cast down the tired work of an uninspired hand, unwilling to make full use of his power.

What do I expect of a weary god, of my weary self?

Do I expect to spy Mitch across this crowd, in *djellaba* selling candied nuts from his cart, weighing them on an old brass scale, ten dirhams the hundred gram, pouring them into funnels fashioned from squares of last week's *Le Matin du Sahara*? To see MJ in the ragged shoeshine boy whose eyes dart constantly towards our feet and whose brush knocks hollowly against his wooden box to announce his trade? To find Ardis crouched before a basket heaped with henna, her own hands stained dark orange once a week with the fine green powder to keep them smooth and soft? To discover Lily making a repeated moan, as she rocks herself back and forth beside her tray of sweet fried pan-cakes, which sounds, if I bend near, like *oumn, oumn, oumn*?

I enter the narrowest street before me. It is roughly cobbled and nearly dark, with sewage gleaming down its centre, and closed doors, unnumbered, to either side. Someone going the other way, a man, bumps my shoulder and mutters an Arabic greeting or apology or insult. The alley bends several times, inter-sects equally dark, narrow passages, then comes to a dead-end at a high stone wall. There are no known or unknown faces visible in the darkness, and the noise I have left has been lost behind.

After MJ disappeared without a trace in 1977, unlike Mitch not dropping even a passport as clue to where he vanished, he might as well have stepped off the edge of the world, or simply dematerialized into something less solid than atoms. We lost MJ in the truest sense of the word. For years I was unable to summon even a vague feeling that he was still alive or long buried, and even his strange and partial reappearance in Paris during the eighties didn't really alter this. He was gone and he left only blank space behind: both the air near me and the air beyond my vision were emptier. Later, though, I was able to imagine MJ in various land-scapes, and while I knew these images of my heart and mind bore no relation to the actual place where MJ had died or still lived, they helped me to see my brother once more.

I pictured him especially in a particular town I know on the Pacific coast of Mexico. It happens to be a place where I was once happy. There is not the slightest reason for me to believe that MJ ended up in that or any other town in Mexico; he never spoke of Mexico with special feeling, or even, as far as I recall, mentioned it more than half a dozen times in passing. But I like to imagine him in the plaza of this town in the evening, seated on one of the benches there, with the name of the person who donated it inscribed on the bench's back. Around MJ paths twist through trees and shrubs, lit softly by lamps during the evening, and at this hour blossoms open to release scent into the air, adding it to the salt on the breeze that rises from the Pacific. Children play shrill hopscotch in the space before the bandstand; young girls in ruf-fled dresses slowly circle the outside of the square. I can see MJ's eyes, the arc of his throat, how he looks at thirty-three. I can hear boys, standing with hands hidden in pockets, beneath the trees, call to the circling girls, and I hear, too, more distant voices on the soundtrack of the film playing at the Cine Tropical in the town above. It is always a love story, about passion and betrayal, separation and reunion. A white horse wanders towards the edge of the square and nibbles sweet grass growing there. MJ watches the white horse and I watch MJ.

For me, MJ will always be in Mexico. And that is because we need, by some trick of the human heart, to believe that the people gone from us inhabit a place we know and, always, love. A place transformed by our love into a place distinct from, in this case, any number of plazas in any number of small towns poised on the Pacific coast of Mexico. Our love for the place, intensified through our love for the lost person we wish to see, sharpens our vision of it and finds in it numerous minute details invisible to the unconcerned eye, which combine to make it the place we love, as the smallest lines and scars, also indiscernible at a casual glance, transform the face of our lover into a unique place, unlike any other, no matter how indifferently created by no matter how weary an artist.

I retrace my steps back to the crowd and re-enter it. Too many people pass in both directions for me to notice their faces and to know if, in fact, they are familiar faces. My sight fixes upon a stall with no customers before it and with wares not easily identified: tiny burlap bags overflowing with various unrecognizable contents. At first glance they appear to be spices, ground or still in leaves or lumps; a closer view reveals perhaps bits of hair and dried entrails and skin and dung lying loosely or tied with thin twine into oddly shaped bundles that would fit in the palm of my hand.

The woman before the stall is old and small. Her eyes are dim. Often I have noticed that, particularly in poor countries, it is only the old who appear kind; difficulties of existence do not permit the young the luxury of kindness or the security to feel concern for others. Only the old, who have somehow survived life's difficulties, and in the end resigned themselves to them, can achieve kindness as well as wisdom.

"*Qu'est-ce que c'est la?*" I ask, pointing.

She doesn't speak French. She looks at me. There is a blue cross tattooed or painted on either of her cheeks. I stare at the blue crosses. Have I seen this sign before? Where and when?

"*Bon soir, monsieur.*" The voice belongs to a middle-aged man who has materialized by my shoulder. He is thin and balding, and wears European clothes and thick glasses. His eyes appear both very clear and very blurred behind the glass.

"You are curious about the *tseuheur*, the magic? Some, *le noir*, is dangerous. Some, if not precisely amusing, is of interest. For instance, this." He picks up a small handful of what looks like a moist paste, made of finely chopped leaves, which has been moulded into odd-shaped lumps.

"You wish to dream?"

I have to laugh. That is the last thing I wish or need to do. I have wasted enough of my life in dreams. I have spent years dreaming of love, dreaming of peace, dreaming of the day I could stop dreaming, dreaming of waking to find the dream has ended. Why else have I travelled to North Africa except to free myself of the dream into which my father sank his children?

"The dream teaches one many things of value. The dream may show one the path when one is lost, as I am certain monsieur knows. One recognizes the path where for much time it has been beneath one's feet. Please allow me this pleasure. Most kind."

He removes three coins from his pocket and hands them to the old woman. Though her eyes are kind, she doesn't smile. The blue crosses don't shift upon her skin.

"You must mix as much as you can pinch between the finger and the thumb in water that is not cold and not hot one moment before sleep. Then monsieur will dream."

"*Merci.*" I accept this gift I haven't asked for and don't particularly want with a gratitude whose strength surprises me.

"*De rien.*" The man's face slowly turns sorrowful. "Once," he says, "I dreamed. But it transpires sometimes that one day we no longer possess the gift of dream, and no assistance may allow us to dream again. We lose the gift slowly, perhaps as we lose our youth, our beauty, our sight."

The small bag rests upon my open palm. My fingers close around it and grip it hard, until it is hidden in my fist. Looking up, I see the man's back move forward through the crowd, away from me. Bodies close around him quickly and he is out of sight.

I suppose he means that with this stuff you don't only dream but remember your dreams. Well, during a life of dreaming I've experienced every narcotic known under the ecstatic moon. Opium and heroin, cocaine and LSD. All the pharmaceuticals, all the hallucinogens. The capsules, the powders, the herbs, the pills. Even Spanish Fly, in Cádiz once. What difference can this apparently legal substance bought from the market in El Jadida possibly make now, when it's much too late to play the virgin?

And much too late to deny the memory of dreams.

Returning to the Hotel de Provence, I look around me closely. I must be able to describe what is here for someone I love. He has to see how at ten o'clock in El Jadida merchants pull down grids of metal bars which gratingly protest the closing of stores. He must see how at this hour sidewalk vendors wrap unsold scarves and books and shoes spread on the ground back inside black plastic garbage bags until tomorrow. The cafés are still crowded, while the crowds outside have begun to thin. Young boys and old men hold hands in the Place; the touch appears one of innocent affection. A breeze has risen lightly from the Atlantic, still unseen somewhere to my left, disturbing scraps of litter on the ground. The evening is cool, the sky without stars.

# iii.

The next morning, glancing at my image while shaving, I remember once meeting, on the road north of San Diego, a beautiful young girl who had been sleeping in doorways in New Orleans before crossing Texas towards this sunny afternoon in California. She said she was nineteen and looked, in the clear light of a California afternoon, carefree and windblown and blond, until her face presented, only for a second, an angle in which every cold, wet night in a New Orleans doorway was clearly visible. After a certain point these revealing angles multiply and a suspicious odour clings to you that can't be eliminated with even the best efforts of housekeeping. Employers would sniff me out at the start, hire me without illusions. I was similar to many who work, often under the illegal table, badly paid jobs with poor working conditions. Not much is expected of you; they can't get anyone better, not at your low price. They'll put up with you if you're a little unreliable, not quite on the mark, somewhat dazed and damaged from too many nights in New Orleans doorways. They know you won't be around long. By September you'll be picking apples in Oregon, or grapes in the Loire.

The lovers I had before Jose also knew I wouldn't be there long. We pretended without conviction that I would stay indefinitely, even permanently, though every sign pointed to an opposite, more imminent conclusion. There was never mention of what we would be doing in, say, five years. It was clearly understood that by then we would be long separated, out of touch, probably unsure where the other had gone. I occurred between your serious lovers; you were the only kind of lover I had. I usually left the men I briefly lived with on a grey, cloudy day. While you are at work, I pack my bag and call a cab. Perhaps I leave a note, but there is not much of intelligence to be said when you leave abruptly and secretly on a grey, cloudy afternoon. Whether you return to a note or not, my departure isn't entirely surprising. You never really trusted me and were right not to. It won't take you more than a week to no longer notice the space I leave empty, which I filled only partly, and with the less important pieces of myself. I learned early on to leave little evidence behind, especially evidence that will not be searched for or puzzled over.

It was essentially the existence of a bohemian who fails to produce or even attempt art, or of a fugitive on the run from no definite crime. More exactly, it was the life of a secret agent uncertain of the nature of his mission; although both its details and larger purpose remain obscure, he lives faithful to the code, evasiveness and secrecy drilled into him so thoroughly that by now he practises them by reflex. He could, perhaps, have been sent to a place like El Jadida under an artful alias, a convincing but false passport, and a good cover; he is prepared to take the cyanide rather than reveal his secret mission, which will be whispered to him by the young Moroccan in the wine-coloured coat at the reception desk of the Hotel de Provence.

I left you secretly on a cloudy afternoon or without explanation failed to show up for my eight o'clock shift at your bar because there always came a day when the cobwebs in the corners of my room began to spin more thickly and widely each hour, until they threw themselves across me in thick, adhesive ropes, and finally wrapped so densely around me that I couldn't see or hear or breathe. While my hands were powerless to seize a broom to knock away these webs made of images from the past and of images with no reference to a solid, rational world, I was still able to pack my bag and call a cab before it was too late.

Lily, I have also heard the wild dogs calling in the distance.

Listen. They're still calling. From somewhere in the dark alleys beyond the mosque. From somewhere on the Ngondo hills.

During hot, still afternoons, when only wasps disturbed the glassy silence, Lily picked ticks off our dog. On the hard, shaded dirt to the east of the house, beneath the bougainvillea, she held Ginger tightly between her legs and worked fingers through the secret places of his coat. Below his neck, beneath the flaps of his ears, and among the pits of his legs she encountered ticks swollen fat with blood. These she pinched between a finger and a thumb until the soft, tight skin of the sac burst and Ginger's blood spurted over her hands. Picking up the can of tick powder, Lily sprinkled white snow where the pest had nestled; it was supposed to discourage further unwelcome visitors. But a hundred more ticks would fasten to Ginger during his journeys through the brush tomorrow; there were always more than Lily could kill, especially during dry season. Already our dog squirmed unhappily, restlessly. Dissatisfied with our company, he was forever trotting from sight, losing us easily if we tried to follow. Lily told me that Ginger went in search of his tail, which had been chopped off shortly after his birth as a boxer pup. ("It's the custom," Mitch informed us. "Something people do," he added weakly, when our puzzled faces requested a better explanation.) Only the stump of a tail remained, scarcely enough to wag. One day Ginger would return home with his missing tail between his teeth – instead of the usual rats and snakes. Perhaps then he would become our loyal companion, our faithful friend, no longer prone to long disappearances and battles with other dogs which left his torn ears permanent attractions for flies. "They'll drink all his blood," Lily told me, not looking up from Ginger's coat. Lips pressed tightly together, she declined my invitation that we venture down the hill to the main road, where the sugar man sold his cane. He would give us as much as we could carry if we sang something from *Mary Poppins*; all afternoon we could chew the sweet, stringy cane he peeled with his big machete, spit out a trail of exhausted pulp to show where we had been, like Hansel and Gretel in the haunted forest. Still ignoring me, Lily moved her thin, freckled face nearer our dog's coat. She didn't look up when a ripe pawpaw fell from a nearby tree to land with a splitting thud; within ten minutes its sweet meat would swarm with hungry insects feeding so ravenously you could almost hear the click of small, sharp teeth. Now Lily suddenly loosened her legs and clapped her hands three times near Ginger's ears, loudly. He bounded away. My sister held blood-stained hands up to the sky, squinted at them with satisfaction. With broad, sweeping strokes she painted her face with crosses; the marks were nearly the same colour as the earth beneath us. After the blood dried, Lily would have to be careful not to smile, or it would crack.

Our dreamy father had few rules, and these were laxly enforced. Mitch forgot to check the correspondence lessons we were supposed to do in morning, and he wouldn't remember bedtime and brushing teeth and letters to our mother. Another overlooked law was that we three children were supposed to stay together. "There's strength in numbers," Mitch explained. That we did play together, MJ and Lily and I, was strictly due to necessity, for there were no other children at the college – except for black ones who sang taunting rhymes to our backs, or threw bowls of white mush in our faces if we were foolish enough to get too close. Mitch encouraged us to explore as far and wide as we could, and didn't express fear for our safety as long as we were home before dark. "Where did you go and what did you see today?" he would ask eagerly in evening, when night spread around the house and things concealed during day came out to prowl beyond the door. We looked at each other cautiously, chose with care what we could safely tell Mitch. While we often did move across that disturbing landscape as a trio, there were many days when MJ had to lie upon his bed with tightly closed eyes. His head hurt. You could see veins beneath his brow beat with blood angrily trying to get out. When he came home from teaching, Mitch would massage MJ's temples, rub strong fingers into his eldest son's scalp. "It's just the heat," Mitch would say. "It's nothing more than that." With MJ waiting to heal and rise, Lily lost loyalty to our broken group. I would turn to see her nearly out of sight already, one of the old pleated skirts donated by the nuns swishing around her quickly striding legs. If I tried to follow, she would simply walk more swiftly; if I got in her way, she would push me aside – not meanly, but efficiently, as you brush away a branch or vine that blocks your path. I never knew where Lily went alone; upon returning, she would not tell me, and deflected Mitch's inquiries neatly. I suspected she followed the trail above the college, that through the jungle led to where the river roared between rocks. Up there the air was thin and cool, an element that to me felt alien, not quite suitable for human lungs. And there birds cried too loudly, flowers bloomed too boldly, the jungle was too thick. Lily met Ginger by the river, I thought; together they searched for something concealed along its bank. They would be home when they were hungry, they would be home before dark. I never feared Lily would become lost up in the jungle; she was eleven, two years older than me, and I always thought her smart and strong enough to find the way back down to us. I believed that like Ginger she went in search of something missing, an essential part of herself chopped off shortly after birth. What was it Lily hunted during those slow afternoons, when at the house below the only sounds were the ancient gardener's machete striking stones in the yard, the houseboy's croon as he wrung dripping clothes behind the kitchen, the whimper of MJ from his dim, painful room? What would Lily bear between her teeth when she returned?

I'm sure Mitch gave us a dog with the best intentions. "I had one when I was a boy," he said, and then we heard once more about his tough, hardy West Brale youth. Probably Mitch held in his head some clear, focused photograph of three children frolicking with a happy pet. Caring for their dog, the children would learn responsibility; in turn, he would act as comrade and comforter, and strengthen their number. Mitch didn't seem to notice that from the start our attention to Ginger was not reciprocated; we were not that interesting or necessary to our dog. We couldn't teach him to fetch or sit up or roll over and play dead. "He's getting big," Mitch observed happily, as within the door Ginger lifted his head at the sound of wild dogs in the distance. They bayed at a rough beast who slouched through the night. Our dog scratched to be let out, insisted with claws until we had to give in and open the door. Slinking away, he would return in the morning smelling of something rotten, bad. Lily would disregard the stink, pick more ticks from his coat, try to brush it smooth. Perhaps things would have been different in a blander setting, without the scent of wild blood to lure our dog from us. Mitch's hopeful vision might have unfolded more perfectly against a background of neat lawns and fences, tidy sidewalks and maple trees. It was our father's fatal tendency to disregard the landscape upon which he set his fantasies. And to believe that everything was all right as long as we were home before dark.

During those years Lily was taller than MJ and myself, with hair hacked off by Mitch in the shape of a bowl. (He enjoyed playing barber, liked to shave MJ's and mine and his own head right to the scalp, pronounced pleasure in the cool results.) My sister's face was sharp, her new teeth had grown in crooked, scabs always decorated her knees. I was not aware that girls played dolls and house, or dressed up in their mother's clothes; Lily didn't do these things, and never mentioned them. She liked to swim and run and climb the tops of trees. She enjoyed silent activities, such as our visits to Father Joe, the college naturalist, who kept cages of snakes and guinea pigs. The biggest snake – a sly, old boa – didn't like to eat in front of curious children. You had to be very still and patient to catch him strike at the guinea pig shivering at the far side of the cage. Lily looked hard as with a gulp he swallowed it whole. Later I would always envision her studying intensely something right before her eyes, while MJ and I had to turn away. It seems to me that I was usually watching Lily rather than whatever lay before us; she saw for all of us, I think. When at the prison farm they showed us how a cow was killed then skinned, Lily's eyes widened slightly, then quickly narrowed again, shutting the sight inside herself. Later, attempting to butcher the beef back in our kitchen, Mitch scratched his head at the puzzle of sides and quarters, waved the saw in the air, splashed in pools of blood, nearly fainted from fear. Lily worked alongside him; she pointed and advised. From where I hovered with MJ in the doorway, I thought I saw her nostrils quiver, as she breathed in deeply the stench of intestine, the stink of death.

While MJ would sometimes tell stories about where we had lived before Africa and what had happened to us there, Lily refused at this time to discuss the past, and showed no interest in anything not visible in the present either. MJ spoke about the dancing goat on the island in Greece and the little one-armed girl in Spain; he described our mother, Ardis, who was far away in Canada. "She has blond hair and red lips," MJ mused again, while without a word Lily wandered from our secret place beneath the lemon tree. We found her occupied with an army of marching ants. Their file was endless and perfectly neat; two by two they moved with determination towards some destination we could only fathom. You could stir them with a stick or dump pails of water on them, but this interrupted their progress for only the few seconds it took to scramble back into rank. MJ said the ants were marching home. I said maybe they were lost. Lily said they were going to war. We agreed that the ants could strip the flesh from a large beast's frame in seconds. With the blink of an eye bones were picked as clean as a whistle.

"The nuns!" MJ cried in alarm, too late. Before we could escape, a dozen of the Dutch sisters surrounded us; they always seemed to appear almost out of nowhere, and in the most unlikely locations. We would see them filing solemnly across the golf course of the Morogoro Country Club early in the morning, or clustered in the open back of a pickup whirling down the road. Moving with surprising swiftness, they encircled us again, with black habits flapping like huge wings in our faces. For a long time we couldn't distinguish one nun from another; their costumes lent them anonymity. Gradually we learned that Sister Bridgit was tall and thin, Sister Marya short and plump, Sister Elsa always flushed, and so on. They nodded and clucked and patted our heads with concern; in guttural Dutch they discussed us among themselves, seeming to search for a solution to a difficult problem. Then they would attempt several tentative phrases of heavily accented English we could barely understand. "By the sea of Galilea," I thought Sister Anna said. MJ believed they were telling us to prepare for the Second Coming. Lily didn't like the nuns; she wouldn't look at them. From beneath their robes, like magicians, they pulled skirts and blouses sent from Holland to clothe a little black girl. Lily accepted these gifts rudely, glaring at the ground.

Finally the nuns would sigh, pat our heads once more, then turn towards their convent at the highest point of the college, where the jungle began. Sometimes, on our way exploring, we passed the nunnery and heard voices raised sweetly in hymn. Rather than soothe, the song seemed to add a jarring note to the setting, as if there were nothing in this air to receive such words of praise and thanks.

When Lily turned twelve, her breasts began to grow. They irritated her. She picked constantly at the front of her blouse, lifting the cloth that chafed the sensitive spots. I thought she was losing interest in Ginger, but maybe the truth was that he was losing what little interest he had in us. Leaving the house-boy to feed him, we had gone on safari several times and on another occasion made a longer trip when Mitch suddenly decided it was necessary to see Munich without delay. Once, during our third year in Tanzania, Ginger was not waiting for us when we returned to the cement-block house and showed up only three days later; the next time, he was gone two weeks. After that he came around less and less frequently, and between visits I would forget the shape of his nose, the colour of his eyes. Some-times he came home to eat; sometimes we saw him in the dis-tance, among the pack of wild dogs that made wide-ranging expeditions through the area. They ran in a loose cluster, noses near the ground, direction determined by invisible forces, snar-ling at each other. Now Ginger would not come when called; he had forgotten his name. "Leave him alone," said Lily, turning away. "It was a stupid name anyway. He's not the colour of ginger at all." Though Mitch didn't seem to realize our dog was increas-ingly absent, he did appear to sense that somehow things were not the same for us. Something had changed; he tried to put a finger on it. "Do you have everything you need?" he once asked abruptly. He seemed less confident that he held just the right solution to anything like a wild card up his sleeve, and in the evening inquired less brightly about where we had been that day. Lily especially made him uneasy. He suggested she pay visits to Preema, the chic young East Indian woman who lived in the house below ours. Lily stared at him. "Why?" she finally asked. For several moments Mitch rubbed his head, glanced at his watch, hummed. Suddenly he snapped his fingers. "Chess!" he exclaimed. "Which of you kids thinks he's smart enough to beat the old man?"

People began to say the wild dogs were getting out of hand. Their pack grew larger. No longer skulking warily at safe distance, they became bolder, more threatening. All night they would circle and howl around a certain house, trapping its sleepless inhabitants inside. They killed chickens in the village by the college. More than actual damage or harm, they caused disturbance, fear. "Rabies," it was muttered. The Africans wanted to get rid of the wild dogs with axes and machetes. They believed them evil spirits risen from centuries of tortured sleep. They believed them demons escaped from nightmare. One night we listened to the wild dogs tear apart Preema's pet monkey. "Go back to sleep," said Mitch, a black shape in our bedroom door. The monkey's screams died; MJ moaned in his bed between Lily's and mine. His headaches were worse, though the Morogoro doctor, a proud graduate of the Bombay Institute of Dental Hygiene, had promised he would grow out of them. Lily slipped from bed and stood before the window, face pressed against the wire-mesh screen that was supposed to keep out insects and snakes. "What are you doing?" I asked. Lily's nightdress, another gift from the good Dutch nuns, was too short around her thin, scratched legs. It gleamed in the darkness. "Where are you going?" I whispered, as Lily's bare feet padded from the room. I heard the kitchen door click open, then shut. In my safe, hot bed I fell asleep, while outside Lily roamed in search of secrets contained in the carcass of a mutilated monkey. I dreamed I saw her eyes burning yellow in the darkness, her mouth frothing white, her nose smeared thickly with blood.

What did I see, what did I dream? Later I would never know for certain if I ever really saw Lily poised at the edge of the sisal field below the college, a circle of wild dogs dancing around her, leaping up to snap at her face. Back straight and arms folded across her chest, she stood still amid the whirling beasts. Did her lips move? Was she speaking to the dogs? All at once she turned on her heels and ran. The dogs took after her, barking madly; they were hunting Lily or they were following Lily. The pack entered the sisal that grew taller than my sister. All I could see was a dense green field, with no hint what it contained, unfolding still and calm before me. Troubling my eyes.

Later Lily refused to remember anything about Africa; after we were safely back in Canada she would barely admit we had ever lived there at all. In Brale my sister said she couldn't recall our chameleon with the leash of string around its neck or our hunts for frogs in the gutters above the college church. Or seeing the Milky Way creamed above the Serengeti, when in the middle of a night drive home Mitch stopped the car and insisted we get out to view the sky. "The stars are closer when you're in Africa," he told us. I still believe that, as I continue to believe many of my father's patent untruths. But Lily denied knowledge of the shape a baobab forms against the sky and the shriek of a colobus monkey when you pass through the jungle below. At sixteen she put on a disguise of makeup and drank homemade wine with Italian boys down by the Columbia River. Now her hair was long, covering her eyes. From beneath bangs Lily watched Ardis warily, sniffing at our mother from safe distance, trying to determine if this stranger posed danger. "Go back to the loony bin where you belong," she snarled when Ardis said she must be home before dark. Our mother retreated behind the closed door of her room again; in the basement MJ watched another hour of TV. Despite a battery of tests and medications, his headaches were never diagnosed or treated with success; clearly they were due to something more than just the heat. MJ was unable to heal and rise; he couldn't attend high school frequently enough to graduate. At eighteen he disappeared on his way to Montreal, where he was headed to look for work. I think he couldn't stand for us to see the veins still throbbing with angry blood beneath his brow. He needed to lose Africa, to lose us. I continued to believe that a dark continent lay hidden just beneath our skin; with a sharp knife you could peel away a layer to discover the rich taste of mango, the smells of charcoal and dust and rotting fruit, the mocking laughter of hyenas in the night.

Perhaps Lily was searching for these things when she used the razor on herself. By this time – like MJ, like Mitch – I had left behind the Brale house beneath the reeling crows, beneath white powder sprinkling through the sky. We went our separate ways, gave up on the promise that there is safety in numbers. Only Ardis remained behind when Lily entered the psychiatric wing of the Brale hospital. ("Jesus," Mitch wrote to me in London. "We should have the family name engraved on a door of that place.")

During the next three years, while Lily was silent, I sometimes thought of Ginger. By the time we had left Morogoro he was no longer ours; he had become one of the wild dogs. He never came back to the house of cement blocks even to eat, and would have sunk teeth into our hands if we had reached out to pet him. Once we heard disease had swept through the pack of dogs; for a while their number did seem smaller, then they appeared as populous as before. Several times, in the car, we might have seen Ginger loping along the ditch beside the main road. We weren't sure. I thought yes; Lily disagreed. "He's dead," she said. "He died a long time ago. He's not coming back."

When I finally heard from Lily, in 1981, she said she had found

Jesus; intermittently He allowed her to leave the clinic and live with Ardis in the Columbia Avenue house below until the burden of her sins drove my sister back to her cold white room upon the hill. I couldn't help but think of Jesus wandering lost amid the bamboo shoots beside the Ngong River, impractical white robes tangled in vines and roots, waiting for Lily to find Him and to bring Him home before dark. My sister would hardly see me when I visited Brale in 1986 and 1988, on both occasions retreating into the hospital just before my arrival and remaining there, nearly incommunicado, until I left. Upon my return to Europe she sent me poorly printed religious tracts and urged me to become saved before it was too late; through postcards mailed to me from Thailand and Indonesia and Sri Lanka, I understood that Mitch also received warnings of a Second Coming. With Ardis and Jesus and medication, Lily apparently still waits in Brale for its occurrence. Beside the cold, swift river they attempt to pass calm years made up of cleaning and dusting and other careful rituals. The last time I heard from Lily, in 1990, she enclosed a photograph of herself. I couldn't recognize this woman with puffy face devoid of freckles, with hair pinned into a neat bun, with untroubled eyes. Lily looked without smiling into the camera, as if afraid her face would crack. As if parting her lips would allow a wild dog's howl to swell the air.

It seemed, in Sevilla, that I moved safely from the sound of the wild dogs' howls, and from their sharp sense of smell that had always tracked me down before, no matter how quickly and far I ran. It could have happened anywhere, but for mysterious reasons probably having to do with time and distance it happened in the Virgen de la Antigua. A door opened before me. All I had to do was walk into a room that in its peace and calm was unlike any room known before. In Sevilla my *piso* was more comfortably and completely furnished than my previous homes, where I wouldn't bother with pots and pans and shower curtains because I would soon be leaving. Reyna, the belly dancer, helped arrange and decorate the rooms during her 1989 springtime visit from New York. She had talent for more than romance and dancing: it was easy to see that she had squinted at any number of small, unsatisfactory places and without much money fixed them up, made them work. While Reyna offered instructions concerning love, we painted the furniture red and black, with curtains fashioned a sleeping alcove off the wide hall, discovered the best place for the couch, table and chairs. It was a small apartment, actually maid's quarters to the large, unoccupied apartment connected by a locked door; but it was a place you could be happy in, with lots of morning light and plants on the window-sills and garlic hanging in the kitchen. For once I had a telephone. Though it didn't ring often, Ardis was able to call from Brale to ask what day it was, to ask me her middle name.

I waited for cobwebs to begin to form.

For fragile reasons that I didn't understand, and was afraid to investigate, the corners stayed clean.

People I had known in other places came to visit. Reyna returned for another April to find I had begun dance classes in the Macarena, joined one of the clubs that rowed on the river, and discovered Jose. "You can still catch," she told me, approving of Jose, admitting that in him there was at least one Sevillano with brains as well as looks. On her best behaviour, she dressed up and flirted and danced for his attention. "Take good care of him," she warned me before returning again to Manhattan. "And you take good care of him," she told Jose in the same deadly serious tone, turning to regard him from behind dark glasses.

When there was not company I wandered in sunshine along the river, towards the Triana gym, and watered my plants and swept my rooms between English students in whom I one day hoped to feel more interest. Jose finished work, and stopped by at his mother's to shower and change; then he arrived at my door with a litre of beer, chestnut hair newly washed and combed, and skin smelling cleanly of soap. I prepared pasta and *salade niçoise*. He set the table, lit candles, put on music. Later we sat on the terraces of the Guadalquivir, or visited the Alfalfa bars, before crossing back over the bridge towards home. Time always passes in different ways in each place and season; here it ran quietly and steadily and slowly as the dark river below us, where we paused upon the Puente San Telmo, and colours wavered upon the surface of this time with the same brilliance as the reflections of neon upon the water. Two years passed while we paused upon the bridge.

"I'm not leaving," I frequently told Jose, after he knew and feared my history.

"Because you're happy," I replied when he asked why I needed him near.

Because you are happy and because you were born right on this street, only five blocks away, and because you didn't eat *salad niçoise* from Royal Hotel room service in Manila when you were ten years old.

Because you spent your teenaged years on a rowing team that practised on this river, that widened your shoulders and strengthened your back, that narrowed your eyes permanently against the sun.

Because, though five years younger than me, you have some-how acquired the patience I lack, or have enjoyed it all along. You can be patient for both of us when I waken confused because the landscape has not altered overnight. You are patient when I am disbelieving, as if all of this, including you, were a fantastic dream, another mirage.

It looked like, one day, fully re-indoctrinated, I might even buy a television. Yet after three years I was still wary of wild dogs and cobwebs. I still felt unsafe: your strong arms did not always have the power to keep old fears at bay. There were times when it seemed that my quiet life was only the thorough performance of the undercover agent, who understands the necessity of creating an illusion of an unremarkable existence in order to conceal his secret, dangerous mission. Jose knew only part of my previous dark and covert operations. "I understand," he said when I began to explain what I had done and why it had seemed necessary. "But please don't tell me any more."

I glimpse an airplane flying through the sky and my performance slips. I remember driving across the desert from Palm Springs with the gas to the floor, trying to make as much distance as I can before dawn, trying not to glance at the loaded revolver on the seat beside me, trying not to think about what happened in Palm Springs. When I can't forget what happened in Rome and Mexico and Palm Springs, I find myself walking quickly between the walls, unable to hear what Jose says until he grabs my wrist, stops me, speaks louder.

"Today is Tuesday," he says. "I'll be back on Friday."

Then he would walk quickly out the door and leave me this necessary time to think about the sun setting behind the pyramids and making love on the dark cliff above the sea on Formentera and that café in Paris where I could go for a meal when I was hungry but without money. While Jose went out for a drink with his mother, and saw the friends he neglected for me, I walked between the walls and travelled through all the places and incidents and people I had known, until the long journey finally ended and I found myself, exhausted but more peaceful, back in Sevilla on Friday, with Jose opening the door amid the scent of clean soap.

"I'm back," I said.

"I hope you missed me," he said, not smiling.

"I didn't leave," I said, not smiling either.

"Neither did I," he said, moving near.

iv.

In the afternoon, I emerge from the Hotel de Provence and move cautiously through the streets. That they are not the dirt roads of Morogoro, boulevards of Los Angeles, Sevilla cobblestones or Mitch's Hanoi haunts takes me slightly aback. This town is not simply a figment of my imagination. And at this hour its streets are fairly quiet, nearly empty. The air stretches through relative silence. A kind of stupor reigns.

An island of neatly trimmed lawn and beds of flowers floats between the lanes of the boulevard Mohammed v. To one side of the Place, the post-office building stirs after the long pause of afternoon. I step inside and mail a letter of inquiry to the Canadian consulate in Rabat. Leaving, I pass a man settling before a very old manual typewriter on the deep porch. For a fee, I think, he writes letters dictated by people who need to send news.

At the far end of the Place, to my left, lies the Café-Restaurant Scheherazade, which I have chosen for my meals. The place is small and shabby; the food is simple and inexpensive. I can eat *salade niçoise* and *tajine de poulet* in the early afternoon, and there is *harira* at night. So far I always sit at the same table, just within the open doorway – all the tables are covered with sticky plastic cloths – while starving cats twine around my legs. Occasionally, I will remember to wave at the persistent flies crawling over my skin and food.

Ahead of me, the large stone structure housing the civic government flutters with flags. Along the sidewalks, shopkeepers roll up the metal barriers that protect their closed stores; the sound scrapes the air, breaks a spell. All over town shutters are opening upon the slate sky; dreamers groggily shake themselves awake for the evening. Soon the cafés will fill again as darkness falls. The promenade along the shore will become popular. The main streets will turn bright with light.

Now the port slumbers before me. At a distance, to my left, the *quartier portugais* waits for me to enter its maze, dares me once again to find my way back out into the kind of ordinary light that fills this November afternoon. Directly across from the port, facing it, stand several old hotels. A tainted reputation clings to them; they are seedy places by the water where acts of prostitution and perversion might occur. Shady proprietors lean in their doorways or their vacant doorways are dark with shadow. Stone steps rise abruptly from the entrance to the illicit, shuttered rooms above. A mattress on the floor, a blanket twisting across it. The bucket of water in the corner. Strangled moans and sighs.

Something bright – gold or silver – flashes in the corner of my eye; it is alluring enough to turn my head. I see a blond woman step through the dark doorway of the Hotel de Marseilles. She moves into the shadow. The door closes behind her.

I hesitate on the sidewalk across the street. Gulls squawk overhead; a chill wind blows in from the Atlantic. Dodging between a donkey cart and a moped, I approach the hotel and try to open the door. It is bolted from inside. I knock several times; once painted blue, now peeling, the wood is faded and filthy. Two passing boys look at me, nudge each other, say something with a laugh. I listen for a sound on the other side of the door. Silence. I turn and cross the street again, then set out on the promenade as it leads away from the town. Glancing back once, I see a shutter in an upper window of the Hotel de Marseilles slowly close.

Dusk begins to fall. The lamps above me flicker hesitantly, then elect to stay on; ahead, they curve past the fragrant beach cafés. On the shore below, a photographer poses motionless at the edge of the sand. A dark silhouette against a darkening sky. Far in the distance, beyond long stretches of black shore where few people venture at night, shine the lights of Azemmour.

Dagmar or Anke or Ardis.

You have to call her something.

When I return to the town, it must be nearly midnight. I am hungry and cold. I have been down on the dark sand, past the lit promenade, for hours. Only a few stragglers remain in the cafés. The Hotel de Marseilles leaks no light. Its upper windows are shuttered; the building appears abandoned or asleep. From far away a cock crows the hour. The empty streets of El Jadida shine with ghostly light.

"You're back," says the room in a mocking voice.

"Long time no see," it smirks. "I knew we'd meet again."

I glance briefly around Room 5 of the Hotel de Provence. I know it already. Despite slight or not so slight differences, it is identical to Room 253 of the Gilbert Hotel in Hollywood and to Habitación 900 of the Hotel Carlotta in Mexico City and to any *chambre* in any Hotel California in any European city. They are all essentially the same room; the rest is cosmetics.

How something in the voices of people across the wall makes me want to know them or not. How the pillow I toss upon when I hear those voices bears invisible, microscopic remains of every stranger who has tossed anxiously upon it, despite the best efforts of housekeeping. How the mirror in the morning reveals a face I would pass without recognizing in the street.

It's all the same room.

I am not certain how long I will be in this familiar hotel room in this medium-sized town on the Atlantic coast of North Africa. Like the poorly informed secret agent, with knowledge of only a single dubious lead – a passport discovered somewhere in the sand – I must wait in readiness to receive the details of my mission. Still lying at the bottom of my blue bag is the background data for my assignment. Now I spread photographs and letters, timetables and room-service menus and a black daybook across the bed. I sift through them until I find what I am looking for.


The last postcard from my father depicts, on one side, a colour photograph of the Portuguese ruins at El Jadida. The structure, apparently once a fortress, is viewed from sufficient distance to permit a wide border of deep-blue sky above; but whether this structure rises from the centre of barren desert, sprouts above lush jungle, or clings to the top of a cliff is impossible to tell. For all the postcard's photograph reveals, this citadel could be anywhere.

The front appears impressively solid for its four hundred years, and made of some kind of pale (faded?) stone obviously weath-ered by sun, rain and the salt wind of the Atlantic; yet it is a non-descript front, as blank as a featureless face, with no watchful windows or cunning detail for the eye to contemplate with delight. Where are the ramparts, the bastions? In the centre is a wide, arched entrance yawning open in invitation, and what seems only shadow in the interior beyond. Possibly the shadow conceals fascinating contents – artifacts and instruments, weap-ons and tools – old objects of historic as well as artistic interest. One somehow doubts this.

I know that the interior of this citadel, or rather the cistern below it, once so dazzled Orson Welles that he was compelled to film it for one of his many unfinished motion pictures; the quality of the light within this cavernous, vaulted chamber moved him deeply, it seems. It was for Welles, and for many others before and since (for my father?), a mysterious, haunting kind of illumination, whose effect is achieved by the interplay of sunlight, entering a single, oculus window, with a layer of water beneath the stone vaulting. One imagines a constant dripping, a magnified echo of water hitting water. A sound that suggests more than itself and resists easy interpretation at once. It spreads between stone and through what is, by all accounts, the sort of ambiguous light in which the moral actions of a man, often suspect and always open to interpretation as they are, might unfold in a highly cinematic way. A way with precedent: Orson Welles has already splashed through the dark sewers beneath Vienna as Harry Lime, the good friend gone corrupt in *The Third Man*, a few months before emerging from the citadel in El Jadida to exclaim upon shadow and echo and light in a voice that trembles with emotion.

Studying the last postcard from my father, I wonder if Orson Welles was a man often moved and easily compelled, for these ruins appear quite without interest from both an architectural and photographic point of view. Even the word "ruins" seems a misleading exaggeration to describe a structure that has, apparently, escaped the ravages of time to a remarkable degree. Is the uncredited photographer the same photographer who roams the beach at sunset? I will soon come to wonder. Is he to blame for making this sight so wanting in interest? Is it his choice of angle and lens and lighting that are at fault? – if indeed he used a camera more complex than the one he carries at the shore, and had such choices to make. Was he bored or uninspired or suffering a headache on the day he snapped the shot? Or was he, simply, a man lacking talent, an artist unable to do justice to his subject? If presented with the real thing – the citadel rising solidly before me, the cistern spreading eerily around me – might I be as moved as Orson Welles, as impressed as my father?

The caption on the postcard's reverse, in three languages and small print, in the upper left-hand corner, is as flatly prosaic as the photograph it describes.

*Portuguese Citadel, El Jadida.*

*La citadelle portugaise, El Jadida.*

*Il sejahrig ajneebah, El Jadida.*

The message on the other side – seven words in black ink to the left of my Sevilla address – is more ambiguous:

*Greetings from the end of the world.*

I picture my father standing on the sidewalk of boulevard Mohammed v, before El Jadida's single souvenir store. He slowly turns the rack of postcards in the doorway; the rack is somehow unbalanced and teeters dangerously as it moves. It creaks and groans, as if unused to being set in motion. This may well be the case, for it is the off season in El Jadida, and for four months there have been few tourists to pluck coloured cardboard pictures from this rack. Quite possibly the stock of postcards has not been replenished since the summer season; the rack is far from full, with a depleted look, and the few cards still haunting it are faded from sun, splattered by rain. These are, I imagine, the least interesting postcards, poor ones passed over by the summer people. Long gone are choicer cards presenting, for example, the interior of the cistern, that mystical place which has profoundly affected so many. Really, my father may have very little choice of postcards to send me from El Jadida; only the most ordinary scenes of shore and sea, market and mosque – the least telling details, the most vapid panoramas – survive.

Or perhaps the rack was, in fact, crammed with postcards when Mitch selected a last one to send me. Quite plausibly, he was in a hurry when he made the choice; he left it too late. Say it is nearly evening in El Jadida. The light is fading quickly; in a few seconds, only as long as it takes a star to fall, the sky will be completely dark, and then the streets will empty with astonishing speed, as if night were dangerous, an element to be avoided at all cost. In January a cold, dark wind blows upon El Jadida from the ocean, and people from other places, Europe or America, do not promenade its streets, linger in its cafés, prolong the evening with mint tea beneath the lamps and palms. Already the owner of the souvenir store is eager to close; he brings newspapers from Paris and London, only five days old, inside. Because of dimming light and hurry, by mistake Mitch picks a postcard of the citadel's exterior instead of one of the cavernous cistern below. He chooses the wrong card.

It is equally possible that Mitch was thinking of something else as his hand reached out to select a postcard from that rack. Certainly enough weighs on his mind: behind him lies the long, confused journey to this medium-sized town on the Atlantic coast of North Africa, a path indiscernible during the making, camouflaged to prevent anyone following, perceptible with difficulty only now, looking back, when it has nearly faded. Years of circling and searching and failing to find are about to come to conclusion. Suddenly the unclouded sky above El Jadida becomes suffused with an intense light, the kind of magical light that occurs – rarely, briefly – just before dusk at certain latitudes in certain seasons. For a moment it seems possible to see far into the sky, to its deepest end. What is there? Mitch lifts his head and looks above: this is the light of his age-old dream. Then the mosque's bell begins to clang; Mitch's head jerks at the sound. Allah is waiting, it is time to pray, another lesson of the Koran must be taught. Figures urged by the bell scurry by and Mitch's hand reaches blindly for the last postcard he will send me.

Or could it be that Mitch was indifferent to the various scenes which decorate these cards? Only the message he writes on the back will matter? Any gaudy photograph will do? Ocean, shore, citadel, cistern: in the end it's all the same?

Of course I am not sure if Mitch actually entered the citadel and cistern, or even knew of their existence. Given his tendency to overlook the principal point of interest of a place, it is not impossible that he spent three weeks in El Jadida unaware of its most impressive feature, its only claim to fame. People always described my father's gaze as intent, and they were correct insofar as his eyes usually focused sharply upon whatever lay before him, as if no detail of his surroundings could escape his notice. In fact, what lay before Mitch was always what he dreamed and never the principal point of interest; it was this mirage that formed the object of his intent regard. Very likely the El Jadida through which Mitch wandered during the final days before he disappeared is not to be discovered upon any picture postcard, no matter how superior, or upon any piece of film by Orson Welles. For Mitch this last city might just as well have been Jerusalem or Moscow, Babylon or Rome. Any Atlantis, El Dorado, Xanadu.

Perhaps my father bought the last postcard he would send me in early morning, not late afternoon. Perhaps dimming light and descending night have no part in the story at all.

Sometimes I believe I know exactly what was running through Mitch's mind while he walked between the Café des Amis and the Café-Restaurant Scheherazade on those January nights in El Jadida. At other times this man who strolls through my dreams is a stranger never seen before, and I have no idea what he will do next, where he will go tomorrow, or the reasons for any of his actions. With each consideration of Mitch's last days in El Jadida, a more tantalizing possibility looms in my mind, and, fickle devotee, I reject the previous one. And there have been occasions in the past week when I think: Who gives a damn what happened to that man. Leave him to his fate. Let him go to hell.

At the moment, I feel I know a good deal more about Orson Welles' time in El Jadida than I do about my father's. I can see Orson Welles more clearly there. I can hear that actor's rich voice, gloriously theatrical, boom down the boulevard Almouhit and fill the Place Moussa. Welles puffs cigars in beach cafés which bear wistful resemblance to the Deux Magots, the Flore, or other Parisian places. In 1950 he is stout but not yet impossibly so; it is hard to tell, from his exuberant air, that he is juggling a restive cast, stolen equipment, and insolvent Italian backers for this current, quixotic project. Through the streets he strides indiscreetly, entourage in tow, scattering Jewish shopkeepers in the *quartier ancienne*, tossing coins to beggars who in the dust swoon with disbelief, gesturing expansively and maintaining a continuous flow of talk, a whole river of words that does not run dry, at least not in El Jadida. (In fact, this stream of words will not end for thirty-five years – in, appropriately, Las Vegas.) A thwarted dreamer? A stunted giant? Certainly a vibrant weaver of projects and schemes, visions and plans – few of which will be realized. Like Mitch, Welles is essentially a dreamer; unlike my father, a dreamer for whom in the dream's telling may lie its satisfaction.

In El Jadida I imagine my father was mainly silent. Uncharacteristically silent and alone. A silent man of medium height and build peering intently at a rack of postcards in the dimming light of a North African winter evening. In the afternoon he walks the shore alone. Often he is the only patron of the dining room of the Hotel Mahraba; if stray off-season tourists enter while Mitch is there, they invariably choose a distant table, and, sensing that privacy is important to this man, do not nod or lift glasses in his direction. Indeed, everyone in El Jadida seems to respect Mitch's need for solitude to a remarkable degree: beggars spare him whines and street children do not persist in showing him the way to *la cathédrale* (which is not difficult to find, and even hard to avoid – but there is little else, besides the citadel, to guide the tourist to in El Jadida). Without an entourage Mitch wanders the medina, where the narrowness of streets casts them in permanent shadow and coolness. He looks without pausing into windows, then enters (randomly?) a low doorway. He is in a large, square room with sand-coloured walls of plaster and a cement floor covered with scattered rugs. In one corner a woman bends over a table and with deft fingers picks chaff from a pan of wheat. In a basket by her feet, a baby cries. The woman, who is unveiled and young, glances at Mitch, once, then returns her eyes to her work. "Where am I?" Mitch's face asks, but his question is not urgent, almost idle, as if he does not expect or even want an answer.

Back out in the street he becomes increasingly lost in the old town's twisting ways; yet Mitch does not stop to ask directions of shopkeepers in halting French, or to pause on corners to try to gain his bearings. By this point in his life Mitch has wandered lost through the back streets of any number of strange cities; he is notorious for his appalling sense of direction, his inability to fix in mind landmarks which might later steer him straight. We liked to joke that Mitch could get confused a block from home. (Ardis, on the other hand, could weave her way unflappably, as if born there, through *favelas* of Rio or Calcutta slums; her bearing implied that such mazes were nothing compared to the labyrinths of the mind she negotiated every day.) While some weaknesses may be overcome through time and experience, or repeated exposure to a difficulty, Mitch's tendency to become lost, apparently present from birth, as much a part of him as his name, his jet-black hair, was not vanquished even partly as it was tested over and over in always alien landscapes; yet this handicap did not, obviously, make him stay from fear in one known place and not venture to others. By the end of his life Mitch gives the impression of one so used to being lost that it is for him an ordinary event, almost the natural condition of man. Perhaps this is why his figure does not arrest attention in the *derbs* of El Jadida, those alleys where a stranger, particularly a Westerner, and especially one alone and lost, is not an everyday sight.

"There's no such thing as being lost," Mitch would inform me, for instance, as another *autobahn* fled beneath our wheels in 1971. My father especially liked to share his philosophy while driving. The highway expanded something inside him always and he could see farther when in motion; for other people it is ocean or mountain or sky. While Lily and MJ doze amid luggage in the back, I am in the seat of honour just behind my parents, the crumpled map an object of musing across my knees. Mitch's body seems loosened and enlarged by our motion. Ardis stares tensely at the road, unblinking, as if she must keep her eyes upon this highway or it will vanish from beneath us, and we will find ourselves driving through the sky. "You missed the exit," Ardis suddenly tells Mitch, without turning her face towards him or lessening the intensity of her vigil over the road. I check the map and see that she is right again. While Mitch is fascinated by cartography, poring over his vast collection of atlases for whole evenings, he appreciates a map as an object of art or a thing of beauty, and not of much practical use during our journey. Now, for a moment, Mitch appears crestfallen behind the wheel; but he keeps driving, and soon looks again as if he knows exactly where he is taking us. No, we have not missed Munich, we have not gone past our destination, for Mitch knows of a secret exit, unmarked on any map, that will take us exactly where we need to be.

And now Mitch has been declared lost.

Not dead.

A subtle difference.

Sometimes, in the copies of consulate letters and faxes sent to me by Ardis, they use the word *missing* instead of *lost*.

If a body is not discovered, if no remains at all are found, it appears that a death cannot be declared until a certain amount of time (which, at least in North Africa, seems to vary from anywhere between six months and two years) has passed. Only then can a next of kin formally request, by means of a particular form filled out in triplicate, that death be pronounced. An official death, as opposed to the unofficial kind.

Ardis will probably refuse to make this request, as, I suppose, will I. Lily and MJ are, in different ways, unavailable for the job.

So Mitch is still not, officially, dead. Nor can he be lost, since there is no such thing as being lost. He simply disappeared, six months after mailing me a postcard depicting the citadel at El Jadida, bringing to conclusion, upon the Western Sahara, a gradual disappearing act set in motion more than half a century ago.

To disappear. The verb is not irrevocable. To complete its action does not preclude the possibility of performing its opposite. To reappear. One day Mitch may spring back into sight in Oslo? In ten years I will receive a postcard presenting a colour view of the Grand Canyon?

Did my father intend for the postcard he sent me from El Jadida to be the final one? For him it may have represented only another of the numerous cards he mailed to me from the myriad of places he found himself. Of no more weight than the one of the pyramid at Chichén Itzá I received a year ago, or of the Taj Mahal the year before that. On January 17, 1992, Mitch still imagined sending me countless cards in years to come, cards of all sizes and shapes, cards showing all sorts of scenes, cards from Reykjavík and New Orleans and Johannesburg, an unending series of vistas and panoramas, with an infinite variety of stamps fixed to them, never a final card, a goodbye card. Mitch did not realize that he was sending me a last clue for endless speculation and scrutiny.

As I feel baffled by all the uncertainties of my father's last days here, I seize upon hard facts and take comfort from them. I carefully read the oddly written tourist pamphlets in the lobby of the Hotel de Provence. It helps me to have no doubt that El Jadida was once called Mazagan by its Portuguese settlers, who definitely built the citadel and cistern in the early sixteenth century. At that time the harbour was important, but when the Moors recovered the town in the middle of the eighteenth century, the harbour silted over, and is at present too shallow to permit the entrance of ships. The name El Jadida, given the place upon its retrieval from the Portuguese, means, in Arabic, the new one.

These facts are beyond dispute.

If Mitch mailed the postcard the day after buying it, I can be certain, from the postmark of blurred, barely legible black ink, that he stood on the sidewalk before El Jadida's single souvenir store on January 17, 1992.

A Friday. "Substantial evidence" (in the words of the Canadian consulate) points to his leaving El Jadida that Sunday. January 19, 1992.

Or did my father choose this postcard with careful deliberation after all? Perhaps he felt it appropriate that the last image he would send me would show an open doorway filled with shadow, with no hint of what the shadow conceals. He wanted me to wonder and never know for certain if the interior beyond the doorway contains dazzling mysteries that could move me the way they moved Orson Welles. Or to wonder if it conceals nothing. He wanted me, finally, to travel to El Jadida myself and to visit the Portuguese ruins and to enter the citadel's door and to discover firsthand what, if anything, hides within the shadows there.

I would see the amazing light within the cistern.

I would hear the echo of water dripping upon water.

*Greetings from the end of the world.*

I notice that, at the end of the third word, Mitch's ballpoint pen stuck or ran dry. I picture him, sitting on the edge of this bed in the Hotel de Provence (it is all the same hotel, the same room, the same bed), waving the pen through the air in order to make the black ink flow again. He looks around the room in search of another pen, or even a pencil. Seeing none, he waves the reluctant pen again, it works once more, and Mitch is able to write the last four words of his final message to his second son. His handwriting is easily recognizable; one might describe it as strong and determined, but with enough eccentricity to give it style. It appears no different than the script he employed all his life. There are no unusual quirks to betray that the hand which forms these final letters is guided by an especially wrought-up being. An analyst of handwriting might, from just these seven words, be able to describe Mitch more clearly than I could ever do, and to define, particularly, his state of mind on January 17, 1992. But anyone can see that there is room enough for many more than seven words on this card; the extra space questions with its blankness, reminds that much more could have been said. There is room for thirty words, in Mitch's handwriting. His message requires only seven.

*Greetings*, he wrote.

Not farewell.

Though a dreamer, Mitch was always deliberate. His fascination with cold facts and hard data is a part of that; he was a precise fantasist, with sharply etched outlines to his illusions. All appearances to the contrary, the existence Mitch pursued was never ruled by the accidental, and he would not leave me, because of a moment's inattention or oversight, to feel completely lost in regard to his life. Yes, he taught me to imagine and to dream, but he instructed me also that we can place our faith in solid, visible things.

Such as a colour postcard depicting the citadel at El Jadida.

On the morning of January 17, Mitch finishes his *café au lait*, then walks to the *bureau de poste* in the Place Mohammed v. He buys a 4.50 dirham stamp which bears the face of Hassan II, with typically neutral expression, upon a background of pale green. Mitch sticks the stamp upon the small box in the upper right-hand corner, just above where he has neatly printed my address in Sevilla, then slides the postcard through the slot of the mailbox labelled *Étrangers Avion*. Upon the porch he pauses without turning his face towards the hooded man to his left, who bends over the battered portable typewriter and taps the dictation spoken, in Arabic, by a client at his shoulder. The taste of the stamp he has just licked, neither sour nor sweet, lingers in Mitch's mouth, spreads with his saliva, dissolves through his blood. During the previous night, another night he did not sleep, Mitch has moved closer to his end. He can see it more clearly now. From the post office he emerges into one of those mornings in El Jadida, which occur all year round, when the air is so transparent you feel you can see through it forever, all the way to the end of the world.

I drop the postcard.

It is clear that this damned hotel room isn't going to show me anything. Perhaps the midnight streets of El Jadida will offer me more.

Down at the reception desk the young Moroccan in the wine-coloured coat who checked me in seems to have been waiting nervously for my appearance.

"My name is Mohammed Lasfar," he says insistently when I'm a foot away, about to pass the desk. As if this were the most essential information in the world, as if this were all I needed to know in my lifetime. Mohammed Lasfar stares at me. I think he has something more to tell me. I wait for him to speak further, shrug, begin to move away.

"Please," he says. "One moment." He glances furtively around, then leans towards me. "Room 5 is a good room," he says in a low voice. "Fine enough for anyone, yes? Fine enough for one's father, for instance. One's father would enjoy staying in Room 5 for three weeks during January, I believe."

His eyes return to the ledger before him with such abrupt finality that I understand he has finished speaking for the moment, and possibly forever, upon this subject.

Of course.

Naturally Mitch would choose the Hotel de Provence, the finest in El Jadida, the only one to offer the possibility of leeway. Of course I have ended up in the room where he ended up. Of course it has worked out just like that.

## V.

In El Jadida I come to know when the *muezzin* will call from the mosque, find myself listening to his *azan*, grow used to this pattern of prayer. I begin to realize that here it rains secretly during the night. In the morning puddles shine below the sidewalks and shimmer in the *derbs*, though the days are blue and clear, with equally untroubled evenings. Lying awake, during my first nights in El Jadida, I listen for this invisible rain but hear only wild dogs barking in the distance. I walk at night along the shore, when the photographer and his camera have abandoned their usual place beside the waves. The dark ocean is often turbulent and loud, and shadows float across the sand. They mutter as they pass, muffled and obscure; what they tell me is inaudible because the ocean crashes, sighs, crashes. Go back, I imagine they say.

As I drift through the town during the afternoon or evening, I become aware that Mohammed Lasfar is frequently near. He walks on the other side of the boulevard Mohammed v ; he leans in a dim doorway by the port. He hovers near the last lamp-pole on the promenade. At a table before the Café Rosé, he looks out at the ocean, turns to watch me walk by. Sometimes, on the dark beach late at night, though I know that at this hour he is behind the reception desk at the Hotel de Provence, I believe that Mohammed Lasfar is near.

One day, mailing a postcard to Reyna, I again notice the transcriber who conducts business on the wide, deep porch of the *bureau de poste*. He is poised before a small table that bears an old Olivetti with its insides exposed: a relic from the past. An untidy queue clutches unwritten messages that need to be typed into letters by this man, that need to be sent to the north, south or east. I stare at the man. He is hidden inside an undistinguished *djellaba*, probably late middle-aged, someone I might pass on the street without seeing. His hooded eyes glow in shadow. The sound of his keys taps the air. He types neither quickly nor slowly; he types steadily, for hours, apparently oblivious to time, performing an ancient ritual. His fingers flutter before the paper as if by their movement encouraging a spell that will realize in words the substance of visions and dreams. In early evening, he suddenly packs his typewriter in a cardboard box tied with string and walks quickly from the porch. I follow him through streets that lead behind the comparatively orderly façade of El Jadida where a labyrinth of narrow alleys remains Stygian even during the day. His sandals slap softly against the cobblestones. Despite his burden, he slips with smooth, swift grace; he floats into the dimness before me. Stumbling behind, I try to keep up. He turns at the next corner. When I turn the same corner, a moment later, a dark, empty alley leads before me; not even an echo of footsteps fades up into the sky. The cobblestones are still wet from the previous night's rain; they glisten in the light from a single dim lamp set into the stone wall at a distance down the alley. I wonder if the transcriber vanished through one of the closed, silent doorways to either side. Where has he gone? In the alley ahead, the lamp beckons me forward.


What do I expect?

Swarms of detectives? Packs of bloodhounds? A general state of emergency?

El Jadida appears unaware that a man who has been declared missing was last seen here. There are no signs that the Moroccan authorities are conducting an active investigation into the matter. I inquire at the police station near the port; guarded by armed sentries with inscrutable expressions, it is strangely silent beneath the red and green flag whipping in an Atlantic breeze. A listless atmosphere pervades within. For an hour I wait to speak with an uninterested, irritated official in a grey uniform. He directs me to a second office, on the next street, where an equally uninterested and irritated official in a slightly different uniform directs me to another nearby office. At the end of a long afternoon, I am left with the impression that there are a dozen police offices in El Jadida, each handling a slightly different aspect of law and order, none having any knowledge of my father's case. I imagine papers and records concerning Mitch growing in dusty piles on desks, shuffling unread or immediately forgotten from one office to another, becoming lost in circular transfers, orbiting endlessly.

Late one night, returning from the shore to the Hotel de Provence, I ask Mohammed Lasfar what he meant by his earlier remark that Room 5 was good enough for one's father. He assumes a wary, secretive expression and professes not to understand what I'm talking about. The other desk clerk looks blank when I mention, another day, that my father might have stayed at the hotel when he visited El Jadida last winter. I mean to bring up the subject with Godfrey Bridgeport, the owner, but he always seems to vanish into the private rooms behind the lobby upon my approach, as if avoiding me.

Every few days I enter the *bureau de poste* and ask for poste restante letters. The man behind the wicket shakes his head in a
forceful negative, almost suggesting that the possibility of my
receiving letters was remote, at the very least. Finally, one morning, he hands me a postcard from Reyna in New York. A letter
arrives from Jose in Madrid. From Ardis I receive a copy of the
vice-consul's letter which confirms that, as far as is known and as
she originally told me in Sevilla, Mitch was last seen in El Jadida.

When the Canadian consulate in Rabat still doesn't respond to
my inquiry about Mitch, I negotiate the complicated procedure
for telephoning from the *bureau de poste*. An embassy employee
tells me that certain kinds of information can't be given out –
especially not by telephone – without authorization. How does
she know that I am, in fact, a next of kin? She has no knowledge
of a letter of inquiry from a missing Canadian's son in El Jadida.
The family is being notified according to procedure and will continue to be kept fully informed as events unfold. If indeed I am
this party's son, I will in due course and through proper channels
receive all information as it becomes available.

I swear and hang up.

I decide to call Ardis in Brale. It takes several hours for the collect call to go through. I wait at one end of the dim, cool room
and hear the sound of typing from the man on the front porch
outside. The queues before the postal wickets twist and coil anxiously; even the purchase of a stamp may possess a desperate
urgency, accompanied by sudden wails, abrupt skirmishes, suspense. When my call is ready, I re-enter the battered, old-
fashioned telephone box. I hear Ardis say only "Nothing. No
more news" before our line is cut.

I inspect Room 5 once more for traces of Mitch's presence.

I look again at the documents I leave spread across the small
table.

Soon I will be forced to wander into cafés and stores to ask
the proprietors if they recognize the face in my most recent

photograph of Mitch, taken fifteen years ago. I will have to plead with beggars and cripples for help with my search. On bent knees in the mosque I will pray to Allah for assistance.

I continue to work into casual conversations with strangers the mention that last winter my father was in El Jadida. For a while, people seem faintly curious about my presence in El Jadida. They stop to talk with me in the street and on the shore. They approach me in cafés. The young men want to discuss visas; they all dream of escaping El Jadida and venturing to another country, it seems. Then people slowly appear to lose their mild interest in me. When I do ask them about my father, they speak only of the secret rain.

Later they would remember that winter in El Jadida for the rain which began to fall in late October and continued off and on until March. It was not unusual to receive intermittent rainfall during these months, but the precipitation that winter was memorable because for two years there had been little. Crops were hurting in the fields, a kilo of oranges cost half a dirham more in the market, and beggars in the Place were more numerous. Usually the welcome rain fell during night, while everyone was sleeping, and this transformed it into a secret occurrence. People would waken to clear blue skies and expect to see the street dry with dust. There was always a moment of surprise and wonder when they glanced out windows and saw that the pavement was wet, with puddles shining in the *derbs*. Sometimes, during that startling moment, they wondered if other unknown events transpired while they slept in darkness, and if evidence of those unwitnessed happenings were also left behind.

Yes, it was another quiet winter when breeze blew in from the ocean; regardless of rain or drought, the market hummed with shrewd exchanges and the cafés in the Place were full even during the holy month of prayer and fasting, when between dawn and dusk abstaining customers sat before empty tables and listened to the television convey the sixty lessons of the Koran. And it was the time when young men of the town dreamed of far away; they envisioned themselves living and working in the north, out of sight, among the infidels. In the Café Sables d'Or and the Café Rosé they held desultory discussions on how to secure the difficult visas that would permit them to sell flowers in Italy or to wash dishes in Germany. With luck they might leave El Jadida to return as visitors who frolicked for a summer week upon the sand before departing for more promising places again. They could not imagine why anyone would stay in town if they had a choice, especially during the quiet winter of strange and secret rain.

Indeed, few tourists visited during this season, and usually they remained only one or two nights in town. During the middle of afternoon, when boys did not play soccer on the sand, the beach was empty of strolling dreamers from far away, and strewn with garbage that would be picked up in May, before the crowds from Marrakesh and Casablanca, as well as from foreign countries, descended upon the town for summer. At evening the tourist cafés with expensive prices and English menus were deserted, and their forlorn waiters leaned in doorways to gaze down the street without hope. The promenade along the shore was equally empty after ten o'clock, and like all abandoned places appeared to exist in waiting.

This was also remembered as the winter when several strangers visited, at different times, and remained longer than was customary. Passing them in the street, people would register surprise that they were still in El Jadida. The first *étranger*, an older man, stayed for three weeks in January; the second man, much younger, arrived months after the first departed, and remained slightly longer; in fact, a whole summer separated these visitors, but a trick of memory persuaded minds that they inhabited a single winter, not two.

Both stayed at the Hotel de Provence. Both wandered the streets and shore alone, neither picking up acquaintances among the boys anxious to practise English or other languages of more promising places, nor seeking the company of visitors who passed briefly through the town. Neither carried a camera, or visited the cathedral, citadel or cistern in the *quartier portugais*. Neither said why he had come to El Jadida during the quiet winter or why he stayed for longer than one or two nights of secret rain.

These strangers were also different in many ways. Besides the most noticeable fact of age, there were dissimilarities perceived by only more curious and observant eyes. The older *étranger* always gave coins to the beggars in the Place, while the younger never did. The older man spoke poor French; the other knew French and also Spanish well. The younger man smoked in the street and wore a silver chain around his neck. His predecessor wore a wedding band of gold around one finger of a hand that never held a cigarette. One drank his café *noir*, the other *au lait*; one with sugar, the other without.

Also, it was observed by some, these two visitors did not walk in the same fashion in the street. The younger *étranger* always appeared to search for someone in mid-distance, beyond unnoticed passersby who glanced into his face; he seemed prepared to greet somebody on the other side of the street or Place even when no one was there, even when this invisible acquaintance was never reached but remained at mid-distance before him, as an elusive spirit, or tantalizing ghost. While the older man also gave the impression of being oblivious to people nearby as well as at mid-distance or beyond, he did not appear expectant of coming upon a known face, corporeal or otherwise, in El Jadida. Sometimes, seeing in his face an approximation of the peace that comes with beholding the world beyond this world, people were reminded by this older man of their holy teachers, though they knew quite well that no *giaour* was blessed with faith. Both visitors, by their seeming blindness to the town's inhabitants, made these people feel like ghosts in their own streets, or only atoms of evaporated moisture floating through transparent air.

There were several people, like Mohammed Lasfar, who worked at the reception desk of the Hotel de Provence for two thousand dirhams per month, whose contact with the visitors was more immediate and extensive, and who dwelled upon them longer. These people sometimes received, in the middle of day, an image as clear and unexpected as the memory of a dream. They saw the two *étrangers* walking towards each other in the dark, wet street, otherwise deserted, and silent except for their footsteps and the rain. Their unprotected heads were soaked and drops of rain rolled down their faces. They watched each other intently as they approached, and several times stepped into a puddle, unaware of their feet, unaware of anything but the other drawing near. When they reached each other, the figures halted. A foot of darkness and rain separated them. Without speaking they looked into each other's eyes for a moment that lasted as long as the echo of a bell. Difference in age, and distinctness of face and form, dissolved. With the same expression they regarded one another in the splintered mirror of raindrops. At the same instant they each proceeded in the same direction as before, now stepping where the other's feet had stepped one, two or three minutes ago. Moving farther apart, they did not glance behind to see each other's back slipping into darkness as silent as sleep.

Later, the differences between the two visitors vanished, like the rain before dawn, and then people began to believe that only one *étranger* had remained for an unusual length of time during those two winters conjured into one. This single stranger possessed qualities of both men, and was envisioned in various ways, according to the heart and mind that considered him. Some remembered his kindness to beggars, some his cigarettes in the street; there were those who recalled calm eyes, others who saw a silver chain shining around a neck. Finally these two strangers, merged into one by memory, were both associated with the notable rain of that doubled season. When they woke in morning people would often think of the twinned visitor upon glancing at the wet, wondrous pavement and the puddles shining in the *derbs*. They would recall him as a secret occurrence of darkness that ceased with light, leaving no sign of passing behind. Although no one still knew why the stranger had come to town, or what he did while not walking along the shore or in the street, they carefully watched the ground beneath their feet for some time afterwards. Even in April, when the streets were once more dusty, they searched for sight of a silver chain or a band of gold glittering under clear blue sky.

By summer, when the visitor had been gone for months and the town was crowded with too many unknown faces to notice any as individual or unique, this single, solitary stranger to El Jadida was forgotten even by those who had envisioned him most clearly, even by those who recall their own lost father or lost son approaching through the wet night, and they remembered only the secret rain.

## vi.

"A charming chap," enthuses Godfrey Bridgeport. "A delightful companion. I only wish he could have stayed with us longer."

Five minutes ago I stole up behind the owner of the Hotel de Provence, whose head was bent intimately towards the late-afternoon desk clerk. At the sound of my voice, a sloppy, seedy man, somewhere in his fifties, spun around. His face flashed with alarm, then swiftly became bland. He looked for a moment at my outstretched hand before he limply shook it. "I think my father stayed here last winter. Do you remember him?" I asked.

Apparently, Godfrey Bridgeport has been unaware that I am the son of delightful, charming Mitch. Immediately brightening with pleasure at the news, he insists we become acquainted – right away, this very evening – in the otherwise deserted sitting room off the hotel's entrance. On the glass table before us rests a silver pot of Earl Grey tea, heavily flavoured with the chlorine that permeates the local water supply. Tattered copies of *Der Spiegel* and the London *Sunday Times* book sections, dating back several months, are scattered beside our cups. In the corner of the room a colour television snowily, silently emits a soccer game. I shift several inches away from Godfrey Bridgeport on the red plush sofa.

"Unpardonable," he repeats. "That you have been our guest all these weeks without my realizing your identity. Apparently, young Lasfar made the connection with your father as soon as you arrived, but for some reason obscured his knowledge from me until now. He concealed your father's *fiche*. I haven't the slightest idea why. After twenty-two years of what one might call intimate contact with these boys, I still fail to comprehend the native mind. Unfathomable. I've simply given up."

The next thing I know, he's going to call them *kaffirs*. Isn't he aware that in 1992 one doesn't call the citizens of any country natives and boys? These terms had already been abandoned by the time we arrived in East Africa at the end of the sixties. I don't like this man who has simply given up, not at all. I haven't the slightest desire to form his acquaintance over cups of chlorinated Earl Grey tea on a red plush sofa.

Godfrey Bridgeport sighs. "Of course they steal," he says fatalistically. "And they deceive one constantly over matters of utter unimportance. They also misplace the *fiches* of our guests, hence my lamentable failure to have appreciated who you are. If I had seen your *fiche*, I would have known at once." He considers me out of the corners of eyes laced with small red veins. "No," he shakes his head. "I can't see that you resemble your father, not really. Such a mature, handsome fellow. You can imagine, here in El Jadida, that he appeared like a breath of fresh air. A drink of cold, clear water when one is simply dying of thirst."

"I haven't seen my father for a long time," I say, excusing my inability to gush over his virtues.

"Yes, a breath of fresh air," Godfrey repeats musingly, as if I hadn't spoken. Obviously, I won't have to work to keep up my end of this conversation. I'll only have to nod occasionally and try

138

not to sneeze from the amazingly powerful aroma of gin that swims around this man.

"I try to get home every five years or so," reflects Godfrey. "But England has changed, and not for the better, I'm afraid. I scarcely recognize the old dear. More natives than the Marrakesh medina. Sad, quite sad."

"I'm not sure why my father came to El Jadida," I say leadingly. "How did he pass his time here?"

"One does not question the appearance of a rainbow after a storm," chides Godfrey. "One is grateful, one is happy, one is –" He waves his arms expansively, unable to articulate all the powerful emotions that flood one when one meets Mitch.

Godfrey adopts a tone of simplicity. "He was beloved, he was adored. The natives worshipped him. In fact, my Mohammed Lasfar neglected his duties to trail like a lost puppy after your father." Godfrey's voice sharpens. "I'm afraid I had to reprimand Mohammed Lasfar in the strongest possible terms. Well, one must keep after them day and night, mustn't one?"

I force myself to remain sitting with an attentive expression beside Godfrey Bridgeport. He declines to respond when I ask whether he has been questioned, by Canadian or Moroccan authorities, about my father; this bored dismissal of the topic suggests that it is meaningless to himself and therefore essentially unreal.

"Regrettably, not all the audience fortunate enough to attend your father's lecture was able to appreciate its many fine qualities," Godfrey mourns.

"Lecture?" I have lost track of my informant's monologue.

Godfrey suddenly claps his hands and in Arabic shouts in a high-pitched voice of surprising force and volume.

"Surely you know," he reproves me. "A distinguished speaker like your father. It was a privilege to have the opportunity to hear his views, but, as I say, quite unfortunate that not all in attendance were capable of appreciating them."

The young dining-room waiter appears with a piece of paper, hands it to Godfrey, then backs bowing from the room. The lids of Godfrey's eyes slowly lower as he gazes at the waiter's retreat; for a moment he seems sunken into a spell. Then he shakes his head and, with a flourish, delivers the paper to me. It is actually a small poster.

L'ALLIANCE FRANCO-MAROCCAIN

PRÉSENTE

MONSIEUR MITCH

QUI PRÉSENTERA SON LEÇON

"L'HISTOIRE COMME METAPHORE"

SALLE DE PROJECTION

AVENUE DE HASSAN II

SAMEDI, 11 JANVIER 1992

"Here in El Jadida," Godfrey explains modestly, "we do our best to preserve some fragile association with the world of ideas, art, civilization. Now and then the Alliance brings in the odd third-rate speaker, the occasional Chabrol film. Certainly we do not often have opportunity to find in our midst someone of your father's intellectual calibre and academic standing. A full doctorate from the Sorbonne is nothing to be sneezed at."

"My father has always had original theories," I cautiously admit. "And he has never been shy about sharing them."

"It is his style of speaking that is most appealing, isn't it?" notes Godfrey. "Oh, I'm afraid I am no sort of intellectual. Most of your father's complex ideas sailed far above my head, sadly. But one could admire the zest and enthusiasm with which they were presented. Such an engaging presence, such real charisma. Has your father ever acted professionally? I wondered. I'm positive there was no need for the fuss that certain Alliance members raised when he delivered his lecture in English. He chose the language most suited to his particular material, I dare say. I fear, however, that English is beyond the grasp of most of the Alliance, poor dears. Several requested a refund of their admission. And I must say I was properly embarrassed by the outburst of booing that interrupted your father precisely when he reached the climax of his talk. You know, one may educate them, one may dress them, one may even drill some manners into their head. But, when all is said and done, natives they remain."

"Mitch has been booed before," I assure Godfrey. "What is history a metaphor for, according to my father?"

"Heavens," exclaims Godfrey. "It was quite beyond me. Yet I suspect that in the end it might have been for the best that our Alliance was not equipped to understand your father. I'm afraid no one could call them freethinkers. Some of your father's views were of an expansive, if not controversial nature, as far as I could make out. That bit about the sadomasochistic nature of the sexual relationship between Napoleon and Josephine – even I was startled."

Godfrey pauses and frowns. "That business of the bill. Water under the bridge, I say. It was a rare privilege to enjoy the pleasure of your father's company. One could not place a price on the agreeable moments we passed together in this room, chatting just as you and I are now. I'm only sorry your father had to leave without saying goodbye. At the moment of farewell, I feel, one is able to express emotions which do not easily emerge at other times. Of course, I knew he would be leaving El Jadida soon. I understand his presence was required further south." Godfrey utters a tinkling laugh. "Imagine your father in one of those desert towns. They'll be swooning in the streets."

"And I'm swooning with sleep," I say, rising.

This conversation has tired me. It wearies me to learn that until the end Mitch still practised leeway in hotels and still viewed history as metaphor and still charmed everyone who crossed his path.

I force myself to look again at Godfrey. He grimaces or smiles at me. His teeth are black or yellow or missing. Small veins have risen upon his red, mottled face. There is something unkempt about him that has nothing to do with his clothing or what remains of his hair. Something loose, slack, furtive. Twenty-two years with the natives in El Jadida. You're not doing so bad, Godfrey. In fact, you're holding up admirably, in spite of the natives and the boys. I'd look as washed up and defeated as you after just a year in this place. Yes, I tip my hat to you.

Godfrey doesn't notice me leave the room. He is busy removing a flask from his pocket and pouring gin into his teacup. Laughing softly, he shakes his head back and forth. "Swooning in the streets," he giggles. "Simply swooning."


I snap on the light in Room 5 and suddenly no longer swoon with sleep. It isn't late. Crossing to the French doors, I step onto the balcony. The street still bustles below. The air is cool and dark and aromatic. Streetlamps glow among the trees along the sidewalk and the leaves shine. I breathe the scented air deeply, then turn inside the room. Sitting on the edge of the bed, I listen intently for the secret rain. A bell tolls from the distant mosque. My head lifts at the sound. Didn't the time for evening prayer pass several hours ago? Is it already time to pray again? What will we pray for this time, Godfrey Bridgeport? And who will listen? I rise from the bed and move back onto the balcony. The street is becoming quiet. Soon only isolated figures – mostly young men, lonely in number – will linger on the corners and on the steps of the bank across the street. I wait for the quarter moon to ascend. Then the streets are deserted and silent.

I am standing in the middle of the room. Suddenly, the room seems much too brightly lit. I don't know what will happen next until I see it occur: instead of flicking off the light, I bend before the night table. My left arm reaches forward. My left hand opens the drawer and takes out the burlap bag containing the dream potion from the market. This is already happening, I can't stop it now, it's much too late for that. I mix a pinch of the substance into a glass of lukewarm water. I stir and wait. It doesn't dissolve very well. You must believe, I think. Have faith. I drink it in one large gulp. I expected a bitter flavour: an acrid aftertaste. But this tastes of nothing at all. As if it weren't there.

I turn off the light, climb into bed, fall into dreams.

It was not easy to find the tattoo artist, though his skill was renowned throughout the town and far beyond. Away from boulevards and cafés, away from lights and crowds, he lived among the narrow, twisting alleys behind the *quartier portugais*. These were lit only by weak lamps attached infrequently to cold stone walls, and after dark, rats roamed freely within the gutters and the waste. Few people passed over the rough cobblestones then; occupants were silent, if not sleeping, behind closed doors to either side; the doors were unnumbered as the alleys were not named. Except for a cat's sudden scream, or the squeak of a bat, there were no sounds but my footsteps and heartbeat echoing against stone. I knew it was only possible to find the tattoo artist on a night without stars, when he did not prick coloured constellations upon the black skin of the sky.

Yet a sign did not hang helpfully upon the artist's door; nor did the door stand open in invitation. Within the labyrinth the tattoo artist's location itself remained as elusively unfixed as a fugitive's, though it was purported that his room was always the same bare, cement space illuminated by a candle, half-burned, whose light transformed the ancient dyes and needles into substances sheened with gold. If you could discover the secret way to the tattoo artist, the path of your life would be forever changed, it was averred in the tone of absolute certainty only ignorance can evoke: nothing and everything was known about this man whom the mute would describe in clear, precise detail if only they could speak.

Perhaps he strolled through the *souk*, unrecognized but not disguised, to hear the stories told about him – all contradictory, all unproven – when we wearied of discussing the sixty lessons of the Koran and the reason for changing tides.

In the town we all grew up with mothers' dire warnings that if we were not careful the tattoo artist would etch hideous, permanent pictures upon our sleeping skin. Later we learned that possibly his designs could attract the ideal lover who would not waver, who would not stray. Some said he substituted poison for ink when sought out by an evil man and some suggested that in certain worthy cases his handiwork could cure sickness and even extend life. There were those too who claimed that his instruments were the tools of Allah, and his images the Prophet's revelation. It was agreed that one needed to seek the tattoo artist at the correct time of life: overly tender skin would fester, blister and scar beneath his needles, while tough and weathered flesh would break them. The tattoo artist was a Jew from Essaouira, a *marabout* from Tarfaya, a Berber murderer or thief. Perhaps he was a distant cousin on your mother's side, the beggar disintegrating with leprosy before the Cinema Le Paris, that pilgrim glimpsed yesterday on the road to Azemmour. Stories shifted like Sahara sand blowing through the *derbs*, and changed shape and form from one day to the next, according to the wind. I did not puzzle at never seeing an example of the tattoo artist's work during my yearning youth: by the time I grew into a man and felt compelled one starless night to seek him for myself, I had come to believe his design remained invisible upon a subject until that being stretched his soul into a canvas tight and strong and broad enough to display the beauty that it held.

I had to ask infrequent strangers hurrying through the alleys for directions. Often they would not pause to answer, or only muttered brusquely that they didn't know; many spoke a dialect I hadn't heard before and couldn't understand, as if they came from the other side of the Atlas Mountains, or far beyond the

Rif. If I knocked on a door to ask my way, those inside remained silent, or with a shout warned me away. Increasingly, I remembered how it was said that numerous people had vanished in search of the tattoo artist; whenever some restless, dissatisfied soul disappeared from our town the presumption was that he had passed through the gates of the *quartier portugais* and had not emerged again. Some said these narrow alleys, dark even during the day, teemed with lost spirits who on starless nights reached out with hungry bones of fingers for anyone foolish enough to seek the tattoo artist they had failed to find. This was home, it was rumoured, to countless beings fallen into disappointment and despair, and that they sought consolation in narcotic and carnal pleasures was evidenced in sweet smoke and moans rising into the blue sky above our sensible town. "See what happens," mothers warned their discontented children, hoping one day these offspring would grow to feel happy with the prospect of a perfectly satisfactory, harmless tattoo of the kind offered every day and at reasonable price in the market; for example, a green cross of Islam, or a yellow star of hope.

I wandered until north and south became indistinct, and time and distance without proportion, before I found someone who would help. She looked at me with cold, suspicious eyes under the lamp where we met, and appeared undecided whether to speak or not. Slowly a knowing smile twisted her face, which was scarred and disfigured beneath heavy powder. "The next crossing," she finally said, placing ironic emphasis upon each word. "The third door to the left." Then she turned and walked swiftly away, drawing a scarf more closely around her head, leaving light, mocking laughter behind.

The tattoo artist did not answer my knock, but when I pushed the door it opened. In a room off the entrance he sat on a wooden bench between the small table which held his instruments and colours and the chair in which his clients sat when not required to lie upon the floor or to stand erect to receive his mark. He was

145

looking in my direction as I entered but did not rise to greet me. The old man wore a dark robe, with a hood concealing whether his hair was black or white or disappeared, and partly obscuring his eyes. The garment made it difficult to know his size or shape; his fingers, unadorned with rings, were long and thin. No tattoos were visible upon the skin left uncovered by the hooded robe. Appearing absorbed in thought, and scarcely conscious of my presence, the tattoo artist did not speak.

I sat in the chair and explained that I wanted a tattoo unlike any other in the world. Commonplace tattoos – a lover's name or initials, an eagle, snake or lion – did not interest me, less the heart, the arrow, the bolt of lightning; nor did I desire even a rare symbol of obscure significance. I wanted a unique tattoo, a singular tattoo: a shape that would clearly reveal to the world exactly who I was, and how the design of my being was in many minute ways, indicated in his etching, different from all others. If I did not know how it looked or what it was named, this was because the mark I wished for did not yet exist except within the tattoo artist's imagination. There was only one thing I knew for certain: it should be imprinted upon my heart.

The tattoo artist listened, then left the room by a door at its rear. He returned to set a tray holding a small silver teapot and three glasses on the floor. After a moment he poured pale tea into two of the glasses. Steam began to rise. Suddenly I wanted to tell the tattoo artist many things about myself: where I had come from, what I had seen and done, whom I had loved. I needed him to know how long I had been anticipating this moment, and how difficult it had been to find him, and how the doubts I had once felt about receiving his mark were vanished. He should hear me and see me, I believed, to know exactly what tattoo to place upon my skin; but the artist only watched the rising steam, seemingly uninterested in the material he had to work with, and I could not interrupt his silence. He turned to shift the candle slightly, then studied the shadow it cast upon the wall. He sighed once.

Removing a small square of paper from the folds of his robe, he untwisted it above one glass, spilling white powder. He handed me the glass. I drank its hot contents quickly, then loosened my shirt and lay on my back. The cement below me warmed as I fell asleep.

It was cold when I awoke. The candle still burned halfway down. The tray that held the teapot still lay on the floor. One glass was empty, one glass was full, the third was gone. There was a burning sensation at my heart. I bent my neck and saw my tattoo. At once I knew I had never seen this shape before. It was unique. I did not know what the small shape symbolized; it called nothing definite to my mind, yet seemed at once to suit me and to describe me. Was there a suggestion of a wave, a hint of an eye, an allusion to an outstretched wing? Fastening the buttons of my shirt, I watched the tattoo artist use a wet cloth to wipe his needles of dye. When they were clean, he replaced them exactly in their former position on the table. He stared at his instruments with an expression that contained amazement or horror or pleasure, or a combination of these three emotions. He was unable to hear my thanks or to receive my offered payment, and I left his room.

For several years I was pleased with my unique tattoo, though long after the pricked skin healed it continued to burn in such a way that I could never forget its presence. When exposed it caused astonishment and envy, and those with apparently ordinary tattoos sought my companionship and approval. My mark became famous in the town and occupied a central place in conversation. On the corners old men argued endlessly over its meaning and at the shore small children tried to trace its outline with sticks upon the sand. Seers used the shape to predict the future. Holy men proclaimed it visible evidence of Allah's touch. In the dark, lovers pressed lips against those brilliant colours; tongues travelled its contours, and tried to lick it off my skin. There was a season too when many youths attempted to have my tattoo copied onto themselves by the everyday tattoo artists in the market; these imitations, however skilled, were always inexact, and appeared somehow grotesque. During this time I felt that even with my shirt buttoned to my neck it was possible for passersby to see through cloth to the colours stained upon my heart.

Later, though unchanged itself, my tattoo seemed to evoke a different response, such as distrust or pity or fear. My fellow townspeople fell silent when I approached down the street, and mothers placed hands over childrens' eyes to shield them from the sight. No longer did lovers line up to lie with me upon the sand; perhaps they realized their kisses could not erase my mark, less swallow it inside themselves. Now I was lonely, and separated from those around me by what I had once hoped would permit them to see me clearly and know me intimately. I tried to keep my tattoo hidden, as if it were ugly or obscene, wearing a heavy burnoose as armour even during the hottest season. "I hope you got what you wanted," my mother said, as another wedding procession wound past our door with its bright song of union. Ashamed of my mark, I wished it to fade or wash away, or to alter into an unremarkable design. At night, dreams concerning an undistinguished existence, with an unbranded aspect, afforded me brief release; awakening at morning brought more bitter disappointment. When I offered tattoo artists in the market large sums to remove my mark, their refusals were nervously adamant, and I was driven to prowl the dark alleys behind the *quartier portugais* once more. Hoping its creator could alter or eliminate the unwanted design, I searched for him on many starless nights, yet in those narrow passages encountered only yearning youths with blank, unmarked skin. "Go home," I told them.

One day my tattoo suddenly began to burn more searingly, as if freshly pricked upon my skin. Now the pain was so sharp that it would not permit me to sleep or dream or pray. At this time I gradually began to wonder about the tattoo artist himself, seeking to recall every detail of my experience with him, and to find in that memory some clue to the meaning of my mark or a way of living with it. I mused upon the possible landscape of his past and the likely contours of his present. What were his intentions when faced with the canvas of my skin? What desires urged him to use dyes and needles upon me in one way and not another? This was the period when I hoped to understand the implications of my mark by knowing the being who had placed it there, as we turn our eyes above the clouds to contemplate the force that works upon us here below.

In this way my long journey began. First I roamed the town itself and then the towns nearby in search of someone with the same tattoo as mine. I had faith that at least one other being in the world wore that brilliant shape that hovered over my heart; even accidentally, even a single time, it must have been created before. It had to have a twin. As years went by and my search did not end, I journeyed farther from the town, crossing mountains and valleys, deserts and plains, rivers and oceans and streams. In distant lands I saw many things and met many people, but the single shape I hunted for did not appear before my eyes. I believed, still, that when it finally occurred our meeting would possess the symmetry and grace of a balanced equation: my mark would vanish beneath his gaze as his would dissolve under mine, and we would no longer each feel the same constant pain. "One glass was empty, one glass was full, the third was gone," I repeated as the road stretched far before me.

Though my end is growing near, I continue to roam from place to place in hope of discovering someone marked like me. The tattoo still burns above my heart; I have not grown used to its ache. While the colours of the world have faded, and stars dimmed with my faith, the tattoo flames as brightly as in the beginning. Now it is many years since I have been to my town, and I do not know if my family and friends still live. I do not know if the tattoo artist still hides within the dark alleys behind the *quartier portugais*. I do not know if he still pricks his stained needles into flesh, scarring it differently each time, leaving upon our hearts the unique designs from which we seek release.

I waken dismayed.

What kind of dream was that? Please. Not the same dream of dark alleys and permanent marks and endless journeys. Not again. I don't require a potion from the El Jadida market to come up with those old, worn-out images; I can manage them quite well on my own. Where are fresh revelations to tell me what I need to know in this particular place, at this particular time; some sign to point me in the direction of my father? If this potion isn't going to provide me with more valuable information, I will throw what remains of it off my balcony at the Hotel de Provence, scatter it on the morning breeze. Let it fall upon the streets and people below. Let me have their unknown dreams instead.

# vii.

Fixing my eyes at mid-distance, I still hope that someone emerges from the placid landscape to inform me that in El Jadida Mitch caused scandal by tanning nude on the beach, weaving drunkenly through the street, or paying a young woman to remove her veils in his (my?) room in the Hotel de Provence; but I spy only old men slapping worn cards in café games of seventy-one and starving cats cringing at the entrances of alleys and boys playing barefooted soccer on the beach, their field etched with sticks into the sand, their goalposts fronds torn from palms during the windy nights. The eyes of beggars and cripples, which as a child I believed contained secret messages, only plead for comfort and money I do not have to give. I continue to notice with interest the man who types letters for the illiterate on the porch of the *bureau de poste*. The man who with a Polaroid camera waits at the beach for young couples wishing to be photographed at sunset. And Mohammed Lasfar, in his wine-coloured coat, who when I enter the Hotel de Provence an hour before dawn, casts dilated, dreamy eyes from the reception desk and wonders if it was raining at the shore. "Did you see the rain?" he asks.

And now Ahammed and Abdul, whom I do not understand.

We sit upon cushions on a thinly carpeted cement floor. The walls of the room, also cement, are bare except for several photographs, torn from magazines, which display expensive cars and blond fashion models and forgotten pop stars of the seventies. A silver pot of mint tea steams beside a small glass bowl, containing a crumbly mixture of ground almonds prepared with honey, on the low table in the centre of the room. The candlelit space is ordered, uncluttered, minimalistic: a portable radio, a small stack of textbooks in French, several piles of neatly folded clothes and blankets, a few dishes, toiletries and odds and ends. Two *m'tarrbas*, for sleeping, are pushed against the walls while not in use. Beyond the door lies a patio, off which lead four or five similar rooms, each inhabited by people unrelated to those in the others, and a communal bathroom and kitchen.

At first pleasantly bored by the company, I find myself looking often at the glass of mint tea, too sweet for my taste, in my hand, then at the glasses held by my new companions. I study the level of liquid, higher or lower, in each, and observe how in candlelight it appears more gold than green. The vision subtly stirs me, for a reason I do not understand.

Ahammed and Abdul are students, nineteen and twenty respectively, from towns several hundred kilometres from El Jadida; like two thousand others, they have moved here to attend the university. In the street, where I was wandering after my evening bowl of *harira* at the Café-Restaurant Scheherazade, they approached with an invitation for tea. Now I usually decline such offers as graciously as possible; after accepting one or two initial invitations, I am certain that the encounter, however harmless, will prove unrewarding. Inevitably, it seems, the conversation must centre upon the seven requirements for obtaining a visa to live and work abroad (I already know these qualifications by heart) and the possibilities offered foreign students by European or North American universities. Surely I can somehow assist in securing a work permit or student visa; surely it is not possible that I am in need of assistance myself, in my own way with as little choice and opportunity as these earnest young students: my powerlessness is patently disbelieved or, because others where I am from clearly achieve power with ease, scorned.

In fact, this visit over tea proceeds exactly upon such familiar lines. I become weighed down by the false, naïve expectations of these two tense young men. Impressing upon me the difficulty of their studies, they obviously feel a need to succeed at university because of the sacrifices made by their families, in Tarfaya and Tan-Tan, to send them here; at the same time, they do not hope that successful completion of their studies will offer any sort of real opportunity. Again I listen to a litany composed of a need to flee a hated king, to break away from a society of limited choice, to slip from a land lacking possibilities. Once more I suspect that the air above El Jadida, apparently clear and cloudless, is actually thick with longing, heavy with frustration, dripping with dissatisfaction.

Now more impatient than pleasantly bored, I try to draw Abdul and Ahammed into topics that interest me more.

"Have you been to the desert?" I ask.

The question makes them uneasy; they glance worriedly at each other. I wonder if my French is incorrect or if this apparently innocent but somehow inappropriate question has insulted their hospitality. At once withdrawing from the conversation, Abdul gazes at the blank wall before him and slowly sips tea. Ahammed, who all along has seemed the more relaxed of the two, offers me a standard response: "Fès is interesting, Marrakesh is interesting. All our imperial cities are most rewarding for the visitor."

Once again I feel blocked by a wall as solidly impenetrable as the cement around me. Fès and Marrakesh are interesting, the imperial cities are all worth visiting: I am being provided –

politely, automatically – with the answer Ahammed believes I seek. For some reason, people I have so far met in this country seem unable to consider the possibility that there may be several answers to a question. Is this because they believe all infidels are the same, with a single desire, only one intent? They cannot believe that one set answer will not satisfy me, unless I am perverse? They suffer from a lazy imagination? An inability to empathize?

"What is the desert like?" I press, risking the frown that usually follows a request for information deemed unsuitable for the *giaour*.

"I must pray," Abdul says abruptly, exiting the room to wash himself before, in the patio, kneeling towards the east.

I have studied a Moroccan map. In the Hotel de Provence, I have spread it across my bed and, my father's son, mused for hours upon its details, memorized roads and towns, mountains and desert. Temporary lakes. Generally passable roads. *Piste pour tous terrain. Cours d'eau intermittent.* Tarfaya and Tan-Tan, the hometowns of my hosts, are located, I know, near the northern edge of the Western Sahara, on the only real highway leading into the south. Mitch would have passed through them in travelling from El Jadida towards Smara, farther south. It was only when Ahammed and Abdul had told me where they are from that I accepted their invitation to tea.

"The desert is difficult," Ahammed responds cautiously. "It is without interest. The people there are uncultured, and have not studied at the university. They know little about the world. There is no scenery, nothing for the eye." He trails off sadly, then brightens. "If you visit Tarfaya, my family will be most pleased."

"I am going into the desert," I insist. "I will try to go as far as Layounne, maybe farther."

"Soldiers," mutters Ahammed. "There are only soldiers and sand in Layounne. The war."

What? This catches my interest. I am unaware of a war in

southern Morocco. The Western Sahara is a hot spot? The centre of a guerilla movement? A little action, another operation, one last opportunity for Mitch to place an iron in the fire?

Still with reluctance, Ahammed continues to explain that for more than fifteen years a dispute has simmered over the territory, once dismissed as barren, that lies south of Morocco. Phosphates, he says. It was because of rich reserves of phosphates that Hassan II invaded the abandoned colony in 1975 and seized control of its northern two-thirds.

"Many of our people moved down there," Ahammed goes on to say. "We called it 'The Green March.' But Mauritania wanted the area's southern third. And the Polisarios, the guerrillas, wanted to make the whole place an independent Western Sahara state. Algeria and Libya supported their struggle and the war began. The Americans gave us dollars and we built the biggest sand wall in the world across the desert to block off our enemies. Yet, despite the Americans, there was not enough money to keep fighting. The phosphates were not as rich as we had dreamed. So we agreed, in 1991, to a ceasefire with the Polisarios and so the UN arrived. They say the UN will supervise a peaceful referendum. They say the people in the Western Sahara will have a choice between Polisarian independence and Moroccan rule. They say it is quieter there now. But most of our army is still down in Layounne and further south, in Dakhla. And the road south of Dakhla is still mined.

"It is still dangerous," says Ahammed, as Abdul re-enters the room with his hair wet from ablution. Ahammed breaks off awkwardly, as if he has been discussing a taboo topic. An embarrassed silence follows.

"What's that?" I ask to break the tension, pointing to an especially thick book, its dark leather cover embossed with Arabic characters in gold. I am surprised I didn't notice this book before. Positioned carefully on the floor, apart from other articles, it seems to possess special significance, perhaps as the only object in the room that is treasured for its beauty as well as usefulness. As I gaze at it, the book seems to radiate force; in the room's still air, the candle flame wavers towards it.

"The Koran," says Abdul. I notice now that his eyes appear unusually moist, as wet as his hair.

"Abdul has a gift," remarks Ahammed. "He knows the complete Koran by memory. It is most unusual. Even the old teachers in the *medersas*, and the *imams* in the mosque, who have studied the Koran all their lives, do not usually know it entirely by heart. There are very few with this gift."

He crosses the room, picks up the book, opens it.

"Listen. I will begin a sentence, any one at all, and Abdul will complete it."

Ahammed flips pages at random, starts a sentence, then pauses to allow Abdul to finish it. After they do this several times, Ahammed turns to me and, switching back into French, says, "The Koran has sixty lessons."

Abdul has not paused in his recitation to allow another passage to be cited by Ahammed. Now with closed eyes, he continues to recite steadily and quickly, with no sign that he will not carry on indefinitely, or at least, perhaps, until he has reached the end of the holy book tomorrow.

I do not understand.

I glance down at the glass of tea in my hand, realize it has grown cold.

Abdul does not seem to recite with emotion; this appears a mechanical exercise, a trick, though my impression may be false. Quite possibly I am misinterpreting his tone of voice; it may well not be a monotone, without inflection, only vocal gymnastics, a rapid series of sounds without meaning even to himself. Perhaps he is simply spouting gibberish – though sacrilegious stunts don't fit my initial impression of him. Ahammed stands with the Koran in his hands, a proud expression on his face, like the owner of a pet performing accomplished feats. For a while I listen intently and attempt to pick out a single word from Abdul's drone but then give up, allow the words to wash over me, abandon myself to the sound. Slowly I feel released from the obligation to understand, to interpret. The room feels extremely peaceful, as still as if it were silent; greater silence spreads beyond. Are the neighbours sleeping, or do they listen in silence? Is Abdul still reciting, or do his lips merely move mutely now? He appears entranced, as if he could not stop even if interrupted, even if a bolt of lightning suddenly split this space in two. Why does Ahammed still stand? I wish to lie down, rest my head upon a pillow, close my eyes. To sleep in this silence that is not without sound. As the desert also is not without sound, though you may feel there is only silence upon it.

I am at the door without knowing my body has moved. Abdul continues to move his lips; Ahammed still stands and watches him. Neither seems to realize that I have altered my position, that my glass of cold tea has dropped and spilled upon the carpet.

"I don't understand," I say before I open the door, then close it behind me.

One glass was empty, one glass was full, the third was gone.

It takes me a while to find my way back to the centre of town. Disoriented, I walk first in the wrong direction until, seeing the mosque loom before me when it should be at my back, I turn around.

I have not seen Mitch since he departed Brale six months after MJ's disappearance and six months before I also left Brale, immediately upon graduating from high school at sixteen, to begin my own journey, in England. Mitch said, in December of 1977, that he had to find his eldest son since no one else in the country seemed interested in the job. The RCMP were utterly disorganized, completely useless, a national disgrace; they couldn't find an elephant in a china shop, swore Mitch. They certainly weren't doing all they could in this case. They definitely weren't providing the kind of assistance that he, a law-abiding taxpayer, deserved. In fact, according to Mitch, the RCMP were downright impolite, intimating that, if they were his son, they too would move to Montreal and not send home a forwarding address. Anyway, they said, MJ was eighteen, legally of age, free to go where he chose with as much privacy as he desired, unless clear evidence surfaced to indicate police intervention was warranted. As for that MLA Mitch called about his boy, he was curt, abrupt and unsympathetic. Well, what could you expect: a politician, and a Socred at that. By God, Mitch would probably discover MJ within twenty-four hours of stepping off the plane at Laval; he knew his flesh and blood better than anyone, he could locate his boy in outer space if need be, he would go to the ends of the earth for the sake of his son. A few weeks. He would be back in Brale with MJ at his side within a few weeks tops, rain or shine. Did anyone want to put money on it?

Although Mitch did fly to Montreal, where he twice called to inform us he had turned up several very promising leads, and sent a postcard presenting the faculty of science building at McGill, he did not return to Brale within a few weeks, rain or shine, with or without MJ at his side.

In fact, he never came back to Brale again.

In fact, from Montreal he flew to Montego Bay and from Montego Bay headed for Miami. We received postcards and collect telephone calls from both places in which Mitch assured us he was hot on MJ's trail. You could almost say MJ was there in his hand, he was that close. From Miami my father continued south. He communicated with us from Colon, Caracas, Rio de Janeiro and Lima during the next four months. Mention of the search for MJ gradually descended into the postscript of his messages, then disappeared altogether. Perhaps it was to be understood without saying that he still hunted for MJ; but I, at least, never understood without saying a single action of my father.

I believe that Mitch intended to leave Brale, on his own and for good, well before MJ had disappeared the previous summer.

There had been signs.

The four years in his hometown, since our return from wandering in 1974, had clearly not been happy ones for Mitch. From the start he didn't enjoy his teaching job at the high school, beside the hospital, on the hill; there he was not head of the history department, and was forced to follow a curriculum that clashed with his vision of history as an act of imagination, or a re-invention of what has been forgotten. At dinner he fumed over the jackasses he had to work with and the dope-smoking, hormone-addled teenagers whom he found it patently impossible to teach. This was education? No wonder the country was going all to hell, Mitch ranted, in the same way he now ranted about the Canadian political situation and the Canadian welfare system and the whole damned Canadian mentality. I remembered Mitch, during our years outside the country, reminding us frequently never to forget where we came from; Canada, he had said then, was a noble land, the envy of all the world, the finest country ever to raise itself upon the grand foundations of democracy.

His sisters reminded Mitch that he was lucky to have a job at all; if his old friend Andy Soles hadn't put in a good word for him at the high school, he might never have walked into that position at all, or at least not immediately upon returning to town after a six-year absence. And let's face it, Dorothy added, the money it brought in was pretty essential at the moment. She and her sisters didn't mention that they had helped Mitch get back on his feet when he'd first come back, when he didn't have a penny to his name.

Mitch banged his fist on Madeleine's kitchen table and shouted that Andy Soles was no friend of his in the first place, and in the second place they could shove that job right where it belonged. In the third, fourth, fifth and sixth place, every one of his sisters had thrown themselves away on men not good enough for them, men as dull as dishwater, men unworthy to lick the shoes of Brale's four prettiest, liveliest girls.

No one dared point out that Mitch's sisters had married men who were decent husbands, good fathers, and well-liked, agreeable people. Madeleine could still not forget how, twenty-one years ago, Mitch had spoiled her wedding day with that outburst in the church, though of course his intentions had been good; Mitch's heart always was in the right place, she wasn't denying that. Dorothy, for her part, was naturally upset when, returning from her Reno honeymoon in 1956, Mitch asked if she were certain of John's fidelity. "For crying out loud," she had exclaimed. In fact, the two older sisters had left high school early to undertake undesired secretarial jobs so that Mitch could attend university on the Coast at a time when the family finances were still shaky. They all adored him, especially after little Donald died, along with their father, in the 1960 fire, leaving Mitch their only brother. Although neither his sisters nor their husbands particularly cared for Ardis, whether she was well or not, they had constantly helped her out, from affection for Mitch, during our six years away from Brale. Chas handled her legal affairs, George her finances, and Ivan and John provided practical assistance with the house. Twenty years later Ardis's brothers-in-law would still drop by the Columbia Avenue place to shovel sidewalks after a heavy snow, and their wives never stopped driving over to pick up Ardis for Sunday dinner, however awkward her company always was for them.

"For crying out loud," the sisters exclaimed in Madeleine's kitchen now.

Mitch looked at Jeanette, whose married surname was Catalano.

"Catalano," he pointed out, "is an Italian name, is it not? Have you heard of the Italian mafia? It exists here in Brale; any fool can see that. Who do you think owns this town, runs this town, keeps this town in the Dark Ages?"

Jeanette sighed. There was no use explaining to Mitch what he already knew: half of Brale was of Italian descent; Italians had come to Brale to work in the smelter on the hill, just like their own father; if most of the town's businesses and real estate were Italian-owned, this was only a natural consequence of the population's large Italian proportion.

"The Pope," Mitch muttered darkly, "is behind it all."

His sisters glanced nervously out the window towards the back lawn, where their husbands were playing bacci.

It was unwise to argue with Mitch during those unhappy years in Brale. Normally a whistling, singing man, he also possessed the dark streak, handed down by a moody mother, and shared with two of his sisters, Dorothy and Kay. "It's that Greek blood," the other, less temperamental sisters would say, shaking heads before the undeniable, unalterable fact of it. There was nothing you could do when Mitch, like Kay and Dorothy, began to stomp around the house muttering to anyone within earshot – and everyone was to blame – that no one in this bloody family thought a minute about him, never mind gave two cents for his happiness. He had wasted his life on people who wished him dead; he didn't know why they didn't get out a gun and shoot him in the heart. Hell, the way they treated him, it amounted to the same thing. Any way you looked at it, they'd be doing him a favour. They could sing at his funeral, dance on his grave, celebrate that he was gone at last.

You couldn't do anything except stay out of the way and hope you weren't trapped in the car when these spells, which Jeanette always insisted were chemical in origin, fell out of nowhere, upset everyone, then vanished just as suddenly and mysteriously as they arrived. These moods seemed all the blacker because they descended upon people usually lighthearted and laughing, able to charm the pants off a pauper, all white teeth and broad smiles, pranks and jokes and songs.

"His difficult marriage," Mitch's sisters rationalized when, after 1974, his moodiness deepened. "All that travelling with those children," they mused. "The strain."

Between 1974 and 1977 Mitch's dark mood seemed unbroken by sunnier emotional weather. Scowling and swearing, he was almost unrecognizable to us, and seemed even to have altered physically, appearing shrunken, thin, no longer handsome. Lily, MJ and I avoided our father as much as possible. We viewed him now as the crazed captain we had been too weak to mutiny against during the six years we were, upon his ship, forced to float across dangerous, frightening waters. When that imprisoning galleon finally caught fire (was it Mitch himself who set the blaze?), we had somehow managed to scramble into a lifeboat, and from it watched our father, still on board among the shooting flames, shake his fists across the water, shout that we were cowardly traitors to abandon his sinking vessel. In the lifeboat we were in less danger, but still not safe; rescue would not come, we knew, until we drifted into calm harbours, far from Brale, protected from Mitch's sight. Meanwhile, in our cramped, uncomfortable lifeboat, we studied.

Until 1976 we spent afternoons and evenings, and all of weekends, in the basement rumpus room with homework. Upon returning to Brale we were placed in classes with children two years younger than ourselves; at first we had to work hard just to keep up with them. We spread notebooks, texts and pens upon three card tables and worked in silence. The rumpus room possessed a subterranean quality, with only several small windows set high upon the wall, at ground level, to fill the room with dim, murky light during the daytime. The room was sparsely furnished with a shabby couch, a threadbare carpet that once adorned the living room upstairs, and a television we never watched. Mitch had instilled in us the notion that we were far more intelligent than other children; it bothered us that, in Brale, quite the opposite appeared true.

We studied constantly, fiercely, desperately; long after Mitch and Ardis had retreated to their upstairs bedroom, we were still memorizing what we should have learned five years before. Unravelling mathematical formulae, chemical equations, and historical puzzles, we created a universe of new information that was as complex and intricate as our private card games of the past. Our faces, pale from lack of sunlight, strained with concentration.

"You have to," MJ insisted when I said I couldn't understand the problem before me.

"Do you want to end up like him?" Lily asked.

We studied to catch up, and because we didn't know how to make friends or join clubs, become members or fit in. It seemed too late to learn how to skate, ski or play hockey. Our lack of knowledge was enormous; we could fill in only so much of that huge, dark space. Pragmatically, we determined upon what areas of ignorance could be eliminated with swiftest, most useful result. Although teenagers, we didn't attend school dances, stay out late, smoke or drink or dabble with drugs. All that seemed frivolous; there wasn't time. Classmates and neighbourhood teens initially tried to befriend us, but quickly gave up before our puzzled faces and blank silence. To MJ, Lily and me, their language was as incomprehensible as Swahili, their behaviour as strange as a Massai tribal dance. After Sunday dinners at the homes of Mitch's sisters, declining cousins' halfhearted invitations to share a joint down by the river, we sat rigidly among our aunts and uncles, and digested unfamiliar roasts and gravies and rich desserts; meals in our Columbia Avenue house consisted mostly of sandwiches and canned soup prepared with effort by Ardis, or thrown together by Mitch or ourselves. As much as possible, we avoided sight of Mitch and Ardis, who sat side by side across Dorothy's or

Madeleine's living room, not quite touching. They appeared to us a strange conjunction we could never bring together in our minds. I always thought, during those Sunday dinners, that an unpleasantly pungent odour, composed of dust and overripe papaya and the decaying flesh of mutilated monkeys, clung to us, and festered upon the antiseptic skin of every Brale room we entered; it seemed to no avail that the three of us had, since 1974, taken to showering a dozen times a day – and Lily even more often – until our skin possessed a permanently scraped, raw aspect. Sometimes, late at night during winter, after our eyes had become red from spending hours over schoolbooks, and when we knew the streets would be safely deserted, abandoned because of the cold, we went out to walk. Our progress along the icy side-walks cautiously, painfully slow, like the awkward, unpractised steps of small children just learning to walk. We created our winter wardrobe from layers of old garments discovered in trunks hidden at the back of the furnace room; perhaps they had once belonged to our dead uncle, or to our father and aunts, in the fifties. The scent of mothballs crystallized around us. Our lungs gasped unaccustomed sub-zero air. "It's like the moon," said Lily in the falling snow; it glittered beneath streetlamps, in the light thrown from mute houses to either side. Occasionally, one of us would make a snowball and toss it at another; we would try to laugh and play amid the snow, but our attempts were tentative, as gingerly as our steps, and our voices, perhaps because of the snow, sounded strange to us, one moment muffled, the next ringing, bright. Flakes decorated our figures and melted upon our faces, and I believed, foolishly, that if I allowed my brother and sister to move even three yards ahead of me, they would vanish into the white landscape, become lost to me. We were alone, and together, still.

Eventually not only did we catch up to students our age, but, with week after week of intense effort, it appeared that we would each end up graduating at least one year early from school. All that changed, in 1976, when MJ and Lily began to pursue their separate fates, and, in the end, only I received a diploma from Brale Senior Secondary.

In the photograph it is clearly Christmas, for the family poses before what must be (extending beyond the upper reach of camera eye, and from one side of the frame entirely to the other) an enormous pine decorated heavily with gaily coloured balls and silver tinsel suspended in descent, as well as electric lights, red and blue and yellow, strung from branch to branch; indeed, as background the tree dominates to excess, distracting the eye from the five people posed stiffly before it. Kneeling in a jagged row upon a carpet shaded somewhere between grey and blue, not quite touching each other, apparently holding themselves apart, they are, from left to right: a thirteen-year-old boy; a girl, two years his senior; a man and woman of early middle-age (or is she much older, or only much more worn?); and another boy, sixteen. Here and there, in spaces between these people, and at the sides of the frame, appear glimpses of gifts, unwrapped that morning and still brand new. According to custom these must be left on view beneath the tree until Boxing Day; clothes, for example, tried on after the wrapping paper has been torn, are refolded neatly, and placed back upon the white cotton batting spread beneath the tree to represent snow. A sprinkling of fallen needles suggests that, unusually, insufficient water has been added to the round metal cup, in the centre of the stand, that holds the trunk. Because the man in the photograph, Mitch, lost his father and younger brother, fifteen years ago, in a fire caused by a Christmas tree, it is not often that either he or his sisters, in their respective homes, pay anything less than strict attention to the possible danger of a drying tree.

165

Madeleine, the eldest of those four sisters, owns, with her husband, Ivan, the house which provides the setting for the photograph. With her sisters, she takes turns hostessing the whole family through the holiday season: this year, Jeanette had Christmas Eve; Dorothy will take Boxing Day, tomorrow; and Kay will do duty on New Year's Day. (For New Year's Eve, the grown members of this extended family reserve a table together at the Columbo Lodge; their children are, on the last night of 1975, old enough to fend for themselves.) At the moment, Madeleine finishes cleaning up in the kitchen (her sisters assisted with the main part of the work) after the dinner for twenty-four. Now and then she appears – aproned, tea-towelled – in the entrance of the living room to keep an eye on proceedings; she must perform the role of sensible sister, as well as hostess. Like Jeanette, Dorothy and Kay, she wears, this year, a pantsuit made of synthetic material adorned by one or two pieces of costume jewellery, and her short dark curls have been set for the occasion, her face made up lightly with lipstick and rouge (not eye shadow, not mascara). The majority of her guests range upon couches placed against the walls, though some of the children (most are in their teens and will, in several years, rebel against attending these functions until, after several more years, they reappear with spouses and children themselves) must sit on the carpet, or on the slate surface in front of the fireplace, which is, despite the season, empty of flame. (For Madeleine, the attractions of a fire do not sufficiently compensate for the bother of wood, cinder and ash, or for an unarticulated fear of smoke that wavers dimly in her unconscious; besides, the basement furnace warms the house more than well enough.) These couches, along with the end and coffee tables, and the lamps, were bought a dozen years ago from the town's single department store; of no particular style, they are, from one sister's house to another, remarkably similar, making it difficult for an inexpert eye to know which home serves as the setting for this photograph.

Curtains conceal the wide window at the front of the room; beyond, snow falls silently through darkness (it is nearly eight in evening now), as it also sifts, seven miles away, upon the graves of Madeleine's parents and younger brother, never mentioned or visited during this season, in the mountain cemetery.

The sisters' husbands bear responsibility for photographing, as they also drive their families to and from these functions, carve turkeys before the dinners, and offer inlaws, for refreshment, a choice between beer and wine. (Hard liquor will not feature in such occasions for another five years, when the children are safely grown, the mortgages completely paid.) The photographs are not taken, however, without considerable, time-consuming contribution from onlooking wives and children; in fact, the process requires as long as half an hour for each family. Even after a group has finally been assembled (invariably a teenaged child protests posing, and must be cajoled into participation; inevitably their mother at the last moment feels compelled to dash into Madeleine's bathroom to adjust makeup or hair), onlookers call out detailed, extensive comments concerning the subjects currently under scrutiny. The group being photographed will be advised a number of times to rearrange itself this way or that; it will be pointed out, for instance, that Caroline's or Susan's expression seems inappropriate, and always Chas must be warned not to wink, Dorothy not to frown, Donald not to pinch his sister, Karen. Such advisories form a fixed feature of the ritual, as much as the initial coin toss that decides the order in which families are photographed, and are made with delight, in teasing, as jokes permitted by affection, allowed among close relations. Not until Kay, the most critical sister, offers the final, approving nod can a posed family be urged, one last time, to smile; then the four brothers-in-law press buttons causing shutters to whir and flashbulbs to explode in a round of light that dazzles the subjects, at least one of whom will reveal closed eyes in the resulting photographs. Only now will coffee be served, with ice cream and pie, and willing players gathered around the dining-room table, tonight extended with extra leaves, at the rear of this space, beside the kitchen, for games of cards and dice that continue until almost midnight, unless snow keeps falling heavily and concern for driving conditions prods families to depart early for their homes, scattered around Brale, and in nearby smaller towns upon the mountain road that winds past the cemetery, silent and white in darkness.

But a difference marks the way this last family of five is photographed. Onlookers attempt a few strained jokes and teasing remarks, then fall entirely silent; even Derek and Jeffrey, who have been rough-housing in a corner, are quiet now. A feeling of chill enters the room, as palpable as if cold air has somehow penetrated Ivan's storm windows. Madeleine pauses in the doorway, with her presence (though she is only five thin feet tall) commanding nothing to go wrong. Jeanette – suddenly, pointedly – stubs out the cigarette she has just lit; smoke curls upward from the ashtray, hovers like a spirit in the air. Everyone watching in this room knows, but would rather not consider, that for six years this particular family attended Christmas dinner neither here nor at another sister's house. (Did the father and children enjoy Christmas at all during that time? Even Madeleine is not sure where they always were, what exactly happened to them there.) No one observes aloud that this presently posed family dresses disturbingly unlike the others, except for Mitch. His wife, Ardis, wears a sleeveless black dress, unadorned by pin or brooch, that exposes dead white arms with muscles twisting like ropes beneath the skin. Her face, deeply lined, is without makeup, and her hair, its grey unique to the room, stands wildly around her head. Earlier, she declined both beer and wine, and spoke as little as she ate. (Madeleine would feel offended if anyone else acted in this manner; but all her sisters-in-law make allowances for Ardis, for all five members of the family in front of the tree.) Her lips press tightly together, unable to attempt a smile or frown, or any

168

expression at all. While other boys in this room sport, in 1975, hair of medium length, the two arranged on either side of Ardis, MJ and Richard, have, like their father, closely cropped heads. Their features appear peculiarly unformed or stunted for their age; their eyes are dull, expressions withdrawn. Their sister's bangs hang over her eyes, yet no one suggests that Lily fasten them up with a bobby pin or barrette. All three children model clothes extremely out of fashion; perhaps they date from as long ago as the fifties. (Jeanette believes she recognizes Lily's pleated skirt as one of her own, long believed lost, presumed disintegrated, now mysteriously resurrected.) The scent of mothballs cuts sharply through that of pine, of perfume emanating from Madeleine and her sisters, of coffee brewing in the kitchen. Only the father manages to smile, though even his expression is odd, seeming directed, past the cameras three feet away, to far beyond the cemetery on the mountain, to thousands of miles from Brale. Before Kay can give her approving nod, Ardis suddenly says, in a harsh voice, "Take it." This time even onlookers start at the barrage of four flashes. Only Ardis, staring directly into the cameras, does not blink. Silence follows. The enormous pine seems to swell, disturbingly, even larger as this silence stretches, and smoke scorches several imaginations. When the mantelpiece clock strikes eight times, the sound fails to bring relief, but tolls, somehow, with inordinate solemnity. While the sound echoes, it seems possible that all inhabitants of the room – those still assembled before the tree and those still looking on – will remain frozen inside its frame, fated to portray permanently this eight o'clock on Christmas Day, 1975. As if, therefore, no further photographs will be taken in coming years. As if this will be the last photograph of all. In a way, such is the case.

As it turned out.

In the end.

Finally, my memories of Brale itself are vague, despite two visits back there in the eighties, as if those visits were to a town unconnected to the one I had inhabited in the foreign country of the past. With difficulty I try to recall the position of Bay and Cedar Avenues, the location of The Gulch, Cominco Arena, Gyro Park. The only part of Brale I remember clearly is the neighbourhood rising sharply above its downtown, on the west side of the river, across the bridge from Columbia Avenue. In stuccoed homes, built upon the face of an almost vertical slope, lived many of the old Italian families which Mitch seemed to feel maintained a sinister grip on the town. They were small, modest houses, swarming in summer with vines of grapes that became homemade wine in basements. From them drifted scents, garlic and olive oil, that I breathed in deeply while, with the help of closed eyes, I imagined that I was far from this (for me) dreary, unsuggestive place; somewhere, perhaps, in Tuscany, where in 1967 fountains spilled water upon dusty squares of *cittadinas* sprinkled over the scorched hills a man and three children wandered, between a rainy winter in Paris and a rainy winter in Rome. And from the windows floated, too, music of a language my mind only dimly recollected, scarcely understood, from eight years before; Italian twined above the hot, steep streets of West Brale where, in 1975, people who had never learned English still lived. During July and August old women in black bent over miniature backyards, cut into the hill, teeming with brilliantly red tomatoes, twisted calabazilla, enormous, elongated squash. On either side of me, closed curtains twitched; the thin slice of a face, or only an eye peered from behind as I passed. Watching over everyone, rising from the hill across The Gulch, pointing high into the scratchy sky, the smelter's tall stacks puffed black smoke day and night. Except

170

within this blooming of olive oil and garlic and grapes, it left an acrid, metallic taste in my mouth.

Back at the Columbia Avenue house I had to pass through the kitchen to descend the basement stairs. Ardis sat at the kitchen table and moved the salt and pepper shakers back and forth, searching in vain for some way of arranging them that would bring her satisfaction and, perhaps, peace. She didn't look up as I paused uncertainly beside her.

"It's hot out," I said at the end of August.

My words sounded awkward, puny, thin. I never knew what to say to my mother, or how to phrase it. I was only beginning to understand, through a word dropped here and there by my aunts, what she had been through while we were away, and why she still retreated often into the master bedroom for several days, still stood at the kitchen sink, gripping its edge tightly, as if she would fall over if she let go. Sometimes, in the heart of winter, she would call Lily, MJ and me into the kitchen, where a glass pitcher of brightly coloured Kool-Aid waited on the table; intently, anxiously, as if we were toddlers instead of teens, she watched us drink her offering. Or, in the middle of summer, she carefully made us mugs of steaming cocoa. Or, in the middle of the night, she raked leaves. In the basement bedroom I shared with MJ, I listened to the sound of metal teeth scrape the back lawn, and envisioned Ardis moving beneath the big maple, shifting piles of leaves which smelled dark and cold, like the essence of autumn, gazing steadily towards the ground beneath her feet, not glancing at the silent house, illuminated only by a back-door light behind her, or at the houses looming in similar silence across the fence, throughout the block. I wondered if MJ and Lily and Mitch also lay awake and imagined a slight breeze, holding hints of both the river and the mountains, shaking leaves above Ardis, spinning several more upon her head. I did not grow more comfortable with my mother during those years; but, more and more, when I saw her nervously bite her lip, I felt my own lips ache tenderly.

"Go away," she said in a low voice, still not looking up at me when I paused beside her in the hot August kitchen.

I knew she didn't mean for me to leave her alone at that moment. She was telling me to leave this house and this town as soon as I could, right after graduating from high school, for my own good if not for hers. She was pleading for me to travel as far as I could from the sight and smell of Mitch's burning ship. Urging me to escape the traces of white-hot current that still sizzled through her brain. Warning me away from the dangerous blaze that roared day and night within the smelter on the hill.

"Go away," she said.

I started down the stairs. Below me, I knew, MJ and Lily pored over schoolwork in the rumpus room, and would glance accusingly at me for wandering away from our studies, even on a sweltering August afternoon. In his office or in the furnace room, Mitch hovered down there also. Indeed, it seemed that the house was divided into two distinct countries – an upper and a lower land – with separate populations. The ground floor held my parents' bedroom, Lily's bedroom, bathroom, kitchen and living and dining rooms. Except for meals and sleep, it was given over to Ardis; rarely did the rest of us loiter in the living room or play cards at the kitchen table. Ardis, for her part, descended to the basement only when we weren't there. If she wanted us, she stood at the top of the stairs and in an uncertain voice, doubtful that anyone was there, called down to Mitch's office, MJ's and my bedroom, the rumpus or furnace room. Occasionally, returning from school, I would discover evidence that Ardis had visited the basement while we were away. Upon my bed lay a pile of damp clothes she had washed but forgotten to put into the dryer, or I found my bed made tightly, in the hospital fashion, so that it was difficult to climb into.

From our card tables in the rumpus room, MJ, Lily and I would hear the clatter of Mitch's typewriter from behind his closed office door. He often shut himself in there directly after supper and forced his big, battered Olivetti to proceed in fits and starts, rapid and loud as gunfire, with long silences in between. Instead of correcting his students' history papers, he composed letters to farflung contacts in order to keep an iron in the fire — even though it appeared that he would be stuck in Brale for good. Or he wrote letters that were never published to the editor of the Brale *Daily Times* to protest the newspaper's outrageous moral hypocrisy, its pathetic local bias, or its unpardonable Italian slant. Above us, when Mitch's typewriter paused, we heard Ardis's light step as she walked back and forth between the living room and kitchen, in search of something she had forgotten. At other times, when she shut herself in her bedroom, there was only silence above.

Later in the evening, Mitch left his office and disappeared into the furnace room, where amid the smell of oil and dust and damp cement he worked on what he called his memory boxes. From the evidence he produced — oddly shaped wooden oblongs with lids that failed to fit tightly and edges that didn't squarely meet — these never turned out anything like Mitch had imagined; they were obviously another bitter disappointment. He became frustrated during their construction, and afterwards smashed them with a sledge hammer into small pieces of kindling for the fireplace upstairs. Studying on the other side of the wall, my brother, sister and I heard Mitch bang away unsteadily, swear when he hit his thumb with the hammer, curse when his measurements of pine and cedar proved mistaken. Often long silences fell upon the furnace room, when it sounded as if Mitch had given up for the night on his dream of a perfect, airtight box.

I imagine, now, my father staring at his materials in defeat, wondering what use there is in trying to create anything worthwhile from them. The expression in his eyes matches the one that appears when he looks at MJ, Lily and me. I see him glance around the chaos of the furnace room, which no one has tried to sort for the past fifteen years. His eyes come to rest upon old hockey sticks and skates once belonging to his brother, before the boy died with his father in the fire. He stares at the large can of pale-green tin, dented and scratched, that contains Donald's universe of miniature spheres, a thousand cat's eyes and agates and plain marbles the boy once rolled upon the grass at Gyro Park in springtime. Sometimes Donald gave an especially lucky marble to an older sister, one of Brale's prettiest, liveliest girls, who would tweak his nose, rumple his hair, and say, winking, "Thanks, sonny boy. I'll carry this in my purse to the Kinsmen dance tonight, for good luck. If Mitch can borrow the Taylor's car and drive us out to the Fruitvale Hall."

The deep freeze next to Mitch switches on, begins to hum, and his gaze returns to his failed attempt to construct an impossibly perfect container to hold sealed memories of four pretty, lively Brale girls, and of a younger brother and Kinsmen dances and a platinum blond Island girl, preserving them exactly in their original form, sustaining permanently precise echoes of voices, essences of perfumes, the feel of Ardis's long, slender hand in his as they wade through the cool shallows of Christina Lake in 1958, minnows darting around their toes.

A furious hammering or the angry rasp of a saw suddenly started up again in the furnace room. On the other side of the wall, MJ, Lily and I didn't bother to grimace at each other; our eyes remained focused upon our schoolbooks, as if we heard nothing, as if Mitch weren't there. We didn't trust him. Because of our father, everything we learned in school required a double effort: 75 per cent of what he had taught us was, we discovered, not quite accurate or completely false, and we had to rid our minds methodically of these incorrect theories and facts before we could replace them with more truthful ones. To this day I still harbour certain outlandish ideas, concerning the causes of the First World War and the physical composition of stars, which I must continually amend in my mind.

Wandering from the furnace room to take what he called a breather, Mitch would hover near us and ask how it was going. We gave him stingy, reluctant answers, and sat motionless while he squinted over our shoulders, refused to allow him to witness our work. In the high school on the hill, after all, we arranged our timetables in order to avoid Mitch's history class, and passed him with averted eyes in the hall. Overhearing students scorn our father's teaching methods or mock his mannerisms, our faces remained expressionless.

Sometimes, while we suspensefully waited for Mitch to leave the rumpus room, he would try to engage us in nostalgic conversation concerning our years away from Brale. "Remember that day at Mombasa when we hired a *dhow* to take us out to the islands to search for shells?" he pleaded. "God, that was a good day, wasn't it? We had some great times. Didn't we?"

We refused to acknowledge that we remembered Mombasa or Morogoro, Manila or Bogata, Paris or Rome; even among ourselves, MJ, Lily and I never discussed the years before our return to Brale. As far as we were concerned, we had been born – simultaneously, as triplets – on September 19, 1974, when an afternoon Japan Airlines flight (one stopover at LAX) touched down in Vancouver.

We couldn't admit to memories of being shocked from sleep in the middle of the night by the sudden flick of a hotel-room switch to find Mitch coldly observing us, shaking his head back and forth in disgust. Our charming father could disappear without a trace, leaving behind a man who regarded us with the flat, jaded eyes of a gigolo who harbours no illusions about love, though out of necessity he practises it every day. "What the hell do you think you're doing?" he demanded at three a.m., in the Royal Hotel, in Manila. We didn't look at each other. We didn't answer that, whatever the time zone or hotel or city, it was our belief that we were supposed to be asleep at three a.m. He would stand in the centre of the room, still dressed in the good clothes he had put on seven hours previously to attend an embassy function or press party, which, in the harsh, abrupt light appeared rumpled, nearly threadbare, with a loose button, a dangling thread, a worn cuff. "Get the hell out of here," he wearily commanded. "Don't bother coming back." In pyjamas we filed out the door to wait in the hall, knowing that after waking us this way Mitch always fell quickly asleep. When five minutes passed, we descended to the reception desk where MJ explained that we had been accidentally locked out of our room. A suspicious clerk accompanied us upstairs and unlocked the door. In darkness we fumbled for our bed and cots; listening to Mitch's deep, even breathing, we went back to sleep. In the morning our carefree, happy-go-lucky father would waken especially prone to offering us adventure, an expedition, a treat. We never brought up, then or later, with each other or with Mitch, those late night rousings, just as, during those years, we never mentioned, MJ and I, waking to hear Lily talking quickly to herself, in a locked hotel bathroom, in a language we couldn't understand. Or how at sixteen MJ suddenly began to suffer his Morogoro headaches again. More and more he lay with closed eyes upon the sagging couch with broken springs, while Lily and I continued to study our schoolbooks; gripping his white face in his hands, MJ struggled to memorize the intricacies of nineteenth-century Canadian politics, fought to ignore the drums beating behind his eyes.

In the rumpus room we remained frozen amid the scent of sawdust in Mitch's hair. Fragrant blond flakes sprinkled upon our notebooks as he regretfully shook his head above us. "They've sure got you brainwashed now," he finally said, pointing to our textbooks, before returning to attempt boxes that would hold memories of real truth.

After a certain point our father accepted that we didn't want him near. He understood that we were uninterested in listening to him expound upon our personal past or upon the true significance of the French Revolution. Learning we weren't prepared to coax him out of his dark moods, he left us alone. Mitch didn't show MJ and I how to shave and he didn't teach MJ and Lily how to drive. At the last possible minute, just before his ship went down in flames, Mitch leaped into the cold ocean, flailed through wild waves towards our lifeboat. When he neared it, MJ roughly shoved him away with an oar. The three of us watched coldly as his head went down once, twice. There was not room for a fourth person in our boat. There was not enough food and water for three people to last much longer. If help did not arrive soon, two of us would have to cast the third into the ocean, or kill and eat him to survive. In the end, only the strongest of us would remain in the lifeboat to pray alone beneath an empty sky for sight of land or rescue. MJ, Lily and I regarded each other coolly, knowing this was no time for sentimentality, irritated by too much of each other's close company in the cramped dinghy. We watched each other through narrowed eyes and calculated who would be strongest when it mattered. We knew we had to keep our plans for escape, from each other and for survival, completely secret. We were aware that if things turned out for the very best – the odds said that they wouldn't – we would never see each other again.

MJ was increasingly felled by always more severe headaches which the Brale doctor could neither diagnose nor banish. They permitted him, less and less, to attend classes or to study, and it became clear, by the end of 1976, that he wouldn't graduate from high school. Feeling theoretical, disinterested sympathy for my brother, I covered my ears and trained my eyes upon a French grammar, glad it was him and not me who moaned in his sleep upon the sagging chesterfield at my side, or across the dark bedroom at night. My own survival demanded and required all my attention; in separate ways, Lily, Mitch and Ardis were themselves forced to concentrate with similar blindness upon how to remain alive: for all of us, anything else was unessential. Though we observed each other constantly, it was only to see how developments immediately around us affected our fight to stay afloat.

Though I shared the basement bedroom with my brother, he offered me no clues that he would soon depart in such a way that none of us would ever find him. He must have planned his disappearance carefully, over a long period of time; he would have needed money, for one thing. He would have needed to imagine the whole thing clearly, over and over, in order to envision the numerous details, critical and minute, that combine to make a successful escape. He had to have lain awake, across the dark bedroom, and pictured above him all the threads of his plan, decided how to tie them neatly together, warned himself to leave none dangling loose. If they resembled the threads of the plan I conjured for myself during those nights, they shone gold and silver in the dark, and seemed suspended just out of reach. Later, when it became obvious that he was prepared neither to return to Brale nor to inform us where he had gone, and when I was far enough from the burning ship to view past danger with perspective, I felt admiration for my brother. He had managed his disappearance well and I never once considered looking for him. I respected his choice because I knew the forces which compelled it; the same forces insisted that I perform my own kind of vanishing act later. At the time, however, I bitterly resented the fact that he had slipped away while I still hadn't.

Nor, at the time, did I foresee what would happen to Lily. That in her own way she would also escape; in her case, into the hospital on the hill, into a separate land of hissing snakes and wild dogs and Judy Garland and Jesus. The signs of disturbance Lily had betrayed earlier vanished upon our return to Brale. In the Columbia Avenue house no one woke to hear her private language tumble over itself behind a locked bathroom door. When she lifted her eyes from schoolwork, stared at the blank, undecorated rumpus-room walls, and moved her lips in silent speech, I believed she was puzzling over sines and cosines along with me. Even after Lily began to stay out all night, in the summer of 1976, to drink wine by the river with boys who had Italian surnames, she still spent as many hours as I did with homework in the basement. I had no inkling that in the back of her bedroom closet the white valise Mitch had presented Lily upon her twelfth birthday, for makeup and love letters, contained among other things pills stolen from Ardis and several razor blades. I didn't know that, four months after I fled Brale, Lily would crawl far back into the furnace room to hide behind our dead uncle's hockey sticks and skates, and our departed father's unsuccessful wooden boxes, where within the smell of oil and dust and cold cement she would attempt her own escape.

Perhaps Lily waited patiently until MJ, Mitch and I were gone before she acted. She calmly watched us leave Brale one by one, in different ways, at almost measured intervals, a cycle of escape; each absence left her freer to take her own leave in the way she chose. Finally alone in the lifeboat, Lily prayed to Judy Garland and Jesus beneath an empty sky, with land or rescue still not in sight. The burning ship, now sunken deep into the ocean but still on fire, made the icy water smoke blackly, and into the air shot sparks that printed instructions for Lily to follow.

Sparks swirled like comets around Lily as she stood in the early dusk of autumn, in 1978, beside a fire in the yard behind the house on Columbia Avenue. Wearing rubber boots, one of Jeanette's old coats, and a scarf around her head, she added more leaves to the blaze and, I think, also offered it the notebooks she had written in while we wandered during 1973 and 1974. From the kitchen table Ardis looked out the window at her daughter. Sometimes, across the yard, Lily vanished into darkness, with the back fence, the chinaberry bush, the crab-apple tree; then she reappeared, as a glowing form or a black silhouette, according to her position in relation to the fire. Lily poked a stick at the blaze, stirred it into greater fierceness. Bending her blackened face near, she made certain that the pages covered with her handwriting were really destroyed. She dropped the stick, thrust her hands deep into her pockets, and lifted her face to watch the sparks burn out two or three or four feet above her head. Seeing her own reflection imposed upon her vision of Lily beyond the window, Ardis blinked, and the two images, of Lily and herself, merged into one. Empty rooms creaked around my mother; below, the basement hummed with silence. It was four months since I had left; for MJ and Mitch longer. October 1978.

Ardis must have risen from the kitchen table and stood at the top of the stairs when Lily's legs, flailing weakly after the pills hit her blood, sent a stack of empty, misshapen boxes crashing down in the furnace room. Ardis must have called down the stairs a dozen times, saying Lily's name like a question she asked the dark space below, before she slowly descended to the basement. Prevision of this moment had always prevented her, in the past, from descending these stairs to look for us, for where we lay bleeding. To reach Lily, Ardis must have passed the doorway to the rumpus room, where a trace of mothballs lingered, with three card tables and a sagging couch, in darkness. Ardis must have noticed, as she approached the furnace room, that to her right the door to Mitch's unlit office stood strangely ajar. Ardis must have turned on the furnace-room light, for the space before her, presently silent, reached forward with darkness relieved only by the small blue pilot light of the furnace itself, by the equally small orange light that glowed on the side of the freezer. Ardis must have paused just inside the doorway, her hand still on the light switch, before she moved forward, towards the smell of fresh blood, the mess of Lily's unsuccessful escape. Only Ardis, I think, could have seen in Lily some signs of this kind of secretly planned escape. The kind of escape Ardis had once attempted herself, and still struggled not to execute.

It was Mitch, of all of us, who had broadcast the clearest signs of involvement in a secret plan. Towards the end of 1976, well in advance of his departure to search, ostensibly, for his missing eldest son, Mitch's mood swung sharply upward. His dark weather vanished and he appeared happier, despite MJ's worsening headaches and Lily's deepening habit of staying out all night, even in December, when the river was numb with cold. My father's changed mood did not seem the result of happy circumstances in the present or of resignation, of accepting the hard truth that he had a wife, a mortgage, and three children still at home. He began to whistle and sing to himself again. I remember hearing "Danny Boy" and "The Impossible Dream," tunes I had almost forgotten. Pausing on the basement stairs, with bright notes circling towards me from below, I thought, "He's up to something."

Mitch abandoned his memory boxes and his letters to the editor of the Brale *Daily Times*. Now he sauntered around the house with hands in pockets and a meditative air. I recognized the dreamy, inward expression on his face, the shining light in his eyes. I had seen him look this way whenever he spread a map before him, planned an itinerary, consulted schedules of planes, trains or buses. Strolling into the doorway of the rumpus room, he smiled for us – Lily and I at card tables, MJ on the sagging couch. Our father no longer approached to stand behind our shoulders and emit the scent of sawdust, but remained at a distance, a handsome, charming character revived after two years of retirement. He watched us as though from far away, with his famous, thousand-mile gaze.

Or he sat with Ardis in the living room, seeming at ease with her for the first time since our return, once more gallant and courtly, prone to compliments and flowers that mystified their recipient. "I'll get out of your hair," he had continually said during the last two years, leaving the kitchen immediately after supper, moving away with nervous swiftness when he chanced upon his wife in the driveway or on the back steps. I had seen Mitch visibly start upon rounding a corner of the hallway and bumping into a woman with grey hair, with lines etched deeply into her face. He seemed as awkward as I, and MJ and Lily, around Ardis. Nearly the only time they spent alone together, my parents, was in the musty bed at night, during the hours which encourage mysterious arrangements, silent pacts.

But now Mitch and Ardis sat close together on the living-room couch, his arm around her shoulder, a photograph album spread open across their knees. For long hours in evening, while they slowly turned the pages, Mitch encouraged Ardis to remember the circumstances and significance of snapshots. "It was a hot July day in 1963," he said. "We had a picnic at Gyro Park. Remember? It was probably Jeanette's idea. The whole gang was there." Ardis turned her face towards Mitch and watched him intently as he explained each image at length. He seemed anxious that she recall the part of their life together that had been eliminated for her by the hospital. I presume now that he wished her to remember him when he was gone for good.

Frequently, he called me into his office across from the furnace room. "Look at this," he said, gesturing towards one of his old curling trophies that I had seen a hundred times before. The room was colder than the rest of the house, with a large desk cluttered with untidy stacks of paper, and shelves he had hung upon the walls, burdened with out-of-date textbooks no one had opened in twenty years. The green linoleum floor felt hard beneath my feet; the smell of old paper filled the cold air. "Last shot in the final end. Three rocks down. I had to curl around a guard, knock two of theirs away, draw onto the button. Impossible shot. I made it."

I had heard this stale story and seen this dusty trophy before, just as I had viewed the high-school yearbook with the picture of Mitch as captain of the debating team, Mitch as the centre of the basketball team, Mitch as valedictorian and award-winning athlete and scholar, Mitch voted the most handsome, popular and likely to succeed. "Look at this," he said, not with his usual bragging tone that made me wish to ask how much it cost to have a false yearbook printed, but in a voice of amazed awe, as if he admired the handsome, popular and likely-to-succeed boy as someone glimpsed from afar, from below, from beyond reach. "Look at this," he said. Though I still didn't trust my father an inch, being unprepared to meet him halfway because there was no halfway with him, I realized that he was trying to show me something more than curling trophies and high-school yearbooks.

"Do you have any use for this?" he asked, holding out a faded cloth letter that had once decorated his basketball team jacket.

"Not really," I said stiffly.

"It's here when you want it," he said. "I've been putting all these things in order. There's some interesting stuff in this room, you know. One day you might get a kick out of what the old man did. Now, everything will be clearly marked. You, MJ, Lily. I don't want any confusion." Mitch frowned for a moment. "The most important papers are in the filing cabinet. The keys are behind the German dictionary, on the top shelf."

*Look at this*, my father told me.

I'm leaving.

(When I departed Brale myself, six months after Mitch, it was without ever having reached to the top shelf in his study and felt for the keys to the filing cabinet, hidden behind the German dictionary. At the time I was uninterested in documents and evidence and proof. I thought I would be able to forget Mitch and to forget the Royal Hotel in Manila and forget the wild dogs of Morogoro. If only I went far enough away. If only I stayed away.

But, years later, when I did return to Brale for brief visits, I

183

noticed that Mitch's office was unchanged, with stacks of papers and old textbooks still cluttering the cold space. But all the rooms in the Columbia Avenue house were preserved in the state they had known upon being abandoned, nearly a decade before. Bedrooms, the kitchen. The rumpus room and the furnace room. Mitch's office. Ardis kept the doors of these rooms closed; apparently, she entered them only to dust. When I opened the doors of these rooms, I was greeted by the smell of mothballs, a trace of smoke, time suspended. A book of poems by Wallace Stevens in the case beside MJ's bed. A white valise, open and empty, in the closet of Lily's room. A map of the world taped to the wall above my bed. Though I had gone far away and stayed far away, I had also grown steadily more curious about Mitch and about the foreign country of my past. My right arm was ready to reach to the top shelf of Mitch's office. I fumbled behind the German dictionary for the filing cabinet keys. I took the contents of the cabinet with me when I left Brale later that week to return to Europe.)

Mitch had been gone for months before we discovered the arrangements he had made for a permanent absence. At the cluttered desk in his cold office, with the sound of his wife's footsteps above his head, he had planned carefully, thoughtfully, rashly. He had composed and mailed an official letter of resignation to the school board, denouncing its antiquated, narrow-minded educational policies. He had cashed in his teacher's pension; it wasn't much, just enough to pay off the remainder of the mortgage on the house, which he had deeded over to Ardis. With his lawyer he had arranged to sell his share in his parents' house, damaged but not destroyed in the fire of 1960, that he owned equally with his sisters; in a year, whichever sister who wanted to would buy him out at the current assessment value. The money was to be deposited in an account he had set up in Lily's name.

He had said goodbye.

*I won't always be around to save you from this, that or the other thing,* our father warned us beside the Indian Ocean in 1970.

*I won't always be around to save you from yourselves.*

To save you from the memory of myself.

*Look at this*, my father said when he told me goodbye.

I'm still looking at this.

# viii.

*Greetings from the end of the world,* I write Jose, on the back of a coloured postcard depicting an exterior view of the citadel in El Jadida. It has been three weeks since my arrival here. While I wait with decreasing hope for some word from Rabat, I hear from Jose that he has found a job in a small Madrid bar, mixed with gay and straight clientele, in the Calle Horteleza. From nine in the evening until two in the morning, and later on weekends, he stands in the doorway, as the bouncer. He has moved out of the *cuartel* and into a shared apartment discovered through new acquaintances from the bar. In the morning he calls the military garage to learn if the general he has been assigned to protect has ordered the car. If the general is not going out, Jose is free for the day.

This is really the first time he has lived away from home, away from Sevilla. Madrid is, I know, a huge, swift, disorienting city, especially compared to tranquil Sevilla. Working at the bar, Ras, Jose will probably meet many new people; he will enjoy new experiences and learn new things. It will be good for him and for us. He needs to learn, on his own, some of the things I had already discovered before meeting him; there were times he felt lacking in experience compared to me. I would point out that, in turn, unlike him, I didn't possess the particular kind of knowledge that comes with staying in one place for a long time. Isn't the whole point of two people joining together that each makes up for what the other lacks?

Still, when we meet again Jose will be richer for his time in Madrid. We will be more equal. Next summer, after receiving his *blanco*, the paper that states military service has been completed, he will be able to go back to school or find a better job; perhaps I will end my career as indifferent teacher of English and return to school myself. We will stay in Spain or move to Canada. We will travel together. We will go on.

Or in Madrid Jose will meet someone else. Someone less difficult than myself, as happy as he is. This is a calculated risk we are both taking. I feel for the silver chain below my throat, close my eyes, slide its clasp back to the proper place behind my neck.

Instead of visiting the cistern, citadel and cathedral, Jose, I have carefully searched Room 5 for signs that Mitch in fact inhabited it. If he left El Jadida nine months before my arrival, and if the room were occupied by a different guest or pair of guests each night during those nine months, this means as many as five hundred and forty people have stayed in Room 5 since my father. Unless I encounter evidence clearly and specifically tied to Mitch, it could belong to any of those strangers. They might themselves have removed a clue he dropped, or it could have been eliminated by the pair of maids who at ten each morning knock on the door to trail mop and broom vaguely across the floor.

The room offers no clues. As far as I can tell, Mitch did not deliberately or idly scratch his initials or a longer message upon any surface of Room 5. The dim corners and the floor beneath the furniture, obviously untouched by the maids for at least a month, also fail to reveal, for instance, a scrap of paper, a book of matches, a ticket stub. In the evening I stand upon my balcony and in the air smell something as sweet as ripe dates, as sharp as paprika, and I wonder if these scents of Africa, strong and pervasive and untouchable, are the only clues I will discover in El Jadida.

*Don't look for your father.*
*You've already found him.*
*Go back.*

And I wonder, Abdul and Ahammed, if there are sixty holy lessons, written in a language I do not understand, which I must learn before I am ready to leave this room and travel farther south.

If there are further dreams I must experience, with assistance of a potion I did not ask for and do not wish to take again (it has remained untouched, in the drawer of the bedside table, since my single, initial dose), before I will awaken to discover the landscape altered into dune and sky and burning sun.

If The Lost Oasis is, rather than a miracle upon that sand, a Polisarian code-name for one more covert action in the struggle for independence.

I still haven't received reply to my written request for an interview with the official at the Canadian consulate in Rabat. According to a note from Ardis, which reached me here yesterday, no progress in the matter has yet been conveyed to her despite what I was told. My mother mentioned that Mitch's final effects (gathered here in El Jadida? or east of Layounne, near Smara, where his passport was discovered?) will remain at the Rabat consulate until claimed by me, or, if she requests, shipped to her in Brale. These would, I imagine, consist only of a few articles of clothing, several tattered paperbacks, one or two mementos of recent times and places unknown by me. Anything of value has surely been stolen, or has disappeared with Mitch into the desert.

✧

"Sometimes one remains too long in El Jadida."

I don't wish to see who this voice beside me belongs to. I wish only to buy one bar of soap and one tube of toothpaste from the stall before me, and I have exactly seven and one-half dirhams to spend.

"Sometimes one remains too long in El Jadida," the voice repeats in exactly the same tone, as if it were a recorded message that will play *ad infinitum*.

I turn and see beside me a middle-aged man wearing Western clothes. He regards me with steady patience through thick glasses. Where have I seen this man before? He appears familiar, from a long time ago.

"Monsieur has dreamed?" he asks.

Of course. The dream man.

"I always dream," I answer curtly. "I've been dreaming all my life. Tell me, is there something in this *souk* to prevent me from dreaming? That's what I really need."

"And has monsieur found the tattoo artist?"

"Monsieur is not looking for the tattoo artist. Monsieur is looking for Palmolive and Crest."

"He lives nearby," the dream man says. "Over there." He gestures towards the *quartier portugais* to our right. "Would you like me to take you to him?"

"Why?"

The dream man smiles. "Everyone wishes to find the tattoo artist, no?"

All at once I am aware of the scent of mint. I glance down and see a woman spreading bright green sprigs on a sack near my feet. Fresh but dense, the scent is cleaner than that of any bar of Palmolive. It makes me want to close my eyes. *Jose.* The word shines in darkness, hangs in my mind, a star.

"Let us go." The dream man walks from the stall, not looking behind to see if I follow.

"*Menthe*," says the old woman at my feet, holding up a sprig of green. "*Menthe, menthe*," she croons.

I take the mint and follow the dream man. He walks quickly; it is difficult to keep up, and several times I nearly lose him in the crowded, narrow passages of the *souk*. We pass stalls offering gold and stalls offering silver; the precious metals gleam in dim light, like lures cast by fishermen into deep, dark water. Then we are passing beneath one of the arched entrances of the thick, high walls that surround the *quartier portugais*.

Immediately the noise and crowds of the *souk* are left behind. A narrow cobblestone street, walled with three-storey buildings on either side, stretches empty and silent before me. I can't seem to catch up to the dream man no matter how quickly I walk; he remains a dozen paces in front as we turn corner after corner into always narrower, dimmer streets. Several times it appears that a dead-end waits before us. Then an arched, low tunnel opens in a wall, and with bent backs we proceed into another silent, empty street.

I notice that all the doors are closed and the windows shuttered on either side. Why are there no people about? It is the middle of afternoon. There should be children playing, women sweeping, men smoking on the corners. And why is it so dark in here? I pause and look upward. The blue sky appears miles overhead, as if the buildings were a thousand, not three storeys tall. I realize grimly why I have avoided visiting this part of town before.

The *quartier portugais* is not large. If I want, I can turn around and with a little effort find my way back to the *souk* to buy Palmolive and Crest for seven and one-half dirhams. After all, there is no such thing as being lost.

The man has paused a dozen yards before me. Doesn't he have anything better to do? Surely he can dream up a more enjoyable way to pass an afternoon than leading a somewhat brittle *étranger* around dark alleys.

"I have only seven and one-half dirhams," I warn, nearing him.

The dream man smiles sadly. "Money is not necessary," he says, then enters the doorway before him without knocking. There is no sign above it, I notice.

I follow. Of course, it's completely dark inside. Though I haven't closed the street door behind me, after three steps I can't see a thing.

"Wait."

I hear the dream man's voice to my left. His glasses shine in the darkness. The gleam reminds me of something from long ago; I try to remember what as his footsteps move away. Apparently, he is walking deeper into the building, perhaps through a doorway to another room. Absolute silence and darkness follow. I hold the sprig of mint near my face and crush it between my fingers. The cool scent immediately multiplies in intensity until it fills the room like water. Palmolive, I think vaguely. The word seems to have lost all meaning in the dark. Crest, I say to myself, noticing that this word too has become a mere shape of sound within myself.

I will count to ten and leave this room. I will turn around, walk three steps, pass through a doorway and into a street. A simple physical process.

I begin counting. One, two, three. Each number falls into my mind like a stone dropping into a dark well. Four, five, six. I hear the numbers splash as they hit water one hundred or one thousand feet below the surface of the earth. Seven, eight, nine. The splashes echo between the narrow walls of the well, bounce between stone, lose distinctness and clarity. They become one loud, continuous roar within the well of my mind. The sound swells until it grows into a physical force with the power to knock me over.

Silence.

I am sitting on a hard, wooden chair. A candle, half-burned, rises upon a nearby table which also holds needles, and small metal pots containing powders and liquids. These objects appear golden in candlelight sufficient to reveal a bare, cement room with dark, shapeless shadows in the corners. Between the table and my chair is an empty wooden bench. On the floor before me rests a tray that holds a silver teapot and two glasses. One is empty and one is full. I lean towards the tray and lift the full glass. The liquid inside it is without scent or colour. I take a small sip. Cold, flavourless.

One of the shadows moves towards me. The dream man looks down at me. His glasses glint; for a second I see a bottle floating on dark water beneath a half-moon. The expression on the dream man's face appears one of concern as he studies me in silence.

There is a burning sensation at my heart. The top buttons of my shirt are unfastened. I look down at the skin of my chest.

The skin above my heart is bare. I look questioningly at the dream man.

"Yes, it is gone," he says. "The tattoo artist has done a good job, hasn't he? He always does. Let me say, please, that it is not easy to remove a tattoo like yours without leaving a scar. Very difficult indeed. Usually there remains some mark, some small sign. I believe one is very pleased, isn't one?"

"But —" I give up. I am certainly not prepared to argue with this man that I have never had a tattoo in my life.

The crushed sprig of mint is still pinched between my thumb and middle finger. With my free hand I rebutton my shirt, then follow the dream man through the door to my left.

Outside the street is darker than before; a single light at the corner illuminates cobblestones, walls to either side, closed doors and shuttered windows. A large rat or small cat scurries by my feet. A dog barks in the distance. I quickly look upward. The sky is dark and without stars. I watch it for a long moment while the dream man's footsteps fade. I lift the sprig of crushed mint near my face and smell cloves. The sprig drops to the ground.

"Palmolive and Crest," I think, walking from the *quartier portugais* towards the brightly lit streets and cafés and stores.

# ix.

"Do you want to change?"

At midnight I stand once more upon the rocks which stagger out of the black Atlantic, far down the shore from the lights of the promenade and cafés I have left behind. A moment ago I removed several pieces of paper from my pocket, tore them into scraps, and scattered them upon the water. At first they whirled like white birds struggling to ascend above the wind, then fell to be dashed again and again upon the rocks at my feet. Now, one by one, they roll beneath the waves to surface occasionally at a safe distance from shore, near my furthest point of vision, or, more often, to sink at once.

Yes, I want to change.

I want to convert, to evolve, to metamorphose, to transform.

To return to the Hotel de Provence from this shore free of more than several pieces of paper. Sufficiently liberated to travel beyond the Hotel de Provence and to open the distant door of a room that is larger than Room 5. A room of infinite dimensions, with walls and ceiling made of sky affording uninterrupted vision.

Turning towards the voice that has just spoken, I am surprised to see a boy behind me. He has hands in pockets, face lifted to the sky, clear eyes. Standing very straight, he is taller than me. Even in darkness, I can't help but see that his body is strong, hard, a force undeniable as darkness and wind. He is one of those boys, fifteen or eighteen or twenty, I have seen playing endless, intense games of soccer on the sand. He is one of the boys I have seen running on long, muscled legs along the road to Azemmour, or performing laborious situps and pushups and stretching exercises at the water's edge. One of the boys, without work or money or opportunity, who seem to throw themselves into physical activity of religious fervour, as compensation. Surrounded by an aura of purity as well as darkness, they inhabit a holy temple of a body at which few are permitted to worship, these boys I have avoided looking at too closely during my time in El Jadida.

I turn back to watch the sinking of what I have offered to the ocean:

A room-service menu from the Royal Hotel in Manila, circa 1973.

An Aereas Argentina schedule of flights between Quito and Rio de Janeiro.

A printout of currency exchange rates from the Banque Nacional de Lyons on October 26, 1973.

It is important that my eyes witness the drowning of these documents. Of these last documents. I need to feel certain that, rather than washing upon the shore to my right or left in half an hour, they have been carried away irretrievably, forever, for good.

"*Voulez-vous changer?*" I hear him ask again.

He won't go away, I know. Even if I ignore him, this boy will keep standing behind me, refusing to take a hint, insisting upon an answer. Waiting for me to reply that this scattering of scraps of paper upon the Atlantic is my way of changing. We all have our own method, each difficult to explain, perhaps ineffectual, merely the best we can do.

His hand reaches towards me. At the edge of rocks slippery with spray, I draw away as much as I can without falling into the ocean. No. Forget it. I haven't come to the shore at midnight for this. I am sorry, but you are mistaken. I am faithful, Jose, never wavering in temptation, and I pray that you believe in the firmness of my belief, in my steadfast devotion.

"Very good," he says, stroking the sleeve of my denim jacket, looking into my eyes with an expression I am unable to interpret. "To change is good."

"Feel," he says, lifting my hand to rest upon his sleeve. Beneath the thin material of his jacket, his arm radiates warmth. During the first week of December, wind blows coldly upon the coast of El Jadida; a moment ago I was shivering as spray dashed icy drops against me. Those arms, one beneath my hand and the other still resting on my own sleeve, would be very warm, very strong around me. They would allow me to forget, for an hour, the reason why I stand here beside the Atlantic at midnight: trying to prepare myself to leave El Jadida, trying to force myself to travel farther south, away from you, Jose.

"It is easy to change," he encourages.

Now his face is near enough for me to see the strong bones rising beneath his cheeks, the straight blade of nose running between a clear brow and full lips parted to reveal white teeth. The kind of features which may seem a genetic accident or mistake or miracle. A cause for celebration, rejoicing, wonder. Like the vision of a tall, handsome Spanish son walking along the Avenida de la Constitución beside a tiny mother stooped in black.

Jose, for weeks now I have stood at night upon the balcony of my room in the Hotel de Provence and looked northward, above the almond trees and rooftops, in your direction. During those hours before midnight – and I know it is one hour later for you, in

196

your separate time zone – the bar where you work is nearly empty and time passes slowly for you, as it does here for me. Though the bar is packed on weekends, on a Monday night, for example, there are not many people for you to greet or bid farewell as they pass through the doorway where you stand. You glance at your watch, then look again down the Calle Horteleza as it slopes towards the Gran Vía. During these slow nights you have memorized the scene before you, just as I have learned completely the view from my hotel balcony. The Banque BMCE on one corner, the Chambre de Commerce et d'Industrie on the other; the gardens that rise above the wall, the stoplight that is always green. I can see you standing in the doorway of Ras because I remember the Calle Horteleza from my visit to Madrid five years ago. Yes, I know the bar was once famous, during the *movida* of the early eighties, haunted then by Almodovar and Alaska when they were still young, still on the edge. Do you remember that song Alaska wrote about Ras? How does it go?

I know the scene before you and I wish you to know mine, so you can see me as clearly as I see you. I want you to see the old women with a line of green dye running from the centre of the lower lip to the chin. How the men, after shaking your hand, touch their heart with the flat of their palm. How at the Cinema Le Paris, Stallone has given way to Schwarzenegger who has given way to Van Damme, as if all our heroes were only active, and did not stand still in doorways or on balconies, fighting in a quieter way.

How the cafés and streets empty early in El Jadida, and when I walk the promenade at ten o'clock at night, beneath the rustling palms, I am unlikely to encounter anyone at all. The dark sand below, its further edge lit by an irregular silver line of breaking waves, barely audible, a sound far back in my mind's cave, appears as distant as another, more dangerous country. Far out upon the water shine lights of a ship; beyond those lights, towards the south and west, the Canary Islands rise from black ocean. If I swam for seven days and seven nights, Jose, I might wade ashore Gran Canaria to inform your father that, all appearances to the contrary, he has been dead for a dozen years. Before me, past the end of the promenade, a narrow road curves along the bay towards Azemmour, five miles to the north, five miles nearer to you. The lights along the road, more sulphureous than the lights of America or Europe, trace the line of the shore, and when they have bended to lie directly before me, they appear like a score of eyes watching from the north. The town behind me has become a huddled mass of dark shapes, with a blinking lighthouse rising above the old Portuguese port. Sometimes, as I walk farther northward, I expect to meet someone just at the point where my vision trails into darkness, for it seems that a figure might lurk there; emerging from obscurity, he walks towards me. We meet, pause to recognize each other, then I continue walking northward, past Casablanca and then Rabat, all the way to Tangier, where I cross the Strait on the path of moonlight that wavers upon this bay beside me. I keep walking, mile after long mile, still northward, through Andalucian groves of oranges and grapes, until at last I arrive at Madrid. Passing the Plaza de España and proceeding up Gran Vía, I turn left on Horteleza. You see me limp towards you, as you lean in the doorway of the bar.

But until now no figure has emerged from the shadows of the promenade or shore to recognize me in passing. I haven't found my father in El Jadida; there have been few signs of him here. I am not yet free to walk five hundred miles to you, Jose. Now I believe that is all that may happen: we will meet, recognize each other, though perhaps without a sign, then continue in our separate directions, move farther apart once more, my father and I.

The boy moves still closer towards me, until our faces nearly touch and I feel the warmth of his breath. "*Changez*," he repeats. Are his eyes gently encouraging, or do they flick over me with cold impatience? Is his voice softly persuasive, or does it hold a cruel, contemptuous note? What forces brought this boy to this windy shore at midnight? What kind of life has he led before this moment? What kind of people have figured in his past? Who is his father?

His arms circle my shoulders, then slide down my back; his hands grasp my jacket, slip it off my shoulders, from my arms. Quickly he takes off his own jacket and hands it to me. He puts on my coat as I put on his. Slightly too large for me, the garment feels thin, worn, shabby – unlike my denim jacket lined with soft red cotton, with a warm red hood. Like most of the Western clothes here, it is probably made from some cheap, artificial material, poorly cut, in a style from the sixties. I suspect I have gotten the worst of this trade, yet I feel no sense of being cheated.

"Let's sit," he says, taking my hand and leading me to a flat rock safe from the reach of the ocean spray. My legs bend and fold, seemingly without my command. I sit on cold stone as if I have given in to something, as if I am no longer required to control or to question what happens to me now. For a moment I think dimly of sodden scraps of paper sinking through darkness; then I am aware only of the warm hand still folded around mine, an unfamiliar scent like savoury smoke wafting from my new coat, the sensation of my former coat touching my side. The ocean roars more loudly. The sound fills me until I feel no distinction between the night around me and myself, between the body beside me and myself.

"It's late," says a voice whose timbre my ears know as well as they know my own voice. Have I spoken without moving my lips? I am pulled to my feet by a hand that I believed was my own hand, that has the same temperature as my body. I am stiff and cold. "Let's go home," says the voice, emerging from a boy who walks beside me across the sand. His arm rests upon my shoulders; a warm, light weight encourages me forward.

"Don't worry," says the boy, as we ascend to the promenade and pass the dark, silent cafés. "The change is good." I feel I have been beside the ocean, far from voices and light, for much longer than part of a single night, and that many changes have occurred within and around me during that time. The empty streets of El Jadida appear different, as if my eyes envisioned them more acutely, or with more intimate knowledge. And my body feels altered in size and shape; then I realize that it is the material surrounding my self that is not the same.

The boy squeezes my shoulder, drops his arm, veers from my side. "Goodbye," he says, before disappearing in my jacket. I watch my own back walk away from me, move towards an unknown life, leave me behind.

By the time I return to the Hotel de Provence the whole town is quiet. In the bright light of Room 5 I inspect my new jacket and wearily smile. It is the grey jacket of a suit, made from something like acrylic, with frayed cuffs, a missing button, oddly cut lapels. In the armoire mirror I stare at a young man who stares anxiously back. We recognize each other dimly from some point in the past; but we have both changed since then. Since that time his hair has grown longer and is sprinkled generously with grey that catches the light. His face appears darker and thinner; the body inside his too large jacket looks slighter. His expression suggests that I have changed also, without indicating whether this change is for the good. At this rate, we will soon pass each other in the street without a glance of recognition.

Suddenly I reach up to the top of the armoire and take down the blue travelling bag that has hidden there for weeks. I begin to pack my few clothes quickly, as if late for an airplane, or in need of swift escape. After a few minutes I sit on the edge of the bed and light a cigarette. I am frightened of travelling farther south, Jose. I know that from now on my journey will be more difficult and more rapid, without weeks spent in a single town, without modestly comfortable hotel rooms. I will be unable to send you a new address where you can write to me. After leaving here, my whereabouts will be unknown to you, and to Reyna and Ardis. For all intents and purposes, I will disappear.

*Hurry back*, your most recent postcard read. *It's getting hard to wait.*

I bet it's getting hard. I imagine you are receiving, in the doorway of Ras, all kinds of offers to make exchanges far more intimate than that of an article of clothing.

Forcing that particular fear aside, I examine with equal dread my stash of dirham notes. My original sixty thousand pesetas has, during these weeks, dwindled to the equivalent of several hundred Canadian dollars. From now on I will have to stay in rooms less expensive than Room 5 of the Hotel de Provence. I will have to live on less food and fewer cigarettes. I will have to exist on the dried entrails of armadillo, the bitter meat of cacti, the insubstantial nourishment of hope.

Or I could remain here. I could continue to eat *tajine au poulet* every day at two o'clock in the Café-Restaurant Scheherazade and each midnight add the black daybook piece by piece to the ocean until every last shred of my troubling evidence was gone. I could continue to send weekly postcards to Jose, Reyna and Ardis. Continue to await word concerning Mitch from the Canadian embassy in Rabat. Continue to experience slightly puzzling encounters with strangers. Pretending I were a tourist, I could visit the citadel and cistern in the *quartier portugais*, and in the *souk* purchase a few inexpensive souvenirs to remind me later of a pleasant, relaxing holiday. And then, when only enough dirhams remained to return to Spain, I could travel north persuaded that I have searched for my father as best I could, with all my resources. Fulfilled that obligation. Done that duty. Put it firmly behind.

"You have to find your father," says Jose on the bank of the Guadalquivir.

"Go," says Ardis in the kitchen on Columbia Avenue.

"Do it," commands the belly dancer, looking up from her makeup table, jabbing the air with a lipstick.

"Sometimes one remains too long in El Jadida," warns the dream man, peering from behind thick glasses.

All right. I glance around Room 5. A black daybook, filled with my father's handwriting, lies on the table. Small jars of lotions and creams clutter the bathroom. Postcards from Jose and Reyna decorate the wall. How startling that the most minimal display of personal objects, with the most fleetingly known impersonal decor, can conspire to make a briefly occupied room feel like home. How puzzling that each departure seems as difficult and necessary and urgent as the original leave-taking, the first farewell, as if for mysterious reasons God created us without the capability of ever learning to say goodbye. You'd think I'd be good at this by now, Reyna. You'd think that I would have mastered at least the skill required to pack bags, walk out the door, and head to the station. Quite frankly, daddy, your Room 5 is overpriced; in any case, I can no longer afford it. I haven't enough to keep paying and paying and paying to learn, here at the end of the world, the sixty expensive lessons of the Koran.

What am I leaving behind here, anyway? The dream man, the tattoo artist. Abdul and Ahammed. Godfrey Bridgeport and Mohammed Lasfar. A boy on a beach. People I have met only once or twice. Strangers who emerged abruptly out of darkness or in light sidled up to offer information I felt ill-equipped to understand, before vanishing like phantoms of my dreams. Cardboard characters summoned from my unconscious only to perform a specific role in my psychological play. Yet the gist of their lines remains elusive to me. What are the sixty lessons of the Koran, Ahammed? How many have I learned in El Jadida? I only know that all sixty combine to form the basis of Islam, and that this word, Islam, means to submit.

Allah, I submit. Rising from the bed, I add my father's daybook to my blue bag; it is the last remaining document, the one I suspect holds greatest significance, the one I am not yet prepared to deliver to the Atlantic. I gather the lotions and creams from the bathroom, pause in the centre of the room, return them where they were. I don't believe they will be of use from now on: they cannot erase the lines around my eyes any longer; they will not be powerful enough to combat the forces of sun and wind and sand. I will leave these beauty secrets of a belly dancer behind for the two hotel maids. And the remains of the dream potion? At the last moment I retrieve it from the bedside table, where it has waited, an untouched, complex temptation, since my single experience with *tseuheur*. Dropping it into my bag, I close the zipper.

Sound interrupts the silence, draws nearer, grows louder. Stepping onto the balcony, I look down into the street. Below, in the first greying of light, I see an old man riding a cart, made only of wheels and a few boards, piled high with oranges and drawn by a small mule. The animal appears much too small to pull this load; yet its hooves knock the pavement brightly, energetically. The air is fresh and cool; a slight breeze stirs. The wet street gleams, though I have been unaware of rainfall during the night.

# III

## The Palm at the End of the Mind

"The palm at the end of the mind
Beyond the last thought, rises
In the bronze distance,
A gold-feathered bird
Sings in the palm, without human meaning
Without human feeling, a foreign song."
– Wallace Stevens

# i.

Persistent knocking disturbs the darkness. Neither steady nor rapid, the sound is interrupted by pauses lasting for perhaps half a silent minute. Just when I believe that quiet will prevail, another loud knock negates the possibility, demands my attention, refuses to leave me alone. Who is it? I call, lying face down on the bed. There is no answer. I rise from the bed and feel my way slowly to the door. It seems far away. I grow conscious of the fact that I don't know this dark room well; its concealed shape and obscured contents are unfamiliar to me. I haven't been here long.

Turning the doorknob, I find that the passage beyond contains deeper darkness. A small figure, presumably a child, stands there. The light is insufficient to tell if it is a boy or a girl. What do you want? I ask. In reply, the child turns and, without looking behind, walks away with a rapid, unsteady gait. As I follow it down the narrow passage, past closed doors to either side, I wonder dimly if this being is injured or crippled. Except for my guide's uneven step, soft slaps against cement, the passage is silent. My own feet seem to make no sound.

After twenty paces, I am convinced that I will be unable to find the way back to my room alone, though as far as I can tell we have proceeded in a straight line. It becomes essential that I keep in sight this figure before me – still only a black shape, darkness made solid – if I wish to avoid being lost. Several times the figure pauses for me to catch up, then continues forward as soon as I am close enough to reach out my hand and touch its shoulder. The passage ends in descending steps, without a railing. I make my way carefully down, fearful of falling a hundred or a thousand dark feet; below, it sounds as if my guide skips carelessly, lightly downward. I try to count each step to preserve a sense of measured distance; after arriving at the twelfth, the shapes these numbers form within my head begin to blur, then lose all distinction. *Twelve.* The sound of the word echoes inside me, an alien noise without substance or meaning to hold onto.

Suddenly the stairs end and the hard surface beneath my feet flattens. I move through a doorway and into the night. The sky is illuminated by a nearly full moon, and scattered with chips of stars. Pale light reveals the child facing away from me to be a boy dressed in a long robe hanging nearly to his ankles, which are as bare as his feet. It is the kind of roughly woven garment, scratchy against the skin, worn in the desert, a thought distantly informs me. *Desert.* The word stirs inside me, followed immediately by the realization that the small town, sleeping or abandoned around me, is poised between the desert and the ocean. At the next moment I become aware that the ocean must be near: the sound of waves heaves now to our right, now to our left. Disproportionately loud, even magnified, the sound washes each thought from my mind before it has barely formed, before it can be pursued. Still turned from me, the boy pauses in front of a black palm whose branches, rustling in the breeze, cast shadows which sway and shift across him. Hypnotized by the sight, I do not notice, for a moment, that the boy has moved away, that I stare at only shadows.

I hurry after him again. As we travel between darkened, silent houses of whitewashed earth, I feel little curiosity regarding our destination. I am prepared to follow the small boy indefinitely. My eyes fixed upon the back of his bobbing head, I am conscious of a longing to see his face, and of how, with each moment, this longing grows into need. I wonder why the broken dirt road, littered with stones and glinting shards of glass, does not appear to hurt his feet. The road slopes gradually downward through a gorge; banks rise on either side, growing higher with each step, until I feel that we are walking deeper and deeper into the earth, and that the ground will never flatten, widen, open upon broad landscape again. A dog trots by, tongue extending from its mouth; there is a sudden stench of decay. The small boy walks increasingly swiftly; perhaps he has forgotten that I follow, for he no longer pauses or glances back. I am not easily able to keep up. Now he seems to flit rapidly across the ground, or just above the surface. For a second, until I blink, I think that he runs on all fours.

He stops so abruptly that I nearly bump into him. The gorge has come to an end; a bank rises steeply before us, as well as on either side. A garbage heap climbs halfway up the bank. The people of the town must throw refuse down here. The boy claws through it, shifting objects undefinable by my eyes. Once he stops to throw a stone to our left; a dog yelps, runs away. He seems to have a clear idea of what he is looking for, the small boy, and precisely where it is buried: his effort is concentrated, focused, determined. The stench of decay becomes overpowering, killing the scent of salt in the air, seeming almost to possess the solidity of a persistent, unwanted touch. All at once I am aware of shivering violently, though I have not realized that the night is cold. The sound of waves grows louder, then fades. A crow coughs nearby.

I am uncertain how long ago the boy stopped clawing through the garbage heap. He has risen and turned towards me, breathing quickly, lightly from his work. His face, just below mine, is near enough to kiss; it shines with anticipation. He has something to show me, something to reveal with pride. I wish to look into his face until I discover something not immediately apparent there, a secret hidden in his features. Desire sickens me. Grasping my hand with surprising strength, he draws me forward three steps to the edge of the garbage heap, directly before the place where he was digging. The pressure of his hand grows tighter, more insistent. I turn my eyes from his face to what lies uncovered at our feet.

A body, obviously of a man, sprawls face down amid garbage. I see the short dark hair of his head, a white shirt stained with blood or dirt, and light-coloured trousers that may be made of khaki. At the moment my eyes hazily recognize the particular material and cut of these trousers, and perhaps the shape of the limbs that fill them, my gaze slips from the man to the discarded objects around him. All at once it becomes extremely important to identify the scattered confusion. Are those bones, just beside his head? Is that part of an automobile tire, by his left hand? Does his right hand rest upon a bunch of rotting bananas? My eyes return to the body. I try, and fail, to recall the vague memory sparked by it a moment ago. Instead, I notice how his left hand curves gracefully around something, how his arms appear flung wide to embrace the ground, how one foot lacks a shoe. I believe that I could stand here until dawn without absorbing everything contained within the few square metres before me. I could look all my life at this scene and still miss half its elements.

I feel pressure upon my right hand again. The sensation of the small boy's touch returns to me as something long forgotten yet intimately known. *Warm.* The word splashes dully into my mind like a stone into a deep well. When the boy removes his hand, I experience a stabbing loss; my abandoned hand dangles in the air, as if unconnected to anything. The boy bends down until he is squatting over the body once more. He attempts to turn the man by pushing at his right shoulder. Apparently, the body is very heavy, for the boy grunts and strains to move it. At last, slowly, the body begins to turn. My attention is caught by the scratching of a palm in the wind, somewhere above my head. I struggle to see the image suggested by the sound: the shredded black of branches waving against a background of fading night and shrinking stars. My mind strains with effort. I notice, in the foreground of this image, in the shadow of the palm, a body turn with the imperceptible slowness of a planet. Fraction by fraction the face is revealed, until it stares squarely up at me, and into the sky beyond.

I turn over and look upward. I gaze into darkness wondering why there are no stars, wondering where I am. My mind grapples with the puzzle. I experience slight relief when I understand that I lie on a hard bed, with a meagre pillow beneath my head, a rough blanket pulled halfway up my torso. The blanket scratches my skin. A strong, disagreeable smell fills the room. The bathroom down the hall, I think. Suddenly, I freeze: from nearby travels a knocking sound. It is irregular, persistent. Who's there? I call into the darkness. No one answers. The knocking ceases, then breaks the silence again. Rising from the bed, I feel my way slowly in the direction of what I believe is the door. I stop. The sound comes from the other side of the room, behind me. I recross the dark space, just as slowly, and feel for a window in the wall. A loose shutter bangs, knocks, bangs. My fingers fumble to hold it still. I gaze out upon rooftops, and gently rolling hills beyond. The desert waits on the other side. It takes me a moment to wonder why moonlight bathes this landscape without entering the window. Pushing away the unsolved problem as having little importance, I fasten the shutter with a hook.

I lie upon the bed again, and, despite the fastened shutter, listen for the knocking to resume. Silence presses around me, as firmly as a hand. My right hand aches. Stinging pain in my feet suggests that they are cut. I lie with my face turned towards the darkness above me. Waiting for dawn, I listen to the rustling of a distant palm.

At dawn I have no clear sense of waking.

Unaware of moving from one state of consciousness to another, I feel that I have lain awake all night to wait for this moment when cracks of light bend through shutters to illuminate feebly the space around me. At the same time, I am stirred by images that seem to belong to the fading darkness and that possess the qualities of a dream. As an unfamiliar room slowly reveals itself, I study these images for plausibility, prepared to spring upon a detail that betrays them to be imagination.

A dark gorge. A body strewn amid garbage. A palm rustling overhead.

It must have been a dream. I must have slept.

At some point, awake or asleep, I rose from the hard bed beneath me and fastened the shutters. Turning off the light last night, I had left the window open in hope that night air would diffuse the heavy smell of the bathroom down the hall. Now I sniff the air inquiringly. It answers that I am still in the Hotel Suerte Loca, still in Sidi Ifni. After several minutes I am able to calculate that I have passed three nights in this room. It is eight days since I left El Jadida. The information emerges upon my mind just as light reaches the far edge of the room, defining its dimensions.

Except for the bed, the room is bare. The floor is made of murky grey tiles; perhaps once brightly coloured, they have faded beneath dirt and wear. The blank walls, painted a disturbing shade of lime green, are smeared with what appears to be dirt; I don't wish to make a close examination and learn that the dirt is, after all, dried blood or excrement. A bulb dangles nakedly from a wire in the ceiling.

My blue travelling bag, opened and unpacked, stands in the centre of the floor. My eyes linger upon the bag and try to fathom its contents, then become distracted by the sight of a large cockroach walking slowly towards it. Two antennae on the insect's head waver as it travels across the flat, hard surface. My eyes shift quickly to a grey jacket hanging from a nail on the door. Puzzled, I try to recognize the garment.

Emerging without familiarity from a third dark night, the room insists that it will remain unknown to me, no matter how long I inhabit it. I realize, in the dawning light, that on each of these past three nights I have dreamed about a dark gorge, a body strewn amid garbage, a rustling palm; yet each time the dream has unfolded as a new experience. Perhaps I will continue to dream the same images every night that I remain in this room.

Or until I recognize the face of the body in the gorge.

Or until I discover that it is me who lies strewn amid garbage, beneath a rustling palm.

Slowly the room becomes more grey, less black. Concentrating upon the sensation of the hard bed beneath me, I search for an explanation of how I came to lie upon it.

Welcome to the Hotel Suerte Loca.

What crazy luck or crazy chance brought me here, Reyna?


From El Jadida the southbound CTM bus carries me through gently rolling fields of tomatoes and corn and wheat towards Safi. The green landscape, dotted with blue cornflowers, appears almost lush; it is interrupted also by the grey of olive groves and, more sparsely, by oak or ash, with red earth breaking through the green to remind roughly of what lies below. Women wearing layers of brilliantly coloured rags, with equally gaudy scarves around their heads, tend herds of goats, sheep and cattle. Mules draw ploughs and carts; crops are being reaped by hand. It seems that I am journeying into the past, a time before machines, a Tolstoy novel. At the side of the road, barefoot boys watch us speed by as if observing, from a great distance and without astonishment, the passage of a space ship, or any alien form of transport. They appear, for the moment they are glimpsed, as figures frozen in a tableau. They might remain there, hoes and scythes dangling over their shoulders, forever. A mist hangs over the fields until noon, casting silver light that causes the landscape to shine with the hallucinogenic intensity of a dream.

As the interior road approaches Essaouira, one hundred kilometres south of Safi, the terrain turns more hilly, hinting at the presence of the Anti Atlas farther inland, to the east of the southern plain, and the green fields give way to sand, the trees to thorny scrub. The landscape grows less populous. Argan trees contain the startling vision of goats who somehow manage to scale the thorny branches to feed on leaves. Glimpsing animals in the air, I feel that from this point the scenery will become increasingly strange and unexpected; soon, perhaps, there will appear camels flying above the dunes, or fish walking along the road.

I stop for the night in a labyrinthian hotel in Essaouira, where young travellers float like butterflies through narrow white streets and land upon cups of sweet coffee in the Place below my room. Leaning out the window, I listen to them evoke twenty-year-old stories of Jim Morrison's sojourns in Essaouira, swap travelling notes about Tétouan, Fès and Marrakesh. Their light laughter sounds more faint when I turn back to the map spread across the bed and measure how much closer one day of travel has brought me towards Smara, towards where my father's passport was discovered on the sand.

After Essaouira, as the road winds farther south towards Agadir, the land reverts to green, with plenty of citrus trees and fields of vegetables once more. I think, with a sense of relief, that the drier area around Essaouira has been simply a brief dream, or some kind of geographic anomaly: perhaps this newfound green, proving more than a final gasp, will seize control of the earth's surface again. This hope is furthered by the sight of Agadir itself, with its high-rise hotels, expensive restaurants and discothèques. I stop to spend the afternoon, surrounded by pink, middle-aged German tourists on package holidays, on a beach which the Atlantic seems to touch with distasteful reluctance. Even these dubious signs of civilization strung along the shore persuade me that concrete and neon might possess sufficient power to delay the desert.

Such is not the case. South of Agadir, the Plaine du Sous vanishes with shocking swiftness, and, at Ait-Melloul, I am presented for the first time with undeniable evidence that only desert might wait ahead. Veering inland again, the road no longer affords reassuring glimpses of the ocean. The eighty kilometres to Tiznit, the next town of any size along the highway, insists upon acceptance of this evidence: now the earth becomes unremittingly flat and dry, without the graceful sweep of dunes to compensate the eye, and with each kilometre there exists less vegetation and population, fewer hints of any sort of life at all. Tiznit itself, surrounded by meagre groves of palms, and thick ramparts pierced by six gates, is dusty and dry; but already any concentration of life or thin comfort inspires a gratitude that would, in the north, seem absurd. Among other effects, I am discovering that a desert landscape evokes intensely pitched emotional responses to the slimmest suggestions of life. Now I view a spindly tree with awe, a muddy trickle of water with elation, the most forbidding human figure with empathy. From here, Tiznit suggests, it will be enough to reach paved roads and cement buildings, market and stores and a few cafés. Pleasant boulevards, picturesque architecture, flowery Places: these luxuries will not be permitted by the desert, where it is as much as can be done to throw up rough protection from sand and wind and heat.

At Tiznit, I have to wait three days for a seat on the single daily southbound bus. From this point, it appears, travel will become increasingly difficult and twice as expensive as in the north. In a dreary cement room across the Place from the CTM terminal, I listen to boys call the names of destinations like prayers. *Tafraout, Tafraout, Tafraout,* they wail until the word loses meaning and evolves into mere sound to summon a distant, perhaps deaf God. I learn that people are often compelled to travel by *grand taxi*, in the form of a battered sedan of suspect mechanical health, with six passengers squeezed into its seats, all heading for one desert town or another. Few tourists seem to venture beyond Agadir; conversely, there are all at once many more soldiers, in dutiful transit towards Layounne or Dakhla, deep in the south. It is already becoming uncommon to encounter anyone who speaks more than rudimentary French, and even Arabic seems uttered less often, as if any speech were an unnecessary expense of energy. The desert radiates a silence difficult to break; the idea of speech grows pointless. What is there to say? inquires the desert. What? demands the infinite, glassy sky.

Travelling the main inland highway from Tiznit to Goulimine, I am at first overcome by a sense of hopelessness; gradually, this evolves into dull acceptance of flat, dry plain unrelieved by sight of a solitary blade of grass, a single tree. Sometimes the road crosses an *oeud*; invariably, this proves only a dry bed of cracked earth apparently untouched by water for months. The landscape is strewn thickly with large stones; this, the *hammada*, appears even less welcoming than sand. These rocks seem the rubble of something ruined, or evidence that God abandoned His work from lack of interest, left these boulders as reminder that His hand gave up on this place. The road runs perfectly straight, and nearly empty; often we travel dozens of kilometres without encountering another vehicle. The horizon looms low. The immense sky presses insistently upon the earth like the transparent top of an oven whose function is to contain and concentrate heat. To the east of the desolate plain, the Djebel Mani rises abruptly and sharply to the sky. On the other side of this forbidding mountain, I suspect, stretches equally inhospitable terrain.

Once, somewhere south of Tiznit, I feel the bus grind to a stop. Unwilling to witness the landscape grow increasingly barren, I am dozing in the heat, feeling the vibrations of the engine that carries me south. I open my eyes. Outside the window still stretches the flat, stony desert. We have halted to let off passengers: a young man and woman, obviously dressed in their best clothes, with two small children, and a baby slung across the woman's breast. It is apparent that these people travel seldomly; disembarking, they execute each of their movements with silent care. The conductor climbs a ladder running up the side of the bus. From the roof, he lowers two large suitcases and a sheep with bound limbs to the young man on the road. The sheep lies motionless beside the pavement, blood trickling from its mouth and nose. When the young man picks it up and throws it over his shoulder, the animal suddenly opens its eyes and blinks. The man reaches down to grasp a suitcase with each hand. Shifting the sling with the baby to her back, holding a child with each hand, the woman moves away beside her husband. Leaving the road, they strike out into the rocky desert stretching towards the west. No buildings or trees lie in sight. As the bus shudders back into motion, I feel something grind like gears inside me.

When I reach Goulimine, the northern gateway to the Sahara, the wind is blowing in gusts which raise dust from the flat ground, causing unveiled eyes to water and itch. Surprisingly large, composed of buildings made of mud dried by sun to the colour of rust, the town sprawls without design or shape upon the desert floor. The place seems scarcely alive, in submission to sun and heat and dust. Dulled from too many hours of monotonous scenery, my eyes are unable to view Goulimine except as utterly without charm. I find the town's only approximation of a hotel. The desk clerk seems startled by the prospect of a guest and suggests, apologetically, that Goulimine is more interesting to visit in July, because then the Blue Men from Tarfaya arrive in throngs to sell camels and to celebrate the successful completion of their business. When he shows me a room, I realize that as I travel farther south each hotel is more grim and cheerless. Venturing outside at dusk, I see a brief flurry of activity, a frantic filling of cafés and shops; once this ends, darkness presses thickly around the town, wind moans steadily through the streets, and the stars above look distant and cold.

The next day I stand before the day's single southbound bus. Spewing diesel fumes as it idles, the bus wavers like something less than solid in the afternoon heat. With a babble of shouting and arguing, travellers negotiate to have bound animals and sacks of grain stowed securely on the roof. If I step onto this bus, I could be deep in the desert, near Smara, by dawn.

Though the wind has died, sand still swirls into my eyes. Three syphilitic camels, kneeling in the dirt to my left, open mouths in wide yawns. Farther left, a group of small children jab sticks at something by their feet. I glance at the bus, see that it still shows no signs of leaving soon, and go over to see what the children are doing. A dead dog lies stiffly in the street. Blood has glued dust thickly to its coat. The children poke excitedly at the animal; they are trying to spear out its eyes. I tell myself that their voices can not really be gleeful. A little girl beside me, noticing my interest, offers me her stick. As my fingers curl around the slim wand of wood, I see the southbound bus groan into motion from the corner of my eye. It leaves a trail of dust that hangs like a plume of smoke in the air.

I drop the stick. With my blue bag I wander the flat, wide streets until I hear voices raised in monotonous, mournful song in the distance. Approaching, I see that they come from a gathering of decrepit *grand taxis*. The drivers chant their destinations, though no one but myself is near enough to hear. *Sidi Ifni*, one burnoosed man moans. I don't recognize the name from my map.

I'm not certain if it is on the way to Smara. From the back seat, three women, veiled so that only their eyes are visible, watch intently to see what I will do. Quickly, I slide in the front, beside the driver.

Like the women, he doesn't speak French. We drive in silence along a narrow, badly paved road that winds into hills which rise towards the west, less sharply and abruptly than the sheer, stony Djebel Mani to the east. I feel a stab of panic. I am travelling west instead of south, moving no nearer towards Smara, detouring sideways from the desert. I am disappointed in myself. I thought I was ready for the desert. For what I might or might not find there.

Quickly, however, my heart lifts, my eye quickens, my nose detects a hint of the approaching ocean. These gentler, western hills are invitingly vegetated with brush scrub and spindly trees and yellow grass. Here and there materializes a lonely dwelling made of mud and brick; upon a grassy slope appears a girl with a large bundle of sticks balanced upon her head. The grass turns greener, the trees more numerous and large. Rising and falling, twisting and turning: such motion possesses previously unappreciated delight, just as the sparse signs of life seem cause for celebration and prayer. As dusk begins to fall, I feel a growing elation of having executed a daring escape from unnecessary danger.

After forty kilometres, Sidi Ifni appears with startling suddenness: one moment we are surrounded by darkness and the next moment we are driving along a flat, dirt road lined with cafés and stores. A considerable number of people walk beneath the arcades. Leaving the taxi, I observe that these people look strangely subdued, as if they are in deep mourning, bowed heavily beneath loss. The streetlamps are insufficiently bright to disturb the darkness to any degree. Turning the corner, I notice that several sidestreets lie completely unlit and that a sizeable number of houses are boarded up and apparently abandoned. At times I think I hear snatches of Spanish in the air.

A Place appears. Surprisingly well-tended, fragrant with

flowers and shrubs, it resembles a Spanish plaza. Paths wind beneath trellises, past stone benches, around a central fountain. Here, too, many of the scattered lamps are unlit, casting the place into a glowing dimness. Several large white buildings, one a closed hotel, stand in immaculate condition around the square. The oddity of stumbling accidentally upon a piece of Spain here in the south is heightened by the emptiness of the square. I lower myself upon a bench. After the afternoon heat of Goulimine, the evening air feels cold. A beam of light, whose source I can't determine, sweeps across the Place, revealing it clearly for a moment, then returning it to dimmer light. The beam travels over me again and again between spaces of darkness. Each time the circling light finds me, I experience a curious sensation that does not seem to be caused directly by the beam.

Wandering back over rough, dark roads, I find myself once more in the populated and lit main street. When I ask directions to a hotel, people shrug. I am struck by their gravity; even the children appear unusually serious. It's the desert's proximity, I think. In the north, these people would act differently. As I reconcile myself to sleeping on a bench in the Place, I encounter a small child who reacts with excitement to my inquiry concerning a place to stay. Suerte Loca, Suerte Loca, he repeats vehemently. Puzzled once more at hearing Spanish, I follow the boy away from the main street and down a road running beside a gorge that splits the town in two. Again the houses become less frequently inhabited; fewer streetlamps function. Moving with surprising swiftness, despite an uneven gait that suggests he is lame, the child almost vanishes into the darkness before me several times. Then he stops and points to a three-storey building at the edge of the gorge.

It appears silent and dark, almost certainly abandoned. The whitewashed exterior has flaked and faded. Many windows are shattered. An Arabic sign hangs over the doorway. Turning, I see that the small boy has disappeared. I push open the door and find

220

myself in darkness. After a moment, a match flares and a candle flame illuminates an old man squatting on a piece of cardboard at my feet. He is paring the soles of his feet with a large knife. Several times he wipes blood from the blade onto his dirty robe. After glancing up at me, he bends his head to his task again.

"Do you have a room?" The words echo in the empty space around me, sounding ridiculous to my ears.

The man sets down his knife, picks up the candle, and gestures for me to follow.

Moving in front of me, the candlelight reveals only the man's hand and lower arms, as if they were unconnected to a body. I feel uneven stone beneath my feet. The candle rises before me, signalling steps; as I ascend them, I count each one. Pausing at the top, I see that the candle now burns at the other end of what appears to be a hallway. The smell of urine and feces transforms the darkness into a thick substance. As I approach the light, the old man opens a door and steps into a room. He sets the candle on the floor. I can make out a bed to the right. The old man repeats a sound several times. When I pull a twenty-dirham note from my pocket and hand it to him, he grunts with satisfaction. Gazing at the candle on the floor, I hear the shuffling of bare feet fade down the hallway, then disappear.

Silence presses around me. There are no sounds of voices in the distance and no cough, creak or drip from nearer by. I experience a clear sensation that the rooms to either side are unoccupied and that I am the only guest in the hotel. Turning, I feel the wall near the door until my hand encounters a switch. My eyes blink with confusion when electric light floods the room, revealing lime-green walls, a floor of murky tiles, a shuttered window and a bed.

I step back into the hallway. The light from my room reveals closed doors lining the passage. Like mine, they are unnumbered and without a lock.

I re-enter the room and close the door behind me. I set my

blue bag on the floor beside the burning candle. "You've been in worse places," I tell myself, sitting on the edge of the bed. It is covered by a rough brown blanket. Lifting it, I see that there are no sheets below. I sniff the blanket and am reminded of a wild animal. I turn off the light. This is the kind of room where it is best to see as little as possible, where ignorance is bliss. Or acceptance, at least. With time, I remember, one grows dangerously used to anything.

All the cramped, confining rooms I have ever inhabited seem to lead directly to this room. Ten years spent inside small rooms prepared me for this present one. Now the relatively spacious, comfortable apartment in Sevilla appears to me as anomalous as a pool of water upon a desert. I remember how, moving into the Virgen de la Antigua rooms, I had difficulty becoming used to the unfamiliar space they afforded. I found myself wandering from room to room in puzzled wonderment, uncertain how to inhabit the space, disturbed by the choice offered by more than one room.

I open the shutters and look out. The moon floats, nearly full, above the hills I crossed an hour ago. Sprinkled stars remind me that I am hungry. The dark gorge below, lined with small, scattered houses, widens then opens up in the distance. The Atlantic glints beyond. As soon as I see the ocean, I hear waves. They sound unusually loud.

Sitting again on the edge of the bed, I experience the relief that occurs upon believing that the worst point has been reached. If the past is forgotten, there is nothing to compare the present to, and it becomes impossible to judge if the present is, in fact, good or bad. I roughly shove an image of the pleasant apartment in Sevilla from my mind; immediately, the thought of Jose replaces it. More gently, I push his image aside. The darkness of the room seeps inside me until I see, within my mind, only a candle flame. It wavers slightly, spits twice, then goes out.

Welcome to the Hotel Suerte Loca.

How did I get here, Reyna?


On my third dawn in the Hotel Suerte Loca I notice again that I lie on the hard bed as if Jose were beside me. My body approximates, as closely as possible, the position it takes when he is there. I curve around his absent shape.

In a moment I will rise from this bed, open the shutters, and watch the sky bloom red above the eastern hills.

In a moment. I need more time.

I will need days, and perhaps weeks, in Sidi Ifni before I am ready to travel into the desert.

And before I can think of returning to Jose. Though I miss him more sharply the farther I travel south, with a physical ache that mixes with the ache caused by hard beds and cramped buses, I need more time before I can return to him drenched with light.

It occurs to me, as a distant aside, that I am no nearer to finding my father.

# ii.

At Sidi Ifni the combination of ocean, hill and desert produces thick fog which rolls off the Atlantic at dawn and creeps up the hill to surround the town for most of the day. Often the fog swaddles the streets and houses like a heavy white blanket; at other times, stirred by breeze from the water below, it prowls like a wispy spirit around corners and between buildings, through windows and over rooftops. During these blanketed hours a hush prevails in the air, as if the fog prevented people from speaking above a whisper, and even near voices sound as muffled as the ocean in the distance. As if they have never grown used to this daily phenomenon, and fear becoming lost a dozen steps from homes inhabited since birth, people creep cautiously to and from the small market and school in the upper town, and the fields that lie beyond. Only in the late afternoon does the fog suddenly burn away to reveal a glassy blue sky that has been waiting above all along. For the few hours until dusk, the sun beats ferociously, making up for lost time, and the baking streets remain virtually unoccupied. Then light drains from the landscape, the sun lowers into the Atlantic, and night falls, moon rises, stars shine. The temperature drops with shocking swiftness and the air possesses a dry desert chill. People scurry through the streets for a brief hour or two, apparently as fearfully as during day. Voices ring with unnatural brightness, and the lights in the main street bravely attempt to prick a vast darkness that stretches from the Atlantic to the west and the Sahara to the east. By nine o'clock the streets fall completely empty and silent; houses stand shuttered, dark, mute. The lighthouse on the cliff sweeps its beam across the upper town and the Atlantic below, and the Place and streets are flashingly illuminated only to reveal their emptiness. Dogs and rats slip through shadows; palms scratch overhead. The large quantity of abandoned houses suggests that many people have been unable to bear the recurrence of fog during the day and desert chill during the night, in spite of the fact that, surrounded by fields, Sidi Ifni seems a haven from barren desert on three sides, and from ocean on the fourth.

During my first days in Sidi Ifni, I am increasingly baffled by the place and by my need to understand it, as if solving this mystery were necessary before solving the mystery of my father's disappearance – in spite of there not being the slightest hint that Mitch passed through the town on his way to Smara, or even, for that matter, any real proof that he travelled anywhere south of El Jadida. The discovery of his passport in the desert might only mean that this document was stolen from Mitch in El Jadida and made its way to Smara without him.

I find myself prowling the streets of this town as if I have been sent here to investigate them. At the southern end, Sidi Ifni perches a good distance above the Atlantic; yet this elevated, relatively flat land is split by a gorge that widens and deepens, dividing the town, until at sea level it opens upon green fields and olive groves and palms through which a coastal road twists towards Tiznit, to the north. In fact, I realize now, this narrow route is the shorter, quicker way from Tiznit, and by taking it I could have avoided the harsh inland journey by way of Goulimine. Here a street runs flat; there it slopes through the gorge, or cuts more sharply into its sides. This suggests to me that existence unfolds on more than one plane and in more than one way; that implication is furthered by the peculiar combination of abandoned houses and larger, immaculately preserved buildings facing upon the Place, by the mixture of Moorish architecture with art deco touches of neat pastel-coloured trim (pinks, light blues, pale greens), by the swirling of both Spanish and French, as well as Arabic, in the air. I wander bewildered through the fog, uneasily enchanted, searching. Despite the freshness of the Atlantic air, the town is thick with atmosphere as any haunted place.

One afternoon I step into the largest building, obviously administrative, that faces the Place. The tiled foyer is pristine and silent and empty, with no signs of activity in the rooms beyond. On a counter inside the doorway, I discover a stack of pamphlets. "L'Histoire de Sidi Ifni." Taking one, I return to a bench in the Place to read.

The pamphlet explains that, long a lone speck of a Spanish colony surrounded by French territory, Sidi Ifni was held by Spain after the rest of Morocco achieved independence in 1956. For thirteen years it remained a Spanish enclave, though to force this situation's end Morocco eventually blocked all entry points by land, sealing off the town except by water, allowing only that Atlantic access. For three years the town was more deeply isolated than ever. Finally, in 1969, Spain acceded to Moroccan pressure and gave up claim to Sidi Ifni. The Plaza de España was renamed the Place Hassan II. A different flag was hoisted above the square.

I look up from the pamphlet. Now I understand why this Place resembles any plaza in any Spanish town and why as much Castillian as French is spoken among its flowers. Beside the administrative buildings, the empty Hotel de Palais looms between the Place and the ocean cliff. Just beyond, to one side, stands the lighthouse; further, at the edge of town, lies a small, abandoned airport. As the fog burns away and the sun appears, I see people moving towards the walk that follows the descending line of the cliff. They gather along the wall and look down at pylons extending towards the anchorage at which ships no longer arrive. Backs to the desert, they look out upon the ocean and know what it means to be forgotten, or neglected, by the world.

Would I even recognize Mitch if I did happen to see him, here in Sidi Ifni, emerging from the fog, approaching as large as life, whistling "The Impossible Dream?"

I'm not sure.

I haven't seen my father since that December day when he left Brale, ostensibly to search for MJ in Montreal, and never returned. While I have lived in Europe, and along the west coast of North America, Mitch has stayed predominantly in southeast Asia and South America; these are, I gather, still the parts of the world in which he operates the best. Where there remains the greatest opportunity for leeway, the likeliest possibility of fortuitous contacts. Where a white North American still embodies, by virtue of the colour of his skin, a certain amount of power.

I know roughly where my father wandered from the postcards he sent me during those years. The postcard remained Mitch's favourite form of communication: it provides sufficient space in which to offer a few tantalizing hints that, if there were more room, he would gladly expound upon in detail. *Letter to follow*, he usually scribbled at the end of his thirty words. If a letter did, in fact, never follow, this may well have been because the possibilities to which he alluded would not hold up under close scrutiny; they existed better as broad brushstrokes of an always unrealized painting on an always unfinished canvas.

For ten years, while I roamed as much as Mitch, the postcards were forwarded to me by Ardis, who received them at the

227

Columbia Avenue house within sealed envelopes. *Please forward*, Mitch printed in capitals beside my mother's address. *Private and confidential*, he added along the top. In whatever small, shabby room I happened to be occupying at the time, I would read my father's words and not know whether to laugh or cry. Lifting my eyes from a postcard of the Taj Mahal to the scarred walls that confined me, I wanted to feel angry or outraged. Instead, my father's elusive phrases seemed to allow me to accept my puzzling surroundings, at least for a while. I felt, when I received a postcard from my father, at peace with discomfort and able to bear hardship. His messages appeared before me like the signposts in a bewildering dream, providing comfort even when they offered directions in a language I couldn't understand. If I was hungry, I would take out my collection of my father's postcards and read them once more.

When I finally settled in Sevilla and Mitch could write to me directly, he still enclosed his postcards within envelopes warning of their confidential contents, presumably to prevent curious postal clerks from glimpsing his highly private words. Such fear was unnecessary: my father's communications remained so vague that they often lacked any kind of basic sense, and even to my experienced eyes appeared as impenetrable code. Certain key phrases did recur. *Things are looking up. Onto something big. Irons in the fire. Promising lead. Excellent contact.* These were the same pet phrases Mitch had cherished more than a decade before; over time, they seemed to have taken on for him the quality and power of a mantra or litany, possessing in their sound and shape a significance that had little to do with literal meaning. One postcard never mentioned what had happened to the former's promising lead or excellent contact; these sure bets were always replaced, in a different setting, with leads and contacts of equal or greater promise.

His postcards suggested that my father didn't alter significantly from when I was a child. As I understand it, he managed to hold onto an eternal optimism, an unshakeable hopefulness. I fail to comprehend how he continued to believe, all evidence to the contrary, in the silver lining of every cloud, in the calm after the wildest storm, in the treasure that waits around the next corner, in the miracle of each tomorrow. I see, in my father, an extreme example of man's capacity for hope, and I still don't know if such hopefulness, apparently unrewarded for twenty-odd years, is a form of foolishness or a sign of deep faith. Perhaps Mitch possessed the kind of unselfish faith that does not expect or require reward, that is its own virtue, a blessing in itself. In Sevilla, when things were less difficult for me and I held real happiness in my arms, I felt bemused by my father's quixotic communications and laughingly showed them to Jose. I am still not sure if I should feel contempt or awe for my father, and I do not know, either, if I should deplore or exalt in the same hopefulness within myself.

Since 1977, Mitch's sisters and wife have each received a single yearly letter, in fact a photocopy of the same letter, dated January 1. This resembled the annual report of a company's board of directors to its shareholders, if it were a company built upon the currency of possibility and hope. In summing up, every year has been a good year, all in all; enormous strides forward have been made, the big payoff is just around the corner, it's only a question of a bit more patience, everything should bear fruit by springtime at the latest. As a matter of fact, you might as well start picking out that fur coat, diamond or BMW right away. Hell, anything you want, the works, the whole damned pie. Money is definitely no object, sweetheart.

Money was never the object for Mitch, not really. When he spoke of the big bundle and pay dirt and easy street, he was not referring to dollars and cents. I think he was speaking about the dream realized and the fantasy made actual in terms that the world could understand. His vision might have seemed more real if he described it as a piece of prime property listed in a realtor's catalogue at a certain price, complete with a tempting description of its stunning views, a guarantee of high resale value, and a clear photograph of the luxurious palms, the pool of blue water.

It is odd that no one received a photograph of Mitch during those years. He was never shy of posing. I haven't the slightest idea how much and in what ways my father has aged since 1977. His hair, still jet black then, may be completely grey by now. There must have formed lines, wrinkles, hollows, sags. Mitch is fifty-seven, around the age of Godfrey Bridgeport. It is hard to say how a transient life would have aged him; from my own experience, I know that wandering tends to wear you more quickly than a stable existence. Is Mitch's body still athletic and strong, or has it become withered, stooped, slack? Are his eyes still flashing, or have countless failed contacts and cooled irons and disappointing leads dimmed them? Is he still swaggering, confident and happy-go-lucky, or has repeated failure turned him tentative and cringing? According to Godfrey Bridgeport, perhaps not the most reliable witness, Mitch hasn't changed much in appearance or manner since the last time I saw him swing a bag onto his shoulder and give a jaunty wave farewell. On my last visit to Brale, I looked carefully at his sisters – especially Dorothy and Kay, whom he most resembles – to see how they have aged, and to imagine how my father might have similarly altered over the years.

His voice on the telephone, the last time I heard it, was as breezy as ever.

He had begun to call me in 1989, when I moved to Sevilla and had a telephone for the first time in years. Whenever I lifted the receiver and listened to as many as twenty coins fall into a pay-phone slot, I knew my father's voice would follow.

"Hello, handsome," he always began in the same hearty voice. "De Gaulle's a disaster. The bloody plane's been delayed an hour. What can you expect from the French? The cancan and kissing: that's all they're good for. But I should be in Kuala Lumpur by dawn. Three days in Paris is plenty long enough for the old man. Remember the winter of '66-'67? Rained like goddamn cats and dogs the whole time, didn't it? Strolled down the rue St. Jacques just this morning. Couldn't remember what the hell number we lived at there. Thirty-seven or seventy-three? What's the matter, sonny boy? Cat got your tongue? Paris has gone all to hell, let me tell you that. They couldn't pay me to live here. This New Europe they keep parlez-vouzing about. A clear contradiction in terms, for Christ's sake. You can't call an old woman a young girl, not in my dictionary. What time is it there? Listen. Watch the mail. Put a letter to you in the box this afternoon. Outlined in detail my agenda for the next six months. Things looking up. Got an iron in the fire. If all goes per schedule in K.L., yours truly will be sitting pretty before you can say the word. First thing I'll do on easy street is hop down and visit you in sunny Spain. Jesus, been a long time. Almost jumped on an Iberia flight last month. From Bonn. There to take care of a deal for a Jo'burg concern. The rand is diving, he has to dump. So I do him a little favour in Bonn. No skin off my back. Expenses today, a contact worth its weight in gold tomorrow. When the hell you making your move? Face the music. Nada happening in Spain. Don't tell me. You've turned into another Stick in the Mud. How's your Jose? Wait a minute. Was that my flight they just called? Delayed or not delayed? Why can't they make up their feeble French minds? Got to run. Remember. Watch the mail, kid. And don't take any wooden nickels."

Sometimes, when he hung up at De Gaulle or Heathrow or any European airport whose relative proximity to sunny Spain compelled Mitch to call his kid, I realized that I hadn't spoken a word. Often I lay the receiver down and continued what I had been doing when it rang. Or I handed the receiver to Jose, saying, "It's for you." From a distance Mitch's monologue sounded like a thin, frightened squeak. I pictured my father leaning into the booth. He is dressed in khaki, with an overcoat slung over his shoulder and one small bag at his feet. He can carry the bag onto the plane, he won't have to wait for luggage at the other end. Still travelling light, still travelling right. One hand covers the ear not pressed against the receiver. His eyes dart from the newsstand to the bar to the departure lounge in search of promising contacts. The monologue picks up speed as it proceeds; his last francs have gone into the pay phone and he has only thirty seconds left to talk. Often the line is cut before he reaches the part about the wooden nickels.

The Sevilla Telefonica informed me that it has no such thing as an unlisted number service.

Once or twice, during those years, our paths nearly crossed.

On one occasion I realized, after the fact, that we had been in Rome at the same time. In 1984, upon arriving in Los Angeles from that city, I had received a postcard, forwarded by Ardis, whose postmark indicated that for at least one day we had both inhabited the Eternal City.

*Hot as hell, swarming with Italians*, Mitch wrote on that card.

As I distinctly remembered, it had been grey and cold on that particular day in Rome, as well as on the preceding and following days.

Perhaps the closest I came to my father was in Amsterdam.

During 1982, living in Berlin, I had mentioned in a letter to Ardis that I would be spending a few weeks in Amsterdam the following month. It was one of those times when I had stayed too long in a place and needed to get away. For too many nights I had gasped for breath as the walls of my small Kreitzburg room steadily squeezed closer around me. A few May weeks in Amsterdam to decide where to move to after Berlin: perfect.

Somehow Mitch discovered my plan. I was surprised to receive a postcard, just before I left Berlin, offering me the use of an apartment in Amsterdam. It wasn't his, but I could stay there; the place was uninhabited at the moment. The keys were waiting in a bar on the corner, where I would be expected to show up for them. Ask for Peter, instructed Mitch.

I warily accepted the offer. I was suspicious of discovering that the apartment's address did not exist, or that there would be no Peter and no keys at the bar on the corner, or that when I unlocked the apartment door strangers would coldly ask me what I wanted. But, as usual, I didn't have much money. I couldn't afford to turn down Mitch's offer.

In fact, the address did exist, the keys were waiting with Peter at the corner bar, and the apartment was empty when I unlocked the door.

"The company owns the place, a business expense, a tax write-off," Mitch had breezily assured me on the back of a postcard presenting an aerial view of Singapore.

It was a spacious, two-bedroom apartment, with broad windows overlooking the street two floors below and affording a view of one of the canals. I had a sense of being in a hotel suite inhabited only briefly and unmarked by its transient guests. The white walls were clean and blank. Although the kitchen was stocked with dishes, the refrigerator was empty. Toilet articles, all with Dutch labels, were arranged with precision in the bathroom. Clean linen covered the beds. Copies of the international editions of *Time* and *Newsweek*, none more recent than three months, lay in a neat pile on the coffee table. While the telephone was connected, it didn't ring once during the two weeks I stayed in the apartment. No mail arrived at the door.

I was unable to form any idea of who owned the place.

Which company? What business?

Better not ask. Never mind.

For two weeks I enjoyed living in more space than I was accustomed to. I found myself walking from room to room without purpose, sheerly for the pleasurable feeling of freedom this afforded. I felt previously blurred sensations emerge into clear light, as if they rose through murky water to float upon the canal beneath the windows. Blessing Mitch, I bought groceries and candles and wine. I haunted museums and churches. I lingered on bridges. From the apartment, I gazed down at the canal and watched it change from grey to blue to violet to red during the course of a day. The water smelled richly dank; the spring leaves above smelled fresh and clean. From nearby a churchbell pealed round, full notes through the mild air.

During the whole time I expected a key to turn in the lock, a face to appear in the opened door, a voice to demand what the hell I was doing here.

This didn't happen.

Passing me on the stairs or as I unlocked the door, the occupants of the other apartments in the building paid me no attention. They seemed used to strangers coming and going from the apartment.

After three days I began to look for clues.

At first my hunt was unsuccessful. No clothes hung in the closet. All the drawers were empty. Nothing seemed to lurk beneath beds, behind couches, in corners. Not a scrap of paper. Not a single thread. Not a hair or crumb or stain. I began to feel that before my arrival every surface had been carefully wiped clean of fingerprints.

On my last full day in Amsterdam, ready to return to Berlin rested and relaxed, I felt almost relieved that I had discovered nothing. I appreciated that the apartment offered up no curiosities to interfere with my attempt to plan what I would do once I left it.

Then I noticed, behind a heavy bureau pushed against a bedroom wall, a small cupboard. Its door was seamlessly fitted; it had been easy to overlook. The cupboard was unlocked, but the black briefcase, its only contents, wasn't. Like a safe, it could only be opened by, I supposed, the correct combination of three digits. For an hour I twirled numbers back and forth, hoping to stumble upon the secret combination by accident. Meeting with no success, I took a knife from a kitchen drawer and began to poke at the lock. By the time I finally managed to pry the briefcase open, the lock was destroyed and my hand was bleeding.

The briefcase contained letters, photographs, documents. Spreading them over the kitchen table, I poured a glass of wine and sat down to examine them.

A photograph of three children astride a camel, with the Sphinx in the background.

A room-service menu, printed in French but priced in American dollars, from the Royal Hotel in Manila.

An Aereas Argentina schedule of flights between Quito and Rio de Janeiro.

A printout of currency exchange rates from the Banque Nacional de Lyons on October 26, 1973.

Reports from the hospital in Brale concerning my mother's mental health between 1966 and 1974.

One of Lily's high-school report cards from 1975.

One of the few postcards I ever sent my father, mailed from Paris to Saigon in 1980.

A lock of platinum-blond hair.

A business daybook, printed in Germany, with occasional entries jotted in my father's hand. MJ's birthday was noted on the page for September 10; Ardis's, Lily's and my birthdays, but not Mitch's own, were also written on the appropriate pages. There were careful lists of expenses, in currencies I could only guess at: toothpaste, taxi, coffee, stamps. And telephone numbers and addresses, beside first names like Bill, Javier, Shorty. Appointments: Ritz bar, 8 sharp; loading dock, dawn. Dispersed among these jottings were longer entries, some covering several pages, in what appeared a code or invented language.

A score of other evidence, some easily comprehensible and some more obscure, that offered me fresh information concerning my family's distant past, as well as clues into the nature of my father's more recent existence.

I spent the night poring over the contents of the briefcase. There was too much to absorb; for the moment, I could only form a rough idea of what was there, and how it might, with

235

further study, provide additional insight into my family and myself. Into the whole crying shame of it all, as Mitch would say. I felt newly confused by information that disturbed my fragile understanding of the past. The crying shame of it all now revealed itself to be far more complex than I had ever imagined, and I felt more baffled than ever in regard to my father's present life. Whatever sense of peace and well-being that I had gained during the past two weeks immediately evaporated.

At dawn I replaced the papers in the briefcase, tried to snap the broken lock shut, then left the case beside my packed bags. After dropping off the apartment key with Peter at the corner bar, I carried the briefcase with my luggage to the station, where I caught the noon train to Berlin.

During the journey I attempted to break the coded passages of the daybook.

Were those references to the shipment of drugs from Medellin to Miami?

Was that an allusion to the sale of chemicals for nuclear arms to Libya?

Did another passage describe a sale of weapons to Iraq?

*Glad you made use of the apartment*, Mitch wrote in the next postcard I received from him, postmarked Caracas.

He never mentioned the missing briefcase, then or later. By this point he had been carrying around or storing in various places its oldest content for four years. They were obviously of some importance to him; he had taken considerable care not to misplace them in the course of a way of life that, as I well knew myself, encourages possessions to become lost. He had to know that the briefcase was gone. He had to know that I had taken it.

Perhaps he wanted me to find the briefcase.

Perhaps he arranged the whole thing to that end.

Perhaps, in fact, the apartment did not belong to any company as any tax write-off.

Perhaps Mitch rented the apartment, upon learning of my visit to Amsterdam, specifically to plant the briefcase in it. He counted on my curiosity. He knew me well enough to be fairly certain that I would discover it. He put his iron in the fire, went with the odds, placed his bet.

Had there been something odd about Peter's manner in the bar on the corner? I had only spoken with him for a few minutes, long enough to introduce myself, chat briefly about the neighbourhood, and receive the keys. He seemed pleasant enough – somewhere around forty, somewhat bland. I gathered that he owned and ran the bar by himself; in an Amsterdam guidebook both the bar and its clientele would probably have been described as typical. Peter had given me the impression that he was too busy serving customers to talk at any length; he did not make a point of inviting me, since I would be staying so close by, to return to the bar and become acquainted with him when he had more leisure. I had sensed that he didn't know Mitch well.

Had there been something odd about the precise placement of the heavy bureau in front of the cupboard? Something that was likely to draw my attention to it, sooner or later?

And was there, sitting on one of the benches along the canal beneath the window, a man wearing dark glasses, with a newspaper before his face?

Three years later I found myself with four hours between flights at the Amsterdam airport. On a whim I took the train into the city and located the street along the canal that I had gazed down upon in 1982. The area appeared different than I remembered, perhaps because before I had viewed it in May and now it was December. For about fifteen minutes I looked up at the apartment in the southwest corner of the second storey; its broad windows were still covered with white curtains. A hand did not part the curtains, a face did not appear to look down to where I stamped my feet in the cold. I walked to the door of the

237

building and pressed the buzzer for 4C. No answer. In the bar on the corner I asked the woman behind the counter if Peter was around. No Peter here, she replied. Three years ago? She shrugged and shook her head. She had owned the bar for only a year. She couldn't tell me anything about the past owners. She was sorry.

You've seen too many spy movies, I told myself on the train back to the airport. Too many movies dubbed into languages you only half understand, with plots only half comprehended. You have become too used to using your imagination to fill in the parts you could not follow. You are too accustomed to creating your own explanations for puzzling endings of stories. It has become a bad habit.

*Look at this*, Mitch told me in the Brale basement in 1977.

One day you might get a kick out of what the old man did.

There's some interesting stuff in this room, you know.

I carried the contents of that briefcase with me for ten years, though somewhere along the way the damaged case itself was left behind. Whenever I took the wrong drugs at the wrong moment, or when the room in San Francisco or Rome closed too tightly around me, I studied those photographs and letters, airline schedules and room-service menus. Even after knowing them in detail, I continued to examine my documents with the hope that a fresh angle might present itself to shine new light upon old events. And when I removed the contents of Mitch's filing cabinet, in 1988, I compared those documents with the others, trying to understand why he left some behind in Brale, why he took some with him, and what the differences between them might suggest.

In particular I have looked, during sleepless nights, at the coded passages of the daybook for 1982. I have never been able to decipher them completely. The longer studied, in fact, the more it appeared that Mitch employed a number of different codes, often moving between one and another several times within a single paragraph; the key that unlocks one sentence does not make the next less obscure, and my comprehension of the whole remained fragmented.

Consider what is not obscure:

Uranium to Libya, Uzis to Iraq, snowbirds to Miami.

Non-clearance flights, black landings.

C-5AS, C-130S, C-141S.

Kilos, grams, metric tons.

U.S. dollars, deutschmarks, sterling.

Dick Z. in Pyongyang, S.P. in Tripoli, X. Dos in Medellin.

Operation. Action. Touchdown. Red flag. Bail out. Bingo.

A certain kind of world, specific and elusive at once, is suggested by these fragments. It is a tightly closed sphere controlled by a few behind-the-scenes players whose manoeuvres are carried out by a small number of operators across a substantial portion of the globe. This sphere exists between cracks of UPI stories and fissures of AP items. It is, I suppose, fragmentary by its nature and from necessity; the connection between, say, a North Korean coup attempt, a touchdown into Baghdad and the rise of a certain stock on the Bonn exchange may not be readily apparent for good reason. And the invisible glue holding together scattered events in Germany, Iraq and North Korea is provided by the shippers and handlers, the operators and go-betweens and middlemen, all in it for a small piece of the action. They would surely not be encouraged to keep daybooks from which even an elusive glimpse of the big picture could be gleaned after ten years of study.

In many cases, the middlemen and operators may not themselves be aware of the big picture.

In many instances, there may be no big picture.

Or so I speculate in an unnumbered room in the Hotel Suerte Loca, retrieving from the bottom of my blue bag the black daybook discovered in Amsterdam, the only piece of evidence not offered to the Atlantic Ocean in El Jadida.

239

*Look at this.*

Everything I know about my father refutes the possibility that he would be able to function in the world suggested by the black daybook. I can see Dick Z. in Pyongyang or S.P. in Tripoli snap their fingers to make Mitch disappear. He falls between the cracks of an action or off the edge of an operation. A man who views history as metaphor is not necessarily suited by temperament to manipulate efficient touchdowns in Baghdad. A man lacking a sense of direction and an ability to calculate exchange rates between hard currencies is not likely the best handler to react correctly to a red flag in Pyongyang. He represents a poor risk, an unreliable factor.

And it certainly requires an athletic stretch of imagination to envision a three-week sojourn in El Jadida as bearing the slightest connection to any operation or action, no matter how minor. Possibly Mitch travelled to El Jadida for a holiday from non-clearance flights and black landings. Possibly he wished to step away from the action for good by emerging from the desert with altered fingerprints, a surgically redesigned face, and the passport of a new identity.

Or perhaps The Lost Oasis is code for a fresh action by Polisarian Front rebels in the Western Sahara.

Perhaps this time the action centres around phosphates, not uranium.

*Look at this.*

I believe that every mirror has the power to cast the same image in a unique way and that every bed may lend the same dream a slightly different shape; similarly, an unnumbered room in the Hotel Suerte Loca might offer insight into the remnants of the Amsterdam documents that would differ from the insight afforded by Room 5 of the Hotel de Provence. That my father allegedly occupied Room 5 but not this unnumbered room would, I imagine, have bearing upon the nature of the revelation occurring within their different walls.

Flipping through the black daybook for 1982, printed on stiff white paper with gilt edges, I notice that references to Uzis and uranium occupy the same pages as careful reminders of MJ's, Lily's and my birthdays.

What are the implications of this juxtaposition?

What is the metaphor for my father's peculiar history?

Why do I imagine him, whether in Tripoli or Medellin or El Jadida, as always alone?

As Sidi Ifni huddles within thick morning fog, I consider the possibility that my father was one of those delusionists convinced that the gum-snapping Safeway checkout girl is an underground operator of the IRA; her chipper reminder to have a good day is actually coded information concerning a Manchester operation. The ROTC acts as a cover for a Palestinian plot to assume economic and political control of the industrialized world. The PTA functions as a covert cell working towards the *majehedin* liberation of Afghanistan. In Mitch's fantasy, Godfrey Bridgeport appears as a necessary link to the Polisarian Front one thousand kilometres south of El Jadida. The Hotel de Provence serves as the pre-arranged meeting place with Polisario commanders disguised as desk clerks in wine-coloured coats.

In the years since 1977 Mitch may have filled fifteen daybooks with notes for the plot of a thriller he planned to write but at some point began to live instead. From Smara he strode into the Sahara with a plastic 1.5 litre bottle of Sidi Ali water, a pocketful of roasted almonds, and the conviction that the Polisarians desperately awaited his arrival with information concerning a recent decision by Khadafy to support their struggle for independence.

In the Hotel Suerte Loca my only remaining piece of ancient evidence seems still capable of expanding in possible meaning, altering in implication, cancelling itself out. Like an organism capable of changing shape at the blink of an eye for survival's sake, my information transforms a delusionist into a sentimentalist from one moment to the next. To study this evidence, both obscure and not obscure, is to experience a dream of walking into a room to find another doorway beckons to a further room, where another doorway urges passage to still a further room, and so on without end. You proceed from room to room to room always with the expectation that the next will hold the urgently required answers that you seek. As it turns out, the next room always proves only another antechamber of the dream.

Call it Operation Lost Oasis.

Night has fallen by the time I close the black daybook. I glance at the window that looks towards the desert beyond the hills. *Hurry,* summons the sand. Aren't you ready yet?

I freeze. Again, a voice travels from a room near mine, or from the lower floor. I listen for footsteps to pass my closed door. The fact that the entire hotel, except my room, is unlit deters me from exploring it now. Tonight I will only huddle once more beneath the brown blanket and try to stay awake until dawn. Not because I fear that someone will enter my unlocked room while I sleep, but because I do not wish to dream again about a dark gorge, a body strewn amid garbage, a palm rustling overhead.

My daytime investigation of the Hotel Suerte Loca has failed to reveal other guests. Most of the rooms, like mine, contain only a bed; some boast just a mattress on the floor. They are, all of them, filthy. Perhaps the hotel acts as a refuge for people without shelter, for beggars who require a protected place to squat for the night. The old man who showed me to this unnumbered room has not returned to ask for further payment. Now I wonder if he had any official connection to the hotel at all. More and more, it looks like the place is not only out of business, but has been abandoned by the town with the finality that renders the forsaken lover invisible. Passing through the gorge below my window, people seem to turn their eyes deliberately away from the building. Even little children refuse to see it with such determination that, I think, they would continue to deny the solid reality of its flaking whitewashed walls even if they bumped right into them.

Increasingly, I feel that the other rooms of the Hotel Suerte Loca contain past versions of myself. A young boy of sixteen who lived in England, an older boy of twenty who lived in Paris. A twenty-two-year-old in Rome, a twenty-five-year-old in California: all these beings, and others of various ages, have travelled with me here. I wish to pass from one grim, bare room to another and tell these young men that there is no need to feel afraid, that there are worse things than waiting. Hang on, I want to urge them. Don't give up. You're not alone.

But I'm running out of money. I live on a *bollo de pan*, a glass of coffee, and a few bananas each day, which I purchase up in the market. Instead of buying bottled Sidi Ali water, I drink from the tap in the foul bathroom. One of the legacies from my East African childhood is a stomach as tough as iron. Also to save money, I have quit smoking. A few days ago, I switched from Best, a decent brand of Moroccan cigarette, to dirt-cheap Casa Sports; the latter contain tobacco blacker than Jose's Ducados, and fall apart when you try to puff on them, or fail to light at all. I gave up on them from sheer frustration, and with difficulty have been withdrawing from nicotine. Nothing's easy, the belly dancer would remind me, swaying before the mirror in Sevilla. Deal with it, she would advise.

Hope is a habit more difficult than smoking to break. Something will turn up. Every cloud has a silver lining and a rainbow appears after every storm. The big payoff waits around the next corner and tomorrow is bound to present a miracle.

I'm not an optimist's son for nothing.

When one of the airplane's engines fails, you take appropriate action. Jettison extra fuel. Dump unnecessary cargo. Sometimes you can trick yourself into believing that this tightening of the safety belt is a spiritual rather than an emergency procedure. Get rid of the dross. Pare down to the essence. How much do we

243

require to live and how much of the dropped cargo is a buffer between ourselves and the world? Can we survive, and even transcend without red plush sitting rooms and tattered issues of the *Sunday Times* books section? To what degree is what we possess beyond body, mind and soul a curtain that blocks our vision? What are the barriers between ourselves and God?

If you have summoned me here to teach me how little man can live on, then you have seriously miscalculated, darling daddy. I already know how close to nothing I require to exist. I have spent ten years in small, shabby rooms like this one learning that lesson over and over again. I have done my time in the wilderness with only bread and water and hope to sustain me.

I do, however, still need to learn how richly a man may live.

Jose and the Virgen de la Antigua offered me a taste, and left me with a longing for more and more and more.


Paris and London.

California and Mexico.

Berlin and Paris and Rome.

Crete, Ios, Formentera.

String the names together and it sounds glamorous. I know that Jose thought so, at least at the beginning. I had lived a carefree, adventurous life before meeting him, he believed. But though I didn't like to talk about those ten years after they were over, Jose slowly came to understand that they weren't as exciting as they first sounded.

When they had ended, I thought of those ten years as a lonely, wandering dream from which I had finally woken. At the time, it didn't seem especially unpleasant or difficult to exist for three to six months in a small room in one city, then spend a similar amount of time in an equally small room in another city. It was something I became accustomed to. I gradually forgot that there could be a different way of living, until my mind lost the ability to perceive other choices. I held onto my existence as the only one I knew. I cherished my life with tenacity; for the less one has, the more fiercely one hangs onto it.

The dominant characteristic of the dreamer is passivity. Lying unconscious in the dark, you submissively observe someone who resembles yourself stumble through a series of events which possess a logic that is particular to a dream. The most outlandish occurrences seem perfectly reasonable and unsurprising. There is no way of predicting what will happen next, no way of shaping the dream's narrative. If the plot turns painful, you can't lift a finger to alter its unfolding. It is impossible to anticipate, at any time, that the dream might soon end, that consciousness waits nearby. Even though the dream is, of course, a creation of the sleeper, and so might finally be thought to lie under his control, this simply does not seem true while the experience lasts: dreaming, we are helpless, powerless, not responsible.

Looking back, this time appears continuous, seamless. Only the landscape changed. The room was larger or smaller in size, higher or lower in relation to the street. It contained a bathroom or the bathroom was down the hall. The bed was wide and soft; it was narrow and hard. Sometimes there was a window. The temperature within the room was hotter or colder. There was sunshine or rain or snow outside. The people beyond the room spoke one language or another. Perhaps there was enough money to buy a bottle of wine. Perhaps there was not enough money to buy a loaf of bread.

Happy? Sad? Such words did not apply.

All these considerations were beside the point, and did not affect the shape or texture of the dream – except as the unseen surroundings flavour our unconscious imaginings in the subtlest of ways, causing one room's dream to vary microscopically from another's. It didn't really matter how the room was furnished, if I was hungry, that I was cold. Whatever the variables, I would sleep fourteen hours each night, then lift myself from

245

the bed to continue dreaming in daylight. If I had enough money to buy a cup of coffee and a cigarette, the morning passed pleasantly; if not, I was unaware that anything was lacking. In slow motion I washed an article of clothing in the room's sink, straightened the bed, combed my hair. At midday I left the room and walked for several hours in the street. I looked into store windows with disinterested curiosity; the displays behind glass appeared so far beyond my reach that I did not even consider longing for them, as I would not dream of reaching for the planets in the sky. The people who passed me on the sidewalk seemed just as distant and untouchable; usually I felt that if I tugged their sleeves, they would turn around to see no one there. When, very rarely, someone stopped me to ask for directions or the time, I became shaken and startled. For several hours I would tremble with an excitement that I could not understand. Often I pretended I did not comprehend the language in which I was addressed. Shrugging, I walked away until my heart slowed again.

On the whole, I felt calm. A park bench or warm sunlight or soft rain provided soothing pleasure and inspired deep gratitude. At certain times – my dangerous days – similar things could assume the power to upset me: a pair of lovers glimpsed across the street, a single phrase overheard in a café, the sight of the moon and stars. A glimmer of another way of living stirred me subtly, like the vision of a galaxy so far away that it is suggested only by the faintest hint of light at the top of the dark heavens. Then I would quickly retrace my steps to the room, close the door, trace circles around the small space, breathe deeply. Soon I became peaceful again, with a renewed sense of the inevitability of my situation. Acceptance filled me like clear, holy light. Once more it seemed pointless and even foolish to struggle against the power of my dream. After a certain, extreme point has been reached, a being lost in snow begins to feel a longing to cease struggling painfully against the cold; as soon as he gives in to that

246

inescapable, frigid force, he starts to feel warm, and finally drifts to sleep in the whitest, heaviest blankets of all.

To dream is essentially a solitary experience. Though two lovers share the same bed, and lie entwined tightly through the night, sleep separates and each dreamer goes his own way in the darkness. Often, for several seasons at a time, no one knew in which city and country I was living. This afforded me a curious sense of satisfaction. I had slipped behind a curtain that concealed me from inquisitive eyes. Everyone, I think, feels uneasy at the thought of being observed during sleep, when we are unguarded and defenceless. During a four-month stay in Vienna, I would be likely to move from one cheap hotel to another several times to avoid witnesses – a concierge, a maid, a valet de chambre – to my solitary state. I could not bear, for example, a *patronne*'s cool scrutiny of my ascent upon a circular staircase towards a fourth-floor coffin in the Hotel Luxembourg. I did not want strangers to wonder about me and I did not want family to feel bad for me. A curious mixture of pride and shame made me alternate the shops where I bought my provisions with careful deliberation in order to conceal the skeletal, thin frame of my life.

Several times a year I sent a postcard to Ardis to let her know that I was still alive and had not, like MJ, vanished off the face of the earth.

*Paris is pleasant.*

*Vienna is charming.*

*Rome is a dream.*

When it happened that Ardis had my hotel address, and could send me a note concerning life on Columbia Avenue, or forward a postcard from Mitch, I experienced the sensation of a hand shaking my sleeping shoulder; the touch registered upon my unconscious mind, but was not strong enough to wake me. After I discovered my father's black briefcase – in Amsterdam, in 1982 – I would take out the cryptic daybook it contained and look through those pages when I was especially hungry or cold or alone. Or, under similar circumstances, I might ponder the mysterious message that MJ left for me three years later in Paris. I would study these carefully until I felt almost comforted, as though they explained my situation in a mysterious way I could not begin to articulate.

Upon falling ill and finding myself unable to afford medicine, during the first of those years, it would become difficult to carry on; then I wished for someone to look after me, an extended hand, help. Or evicted from a room into the street, my pockets empty and all my belongings in my blue travelling bag, I would wonder what would happen to me. Where will I sleep? I asked the air. What will I do? The sky inhaled my questions, absorbed my fear. Soon I learned that in a dream we will survive the most terrible events without apparent effect; we will waken unscarred by mutilation, unscathed by disaster, resurrected from death, for they are only imagined, after all. Pain, illness, discomfort became, for me, as chimerical as singing stars.

Time passed slowly and swiftly at once. A single day could last as long as three childhood years in Tanzania. I could fall asleep in 1981 and waken, the next morning, in 1985. An autumn in Vienna blurred into a Berlin winter bled into a San Francisco spring. Usually I moved from one place to another at the change of season: when winter ended, when autumn began. These moves were not made with the hope that they would significantly alter my existence; rather, it seemed such geographical adjustments were necessary for the continuation of my dream, as if a new place acted as a stronger kind of sleeping pill when the power of the present place's soporific became ineffective.

Wherever I was, there were times when necessity forced me to find some sort of job and to hold it for several months. Those periods of employment – as dishwasher, bicycle messenger, answering service operator – did not really alter the texture of my dream. They seemed, the hours that I worked, as a kind of deeper dream, and I went back to my room after a shift was over with the knowledge that my real, solitary self was patiently awaiting my return. "You're back," he would say, greeting me from his chair by the window. He would not bother to ask where I had been or what had happened to me there. My hours away from the room and from him were unimportant, entirely beside the point. Because I continued to live, while working, as if I had no money, I was able to save much of whatever currency was paid me and quit a job when it became difficult to smile and speak and react to others. With fresh funds, I was able to devote three or six months exclusively to the dream. Needing quick cash to cover a hotel bill or a plane ticket, I could spend several hours in several strangers' arms. I scarcely saw or felt them, the hungry men.

It did not occur to me, during those years, that I might have a bank account or a social security number, a driver's licence or a lease. My only identification was a passport. My only belongings fit into a blue travelling bag.

On my birthday I treated myself to a bottle of wine and a restaurant meal.

At Christmas I bought myself a new coat or pair of shoes.

An occasional movie was a significant event planned for a week in advance, mused upon for a week afterwards.

If I skipped a few meals, I could afford a secondhand book. Always I chose one with many pages in a language that was not my mother tongue; that way, I was forced to read slowly and the book lasted for a long time. As soon as I finished the last page, I began at the first one again, then read the book a third and fourth time too. Memoirs of an obscure eighteenth-century English earl; an exhaustive account of a minor First World War battle; the most turgid nineteenth-century novel: in my dream, every book held equal value and interest, as a way of turning the pages of the weeks.

All events in a dream are symbolic, thus everything that occurred during an uneventful day assumed enormous size and demanded thorough interpretation. In my room at evening I could contemplate for hours an earlier accident of a child in the park, the concierge's greeting as I passed the front desk, a certain song spilling from a bar. What did these things signify beyond themselves? What did they tell me about the world, about myself? Why did the lilt of Peggy Lee and the howl of a wild dog still vibrate in the air around me, after twenty years, as though sound has an unlimited capacity to echo and linger? And why did vanished images — the face of a leper, the shape of a lemon tree — still hover upon my eyes no matter how often I blinked, distorting sight of my present surroundings? Was that the scent of cloves still curling like a halo around my head? What could be done with memories of twenty minutes or twenty years ago when they refused to shrink to tidy, manageable proportion despite the best efforts of time? Yes, I was self-absorbed to an extreme degree, for the world beyond the narrative of my dream lay in darkness: a vast obscurity was illuminated only as I imagined myself moving through it. I was sealed inside sleep.

On some level, I was waiting. I had no idea of who or what I waited for; my mind became incapable of conjuring up the future and what it might hold for me. Love? Comfort? Companionship? At times I felt that the door of my room would open and someone would inform me that the dream was over; but this person was vague in aspect, without gender or name or age, like God. Meanwhile, I was not impatient for the dream to end.

Only once or twice a year would I find myself rocking rapidly back and forth on the edge of the bed. *No. No. No.* A harsh, unfamiliar voice of some *dybbuk* inside my skin protested, pleaded, prayed. I leaped up to stride quickly between the walls. *You're young, you're young*, I heard that guttural voice rasp. I beat my fists against my thighs, slapped cold water against my face, dug the point of a knife into the soft skin of my inner arms. I was trying to wake up. I gazed in horror around the room and wondered how I had got there. Who and what had put me there. The next morning, I knew, I would remember this incident only dimly, as something that had happened to someone else several years ago. The cuts upon my arm would burn insistently, nagging at my mind with an elusive understanding of how they had been put there.

Infrequently, meeting another young man to sleep with, I would briefly escape my room. I would invent a story that explained my life as something that would not disturb him. Pretending to speak Italian, French or German only slightly, I allowed him to interpret what I did not say in the way he chose. My mouth stretched into a smile; light words slipped from my mouth. He would take me to his bed and find himself surprised by my eagerness, unaware of the forces that compelled it. Perhaps I stayed with him for a week, or, in exceptional cases, for as long as a month. Eventually, it became too great a strain to maintain an illusion that would not alarm him. I fell silent too often. I began to think more and more about a small, empty room. He began to look at me with suspicion; invariably, I let slip a detail that jarred discordantly with his knowledge of me. It was time to leave. We had both gotten what we needed. My small room summoned me. During that week or month I had carefully hoarded every one of his caresses and kisses. They would sustain me for six solitary months.

1978 to 1988.

What happened in the world during those years? I didn't read newspapers. I was unaware of even the broadest political and social changes of that time. Later, I would piece together some knowledge of the decade by poring over old magazines. I would become adept at covering up the missing gaps in my information. Sometimes I would falter, and Jose and I would laugh.

"What planet are you from?" he asked, his lips searching my throat.

I have no idea why I was roused at that particular moment – in Sevilla, in 1989 – rather than at any other. Why does any dream end? The dreamer has slept long enough. Sufficiently restored by

251

rest, he is able to face consciousness. An alarm wakes him. Light wakes him. Hunger wakes him. The prince, bestowing a potent kiss, wakes him.

I am not certain if my two visits to Brale, in 1986 and 1988, had anything to do with my wakening.

If my 1988 visit to the Columbia Avenue house decisively stirred something inside me that had first stirred more faintly upon my original return, in 1986.

The basement rumpus room, with three card tables still set up there, now appearing wobbly, too fragile to bear the lightest weight. Twin beds, neatly made up, on either side of the bedroom I had shared with MJ. Mitch's study, on the other side of the wall, with its big, old Olivetti and outdated history books. Its filing cabinet that I unlocked with the keys my father had hidden behind a German dictionary eleven years before. The cluttered furnace room, still smelling of oil and dust and damp cement. The siren from the smelter on the hill at the change of shifts. The cautious questions of Mitch's sisters concerning how I had spent my years away from Brale. Lily's reluctance to allow me to visit her in the hospital on the hill. The weight of Ardis's long, thin hand resting upon mine. Scratched, worn Peggy Lee records beside the living-room record player. The past crashing around my ears. That deafening sound. Something clicked inside my head. Something shifted inside my heart. Did I only imagine, in that house, the scent of cloves curling around me – strangely sharp, like smelling salts?

"Don't give up," said Ardis, when we made our goodbyes at the end of my 1988 visit, before I flew back to Europe and found my way to Sevilla, Jose and the Virgen de la Antigua.

I looked at her in surprise. What did she know about me? What had she guessed about the past ten years? What had she unscrambled from my coded postcard messages that Paris was pleasant, Vienna charming, and Rome a dream? What had she perceived, as we sat together in the living room, both fighting a different kind of numbness, a different kind of dream?

My mother regarded me steadily through clear grey eyes. Her hand reached out to touch my head like a wand.

"Remember that," she said, then turned and walked quickly away, not glancing back as I climbed onto the Vancouver bus.

In retrospect, what seems stranger than the ten-year dream, and why it ended when it did, is that afterwards I seemed so little marked by the experience. As if, all along, there had existed another person, with my name and appearance, who had lived an ordinary, waking life. I simply had to step into his shoes in order to assume his experience and knowledge: how to laugh and make love and live in the world. Almost effortlessly, I was able to form friendships and to chatter in cafés. To open a bank account and to learn how to drive. To think about the future as something I could plan for and shape and determine. To strike a truce with the past.

Peering up at distant, invisible planets, I would remember the ten years of lonely dreaming, and feel nostalgic and appalled at once. Paris and London, I lightly laughed. Vienna and Rome, I mentioned by the way. I regretted those years and I missed them. I did not often mention them except in the most general of ways; more would mean an act of betrayal. Rome was eternal, Vienna a waltz. London was foggy, Paris a city of light. Crazy California. Mysterious Mexico. There was nothing more to those places and those years than that.

Sometimes, strolling beside Jose down the Avenida de la Constitución, I would glimpse someone who I knew, with clear, immediate recognition, was lost far inside a dream. The slow, shambling walk. Eyes fixed upon the sidewalk. A sudden glance up with a blurred, puzzled expression. That inward look. Perhaps the signs were unmistakable only to someone who has been inside the dream himself; a casual observer might think this person was on drugs. Quickly, I would turn to Jose, say something to make him laugh or smile. He loves me, I know, in part because he somehow senses my lonely years with a completeness and a wealth of detail beyond my description. He knows how much he means to me precisely because of those ten years. While he sleeps by my side, I wonder if there is someone, like a dreamer glimpsed in the Avenida de la Constitución, who still bears my name and aspect, who still spends three to six months in one small room or another, in one city or another. Someone who still drifts inside the lonely dream. He is lying alone at this minute. At morning he will lift himself from the bed to continue his dream in daylight. He looks cautiously around to see where he is, to see if the setting of his dream has altered overnight. Of course I would like to open his door, my arms overflowing with flowers and food and wine. I would like to take care of him and never leave him. But, listening to Jose's strong heart beat beneath my ear, I would remind myself that he, that other lonely dreamer with my name, is not unhappy at all. Quite the contrary, in fact. To the point where he might very well slam the door in my face.

I still don't know why I fell into a lonely dream myself. Was that time a deep, dark well I had the misfortune to plummet into simply by taking a wrong, unlucky step one day? Or did I swallow a powerful soporific whose effects did not quickly wear off? I have wondered if someone other than myself administered that potent dose. My father, for example. I idly consider what his intentions could have been. Perhaps he poured that draught down my throat with the best intentions, out of concern only for my good, in belief that this was the very best he could do for me. Or, more selfishly, he desired company in his own lonely dream, and was prepared to do whatever was necessary to ensure that I joined him there.

There?

Here.

Welcome back, says the dream, here in Sidi Ifni, here at the end of the world.

I knew you would return.

What took you so long?

I missed you.

# iii.

Shaking myself awake, I walk quickly through the morning fog towards the garbage heap at the bottom of the gorge. I claw through the refuse in search of something concealed within it. Undeterred by the rising stench, my hands methodically lift rotting substances from one place to another. A young woman, with a baby bundled on her back and a large pot balanced on her head, approaches, pauses to watch me, moves on. A buzzard barks nearby. Much of what I uncover has decomposed beyond the point of recognition; nothing resembles a human form. I finally find what appears to be the tail of a cat, with maggots squirming through the fur. I hold this in the air for a long moment, drop it, then walk away.

Later that evening, the electricity in my room at the Hotel Suerte Loca ceases to function. I buy a supply of thick white candles from the Berber market in the alley sloping off the main street. The candlelight pleases me. The garish green walls dim to a more neutral colour. The bare room somehow appears more itself with only one soft point of illumination and shadows shifting around it.

But the nights are growing chilly; I need a source of heat for my room. I venture to the fields beyond the town and gather an armful of sticks and brush. When I build a small fire in one corner of the room, the space quickly fills with smoke that billows towards the open window. Coughing, I crouch on my heels near the fire. I tear pages from the black daybook and feed them one by one to the flames. This gives me peculiar satisfaction; the activity is its own reward. I wish only for meat to cook over the fire. The next day, the lime-green walls are covered with a light layer of soot. I touch my face, study my fingers, see that similar soot clings to them. This too makes me happy. With each night of fire, my skin and the walls of the room darken further. A scent of smoke hangs heavily in the air, permeates my clothes and hair.

While the last page of the daybook explodes in flame, I hold the stiff, empty cover. My fingers rub its worn surface. When the fire is stronger, I drop the cover into the flame. For a moment it appears that it will not burn. My head lifts to the open window as the cover catches fire. Drums are beating in the distance; I recognize the sound from Morogoro. I move from the fire to the window. A message pulses through the air from the plain beyond the town; it curls around the signal that I am sending with smoke. Just when they seem about to fade into silence, the drums grow louder. This lasts nearly to dawn. On each subsequent night, the drums call a little more loudly, a little more wildly, a little more enticingly.

The drums still seem to echo inside my head during the morning. I sit on a bench in the Place Hassan II while fog floats through the air around me. It parts to reveal trellises and flowers, then closes over them again. Hypnotized by a sense of continual revelation and concealment, I fail to react when a blond woman, pale

257

and neat and poised, appears briefly by the fountain in the centre of the square, before vanishing beneath the fog.

I stop scratching marks on the wall to record the passing of time. Soon afterwards, the marks already there disappear beneath the soot. At that moment I forget how long I have been in Sidi Ifni. From that moment I have always been in Sidi Ifni.

"*Pas de poste*," the man tells me sadly, holding out his hand, palm upward, in a gesture of helplessness.

"What about a public telephone?" I ask, switching to Spanish. Perhaps this man will sound less mournful in another language. Perhaps it is only French that makes everyone I speak to in this town sound forlorn, *triste, lointain, douloureux*.

"No telephone," he says, more sadly.

My informant, owner of the most important store in Sidi Ifni, is middle-aged, thin and neatly dressed in drab Western clothes. Le Businessman. Everything one might wish to buy seems crammed into this single small room. Clothes, toiletries, hardware, groceries, medicine, candy, toys. My eyes flit across too many objects crowded too closely together in insufficient light. A thick layer of dust covers every surface except the glass counter separating this man and myself.

"There are people worrying about me. I must contact them. They don't know where I am."

He shakes his head mournfully. "Tiznit," he says. "In Tiznit there are many telephones, many mailboxes. In Tiznit and in Goulimine."

We stare at each other, as if more remains to be said but neither of us knows what that might be.

"Why is this town so sad?" I finally ask, then immediately regret it. A stupid thing to say. I know how conversations in this country tend to drag on politely once begun. I am too hungry to discuss happiness and sadness at endless length. Also, it is late afternoon, the sun will burn through the fog at any moment; when this happens, I like to stand by the wall above the ocean, like everyone else in town. To watch the sun flame over the water. To feel its heat burn my skin.

"Life is sad everywhere," the store owner replies after a pause, appearing pleased by my question, as if I have said just the right thing. Gesturing vaguely towards the dim, crowded space around us, he implies that it illustrates the sadness of life. "So we drink tea together. Please, sit. One moment."

I lower myself reluctantly into a wicker chair wedged to the side of the room while my host disappears through a curtain to the rear.

My left hand grips the postcards I would like to send. Each identical card depicts a herd of camels, unburdened by passengers or other cargo, crossing from left to right over an expanse of sand bleached nearly white and dotted with scrub. In the background, dunes of darker, richer brown rise gracefully towards crests; they are patterned with tracks of hoofprints circling over each other in confusion. Above stretches intense blue sky with the words "Souvenir du Sahara" written in incongruously elegant white script across it. On the back of each card small type describes the scene: *Maroc infini . . . La caravane passe.*

Today I found these cards tucked into a side pocket of my blue bag. I must have bought them in Tiznit or Goulimine, or somewhere else along the way. My eyes must have been attracted to the picture and my hand compelled to pluck it, three times, from a rack of other pictures. I don't know why. I can't remember what it was like to be in Tiznit or Goulimine. It is becoming difficult to think at any length of what took place an hour ago; my mind slips instead to the sounds of flutes and bells, to the smell of the nearby desert. Writing quickly on the back of each card, an hour ago in the Hotel Suerte Loca, I realized that any words from here would sound ridiculous.

259

*Greetings from the end of the world*, I scribbled beside Reyna's address in New York.

*Letter to follow*, I informed Ardis on the second card.

*Wish you were here*, I told Jose on the third.

It has been weeks or it has been months since I left El Jadida, since I last wrote to Jose, Reyna or Ardis. Standing at the window in the Hotel Suerte Loca, I watch the moon wax and wane above the hills to the east, increasingly drawn by that lunar pull, almost ready to slip from the room, move through darkness, into the east *infini*.

If I were Mitch, and if I knew the exact date, I might have written an identical letter to everyone I know, on January 1: "All in all, it has been a good year. Enormous strides forward have been made, the big payoff waits just around the corner, everything should bear fruit by springtime at the latest."

It will be a month, perhaps, before Jose calls Ardis to ask in fractured English why there has been no news from me, until Reyna calls Jose with the same question, until Ardis contacts the Canadian embassy to let them know that they should add a second name to their list of persons missing in this area.

It should be easier to find two than one, I hear her rough voice say.

"Tea together is good," remarks my host, emerging with a steaming silver pot and two glasses on a tray.

Food alone would be better, I think.

"My wife and child liked tea," he comments. Setting the tray on the glass counter and drawing up another wicker chair, he sits so close that his knees graze mine. "My little girl would walk into the fields to gather fresh mint in the morning. She returned home with more than her arms could carry; one could follow her path by the mint she dropped along the way. My wife was especially fond of tea, for she was from the *palmeraie* where tea is a gift from God. Her uncle was a trader I did business with in Goulimine; she was happy to come to live in Sidi Ifni. For her Sidi Ifni was the centre of the world as this was the largest store in the world. We were happy to drink tea together and we became happier when our child was born to drink tea with us. But my wife missed her *palmeraie*. The water there, she said, is as sweet as if God had dissolved a million grains of sugar in it, as refreshing as the tea in Heaven.

"So three years ago we returned there for the Ramadan. It is not an easy journey, you understand. There are no roads to such a *palmeraie*. It is a question of three weeks with the caravan. My wife knew that most likely this would be her only chance to visit her *palmeraie* in this lifetime. The journey excited her greatly. She would not sleep while we rested in the shade of our saddles in the hottest part of day. When we travelled during the night, she watched the sand with eyes which grew wider with each moment, until I feared that she would catch fever from excitement and not know her family when she saw them for the last time in this life. I do not know if monsieur is familiar with the Sahara. It is a tedious place. It is a place to cross between here and there. It is a place to close the eyes. But my wife was so happy to return to the Sahara that one could not suspect that she had ever dreamed of leaving it. As we drew near her *palmeraie* in the third week of our journey, she began to say that she could recognize certain dunes as though they were the features of her mother's face. I laughed. Yet she continued to tell our child of places here and there around us where she had played as a child. She described sliding down the sides of dunes, tumbling over and over from top to bottom, seeing to the end of the world from the highest crest of sand.

"One night, to the annoyance of the other members of the caravan, she insisted that we stop. She said that across a large dune to our right existed a spring whose water surfaced only during the Ramadan. Mint sprang around it until the last day of the holy month, she said, when both water and plant vanished into only sand again. You have never tasted such mint, she promised. The best mint in the world. I laughed at this fantasy. Mint does not grow in the middle of the Sahara, far from oasis. Also, the dunes shift with the wind each month, and after seven years one cannot recognize the dunes.

"My wife became angry. I did not believe in her and I did not believe in the miracles of God. It is terrible that our child must listen to your lack of faith, she said, forcing the beast on which they rode to kneel upon the sand.

"You must bring back this miraculous mint, I shouted as she hurried across the sand with our child by the hand. You must bring back enough mint for all the caravan. We must all have tea together on the Sahara.

"This was the middle of the holy month. The moon was not large, but even a small moon casts much light on the Sahara, and the stars are very white. My wife and child shone as they slowly climbed the large dune. My anger at my foolish wife left me, like grains of sand trickling through my fingers. When they reached the top of the dune, my wife and child paused. I could hear their bright laughter. The sound must have carried far in all directions and high into the sky. I thought my wife would see from the top of the dune that there was no spring or mint on the other side. I thought she and my child would slide down the dune towards our caravan. I would soothe my wife's disappointment and I would tell her that it did not matter that water and mint did not exist in this place, for soon she would see her mother's eyes.

"But my wife pointed her arm before her, towards the other side of the dune. She cried with delight. Then she and my child disappeared. At once I became alarmed, for I could no longer hear their voices though sound carries far on the Sahara and high into the sky. I made my camel kneel and ran towards the dune. In my fear I tried to climb the slope too quickly and slipped down it many times, until my mouth filled with sand and I could not call my wife's name. When at last I reached the top of the dune, I looked over the other side. I saw only sand below and only more dunes in the distance. In the darkness nothing shone except the stars and in my heart there was no light. I slid down the bank and ran across the sand. My feet weighed a thousand kilos. I could scarcely lift them, as if the sand were swamp.

"After some time I heard voices from the caravan behind me. Several men climbed the dune, and then they helped me look for my wife and child. Going as far from the caravan as we dared, we searched until morning. The next day we made our camp in that place, though it was not a good place for a camp and the other members of the caravan were anxious to reach the *palmeraie*. While they slept, I still searched for my wife and child, though it is dangerous to walk beneath the sun on the Sahara. And all the next night, again with the help of other men in the caravan, I searched too, until my voice had called too long and could make no more sound.

"On the following night the caravan had to continue. I had to leave with it. I had to tell my wife's family about the spring and the mint upon the Sahara. When the next caravan came back this way, I had to return with it alone. I lost my wife and child because I did not believe."

The man pauses and sips his tea. My own glass has grown cold.

"We must drink tea together," he repeats.

I sip cold tea. The man appears neither more nor less sad than before telling his story. Frowning, he adds another lump of sugar to his glass and stirs it briskly.

A customer enters. She wishes to buy Colgate toothpaste. Apologizing to me, my host rises to attend her.

"Thank you for the tea," I say, rising also.

He looks at me blankly.

As I reach the doorway, he calls behind me. "Please. One more thing. When I told my wife's family about the mint in the Sahara, they said that everyone in that area knows about its appearance there during the Ramadan."

Outside, the sun has burned through fog. Heat strikes my head. On the sidewalk to my left, a figure crouches before a small fire over which it is roasting something on a stick. I take three steps and drop my postcards into the flames. The figure lifts its head to look at me. It is a woman. Part of her nose has eroded. One eye has become a concave sore. She has no fingers beyond the knuckle and holds the stick by pressing it between both palms.

Sun beating upon the dusty street of Morogoro, Ardis's voice emerging from the greengrocer's, the lepers moaning and reaching to me from the dirt.

The leper groans. I smell the meat cooking on her stick. I have no money for meat. I haven't had meat or eggs or soup forever. Swooning, I lift my head.

Across the street the cartoon face of a grinning clown is painted in gaudy colours above a doorway. Brilliant red hair, huge purple ears, enormous blue nose, blinding white teeth. *Dentiste*, reads a sign above the drawing. For some reason the picture disturbs me more than the leper at my feet or the story I have heard.

The woman moans again. She is not asking for money. She is not asking for anything. Holding the stick in my direction, she tries to wave it despite her tenuous grip. I squat down and pull a small, charred lump from the stick. I toss the burning meat from hand to hand until it cools slightly, then put it in my mouth. I can't tell what animal it might be from. It is mostly fat. I chew slowly. The leper has managed to spear another small piece of the grey flesh beside her on the sidewalk. I hold the stick over the flames for her. Smoke wafts into my eyes and the leper licks her lips. When the piece is cooked, I remove it from the stick, push it into her mouth.

A herd of goats approaches, bells jangling around their necks. The animals dodge and leap and scramble uncertainly, perhaps

fearfully. No one herds them. Following behind, I savour the taste
– charred, bitter, rich – that lingers in my mouth.

*Pas de poste.*

*Pas de téléphone.*

*Maroc infini . . . La caravane passe.*

Waves roll like dunes of sand through the dusk. Just above the
ocean's roar, I hear a sound from the cliff rising from the shore to
the town behind me. Turning, I strain to see through the dimming light. A number of dark caves yawn upon the face of the
cliff. Darker figures seem to stir in these mouths. I think I almost
hear the same sound as before and almost recognize it as a human
sound. Then the ocean's roar becomes louder.

I turn back to the Atlantic. At the point where the waves
darken into one flat mass of water, something glints. It catches the
last light of the sky, rolls beneath the waves, bobs to the surface
again. A bottle? Something rolls inside me, as if I were seasick. I
look for the shining object to reappear, but it seems to have vanished for good.

I walk quickly back up to the town and make my way to the
Berber market in the alley sloping off the main street. A string of
naked lightbulbs exposes plastic housewares and polyester clothes
spread for sale upon the dust. My eyes wander over the cheap
goods, though there is apparently nothing here I need, nothing
here I want. Then I notice, next to some religious objects, several
tablets of paper and Bic pens. They catch my eye, as if they were
flashing in the dark. Quickly, I bend down and pick up two tablets
and three pens. I start to feel inside my pockets for money, then
stop. I need my few remaining dirhams for bread and coffee. Sliding the worn grey jacket from El Jadida off my shoulders, I hand
it to the vendor "*¿Vale?*" I ask. He nods, without indicating
whether he has received the good or bad end of the trade.

I return to the Hotel Suerte Loca, feel my way up the dark stairs, fumble for a match in my room. The candle flame hisses, wavers, steadies. The room is cold. Glancing towards my supply of twigs and brush in the corner, I wrap the rough brown blanket around my shoulders. For a moment I listen to the drums beating across the inland plain. Beyond the window, the glassy moon bobs in the sky.

*Dear Jose*, I begin to write.

I squint at the words in the dim candlelight. Suddenly, a dog barks from the gorge below my window. I freeze, then shiver.

*Write it for me*, Lily said the last time I saw her.

*Write it for all of us*, she said before she discovered God.

Zanzibar. The Ngondo hills. The lemon tree.

Crossing out the two words I have written, I begin again.

I will write it in order to destroy it.

iv.

At six Richard became fascinated by the idea of inserting messages in bottles and throwing them out to sea. When first
informed by his father of this practice, the boy listened as though
receiving spoken confirmation of something whose existence he
had suspected for a great deal of time – in the same way that Africa
revealed itself daily to be a dream he had envisioned long before
arriving there with MJ and Lily and the father, but without the
mother. Once more his eyes widened then quickly narrowed at
the sight of another secret exposed to light. It seemed the father's
words were themselves a message in a bottle that had been drifting
slowly towards Richard for years, and the way the father happened to mention the subject – casually, almost accidentally, as an
aside – heightened this sensation. The new knowledge bobbed
and glinted upon the fluid expanse of the father's speech, which
now described seven sure ways to catch a falling star.

From then on Richard eagerly anticipated the family's next
journey to the ocean. For the first time, he did not view the prospect of travel with alarm, and the father's intense, erratic desire for

movement now transformed into an unlikely ally. Yet the father had an unfortunate habit of waking his three children in early morning, when mist still wreathed the top of the Ngondo hills and the jungle still dripped, and explaining only then that a trip to Dar es Salaam, Athens or Barcelona would commence in an hour. For several years the boy was always caught unprepared for these sudden journeys; without messages and bottles, he would stare at the Indian Ocean or Mediterranean Sea in disappointment. The surface before him was going to waste; another opportunity slipped like water through his fingers. What if he never had the chance to visit the shore again? Who was waiting across the waves to receive his message right now? On the sand, Richard tilted back his head and gazed across the blue ocean of air above. Without faith he mumbled a brief prayer; it was insubstantial, unwritten, nothing God could see or touch or unfold with His hands.

At home in Morogoro, far inland from the smell of salt and the sight of gulls, he began to ask the father when they were going to the ocean again, so he could have enough warning to make the necessary preparations.

"Soon," the father absentmindedly replied, inspecting one of his big butterfly nets for holes. Suddenly, his face lifted and brightened. His fingers snapped. "Say," he exclaimed. "We'll go to Zanzibar."

"Zanzibar?"

"An island," the father answered briefly, already losing enthusiasm for the idea, now dragging his net experimentally through the air as if he contemplated the capture of a cloud.

"Cloves," he added vaguely.

Richard consulted the atlas and dictionary, then followed the path that led to Preema's house in search of further information. "Here," she said, holding silks and satins to his face, fluttering flags of scarves and saris from her long, thin hands. "In India my mother taught me to hide cloves in closets and drawers to keep my things from smelling of dust and damp."

Richard closed his eyes, inhaled deeply, and saw a spicy land rising from waves, surrounded by water, too far from shore to swim or row or sail to, nearly as far away as the mother frozen stiff in the clinic in Canada, amid the ice and snow.

"I've never been to Zanzibar," said Richard, opening his eyes.

"Neither have I," said Preema, her third dark eye regarding him steadily from the centre of her forehead, not blinking once.

"We're the same," he said, reaching to touch the scar that ran white and jagged as a bolt of lightning across the left side of Preema's face.

One day, when Richard was eight, his older brother, MJ, told him that the family would go to Mombasa in several weeks. The father had decided that they were all a little blue. A week in a hut on a beach would make everyone feel A-OK.

Immediately, Richard began to prepare for the journey. To launch his plan, he felt he needed a dozen bottles with tight-fitting caps. The houseboy would not part with empty, unused ones that sat around the kitchen, and Richard had to roam far and wide to find containers for his messages. Past Preema's and through the brush, down the path towards the sisal fields and up to the tin village beneath the jungle, all around the college patrolled by fat, pink priests: Richard ventured farther from home than he had ever been before. Often he would see something glittering with promise in the distance. Upon approaching, he usually found only useless shards of broken glass or shattered mirrors of mica winking slyly beneath the sun. His face fell. Once more he lifted his eyes to the buzzards and hawks circling the chapel steeple. Farther above in the blue sky, as nebulous as a puff of cloud, a wispy moon waited to shine in the darkness. Preema said that the moon was his mother. "She watches you at night," Preema promised.

When at last he possessed enough suitable bottles, Richard tested them thoroughly in the bathtub. After pushing them beneath the water, he carefully watched them bob back to the surface. Several bottles, not airtight, failed to rise; these he eliminated at once. Splashing the water into waves, he considered whether even the airtight bottles would survive a storm. His eyes squinted at a vast ocean upon which a fleet of brave vessels weathered wind and waves to travel a thousand miles to their destination.

"What the hell's going on in there?" the father called from the hallway, knocking loudly on the bathroom door.

Next he had to compose messages. He spent several afternoons deciding exactly what he wished to say; in order to figure this out, he had to imagine who would find a bottle washed upon the shores of Zanzibar. A sailor or a fisherman. A small girl building castles in the sand, an old man pacing the beach to feel it crumble beneath his feet. What do I want to tell them? he wondered. Will they be able to understand English on Zanzibar? Will they be able to read at all?

He experimented. At first he wrote long missives of several pages that would fit inside a bottle only with difficulty. In them, he offered friendly greetings, a comment concerning the weather, and a detailed explanation of who he was, where he wrote from, and why he communicated. These messages were longer than the letters his father made him write to the mother in Canada, he noticed.

But were they too long?

Brief is best, the father always said. Richard wrote twelve shorter messages, cutting out the weather and anything else that did not seem essential. He varied each note slightly, so every bottle held something unique.

Finally, after more thought, he printed the same single world on all twelve scraps of paper.

*Help!* he wrote.

Everyone should be able to understand that, even on Zanzibar. At last Richard had a dozen good bottles, with a message sealed inside each one, hidden beneath his bed. "I've done every-thing I can," he thought, in the dark going over his preparations one more time for last minute flaws. There was a certain amount of safety in numbers, he believed. If one bottle were swallowed by a whale, and another exploded in the hot sun above the Indian Ocean, ten bottles would remain. If nine of these never reached Zanzibar, or lay forever undiscovered upon its shores, at least one would be found. At least one message would be read. The one in the Coca-Cola bottle, he decided. That's the lucky one.

*Help!*

At first he thought that MJ or Lily called in sleep from their islands of beds that rose, separate but near, across the black water of the room. No. The voice spoke from somewhere closer. Was it his own voice? He listened carefully. Though it sounded like his voice, it was muffled. Reaching over the side of his bed, Richard groped in the darkness beneath until by touch he found the lucky Coca-Cola bottle. Its glass was smooth and strong; its shape clear and graceful. For a moment he held the bottle in his hand and felt more firmly convinced than ever of his plan's ultimate success. Able to ignore the continuing muffled cry for help, he swam to sleep. As he floated away from jungle and snakes and black chil-dren who trilled Swahili taunts, the moon's white hand bent through the screened window and touched his face.

He had tried to make his preparations as secretly as possible. While not difficult to keep the father in darkness, it was less easy to conceal his scheme from MJ and Lily. Watching silently, they offered neither assistance nor encouragement. He knew, though, that they wished him good luck. He also knew that they were busy with plans of their own. In a jar beneath his bed, MJ was sav-ing enough East African shillings to buy three plane tickets to Canada. One day, with Lily and Richard, he would fly away from Morogoro and leave behind the father with his butterfly nets and whistling and shining eyes. Lily's plot was more private; it curled like a snake beneath a flat stone, hissed if anyone came near. While each child worked alone and in his own way, all were intent upon the same end: escape. It was understood that whoever encountered success would share it with the others. Eventually, they would all be rescued.

When it was time to set out for the ocean, the father was irritated that Richard insisted upon bringing a suitcase containing twelve bottles empty except for a scrap of paper sealed inside. "Travel light, travel right," he repeated for the hundredth time. On the driveway of hard, cracked earth he argued with his stubborn youngest child, while MJ and Lily, knowing not to take sides, waited patiently within the white Peugeot. "I don't know what the hell you kids are coming to," the father grumbled, relenting in the end.

As they drove northeast towards Mombasa, Richard often glanced over his shoulder to look at the suitcase of bottles in the back. He didn't respond when first the father tried to tease him about his plan and then, without success, encouraged MJ and Lily to join in a game to guess what the messages said. "Are they love letters?" the father asked. "Valentines?" Abandoning his teasing, he began to whistle "California Here I Come."

As usual, the three children rode in the back seat. They said that they couldn't sit beside the father, in the front, or they would get sick. MJ and Lily looked at their brother without expression; he knew they secretly conveyed solidarity that could not be revealed safely. Lily drew the word *wait* on the dusty window beside her, then quickly erased it. "They won't break," MJ mouthed mutely when the road became rough and the car jolted in ruts. The children stared out the window as Tanzania and then Kenya swirled by in a cloud of dust. When they stayed quiet for too long, the father lifted his hands from the steering wheel and cried, "Look, ma. No hands." The car swerved again; Lily clutched MJ's arm. He's going to kill us, Richard thought.

As soon as they reached the Mombasa beach, he carried his heavy suitcase to the edge of the waves and examined the water before him. It lay flat beneath the hot sun, with no bottles or sails floating upon it. Except for three Africans splitting coconuts with machetes, in the shade of a palm, the beach was deserted. Large grey birds cried overhead. *Help! Help!* they squawked. Richard squinted towards where Zanzibar rose from the Indian Ocean, far beyond his sight.

When the father, MJ and Lily finished unpacking in the rented hut, they joined Richard with towels, pails and fruit. Immediately, he moved a distance from them. "Say goodbye to your brother," he heard the father instruct behind his back. "He's running away." Placing a hand to his forehead, Richard shaded his eyes to see the water better. He decided to walk farther down the beach; the heavy suitcase bumped painfully against his legs. Looking back, he saw that the others were now small black dots. If he held a finger in the air, they vanished behind it.

For a long time he hesitated beside the water. He needed to determine if the tide was ebbing or flowing, and if there was a strong current at this place. Satisfied that the ocean's conditions were favourable, he slowly removed the twelve bottles from the suitcase. At intervals of several minutes he threw them as far out upon the water as he could, paying special attention to the tossing of the lucky Coca-Cola bottle. With contentment he watched them drift lazily from sight. Now it was just a question of time before they reached Zanzibar.

Returning to the others with an empty suitcase and a satisfied expression, Richard assisted in the construction of a large sand castle. Quickly, the father whipped his children into excitement over the possibility that this represented their most successful architectural effort to date. As the most enthusiastic, vigorous member of the team, he urged everyone to work harder, swifter, more fiercely. Then, without his children realizing it, the father

273

gave up on this enormous task; they turned around and saw him pace pensively nearby, hands clasped behind his back, face bent thoughtfully towards the sand or, all of a sudden, thrown up to contemplate the broad blue sky. He remembered aloud all the sand castles they had built upon other shores, and how each had been slightly different in terms of width of moat, height of turret, strength of rampart. "The one in Lagos," he mused. "That was beautiful." The children stopped shaping wet sand into walls and became the father's audience. Against their will, they were caught up in his summoning forth of castles that were not in view, castles that had existed for only an hour in the past; castles that were, for as long as the father considered them, more real than the castle they constructed here and now – which, by this point, had turned into only a childish fancy, unworthy of the father's notice. He could always carry them away with him, no matter how they tried to resist his wile. He could always leave them swept up in something his shining eyes no longer even saw. He could always make them feel foolishly tricked, and once more the children guarded against further beguilement.

From time to time Richard glanced anxiously at the ocean in fear that his bottles may have changed direction upon the water and drifted inland instead of farther out. This concern became acute when the tide turned and began to climb up the beach. Twice in early afternoon Richard walked far along the edge of the waves to be certain that no bottles had secretly returned to shore. How far is it from here to Zanzibar? he wondered grimly.

Sun and sand always made the father playful. "You kids break my heart," he said when he wished to become Robinson Crusoe and no one would volunteer for the role of Friday. Swimming far out from land, as if he were never coming back, he suddenly stopped to splash and shout, in a variation of the drowning game. (In its classic form, this commenced with the father crying for help; then he disappeared underwater, held his breath for what seemed, to the watching children, forever, and only bobbed gleefully triumphant to the surface when he knew that they would, despite previous experience with the stunt, be drowning in panic.) MJ and Lily exchanged a grimace; they privately called the father Big Bawana Show-Off, Richard knew. "I've found a message in a bottle," called the father in a voice turned by distance into a sound as faint as the murmur of the midnight moon. Then he emerged laughingly from the ocean and shook salty water upon his children. Richard shivered when a drop flew onto his arm; the clear, round bead shrank swiftly, disappeared. With MJ and Lily, he silently watched the rising tide approach their sand castle.

"Relax," said the father, noticing the worried look on Richard's face. He flopped down to heave like a fish upon the sand. "Your bottles sank a long time ago."

Richard frowned. Suddenly he pictured his bottles resting in darkness upon the ocean floor. They remained motionless, far beneath currents. Mud and weeds quickly covered them; fish slipped without interest around them. Soon even a diver with a strong light would not notice the black, blunted shapes.

For the first time, Richard wondered about bottles thrown into the ocean by other people. How many bobbed upon the waves and how many rested upon the dark ocean floor? Again he walked from the others to search among crabs and shells and sea-weed at the water's edge. This time he looked for unfamiliar bottles containing unknown messages. What would they say? *Help?* Richard became more and more convinced that his mes-sages would remain undiscovered until he read the words that other people had offered hopefully to the ocean. In his mind the process of discovery took on the precision of a mathematical equation: at the exact moment he lifted a stranger's dripping bottle from the waves, one of his twelve bottles would be found.

The sun burned steadily and the afternoon grew hotter. Stranded seaweed and shellfish slowly rotted upon the shore. The smell was heavy and salty; Richard's head began to hurt. In fits and starts he ran farther down the beach, seeming to spot objects flashing promisingly in the distance; always, when he reached the place, he encountered only glinting waves. Could glass turn into water, as in the Bible water turned into wine?

"We're leaving," the father called from far away at sunset. Richard watched three dots file from the beach towards the hut above, then returned his gaze to the empty water. Now the ocean surface was broken into shadows, reflections and colours in constant, dizzying motion. It became difficult to retain a sense of the water as a single, large body, or to feel confident of knowing even a small patch of it well. The changing light tricked him again and again, until he felt that anything and everything floated before him. Finally, it was impossible to see.

"Once Zanzibar was separate, an island unto itself," he heard Preema's voice echo inside his conched ear. "Then it became part of Tanganika, and Tanganika became Tanzania. Now Zanzibar belongs."

Richard dropped the shell. He returned to where his old, battered suitcase gleamed upon the otherwise deserted shore like solitary evidence that humans had once inhabited this abandoned world. It lay above a patch of damp, smooth sand that had been the site of a large sand castle several hours before. The tide was ebbing, a breeze stirred, and a nearly full moon rose above the Indian Ocean to take its place amid the stars. Richard glanced up at the blank white face, then towards a less distinct glow, beneath shredded palms, where his father, brother and sister were concealed within the hut. Their low, unclear voices reached through grass walls and travelled into Richard's ear as a foreign language he could not figure out; above, the moon floated in stubborn silence. With each moment its light streamed more extravagantly, and shadows became etched with dramatic sharpness into the earth. Grass rustled, waves beat, insects clicked, invisible animals moaned. The air was drenched with dark scent, overflowing with sound, spilling silver light. The swollen night threatened to burst. Why, Richard would wonder in an unseen future, did the father take his children to a grass hut that stood alone upon a shore and offered flimsy protection against the din and dazzle of African nights? Why did he always bring them to places where there was no one else, no frame of reference, no reminder of another reality? After a week on this lonely shore, Richard knew, they would suspect they were the only people in the world, the last beings alive. They would come to believe they were the sole inhabitants of an island, some separate place that still did not belong, another Zanzibar.

Richard carried his empty suitcase into the hut. "I was just about to send out the search party," said the father. He was playing hearts with MJ and Lily on an overturned box beside a kerosene lamp. After the long day of sun, the faces bent over the cards appeared flushed with fever, hot to the touch. "There's rice in the pan," said the father, gesturing towards the one-ring butane stove, not taking his eyes off the cards. As usual, he was winning. He slapped a mosquito on his arm and dumped the black queen on Lily. His bare knees jiggled in concentration. All the children would have to spend their lives in servitude to pay off the staggering debt they accumulated in card games with the father. Within a year they would refuse to play with him any longer. They invented their own games, with rules that the father did not understand and that they declined to explain to him.

Richard didn't eat. His face was set in concentration: as long as he envisioned his twelve bottles, he believed, they would remain safely afloat. (This was only the latest in a long series of pacts he made with God; such bargains would increase in number over the years until it seemed that his entire existence was bound up in promises too numerous to keep but impossible to break.) He strained to watch them sail far from land and beyond the waves, where the ocean unfurled like smooth black cloth. Glass caught the glance of the mother's round white face in the sky; moonlight illuminated the messages sealed inside. *Help!* The bottles floated farther away. They drifted beyond Zanzibar, past the scent of cloves.

"Chumps," said the father when he won another hand.

The bottles disappeared. Richard looked around the hut. He saw the contents of suitcases scattered across cots in a confusion that would increase with every day spent inside the hut and through every disordered year beyond. The rough cement floor was gritty with sand tracked in from the beach. The air was heavy with the smell of salt and kerosene and dried grass. The lamp cast long black shadows, and grotesque distortions of four figures shuddered over the walls.

"You cheated," MJ protested weakly.

The Indian Ocean had become disturbed by the night. The roaring of waves filled the hut. It drowned out an African's voice in the distance, the scratch of a palm closer by, the scurry of rats in the thatch overhead.

"One day this will end," said Preema in a quiet voice pitched below these louder sounds.

"California Here I Come," the father whistled brightly.

Lily looked up from the cards scattered across the wooden box. She peered through the hut's shadows towards her younger brother.

"Write it for me," Lily said in Mombasa in 1970.

Richard listened carefully. Now the cry for help no longer sounded muffled. It had escaped from within its glass walls. At once he knew, as surely as he knew anything, that his twelve bottles had been opened by the ocean. They were sinking to the dark floor below, and their messages cried out as they drowned. The voice sounded familiar, yet it was not his. It did not belong to MJ or Lily or the father either. Richard listened more intently. It was all their voices blended into one chord, he realized. He and

Lily hit the high note, MJ sang the middle, the father boomed the bass. Their cry for help hovered amid the scent of cloves, wavered beneath the watchful moon, then sank somewhere off the coast of Zanzibar.

I curve around the warm, invisible shape of Jose, then suddenly stiffen.

A dim room swims into view, it is seen murkily from a bed, I am lying on the bed. I look warily at the tablet of paper floating like an island upon the floor. Outside the window, the sky is still grey and dense with fog; the afternoon sun has not yet burned through. I blink at porous shadows stirring quietly in the corners. The foggy world beyond the window is equally mute.

## V.

Again the shutters I closed before going to sleep stand partly open the next day. I suspect that once more, during the night, while I was tossing at the bottom of my dreams, someone stole into this room. Quietly, not quite silently, the obscure space was carefully explored. In darkness searching fingers sifted through papers, considered the texture of clothing, lightly lifted objects with which they were already familiar from previous visits during the night. The intruder is accustomed to the atmosphere of these secret visits, unalarmed by the suspense of the situation: it does not freeze or shiver when a dog barks abruptly from quite nearby, just at the edge of town. The intruder glances coolly towards me when, three feet away, I moan in sleep. It floats to the window and opens the shutters I have closed. For a moment it regards the sky above the inland hills, dominated by a large white moon, then glances at me once more, as briefly as before. The dog barks again. There is no hurry to leave this room, no urgent reason to leave me here alone. When the inscrutable purpose of the visit has been accomplished and, one hour before dawn, it is time to go, the intruder does not take anything away, tries to leave things exactly as they were; but the next morning the room always appears altered to my eyes. Things are not precisely as I left them. I can't quite define the change; it stirs subtly at the back of my mind.

A blond woman or a dark-haired man or a figment of my imagination.

Just checking up. Just dropping by.

Waking, I realize that this time something besides the shutter – and something equally obvious – has altered position in the night. The small burlap bag of magic, generally stored at the bottom of my travelling bag, its power deliberately concealed, lies on the bare floor beside the bed. It appears hollow, collapsed, clearly empty.

What happened?

Last night, before sidling from the room, the intruder touched my shoulder, induced me to rise from the bed, enchanted me to move across the dark room. Determined and single-minded and alert, as though accustomed to functioning as eyes, my fingers searched for something in the blue travelling bag. Only they, and the departed visitor, knew what it was. Deftly excavating the small burlap bag, they carried it to the bottle of drinking water on the floor near the bed. They slowly washed the remains of the potion, sufficient powder for a hundred dreams, down my obedient throat. It is an enormous overdose, the kind you never really come out of, not for years at least. I sit on the edge of the bed, last night, apparently awake, prosaic in posture, and consume the draught thoroughly, carefully, thoughtfully. A dog barks in the distance. There is no rush. There is all the time in the world to swallow this lukewarm water, slightly gritty with undissolved particles of potion, while studying the shadow cast by moonlight through the open window. Slowly I begin to feel drowsy. The indistinct room drifts around me; Sidi Ifni spins outside. For a second I envision the intruder moving swiftly through the empty streets, slipping around a corner with one quick look behind its shoulder, vanishing from view an hour before dawn. The shadow on the wall, caused by a certain angling of moonlight into darkness, resembles the lemon tree, dark against the moonlit sky of Morogoro, pulsing amid crickets and frogs and snakes, unfolding at the end of the garden; then the shadow shifts shape, as my eyes begin to flutter closed, until it appears darker than the moonlit sky behind it; its shredded fronds rustle like stiff paper, stir in a breeze so faint it isn't noticeable upon my bare face beneath the tree.

Now I am so far back inside the dream that I can't envision the possibility that one day the door will open again, one day the dream will end, and yes, this time for good.

Now anything can happen; now nothing will surprise me.

Another night. The candle's flame, which provides my room's only source of light, shudders violently and nearly extinguishes in a sudden draught from an unannounced opening of the door. I blink at my unexpected visitor without surprise. It takes me a moment to recognize the small boy with the limp who led me to this hotel upon my arrival in Sidi Ifni, then led me to the body in the gorge during my dream. Tonight he is naked. His body is pitifully thin, with sharp bones that threaten to pierce the skin. Expectant and knowing, his smile resembles a leer.

His eyes dart to my blue travelling bag in the corner. Apparently excited by the sight, the small boy scampers over to it. Immediately, he bends over the bag and begins to burrow into it exactly as he clawed through the garbage heap to uncover the body concealed there. I watch him idly. Nothing of interest remains in the bag. The dream potion is finished. The black daybook has been burned. Glancing between the blue bag in one corner and the charred tiles in the other, I think of Pandora's box with all the misfortunes it contains, with only Hope at the bottom.

Digging deep into the bag, the small boy withdraws something with a flourish of triumph. As if expecting my applause, he holds the small rectangle of stiff paper, coloured on one side, high in the air; then, with a grave sense of ritual, he carries it across the room to where I sit on the edge of the bed. His hands join, palms upward, to form a shelf upon which the rectangle of paper rests like some precious object of an obscure ceremony. I lift the paper from his hands. He bows formally. Quickly, his face becomes knowing again and he makes an obscene gesture with his hands. Turning, he slips from the room and leaves me with the photograph.

Only his shoulders, neck and head loom large in the foreground; for Jose snaps the photograph himself, holds the invisible camera away from his body with equally invisible hands. In the immediate background a dune of sand – empty of footprints, creased by shadows, as clearly ribbed as corduroy – sweeps towards the sky. Far behind lies a hint of valleys and hills tinged grey and blue by distance; a closer view would reveal fields spread with black volcanic ash that absorbs and retains moisture, on this desert island where sparse rainfall is the consequence of miracle, that coaxes crops to grow. Pale gold washes the lower sky and pale blue spreads above, suggesting that this is late afternoon on Lanzarote. Soon the gold will deepen. Soon an evening *sirocco* from the Sahara will burn over the Atlantic – unknown Africa hovers only sixty-five kilometres east across the water – and, in darkness, the sweet *malvasías* will tremble on their vines. But for the moment the hot air is hushed; Jose holds his breath to snap the photograph. After three weeks on the island, his skin is deeply tanned. His face floats in shadow (for the sun lowers from behind); the shadow falls below his neck. In this light his eyes are black smudges that squint downward at their outer corners beneath smudges of similarly black brows. Concealed bones carve his cheeks with slightly deeper shadow. Full and curled and barely parted lips reveal a mouth's inner darkness. Extending beyond the shadow on either side, his shoulders shine in sunlight; gleaming muscle slopes into sinew and bone, appears lush to the touch. Past the photograph's lower edge, beneath the contours of a naked chest, Jose's hidden heart thuds: far to the north, across the water, a lover impatiently awaits his return. His shadow falls, imperceptibly cooling, upon the sand; his unseen feet grip the slumbering ground. Here at night extinct volcanos rumble through his dreams; petrified seas of lava writhe beneath the moon. Two islands away, towards the west, Gran Canaria swims with an unvisited father upon it. Jose's work on Lanzarote is done, the island's market has been researched, the head office in Madrid instructs that he may fly home to Sevilla tomorrow. But the reunion with his lover there will be short-lived: within months Jose will have to go into the army; that will mean another island of separation, another desert of time apart. In May 1992 Jose squints into the camera's lens, peers at the lover who is not there beside him on the sand.

The candle hisses. The scent of soot and ash clings to the air. I didn't bring this photograph with me from Sevilla. I may currently be prone to the hallucinations of hunger and I may be caught firmly inside an overdose of a sleeping draught, but I am certain that I only brought one photograph of Jose with me on this journey – the one, taken upon his graduation from basic training in Cáceres, that shows him posing stiffly in his military uniform. The one that, for some reason, I have recently begun to carry, tucked between my passport pages, in my back pocket at all times.

I look warily towards the blue travelling bag, uncertain what further talismans may have mysteriously multiplied within it, uncertain why their prospect fills me with dread.

Suddenly, I rise and move to the window. The dark gorge yawns below. My hands release the snapshot into the air. Though the ground lies only twenty feet below, it seems that flashes of white twirl through the darkness for many minutes before coming to rest. A black shape scurries like a crab from beneath the fronds of an equally black palm.

For several minutes after waking I do not open my eyes. By the rustling around me, I know it will soon be dawn. Insects noisily anticipate daylight, a cock crows nearby, birds open throats to sing. The earth below me smells dark and cold and clean; the rough brown blanket around me is pungent with animal odour. I feel the shape of a small, smooth stone pressing against my cheek. My eyes open. The sky is still dark; the landscape is slightly darker. Stars are shrinking above the hills to the east, and the moon has already set. My body is cold and stiff from sleeping on the ground. I stagger to my feet.

At once I am fully awake, alert. Several yards away a sheep swings its head in my direction and the bell around its neck knocks hollowly. Beyond, a low wall of stones heaped upon each other traces an uneven line. More distantly, a tuneless wail of prayer commences; one sustained breath rises and falls upon an atonal scale, searchingly, then suddenly stops as if choked. Half a mile away across the fields Sidi Ifni looms white against the sky; only a few lights are visible amid the cluster of square shapes. I stretch my arms as high as I can, wrap the brown blanket around my shoulders, and set off towards the town. The morning fog will not rise from the ocean for several hours. The air is sharp and clear.

More and more I slip from the Hotel Suerte Loca after midnight, when I am certain the town is completely asleep, and spend the hours until dawn outside. I sit in the empty Place, descend to the shore, strike out across the fields. My roaming in the darkness has no clear purpose or direction; now and then I pause, close my eyes, smell the air, change my course. At some point in the night I lie down, wrap myself in the brown blanket, and sleep for an hour. Just before unconsciousness, I envision the unnumbered hotel room containing the empty bed, the blue travelling bag, its scattered contents. These things have increasingly less to do with me. The change of clothing, the remains of my papers, my few toiletries: they belong to someone else now. Returning to the hotel in morning, I scarcely glance at them before throwing myself on the bed to sleep heavily until the middle of afternoon. If they were stolen in my absence, I might not notice.

Each night my ability to see in the dark grows stronger. My feet no longer stumble over the rough ground beneath them. I can smell an animal before I see it now, and by the scent distinguish between donkey, sheep and goat. I have learned where I can pick bananas and oranges and dates from unguarded groves. I know where clear water runs in ditches when I am thirsty. My body has adjusted to little nourishment – stolen fruit, a *bollo de pan*, one glass of coffee a day – and to making every possible use of what it is given; it has even become stronger, as all unnecessary weight has been shed. Each night, drawn by the next unexplored field, I wander a little farther from Sidi Ifni. One dawn, instead of returning to the town, I will keep walking from it.

As I enter the streets, I comb my hair with my fingers; it has grown to the point where it is difficult to keep neat. Spitting on my fingers, I wash my face. I brush fresh dirt from my jeans; stains of old dirt remain. Folded into a square, the blanket fits like a book beneath one arm.

There are few people about. Wrapped heavily in robes – blunted, sexless shapes – they move like sleepwalkers through the street. Carts of produce haven't arrived at the market yet, and the stalls are bare and dark. Though the bakery is still closed, a smell of fresh bread warms the air. The only square of light along the main street belongs to the Café Principal. My step quickens to the sound of voices and music.

The brightly lit room is crowded with men about to set out for the fields. In threes and fours they sit over small glasses of coffee and mint tea. Smoke of tobacco and hashish curls around their heads; waving arms through it, they raise voices over the music to argue, discuss, laugh. This is the time and place when Sidi Ifni lifts briefly above sorrow. The men wear ragged sweaters, torn coats, dirt-stained trousers, gumboots; some have woollen caps, like ski toques, on their heads. I don't have to think about my own soiled clothes, unkempt appearance. Though I recognize many of them from my visit here before each dawn, these men show no sign of noticing me.

At the counter I pay two dirhams for a *café solo*. Before drinking it, I suck the two cubes of sugar resting on the saucer. I never used to take sugar; now my body needs it. I take so small a sip of coffee that it is only a taste on my lips; still, it explodes my senses. Tears slide down my face again today. At first I would feel foolish when this happened – on its own, without warning, unrelated to my emotions. But no one turns to look when I cry; if a glance happens to pass over me, it doesn't linger. Perhaps it is understood that these tears have nothing to do with pain or sorrow. They are a physical response to warmth and light after a night spent outside in darkness. A reaction to the taste of caffeine on my lips and to the presence of people around me. As simple and automatic as a shiver of cold, a yawn of sleepiness.

I close my eyes and lick the salt at the corners of my mouth. When I open them, three men have sat at my table. One is in his twenties, one middle-aged, one still older. They could be three generations of a family: son, father, grandfather. The youngest man reaches across the table to borrow the spoon from my saucer.

In Arabic the other two discuss irrigating the tomato fields; though I can't understand individual words, I comprehend the conversation. The middle-aged man thinks the tomato plants need water for another month; there will be enough rain, the older disagrees. Returning the spoon to my saucer, the young man pulls a blue rag from his coat pocket and, before I can flinch, wipes my face roughly, like a mother dealing with a child's runny nose. I smell lemon on the cloth. The others pause to watch, serious and unsmiling; then they turn their attention from me and continue talking. Something unimportant has passed.

In small groups the men leave the café, swing themselves onto the backs of trucks, ride away. I drink my coffee very slowly, savouring the taste; it must last all day. Touching my fingers to my face, I sniff them. Lemon. In an hour the Café Principal is empty except for the owner and myself. He gathers empty cups and saucers, wipes a rag across sticky tables, yawns. Flies now reign unchallenged in the room. Music still swirls like a dervish around me. Piercing flutes rise higher and higher, driven more and more swiftly by percussion in desperate pursuit. Just before the wild song seems certain to collapse, it ends. An equally frantic song begins at once. If I opened my mouth and wailed in prayer, the café proprietor would not glance in my direction; nor would the flies take notice.

Morning fog steals down the main street by the time I rise to leave. It hangs like cloud several feet above the ground; much higher, the obscured sun must glow. A few women, subdued and silent, make their way slowly through silver light towards the market. I buy my day's bread and return to the abandoned hotel to dream about sleep under open sky.

# vi.

Mitch surveys the bald, scraped realm around another new house and proclaims that things will grow easily here. "Sun, rain, rich soil," he chants, a monarch indicating with one powerful hand his kingdom of infinite breadth and wealth. This lofty gesture says that everything is in the earth; you only have to seduce it upward. Mitch squints into tropical sun; his eyes glint like the mica on the gravel road. In a row beside him three children wait to see what surprise he will conjure next; they can never guess what that might be. Already Mitch envisions fantastic flowers and plump bushes and trees offering unlimited shelter and shade; but these are private pictures he does not wish to share. Now he is kneeling down to rub red dirt between his fingers, to contemplate potential. In the valley below an afternoon train whistles through sisal, and Mitch's face jerks upward, crazy with confidence. "All you have to do is plant," he states, then strides away in big boots that make the gravel crunch. MJ, Lily and Richard are poised stiffly upon unrealized landscape as if tough roots bind their feet into this alien earth, preventing them from moving freely, allowing only distant dreams of escape. Always Mitch believes he can plant them in Spain or Greece or Kenya; they will grow easily anywhere. All it takes is sun, rain, rich soil.

Mitch waves his wand three times, and there is grass around the cement-block house. Three times more makes buds blister, leaves widen, flowers unfold. A father can still change the world that quickly. There is no way of knowing that finally his power will fail, or be revealed as just cheap tricks. In torn shorts, a belt of string to hold them up, this creator bends tenderly over the earth, turning it with expert hands, sure fingers. The children watch his broad brown back, see his wedding ring flash amid the dirt until the sun goes down. Every evening Peggy Lee serenades unpacked crates, croons to their suffocated contents. In the back bedroom MJ and Lily recall aloud other gardens in other places. Are they still growing, those gardens in Greece and Spain and Kenya? Or do they die once Mitch's restless eyes wander towards a new horizon, once those hands travel to touch unknown terrain? They wither like the mother in the clinic, in Canada, in the cold?

One day Mitch plants three saplings into the ground. "Your trees," he explains, stamping lucky circles around the buried roots. MJ, the eldest, has an orange tree, and Lily's is lime. For Richard, always youngest, there is a promise of lemons. Each child is responsible for his own tree: to water it, to pluck insects from the first fragile leaves, to prune branches so they grow shapely and strong. Later, all the fruit will belong only to its owner to do with as he pleases. The children pose tensely beside their future wealth while Mitch hunts the camera in the house. This is another moment that will not last; it must be captured by any means at hand. ("Don't say I never gave you anything," Mitch will later say, scratching his puzzled head, bewildered by his children's unvoiced accusation that perhaps certain essential things were once withheld from them. "What about those trees?" he will wonder, peeking cautiously into the past.) They wait until unable to see each other anymore, MJ and Richard and Lily; perhaps this is preparation for when they will lose each other for good. In darkness three thin voices carol; the song about the circle game twines up into the night, echoes tinnily between equatorial stars. The father can't find the camera: was it forgotten in France, lost in Italy? There will finally be no evidence of what he provided for his children, of what was not enough.

In the nunnery at the top of the college Lily and MJ recite multiplication tables after Sister Anna and capital cities after Sister Ruth. At home, alone except for the silent houseboy, Richard tends his lemon tree. In the morning he runs to see if overnight it has shot up as quickly as the beanstock and is now a ladder to the heavens. He totes innumerable buckets of water across the yard, spills it around his tree, waits on a flat stone nearby. The expression on his face defines expectation. Such hopefulness would be heartbreaking to observe; fortunately, there is no witness. Surely his lemon tree must grow with special speed because of the extra care bestowed upon it? The heavy sun presses like an iron against his head: he imagines an abundance of broad leaves above, protecting him and casting coolness over him. "If you water too much, it won't grow," warns the father, appearing suddenly in his teaching clothes as Richard carries another brimming pail across the yard. Half its contents spill along the way, creating a trail that anyone could follow to find a boy praying beside a stunted tree to some God with a green thumb. (How much water is too much, how much is too little? The boy will spend his life seeking to balance this impossible equation.) Upon that slender trunk he traces certain initials, along with his, within a crooked heart. At supper his head buzzes from sun; he can't eat. "Don't you want to grow as big as me?" Mitch inquires, then waits for an answer. It is, apparently, no rhetorical question; there exist myriad possibilities of who and what this boy may choose to be. Richard senses all the treasure hidden beneath the earth's skin: sunken cities, obscure selves, spirits unseen in darkness. All this may, compelled by Mitch, ascend to shine in light.

When MJ and Lily return from school, Richard invites them into the yard to ponder their trees. He entertains visions of three dancers with joined hands skipping rings around three trees, incanting spells of safe, swift and steady growth. But his brother and sister are reluctant to leave the house unless necessary; in the back bedroom, carefully facing away from windows, they play intricate games that have to do with distant places where no snakes slip eternally past corners of eyes. "What I really wanted was a dog," mentions Lily once, when Richard reminds her of their father's gifts out in the yard. Her thin face and crooked teeth will one day inhabit the same clinic in which her mother currently shivers. "I never asked for any kind of tree at all," Lily flatly adds.

Sun dyes Richard's hair white; his skin becomes faint gold: in shade he appears pale yellow. The boy folds arms around knees, makes a shelf to rest his heavy head upon. Africa is one long dream: he tastes intangible lemons, chews elusive, slippery pulp. (Why is he always thirsty now and why won't water slake this thirst?) Above the dozing boy, just out of reach, dangle golden globes, a whole galaxy of flavour; if he were taller, he could pluck them, peel them, devour them. As it is, he can only view the contents of his dream with proprietor's pride, find slim consolation this way. If there were any justice, his lemon tree would be twice as tall and broad as the neglected trees of Lily and MJ; it would, indeed, be as majestic as Richard sees it in his dreams. Something is not right in how the three trees are equal-sized – still small, hardly taller than Richard himself, with only hints of branches, illusions of buds. It is difficult to believe that although they continue to appear identical, and belong to the same genus, they will one day bear fruit of varying colour and size and shape.

Mitch's gardens insist upon growing with the speed of hallucination, swallowing up space around the house, consuming air and gulping water and blocking out the sky. Does Mitch's garden steal all necessary nourishment from that area, depriving the children's trees of what they require? Richard must poison his father's plants in order to have his hope flourish? Only the death of one may permit the other life?

Soon Richard fears losing himself in Mitch's tangled gardens; they become like the jungle that presses intently around the college, aswarm with wild beasts always on the prowl, too rich in scent and colour, enough to make anyone feel faint. It seems possible that Richard will never find his way out of this maze of twisting paths already choked and leading to no apparent destination. He will wander this wilderness forever, searching for some sign to point him back towards a time when there was order on earth, and no canopy of dazzling green lay between him and the watching eyes above the sky. Then his lemon tree appears before him, something safe to run towards. Its trunk is still slender enough to wrap arms around, but insufficiently thick to fill them.

"*Citrus limonia*," states Mitch. "Be patient. When it finally flowers, it will bloom all year, it will never stop bearing." Mitch peers down at his youngest child. "It will be worth the wait," he vows in such a way that Richard will always remember this promise even as it is broken over and over in a whole multitude of ways. In spite of a carefully nurtured talent for re-invention, Richard will never be able to erase the image of his father's face imposed upon the sky above him like some extra planet, another sun. Now Mitch adds that there will soon be more lemons than Richard will know what to do with. The fulfilment of expectation has its flip side too, Mitch may be suggesting. It would be safer if dreams did not come true? Were cut short, and not allowed to materialize as ordinary, unsatisfactory, more sour than sweet? Richard's mouth puckers, his face twists.

When it's too late to know anything for certain, Richard will wonder if Mitch meant the lemon tree to be some kind of joke. He will learn that, in fact, citrus does not flourish in the sort of tropical climate such as that part of Tanzania boasts; one season of intense rain falling down the Ngondo hills would have killed the tree for sure. Surely Mitch is aware of the climate's unfitness for a citrus crop – even as through long evenings he describes in luxurious detail how Richard's tree will evolve: the long, pointed, pale green leaves; the short, stout spines; the reddish buds growing singly or in clusters; the blossoms of purest white exuding fragrance most powerfully after dusk. Is there something sly, or even malicious, in Mitch's face as from thin air he creates these pictures of a graceful evergreen? Is there some simple lesson here to do with life being one long series of small disappointments, and does Mitch mean for the early imparting of such knowledge, which he himself learned too late, to be his real gift to his children?

Before Mitch decides that Catholicism corrupts, Richard is with MJ and Lily sent on Sundays up to the old mission church where the Dutch priest collects souls in his big black hat. While monkeys screech in protest beyond the stained-glass window, Father Franklin explains that in one God are housed three divine Persons. Father, Son, Holy Ghost: a Trinity. The Son is of the same substance as the Father; that is not disputed. Less easily agreed upon is whether the Holy Ghost comes from the Son through the Father, or from Son and Father jointly. This is perhaps too fine a point for a child who can glimpse no Holy Ghost nearby; yet it is clear to Richard that Father Franklin is not discussing abstract essences or representations. The son closes his eyes against incense, views the father stalking through his creation below. Dwarfed by papayas and mangos that thrust towards the sky, three small trees stand in a row. On the pew beside Richard, in an apparent trance, sit MJ and Lily, whose souls he will not be able to save. The Holy Ghost, invisible in the shadows, whispers acidic promises of divinity.

When the rains arrive there is obviously no need to water the lemon tree, and in the back bedroom Richard hovers near MJ and Lily. Now a mist creeps down the hills in the middle of each morning and until dusk wraps itself around the house. Richard can't look through the window to see his lemon tree, darkened and shined by wet, at the end of the garden. He can only try to remember what it looked like when standing present and real before him. Faith is required to believe that it stands there still.

Already artful at reminiscence, Lily and MJ discuss the past while the heavens leak. Lily says that in Greece the garden was on a cliff and MJ says that in Kenya there was a muddy river where the garden ended. "There were paths among the stones and roses," muses Lily. "And apple trees," MJ recalls. Where was that? In what garden were there roses and stones and apple trees? For every garden outside the window there exists a previous garden; always another room lies beyond whatever walls hold the here and now. So finally Lily and MJ will in their separate fashions wander from sight of everyone, pressing through neglected gardens of the past now gone wild and overgrown, and conquered by weeds and thorns and thistles, in search of that original garden far from where Mitch's skull bleaches beside the mirage of a desert pool. "Don't forget the bench beside the willow," reminds Lily. "Or the swing beneath the oak." Perhaps it is the mist outside that makes her voice sound muffled, something travelling across a great space of time and distance. In the future Richard will wander lemon groves of California and Italy, trample fallen fruit alive with wasps and ants. Then his sister's voice will sift through leaves in the very same way it speaks to him now, recollecting some citrus orchard that reaches fruition only in the gardens of Mitch's mind.

It is the hour when MJ and Lily sigh in unison across the dark room and Mitch meditates to music down the hall. Outside is clear and cool: the rain has ceased until morning, the mist retreated up the hills. Too large and heavy, the axe trails like a plough behind Richard; a furrow follows him from the house, deep into Mitch's dangerous gardens now muddy and slippery and possessed by hoarse frogs. The lemon tree shines in the dark. Its green trunk resists the axe. Anyway, Richard is too young and small for such a task; he should like MJ and Lily be in bed dreaming of somewhere far away where promises bear fruit and the wait is always worth it. Richard doesn't see at once the shape that looms beside him, darkness made solid as spirit was once made flesh. "It isn't sharp enough," explains Mitch, taking the tool from his son. Despite this fact, he is able to sever the lemon tree's trunk with just one blow. It topples, causing not the slightest tremor of the earth. Two trees remain; a trinity is broken. There is the father and there is the son, but where is the Holy Ghost?

# vii.

*The Holy Ghost.*

The pen begins to run out before I reach these words. They are scarcely visible, faint blue ink on paper, almost not there. The pen drops from my fingers. I watch it fall intently and feel satisfied as it bounces on cement. When I rise from the bed, pages covered closely with writing slide to the floor, settle around the pen, lie still. From a nearby room in the empty hotel travels a loud creak that ends almost as it begins.

It must be late. All evening the drums have beat through the dark; the sound reaches from somewhere out in the fields, near the base of the eastern hills, far beyond the town. Just as it threatens to fade into silence, the drumming turns more loud and energetic, in a pattern of continually reversed or challenged expectations. Something is being celebrated. Can it be Ramadan already? I glance at the wall where my row of scratches – my dis-continued calendar – has been covered by soot. I have no idea of the date. I have no idea when the holy month will begin. For me, the time to fast and pray began long ago.

Writing about the lemon tree, I glanced frequently at the open window. My eyes kept lifting towards the night beyond these walls, then returning impatiently to the paper propped upon my knees. *Hurry*, urged the drums. The room makes me uneasy; even the candle's glow seems too harshly, disturbingly bright. My body wishes to stride through darkness, to sleep upon the ground, to waken beneath the sky. *Quick*, command the drums. *Now.*

"I am leaving the hotel," I think after my feet have felt their way down the black hallway and blacker stairs. Now my mind works after my body; realizations occur only when actions have taken place, delayed mental responses do not permit decisions. I must wait to find out what will happen next. "I am going to the ocean," I think as the sides of the dark gorge move past me and the ground slopes downward beneath my feet. This destination surprises me. I thought I would move towards the drums instead. Intent upon their wild beating behind me, I pass a heap of garbage without glancing. The drumbeats grow louder as I move farther from them.

The ocean is nearly calm, with even waves which sway the moonlight upon their surface. My clothes drop onto the sand. I walk from cold air into cold water. It climbs like the snake of knowledge up my skin. I intended to bring the pages about an island scented by cloves, and about a tree promising citrus, and to offer them to the ocean, the water reminds me. I meant to watch them float, saturate, sink. The last pages, I know. The last stories I will write for all of us, I tell Lily, who from a balcony of the hospital on the hill looks down at the lights of Brale, cold and bright as the stars above this ocean. All that is finished, Lily. Over and done with. *Terminado, por fin.*

The cold water wakes me. Already the bare hotel seems a fantastic memory. The empty rooms, the foul bathroom, the dark passage, the darker stairs: a structure out of a dream, solid only in sleep, chimerical. I've been asleep for months. I try to remember what happened before swallowing a dream potion and falling asleep. What happened to the small burlap bag that contained that potion? My mind slips from the question; with other questions, it sinks like a stone through the black water of my mind. The ocean floor – rough sand, sharp pebbles, smooth stones – stirs at my feet. I bob in the water, rise with each wave, keep my head upon the surface, spit salt. My attention fixes upon the next wave rolling towards my eyes. The moon glows directly overhead. My mother's rough voice speaks from far away. *Don't forget me, don't deny me, don't ask me for anything.* A wail enters my ears. I close my mouth and the sound stops. A moment later it bounces off the cliff behind me and echoes high into the night.

When my body has been in water long enough, I find myself shivering on the shore. I rub my skin briskly with the rough blanket from the room; the blanket was chosen, rather than the pages, for this reason, and for purposes equally important but still obscure. I sit on the sand, reluctant to dress. My pores open wider and breathe deeply. A drop of water falls from my hair, slides slowly down my back, tingles. Moonlight transforms my skin and the sand into nearly the same colour. I feel camouflaged.

Chameleon.

I notice something familiar yet alien around my neck. I touch a silver chain. My fingers slide along its links and discover a silver cross.

The chameleon and the string.

MJ found the chameleon at the end of the garden, during our first year in Morogoro. It was no larger than the length of our father's hand. We tied a string around its neck and took it for walks, like a pet. When it altered colour to match the surroundings, this act of camouflage seemed to us a game or a trick; at the same time, the survival mechanism exerted a peculiar power over us, intensely absorbed us, MJ and Lily and I. We wanted to see it happen again and again. The chameleon looked forbidding to me, with sharp spikes rising jaggedly beneath rough, leathered skin. It resembled a miniature dinosaur that had stumbled into the present from a million years ago, and was angry to find itself in a time and place where nothing was familiar, everything was alien. One day we lost the chameleon; perhaps it escaped. One day, a year later, we found it again. We had no doubt that this was the same lizard: the string around its neck, though broken short, was still knotted there. The skin of its neck had grown over the string as the chameleon had grown larger. Now the string looked like an unnatural graft extending from the reptile, an alien part of it. Disquieted, without discussion, as if we had done something wrong, we let the chameleon go.

Newly aware of cold metal around my neck, I slowly dress. The sound now entering my ears resembles a moan more than a wail. When I close my mouth to stop it, a similar sound travels from behind me, where cliffs rise from the shore. Dark mouths open on the face of the cliffs. Holy men live in the caves. Not pausing to eat or sleep, they pray continuously until they die and need to pray no more. In the rear of their shallow caves are scattered the white bones of holy ghosts. I wonder how I know this. Who told me this. I stare up until I see, in several of the dark mouths, points of shining light, pairs of glittering eyes. Though the holy men pray out loud, it is not always possible to hear their voices. Only at certain moments can you hear them. This moment, for example.

I climb into the town and pass the dark hotel. An image of what I have left in the bare room flashes through my mind: An empty blue travelling bag, a change of clothing, two tablets of paper and three pens. At once I know I won't think of those things again. *Travel light, travel right. Leeway.* Streets and houses trail off and fields begin. Before me, where hills rise in the east, drums still beat. My body warms as I walk towards them. I feel sharp hunger inside myself; it suggests presence, not absence. It suggests that I will be able to walk far.

Fire burns in the distance. The sound of drums grows louder;

this is its source. Dark shapes shudder around flames. I smell perfume and animals, smoke and cooking meat. Crouched low to the ground, I freeze. I must not be seen. The dancing bodies twist and flail, inhuman song winds above the drums, kneeling camels cough. With back bent low, I steal away.

Far from Sidi Ifni, the ground begins to rise. I cross towards the road which originally brought me to the town; some forty kilometres away, at the end of this road, a larger town sprawls upon the Sahara. Sand stretches south. I will reach Goulimine by dawn.

My feet make little sound as they walk the winding, narrow road. It rises, falls, then rises again in a pattern of repetition. Sometimes I hear wild dogs in the distance. Once I encounter a herd of goats which leaps away at my approach. Only one car passes. I hear it long before it nears; by the time it is close, I have crouched behind a large rock at a safe distance from the road.

Near the end of the night I pause to rest on a stone. The moon has set. The air is colder and the brown blanket around my shoulders is not warm enough. I reach into my front pocket and pull out a wad of bills. I try to count dirham notes, give up. From a back pocket I remove my passport. Something is slipped between its pages. A photograph of a young soldier. I can barely make out the beret slanted upon his head, the decorative pin attached below his uniform's collar, his unsmiling face. Carefully I return the photograph between the passport pages and walk on.

The sky lightens to grey. Brush and scrub thin, then disappear. The road slopes down towards the desert plain and Goulimine appears spread before me. Smoke rises in straight lines from the town. In the mosque the *muezzin* calls sleepers for the first prayer of morning; long, wavering notes float above hard earth and rocks. The black silhouette of a palm looms against the lighter sky. It stands in a protected gulley a distance from the road. In the still air the fronds are silent; no birds sing in them. I lie beneath the palm and sleep.

# IV

## *The Shadow on the Sand*

"To touch the past with one's hands is realized
only in dreams; and in Morocco the dream-
feeling envelops one at every state."

– Edith Wharton

# i.

Shadow falls over me, blocking out blazing heat and light. I open my eyes. I lie at the base of a palm that rises from a wide gully's floor. A young man stands above me. He wears a ragged, dark-blue *djellaba* that reaches halfway down his shins. The feet below are bare. His left hand holds a stick; his right, a gourd. Nearby, a dozen goats wander between rocks over the hard, dry dirt. The palm's slender swath of shade falls several feet to my side.

The young man looks at me with naked curiosity, as if I were asleep or blind or otherwise unable to see him watch me. He touches my side with one foot. I sit up and brush dirt from my face. Bending down he hands me the gourd; it is made from an animal's cured skin. I hold it to my mouth and swallow warm, sour water. When I hand the gourd back, he fastens it with a thong around one shoulder and says something I don't understand. He points towards the palm's shadow and wanders towards the goats. Turning, he motions to the shade again, then scrambles out of the gully with the goats and disappears.

I move into the shade, fold my blanket, and look around. The sun has passed the centre of the sky. It must be the middle of after-noon. I feel heavy and hot, but when I touch my arm, the skin feels as cool as a reptile's. I hum to hear the sound of my voice, and reach into the pockets of my jeans. I set dirham notes and coins beside my passport on the ground before me. For a while I look at them, touch them, move them slightly. Then I return them to my pockets and climb out of the gully. In the distance Goulimine appears as a neat gathering of rust-coloured shapes upon a lighter background of sand. On all sides the town meets the desert in a clean line of demarcation. Through the sea of small dunes a straight line of narrow, paved road runs to the north and to the south. Road, town and desert appear insignificant; above, lumi-nous and clear and blue, spreads the enormous, dominating sky.

It is too hot to walk yet. Turning, I notice dates scattered beneath the palm. With stooped back I gather them. Some are dried as hard as stones; others, more recently fallen, are slightly less hard. I brush off dirt and ants, bite into them, chew slowly. They are tough, tasteless. Several cars pass along the road to Sidi Ifni, out of sight beyond the gully. Once or twice a voice reaches me from the direction of Goulimine, as if the air contained win-dows that opened for a moment, then closed.

As the sun nears the horizon, it becomes more yellow than white. I leave the gully and start towards Goulimine. I would like to cut at an angle that would meet the southern road a kilometre from the town, avoiding it, but I need food and water. Entering the streets, the smells of gasoline and dust and food hang heavy in the air. People move silently and slowly beneath the shaded arcades. Women with large clay bowls or bundles of twigs bal-anced on their heads stop to stare at me. I spot an empty plastic bottle at the edge of the street. It is light blue, with a plastic cap of darker blue. Sidi Ali, reads the paper label. I pick it up.

At the end of a cul-de-sac women and girls gather before a tap in the wall. I wait until they have filled their containers, then step up to hold my head beneath the water, drink as much as I can, and

306

fill my plastic bottle. Lingering to watch me, the women and girls murmur with approval. In the next street an old woman squats beside a large basket heaped with bread shaped in thick, flat ovals. Handing her a dirham coin, I receive five pieces of bread. I try to fashion the blanket into a sling to carry the bottle of water and the bread upon my back. Making an impatient sound, the old woman rises and moves her fingers quickly over the blanket. I stare at the blue tattoos on her knuckles and close my eyes. As she ties the blanket in a strong knot around my neck, I smell the oil of almonds on her hands. The bread and water rest like an unseen, protected baby against my back.

I walk quickly from the town, anxious to leave it behind. The sun begins to set to the right of the southern road. Traffic consists mostly of large transport vehicles; they slow as they near me, almost stop, speed on. Though the trucks pass intermittently, they make me uneasy. When Goulimine is far behind, I leave the road and strike out across the low, rolling dunes to my right. At first I find it difficult to walk. My running shoes slip with each step; my feet sink to the ankle in sand. I take off my shoes, tie them together by their laces, sling them over my shoulder. Still hot from the day's sun, the sand remains warm longer than the cooling air. It feels at once gritty and soft. My bare toes grip; the sand's give acts as a spring. I walk as far from the road as I can while still keeping it in sight.

The desert darkens and the sky flares. Burnt orange glows near the horizon; deep red blazes above. Every few steps I discover myself paused in disbelief – unable to accept that the sky's colours have intensified still further, unable to move beneath the increasingly fiery threat. I hurry for several steps, then pause fearfully again. It is impossible that the sky can continue to flame without exploding. Suddenly, it turns a point and begins to dim.

Weakened and drained, still frightened, I walk on. Dunes rise and fall below my feet. At one moment I feel disproportionately tall, as if my head extended high into the sky and my feet touched the ground far below; anyone could see my shape looming upon the dunes from miles in all directions. At the next moment I feel so small as to be invisible upon the desert; my motion seems imperceptible, scarcely forward, nonexistent. I am aware of my heart beating in my ears; it sounds dangerously loud. Then I realize that this effect is produced by complete silence around me. I could hear the heartbeat of another being from a mile away. Slowly empty space and silence seep inside me, fill me, take the place of fear. The sky grows deep blue near the horizon, deeper blue above; when night has reached its darkest, it is still not black. Immense and full, the moon rises with dramatic slowness. Stars cluster, drift and swirl in constant motion around me. It seems I walk not below them, but beside them.

I pause atop a dune to eat bread with water. I shiver. The night has grown colder than I expected. Far to my left the occasional light of a car moves down the road. I close my eyes until a map appears before them: I see Tan-Tan, a dot one hundred kilometres to the south; the ocean, thirty kilometres to the west. Rising, I veer west until I am unable to see a light on the road; that guidance has become unnecessary. My direction is clear.

I pause frequently through the night. Without memory I sit in the sky. Desert stretches below. I shake myself back into action, uncertain if a minute or an hour has passed.

The sky begins to lighten. The desert remains black, as if the earth were holding onto darkness, unwilling to let it go. I shrink against the dawn, equally reluctant to become absorbed by light, wishing to curl around myself upon the sand. When the sky reddens in a minor-key variation of last evening's sunset, I am too tired to respond to it. My nightlong exhilaration has faded; with the end of darkness, I have lost an ally, and find myself more alone, less strong. Sharply etched and richly coloured beneath air of astonishing clarity, the desert slowly reveals what has been there all along. In every direction only sand stretches as far as I can see. I have underestimated the desert; it proves more than I thought it was. Somewhere to the east, beyond my sight, runs the road to Tan-Tan; the ocean lies much further to the west. As long as I remain between ocean and road, I cannot became completely lost. Continuing to walk with an eye on the sun's position in the sky, I will eventually reach Tan-Tan.

I am not certain how far away it is. How quickly did I walk through the night? How often and long did I pause to watch the sky? The bottle of water is two-thirds empty; two pieces of bread remain. I have eaten and drank too much. I may not reach Tan-Tan until evening or until tomorrow morning. There may not be enough bread and water to make it there.

The sun quickly warms the air. One moment I shiver, the next moment I sweat. When the sand burns beneath my feet, I stop to put on my shoes and to fashion the blanket so that part of it protects my head. My body longs to lie down on the sand, pull the blanket over it, sleep until dusk. No. If I slept now, I would not waken.

I shrink further inside myself as I walk, retreating as far from the sun as possible. My feet move on their own; the effort is still too great. My head jerks and my eyes suddenly take in the desert. I wonder if I have been walking in sleep. Turning, I see a fairly straight line of footprints smudged behind me on the sand. The desert pales and the sky loses clarity. The air becomes dense with waves of heat. This fierce sun is only winter sun. This heat is not heat at all. This is nothing.

One step. Another step. One more step.

In the desert the shadow is the soul. I glance to my right where a dark shape floats over the sand. Is it a true reflection of myself? More blurred or more sharply outlined? Something larger or smaller? As I continue to watch the shadow, I feel myself float as an equally dark shape over the dunes. I am aware of blank sand where my shadow lay, blank sand where my body walked. I have become my shadow.

I spit sand. Rough, hot grains stick to my tongue and coat my lips. Get up, says a familiar voice. I struggle and fail to recognize the voice, though I know it as well as my own. Get up now, it says more loudly. Dull, sharp blows hit my head. The voice will not leave me alone. It keeps kicking me.

I push my hands against sand and sit up. Looking behind, I see footprints weave towards me in an increasingly wandering line. The sky looms dark before me. For a moment I think that hours have passed and evening has arrived; yet this darkness does not resemble dusk. Gathering thickness, a black storm cloud approaches beneath blue sky. The air fills with a rushing sound and my heart becomes inaudible. Desert lifts around me. My eyes sting. Sand burrows into my nostrils and ears. Blindly, I pull the blanket over my head and with my body seal it to the desert floor. A tight tent surrounds me; burning sand and wind whirl beyond. The blanket tries to pull away from me, seeking escape from the storm. I grip it tighter, bend my neck, breathe the pocket of air before my chest. Breathe slowly, says the voice. More slowly still, it calmly instructs. Now wet your lips with water. No, don't drink. There isn't enough. Only wet your lips and wait. You know how to wait. I taught you that. The storm will pass. Hold onto my voice. Don't sleep. Pray. Pray harder. Pray longer. Hold onto my voice. Yes, it's me. There is no such thing as being lost. Every cloud has a silver lining. Calm follows all storms. Don't sleep. Don't stop praying. Don't stop. Don't.

"Monsieur."

Before me rises the circular staircase to my fourth-floor room in the Hotel Luxembourg. I look longingly at the worn, blood-red carpet on the stairs, the gold paper flaking on the walls, the iron railing that twists and turns like an ageing ballerina's unsteady pirouette. All I want is to climb these stairs and open my door and shut away the Paris streets, the frozen lights, the mocking pavement. *So you're back, monsieur, what makes you think it will be different this time, monsieur, I see you are still dreaming, monsieur, it's been seven years since you began to dream, hasn't it, monsieur.*

I turn towards the voice behind me. Typically impassive, patting the neat grey bun behind her smooth face, eyes turned to the ledger spread before her, Madame Claudel stands at the bureau of her shabby reception. She is flawless in her role as the warden of a prison or hospital. You have to hand it to her, she's really very good, I should applaud you, Madame Claudel.

"You have a message."

She coolly slides a square of folded paper across the dark wood. She does not acknowledge that there is something quite unusual, even singular in this event. Oh yes, during three months at the Hotel Luxembourg I have received numerous messages and all kinds of letters and constant telephone calls. Oh yes, and let us tell another lie, Madame Claudel. I remain at the Hotel Luxembourg in part because Madame Claudel is so perfectly impersonal behind her bureau. As impervious to my creeping through the reception as she is to the obvious deterioration of her Hotel Luxembourg. Far too aloof to glance sharply at me with inquisitive eyes and think: "This young man lives the life of a dog, it's unbelievable how some of these people live, yes, like a dog, you can't believe it, *mon dieu.*"

Or perhaps Madame Claudel does think this kind of thing after all. She may be discreet rather than indifferent. What matters is that after three months she refuses to recognize me. What matters is her superb denial that she has seen me pass in a dreamlike daze through her reception a hundred times.

"What is the number?" she still inquires when I ask for the key.

"Oh yes," she murmurs. "Four twenty-two."

Madame Claudel could say one or two things about the guest in four twenty-two, but that would mean admitting that the clientele in her Hotel Luxembourg is not quite what it used to be. Not like thirty years ago, not like forty years ago, not since the last war.

According to some, 1985 has brought the coldest winter in Paris for thirty years. No, others say, Paris has not been this cold for forty years, not since the end of the last war has Paris been this cold. Since returning to Paris after a year in California, I can't get used to the damp and the cold. I can't get used to the unheated hotel room and I can't get used to the black, bare trees in the Luxembourg Gardens across the way and I can't get used to how icy wind sweeps down the river as you cross the bridges between one side of the cold city and the other. During evening, when I force myself to leave the unheated fourth-floor room, I search the sky above the grey streets for snow. Snow would silence the mocking voices of the pavement. Snow would muffle the cries of children playing in the Luxembourg Gardens across the way. Snow would be something. I wander past the cafés on St. Michel and loiter in St. Germain bookstores and in St. Jacques gaze up at a fifth-floor balcony where eighteen years before three children shivered beside a man who threw his arms into the air and exclaimed: "Look at this, team. We've made it to Paris, for chrissakes. This is only the beginning, gang. You'll never forget this, I swear."

It won't be until years after the winter of 1966 that the shivering children will wonder if this promise were really a threat. They won't be able to forget this no matter how they try. At least one of them won't be able to avoid returning again and again to Paris in the winter instead of going to Turkey or Greece or somewhere else where stairs do not spiral towards an unheated fourth-floor room.

I climb the winding stairs. It is impossible that anyone could leave me a message in the Hotel Luxembourg. No one knows I am in Paris. I set the square of folded paper on the night table. All I can think of is climbing into the wide, sagging bed and waiting for the blankets to warm slowly and to lie beneath their heavy weight until late tomorrow when the Algerian maid knocks on the door and calls that she wishes to do the room, the room has not been done for three days, monsieur, one must do the room, please. All day I look forward to the sensation of my feet unthawing and the warm, slow beat of my blood and long dreams with complicated plots like novels I will never read, never live.

I sit on the edge of the bed and pour red wine into the glass. It is foul stuff. It hits my stomach and warmth spreads quickly through me. The kind of warmth that won't last, the kind you better enjoy while you can. I unfold the square of paper.

*Can't believe I missed you. Will try later. MJ.*

I recognize the handwriting. I remember this handwriting clearly from the days when we sat at card tables in the Brale basement and tried to learn what our father had neglected to teach us and to unlearn what our father had falsely taught us. This handwriting has not changed in the slightest from the last time I saw it. Eight years ago I found a piece of paper, slightly larger than the one I hold now, with seven words in this handwriting.

*Gone to Montreal to look for work*, said the message I found on MJ's card table in May 1977. Exactly the same handwriting. Erect and even and without decorative flourishes. Clear and neat and clean. Like MJ's disappearance itself.

This must be someone's idea of a bad joke. No one has received the least word from MJ since he disappeared eight years ago. My brother didn't tantalize us with hints that perhaps he was still alive, perhaps we could find him if we really tried, perhaps we should persist in looking for him and never stop looking for him.

I descend to the reception and approach the front desk where Madame Claudel pensively regards her accounts.

"Excuse me, please."

She looks up blankly. *Like dogs, mon dieu.*

"Can you tell me who left this message?"

313

"A man." Madame Claudel almost shrugs. "An *étranger*. He asked for you. I replied that you were out. He wrote a message. He left."

"How long ago?"

"One hour. Two hours." Madame Claudel almost sighs. "There is a difficulty?"

A difficulty, Madame Claudel? No. Not precisely a difficulty. That's not *le mot juste*. I wouldn't quite call it that, Madame Claudel.

"No. Thank you."

The fourth-floor room has slanted walls and a sloped ceiling. It feels less like a box than some of these rooms. It contains more dark, heavy furniture than most of these rooms. And if it is unheated, what can you expect for two hundred francs a week? A very good price, Madame Claudel reminds me when I pay my bill each week. A very good price indeed, she repeats insistently, in case I am not sufficiently appreciative of the good price of this unheated room with a view of branches pointing like black bones of fingers above the grey rooftops across the way. Yes, the Luxembourg Gardens are so near that curled in the armchair before the window I can hear the cries of playing children while I wonder why I am back in Paris when I could have gone to Egypt or Turkey or Greece or someplace else where the pavement does not mockingly inquire if I thought it would be different this time, what were you thinking, *monsieur*?

I pour another glass of wine. *Vin ordinaire*. As cheap as it is foul.

A very good price indeed.

I must simply wait. There is no need to get excited. Your brother stopped by while you were wandering past the hollow churches and before the gaudy cinemas and beneath a fifth-floor balcony empty of a man and three children. Under the circumstances, after all these years, your brother will certainly return very soon to see if you are back in the Hotel Luxembourg. Simply wait. You know how to do that, don't you? Wasn't that one thing I taught you well? You can never accuse me of not teaching you to wait, though I may not always be around to save you from this, that or the other thing.

Voices from the next room reach through the wall. This week they belong to a young British couple. While the words are impossible to make out, and the language they form is barely distinguishable, I usually like to hear these voices very much. They are my entertainment when I lie in bed and wait for the blanket to warm and the night's dream to begin. Every few days or weeks new guests with new voices arrive on the other side of the wall; it is like the changing of a cinema program. It amuses me to imagine what the people belonging to the voices look like. Sometimes, passing new neighbours for the first time on the stairs, I am quite surprised. Sometimes the voices don't match the people at all.

I try to imagine what MJ looks like. He must be twenty-six. The age of Mitch when I was born. MJ always resembled our father more than Lily or I did. The same dark hair, dark eyes, strong features. I wonder what MJ could be doing in Paris and how he could have discovered where I stay. I haven't written a note to Ardis for nine months. If MJ happened to contact her out of the blue, she would have no idea that I am in Europe, never mind Paris. Never mind the Hotel Luxembourg.

I imagine my brother passing through Paris on his way from one place to another. He walks along the rue St. Jacques and glances up at a fifth-floor balcony where a father told three children that everything was just beginning. Across the street MJ notices a figure gazing up at the same balcony. My appearance has not changed dramatically in the past eight years; MJ recognizes me at once. Who else could it be? For some reason he does not approach. The peculiar circumstances prevent him. He is not certain if he wishes to reappear after vanishing so perfectly and permanently eight years ago. Instead of crossing the rue St. Jacques, he hovers at a distance, unseen. Just when he wonders if

315

I will gaze raptly at the balcony above all afternoon, I turn and walk quickly away with my eyes lowered to the pavement. My brother follows half a block behind until he sees me enter the Hotel Luxembourg. In one of the cafés on the corner he tries to decide what to do. It is several days before he brings himself to enter the Hotel Luxembourg and ask for my name. Madame Claudel slowly searches through her register. "Yes," she finally says. "Four twenty-two. He has been here for three months, since November. Unfortunately, he is out at the moment. Monsieur wishes to leave a message?"

*Can't believe I missed you. Will try later. MJ.*

I have extraordinary difficulty with this scenario. I have accepted for so long that he vanished permanently that my imagination resists the possibility of a reappearance. Someone's idea of a bad joke. Yes. I look at the message again. I always admired that my brother managed his disappearance so cleanly. He left no nagging doubts behind. No unanswered questions. *Gone for good, good luck, goodbye*: this is how I interpreted his final words. Part of the past slips off the face of the earth. There exists, for all intents and purposes, one less being who remembers the Royal Hotel in Manila, the river rushing through the Ngondo hills, Peggy Lee singing in the Tanzanian night. There is one less person who I can turn to and ask: Did that really happen? Yes, MJ was right. Neat and clean. No traces, no tracks. Unlike Lily and myself. Unlike Ardis and Mitch. All our botched attempts to escape from each other and from the past. Able neither to let go of nor embrace each other. Slipping in and out of view, in and out of airplanes and clinics and chlorpromazine. Tantalizing each other with postcards across the globe. *Letter to follow. Rome is warm. Paris is a dream.*

From across the Luxembourg Gardens church bells ring twice.

MJ won't stop by later, not tonight.

Climbing under the covers, I am unable to dream the plot of a novel that I will not read, will not live. For some reason the voices in the next room irritate me tonight. I want to bang my fist on the wall and shout for the voices to be quiet, please, no voices tonight, I can't bear unseen voices, not tonight.

During the next few days I am unsure whether to remain in the hotel in case MJ does drop by again or to roam the streets in hope of spotting him by accident. On the third day I walk directly to the rue St. Jacques and pause before number seventy-three. This part of St. Jacques is quiet, with little traffic, few pedestrians. Am I being watched by someone I can't see? From one of the windows above, MJ looks down at me? All he wants, in the end, is to see my face once more? Back in my fourth-floor room I eat bread and cheese and listen for footsteps on the stairs, a knock on my door, my brother's voice in the hall. *Open up, you fool.* Then what? My mind can't glimpse beyond the moment that I see my brother's eyes.

After five days I decide he must have changed his mind. He must have reconsidered. It would be a mistake for him to reappear. It wouldn't be for the best for us to see each other again. It would serve no useful purpose for us to laugh about how Paris is just as cold now as it was eighteen years ago, look, MJ, we're still shivering in Paris, is this the beginning or the end?

Well, he could have left another message with Madame Claudel.

*Sorry I missed you again. Must leave this evening. MJ.*

With ten words he could have prevented me from wondering if he were still in the city. He could have saved me from believing that at any moment I might see my brother across the street, from my window, at my door. He could have protected me from being left with one more inconclusive incident and one more unexplained puzzle that my mind would always strain to solve. He could have preserved in me a faith that not all losses must leave a lingering, nagging doubt that they are not for good.

A week later I left Paris for Vienna. I found I was unable to remain in the Hotel Luxembourg. I couldn't accept that perhaps my brother was near, unseen, still alive. It was impossible to wonder what our meeting would have been like. If we would have laughed about leeway and the lemon tree and the pot of gold at every rainbow's end.

I didn't mention MJ's message to Ardis when I visited Brale the next year or again two years after that. She had let him go once; that was enough. Especially when Lily continued to slip back and forth between my mother and the hospital on the hill. As Mitch slipped through the distance, in and out of view. As I did, too.

*Can't believe I missed you. Will try later. MJ.*

MJ, did you mean that it was unbelievable that you would miss me, that you never suspected that you would miss me, that missing me was the last thing you thought would happen?

MJ, did you mean you missed me like I miss the fireflies and Lily's laugh and how Mitch's eyes always looked brightly into the distance?

MJ, did you mean that you will try to see me again in some distant time and place? Not necessarily tomorrow, in Paris, but when I least expect it. When I am wandering down the Paseo de Cristobol at three a.m. with laughter and perfume drifting from the cafés beneath the summer lamps?

Have you seen MJ lately? asked Lily in one of the last letters she wrote to me from the hospital in Brale. The question occurred in the middle of another description of how the wild dogs no longer barked in the night since Lily had found God. Have you seen MJ lately? my sister asked innocently as if this were the simplest question she could ask, as if MJ had often been seen lately, as if MJ had not been invisible for eight and then for ten and then for fifteen years.

*Can't believe I missed you.*

*Will try later.*

*MJ.*

It was to be several years before I could begin to think again of my brother as being lost for good, without expectation of seeing him later. Lost in a way that presupposes neither living nor dead but suggests, rather, another dimension existing side by side with this one, very near yet completely separate, unconnected by tunnel or door or bridge. It was to take several years until I was able, finally, to imagine him (for this other dimension is accessible only through imagination) in some small town or other on the Pacific coast of Mexico. A Mexico of my mind.

Why Mexico?

For no reason except that my vision of my brother must unfold upon some landscape. There must be a background for the face that hovers in my mind. Why not a small town in Mexico where in evening young girls drift around the plaza and old women lean their faces into the night and blossoms reach towards the lamps and boats sail through the stars.

Why not Mexico?

Once my brother and sister and I had a private language built exclusively upon the names of places. For us, Paris and Rome acted as verbs, Rio de Janeiro as adjective, Singapore as improper noun. We learned long ago that this could be the only way to tell our story – through a language where Barcelona means love and Mombasa means sorrow and all gods are summoned by means of prayers that begin something like: Jakarta, Manila, Copenhagen, hallowed be thy name.

And what did Mexico mean?

And when did I forget this secret language?

I came to suspect that the message from MJ in the Hotel Luxembourg was written in a language my brother believed I would remember. A language that reaches through the slanted wall of time. No matter what happened in whatever indecipherable present MJ and Lily and I would discover a way to leave each other a coded message that allowed us to find each other anywhere, at some end of the world. At some end of the world I see Lily and MJ lean towards me and I watch how they grimace at an account of the time Mitch believed that if only we left for

319

Luxembourg tomorrow everything would be all right. That we find ourselves miraculously reunited here or there or anywhere would be no cause for wonder. It would seem absolutely fitting that around us jangle words and music we do not understand; to be surrounded by strangeness is for us the most natural condition. Arabic, Swahili, Hindi: take your pick. And in fact the unknown beyond us makes us appear more familiar and necessary to each other. We say Mitch's name and sigh again; we don't mention Ardis. Always I see Lily and MJ and myself in a circle, with joined hands, facing inward, our backs to the world. I still see us in a circle, even though somewhere along the way, quite far back in the journey Mitch compelled us to take with him, we lost grip of each other and separated, and only I would find myself in the Hotel Luxembourg with voices reaching through the wall and black, bare branches stretching like fingers above the rooftops across the way.

The next time I passed through Paris, in 1987, I didn't stay in the Hotel Luxembourg and I made a point not to stand below a certain balcony in the rue St. Jacques. I didn't want to make it easier for the past to steal up, tap me on the shoulder, then run away before I had the chance to turn around and see its dark eyes floating upon a background of grey stone. I didn't want the past to remind me that it has the power to rise from the grave when you thought it safely buried and to swirl tauntingly around you like a desert sandstorm when you have no food or water.

It stops.

The roaring air suddenly falls silent and still. Uncovering my head, I shake a thick layer of sand from the brown blanket. The sand must have camouflaged me during the storm, making me invisible, transforming me into only one more contour of the desert. The sun has just set and darkness has fallen; cool and calm, the evening denies that a moment ago it was thick with burning sand. The air is as clear as if a door has opened upon a vast room of untold transparency.

How long did the storm last?

A veil has lifted. I never knew the veil was there – for years, nearly always, almost all along – or my eyes were so accustomed to being covered that they forgot there was a time when nothing hung before them, when nothing interfered with their vision of the world. I long to see Jose's face through such unobstructed eyes. To see him for the first time. To see all that he has to offer. Yes, everything looks different; even the empty landscape appears altered. Perhaps the dunes shifted in the storm. Perhaps I fell asleep to waken in this changed place, some Kalahari or Gobi at the end of the world, another plane of desert, one accessible only through imagination or by the baptism of storm. It is no more hospitable or less forbidding, this new desert; but its dangers are familiar, not to be feared, only accepted with respect.

This plane of desert contains my father.

These unveiled eyes may see him.

My grateful lungs breathe deeply. Clear air fills me until, with a curious sense of elation, I feel my body become only clear air, transparent as heaven, no longer a solid shape. I allow myself a mouthful of water and several bites of bread; the act of swallowing seems anachronistic. I look with puzzlement at the shadows falling from the dunes, the enormous moon filling half the sky. What in the unveiled world around me evokes this curious elation? What, visible and near, summons forth a faith that seems to need no object? Who lifts me to my feet and, once more, draws me forward, further, south?

I walk quickly. Dunes swell and sink beneath my feet like sweeping waves while I stand still. I do not need to pause to watch the swimming stars tonight; without looking, I am as aware of their presence as I am of my heart beating not within me but around me, the most distant drum, beckoning. In the aftermath of swirling sand, the baptism and the lifted veil, a door of vision has opened and I am permitted to see what I could not see before. If my father appeared like a shadow beside me, darker than the moonlit sand, I would be able to see his shape where before I would have noticed only loose atoms, shining grains. Now, where there was only darkness before me, a low line of light appears on the horizon, ahead and to the left. The lights of Tan-Tan. Ten or thirty or fifty kilometres away. But visible. Within reach. Near.

Is this what it's like, Mitch? To near the lost oasis?

It's not a mirage, you said. Not hallucination or imagination or dream.

You only told me once about the lost oasis. Remember, Mitch? You knew that you would never have to tell me again. You knew that I would never forget.

For once you were right.

The haven once known and long lost reappears when a pellu-cid door opens in the air. With faith you move through an arch of atmosphere to find that each step takes you deeper into a new dimension. Each moment shines clearer than the one before. Each moment renders food and water less important, until they are unnecessary. Until walking is no longer a straining of muscle and blood and bone. Without effort you move towards the light of the lost oasis. There waits all the food and water you will never need.

The plastic bottle, nearly empty, drops with the remains of bread upon the sand. The blanket floats around my shoulders like the robes of a new religion whose God is summoned by a prayer that begins: Tan-Tan, Tarfaya, Layounne, hallowed be thy name. And Smara is heaven and Dakhla is hell, and from the sand rises a transparent cathedral or synagogue or mosque, reaching among the stars, curving through heaven's vast vault.

# ii.

I reach Tan-Tan towards the end of night.

The town is larger than I expected. Long, straight streets of hard-packed earth run between low adobe houses. The dull-coloured buildings have doors painted bright blue, and are shuttered, silent and dark. Just beginning to stir, the town seems much darker than the desert; only the occasional light, sulphureous and yellow, glows on a corner. Heavily wrapped figures flit like purposeful spirits between the walls. Once or twice I step to the side and allow a cart drawn by a stunted donkey to pass. I wander the narrow streets contentedly, at corners changing direction without purpose. I feel my body reconstruct into matter as solid as the buildings around me; the sensation, halfway between discomfort and pleasure, makes entering this unfamiliar town seem like returning home.

Warmth emerges from an open doorway before me. Inside, a large, bare room without tables or chairs is strewn with straw. A single lamp on the rear wall provides dim light. Men squat on their heels with glasses of tea wrapped in their hands. A goat steps daintily among them. In one corner a man pokes a fire in a stove; he is obviously the patron. Several figures lie against the walls, apparently asleep, with hoods drawn over their faces. The room remains quiet as I settle with my blanket in the straw; only the slow, deep breaths of the sleepers are audible. Those awake are absorbed in their tea and thoughts; below hoods, eyes glow without wavering, as in a sombre spell. The patron claps his hands. In several moments a young boy approaches from a courtyard to the rear. He sets a tray beside where I rock slowly back and forth.

Gradually growing warm, I realize how cold I have been. I glance towards the tray of tea and immediately feel thirsty. I sip the sweet liquid and gaze blankly into the steam. When the boy returns with fresh tea, I ask for a bowl of *harira*. He looks confused and whispers anxiously to the patron, who steps into the courtyard and calls a single word. A woman appears there with a handful of twigs. She blows a coal into flame, adds the twigs, sets a small pot at the edge of the fire. Moments later the boy places a bowl and two pieces of bread beside me. As I dip the bread into broth, I notice movement there. I peer more closely into the bowl. Small white maggots squirm among the lentils. They are only the larvae of flies, saddled with a name of disagreeable connotation, harmless. I try to push them to the sides of the bowl, but they are too numerous. It's only the name, I think, tilting the bowl to my mouth. I sip the warm soup gratefully, moisten the hard bread until it softens. Calvin Klein. I laugh softly to myself. Ralph Lauren. Giorgio Armani. Gucci. *You have to call it something.* Smiling, I wipe the bowl clean with bread. Warmth spreads through my belly.

Beyond the doorway, the sky begins to lighten with grey and the street becomes more lively. All at once I remember that I have walked all night, as well as through the nights before. I lie next to the wall and wrap myself in the blanket. The straw smells dusty and old beneath my face. Above, voices quietly discuss me. They sound far away. Tan-Tan is quiet, I think. In Tan-Tan we are all subdued by knowledge of the desert around us. We don't raise our voices out of respect for the force of that vast silence. I float from consciousness, float towards Reyna. She is dressed in one of her dancing costumes, shining and glittering, swaying to flutes and drums, lashing her long black hair through the air, smiling. I never thought you'd make it, she says without speaking. I've been waiting so long for you. I've been dancing in the desert forever. I'm used to it here. I'm happy here. You could be happy here too.

My eyes open. I have no idea how long I have slept, but feel completely rested. The room is empty and dim; the fire in the stove has gone out. The street beyond the door shines brightly. In the other direction, I see a tap on the far side of the courtyard. I walk over and put my head beneath water, then drink slowly. I look up at the sky. A white ball burns directly overhead; the sky is pale near the sun, deep blue away from it. The woman who heated the *harira* sticks her head from another doorway leading off the courtyard, then vanishes. The patron enters the straw-filled room from the street, with a dead chicken dangling from one hand. He begins to pluck it. Feathers fly around his head and the room fills with the smell of blood. I take a ten-dirham note from my pocket. The patron wipes his hands, looks carefully at the note, ponders for a moment. He claps. The young boy arrives with more tea. I drink it quickly, then leave.

The low adobe buildings of Tan-Tan throw little shade beneath the midday sun, and after a dozen steps I am on fire. I pause to arrange my blanket into a hood that protects my head. Only a few people are in the street at this hour; they walk very slowly, scarcely moving at all, almost staying in place. Their slow motion illustrates exactly the slow motion of a dream. I pass several small stores which appear empty and dark beyond open doorways. In the dust before houses, old women pick lice from children's heads with quick, deft fingers.

Mesmerized by heat, I imagine following passersby to find out where they are going and to discover that we share the same destination. They will lead me to a dim, cool room with a blue carpet on the floor. Reyna sits cross-legged among other women who chatter and nibble sweet cakes. In the idle afternoon, hours before she must darken her eyes and colour her face for another evening of dancing, Reyna sews sequins onto her filmy costumes. The needle flashes, darts, flashes. I scarcely recognize Reyna – not because of her veil, but because the face behind it, relaxed and soft, is unlike the anxiously drawn face I have always seen before. I am happy here, she says without speaking, amid the smudged myrrh.

A loud rumble approaches from behind. I press to the side of the street as a military truck passes. In the open back stand several dozen soldiers in drab olive-green khaki. They look tired and thirsty and hot. Several are hardly more than teenagers, even younger than the soldier in the photograph pressed between my passport pages. One lifts his rifle, looks down the barrel, aims at passersby. "Bang, bang," he cries, like a little boy. Vanishing in a swirl of dust, the truck continues towards the war zone south of Dakhla.

I see no other vehicles until arriving at a main crossroads. There a dozen old sedans and trucks are parked amid travellers with large bundles tied with string. The taxis on one side are headed north; those on the other will travel south: all are dusty, battered, defeated – survivors with sagging springs. I approach the southbound taxis and learn that the fare to Tarfaya, the next town in the desert, is twenty dirhams by sedan or fifteen in the back of a truck. I search my pockets and find one hundred and ten dirhams. About fifteen dollars, I think vaguely, handing notes to a driver, mysterious behind dark glasses and whiskers and head-dress, and climbing into the back of his truck. Five dirhams saved now may mean several meals later. Six passengers already squat on their heels against the inner sides, which extend four feet above splintered floorboards allowing glimpses of the road below. Four of the men are young; two are older. They silently shift bundles to make space for me, without lifting their eyes from the cracked boards. The air grows more heavy and hot, with flies thick on every surface. For an hour we wait while the driver secures passengers to ride with him in the front.

With a lighter, one of the younger men heats hashish sprinkled amid loose tobacco spread across his palm. The older men have closed eyes, as if asleep; the rest of us smoke. The heat in my lungs makes the sun's heat seem less intense by comparison. My body becomes resigned to, even in harmony with the heat – no longer struggling against that force, but sinking into its slow, hot pulse.

The truck jerks into motion. Gasoline fumes and black clouds of exhaust fill the back of the truck at once. Crossing arms over knees, the six men lean forward to rest their heads upon these makeshift shelves, in identical postures of submission. For a while I watch the road run below the floorboards, then stand up.

Tan-Tan has been left behind. Uninterrupted desert spreads in every direction and the sky asserts complete dominance above. Only blue and beige, only space, only this. As if I have been away from the desert for much longer than half a day, I experience the relief of returning to a known place after a long absence. Cool wind blows steadily against my face; the truck vibrates beneath me. Though we crawl slowly over the paved road, the motion seems swift after walking. Signs by the road warn of camels, sandstorms and dunes; they are the equivalent of Canadian cautions against deer and snow and falling rock. Different dangers, the same dangers. Several times the truck slowly nears to a halt because a dune has swept over the road, concealing it.

This is what it is like to fly over the sand, through the air, above the dunes: both smaller and larger at once, the desert reveals itself in a new way. The door in the air opens wider and I move farther through it. Is this an unending phenomenon caused by the unbelievable blue and by the sand below? Does this sensation of continually moving still farther through an always wider door last and never end because no arrival point lies ahead, only

327

beckoning, stretching sand and sky? Is this reaching into the desert an endless process, never finite, a journey of continual discovery without final revelation?

Only unbelievable blue, only raw sienna, only space, only this.

The road turns west, towards the ocean. Soon the air becomes sharp with salt, then blue and white waves appear ahead; no line of distinction marks where the beach ends and the desert begins. Tan-Tan Plage consists of a few roadside cafés crumbling beneath the sun. The truck pulls up before meat roasting on spits. My fellow passengers stir at the sound of grease crackling on coals. We climb out and eat charred meat on squares of frond, paid for by the driver. Then we sprawl in the dusty shade with tea, drowsy as the soft sweep of waves.

"How far is it to Tarfaya?"

The group seems startled that I speak Arabic. A discussion concerning the distance to Tarfaya commences, then quickly becomes complicated. Everyone has been many times to Tarfaya and everyone is certain of the distance to Tarfaya, yet it seems as unfixed as the distance to a moving wave. One hour or three hours or five hours. The discussion widens; Layounne is seven hours away and Dakhla is ten hours away and home is too far away. Happiness is farther away. Happiness is the farthest of all. Like the horizon, happiness is never reached.

The discussion dies without a definite conclusion, and the men around me close their eyes. Two dogs fight over a scrap of meat in the sun. Flies buzz nearby. Waves beat farther away.

"I am going to Smara."

Everyone opens their eyes to look at me.

"Smara is small," the young man beside me states neutrally, leaving me to interpret whether this is good or bad.

"Smara is far," says the older man on my other side.

"There is no road to Smara," adds the driver. "Taxis do not go to Smara."

"My father is in Smara."

The men look puzzled. Have I used the wrong word for father?

"My father," I repeat.

"Yes," they agree with polite disbelief. "Very good," they murmur sadly. "Bless your father."

The truck shudders back into motion. I squat on my heels, though the gasoline and exhaust fumes are nauseating near the floor; all at once, it has grown too chilly to stand up in the wind. Like the other men, I bend my head forward and rest it on the pillow of my arms. I shift awkwardly but fail to find a more comfortable position. Light and heat slowly leave the earth. Unable to view the passing landscape beyond the truck, I have the sensation that we are not moving at all, and will never reach Tarfaya.

There is no choice but to submit; in this situation, Islam is wise. I submit to discomfort and nausea, and to how time seems to have stopped, how this journey seems endless. As the night grows colder, I become grateful for the bodies pressed on either side of me. I need their warmth; they need mine. We sway together in the dark, synchronized. Who are these men, young and old, and why are they going to Tarfaya? What waits for them there? And what awaits me there?

Though unable to sleep, and through unconsciousness escape this experience, I can leave my body: there is always a door to release. I rise a foot above discomfort and impatience to an altitude where they do not matter, where they do not exist. Looking down at my cramped self, in its posture of submission, I am aware of that body's discomfort yet not immediately affected by it, both attached and free. Above, I float like a bird that keeps watch, guides me forward through the night, flies on spread wings above the dark desert. I am able to swoop through the sky and vanish, but out of loyalty and love remain near my self.

Once in a while, when the truck slows to jerk across a broken patch of road, I fall into my body with a thud and open my eyes.

How much time has passed? How far is it to Tarfaya? One or three or five hours?

Tarfaya is far, Layounne is farther.

Home and happiness are farthest of all.

Strong light hits my face. My eyes open, squint, blink. The truck has stopped. A bright beam moves over the other men, who appear to have frozen like wild animals caught in blinding light, then returns to me. I am beckoned out of the truck.

It is difficult to see much. We are at the side of the road, in the desert, beneath the moon and stars. The middle of nowhere. A uniformed man holds a flashlight. Behind him, a dozen feet off the road, stands a small building made of cement bricks. A patrol station, I think, disoriented. A sign of a war zone ahead.

I am asked for my passport. Flipping through its pages, the soldier studies my photograph and essential data, as well as the exit and entry stamps. He finds the photograph of Jose and examines it very closely.

"Who is this?" he asks in French as rough as his voice.

I pause. "My brother."

My brother, my father, my friend. My companion, my lover, my self.

He is disturbed by the fact that the photograph is of a soldier, I think. I sense his curiousity about the connection between the military and myself, and what that might suggest about my travelling towards a troubled area – the uneasy ceasefire between the Moroccan army and the Polisarian guerrillas, south of Layounne. I wonder if he recognizes that Jose's uniform is Spanish, and what the implications of that might be for him, for me.

"Please, follow." We enter the patrol station. The single, small room is nearly bare and badly lit. A stove to one side of the dirt floor provides heat. The walls are blank except for the ubiquitous portrait of the corrupt king. On a cot by the wall sleeps another uniformed member of the Securité Nacional, partly covered by a brown blanket exactly the same as mine.

The soldier sits at a small table. He asks where I am going, why I am going there, how long I plan to stay there. Where have I come from? And before that? What are my parents' names? My grandparents' names? My occupation?

Blinking sleepily, I fumble for reasonable answers. The stove's heat makes it difficult for me to think. I can't stop staring at the gun in this soldier's holster, the braid and medallions on his tan uniform, his shiny boots and beret. The costume of authority; I've always detested it. Don't touch me until you get rid of those clothes, I used to tell Jose, when he came home in khaki from basic training.

I realize that I am not supposed to be travelling in the back of a truck between Tan-Tan and Tarfaya in the middle of the night. This is frowned upon, if not technically forbidden. I am supposed to be lying on the beach at Agadir or exploring the medina in Fès or enjoying the wonders of Marrakesh. If he asks to see my money or luggage, this soldier's doubt will turn into alarm.

He slowly writes down the detailed information I provide. I anticipate him recognizing the name in my passport from the time, nearly a year ago, when Mitch stood in this same spot with a passport covered with many more exit and entry stamps than mine. I hear my father eagerly describe why he is travelling towards a hot spot, energetically explain about irons in the fire and good connections and the lost oasis.

"One moment," the soldier will say. "This name is on a list."

A list of hopeful searchers, of addicted dreamers.

Quickly, however, I recognize this situation as one of those yearning attempts to assert a sense of bureaucratic order and control over a place that defies such measures. This piece of paper containing the names of my grandparents will be used to start a fire in the stove tomorrow or will sit on this bare table for a month. Or it will become lost somewhere between here and Casablanca, somewhere between Casablanca and Rabat. I realize suddenly how small the desert is – or, rather, how few people,

331

especially *étrangers*, move through its vast emptiness. Here there is no crowd to become lost in, no urban labyrinth to become swallowed up by: the desert offers at once no place and every place to hide.

The soldier's extreme interest in my passport suggests how rarely he has the opportunity to study such a document; this is an unusual event for him. He does not quite know what to do, I see in a flash. He is uncertain of the correct procedure in this case. He is bluffing behind his uniform of authority and his official air. It is important that I don't convey I know this. It is crucial that he save face for the sake of his uniform and for the position it represents.

He sets down the pen, takes out cigarettes, offers me one. I shake my head no. The sleeping soldier moans, grunts, sighs, falls silent. The waiting truck idles softly in the distance. I feel the loneliness of this place where only a few vehicles pass night after quiet night.

The soldier studies me curiously. He does not quite believe my explanation: I am very interested in Morocco, I am very interested in seeing as much of the country as I can. I am interested in the Sahara, I am interested in Layounne, very interested indeed.

His eyes are dark, cold, hard. Their gaze is fixed upon mine. We stare at each other. I feel the situation reach the point where it will turn one way or the other.

"You are far from home," he finally says. "Don't go much farther, please."

He rises abruptly and holds out my passport. "Have a pleasant holiday," he says with formal politeness.

I climb into the truck and we rattle off into the night.

*You are far from home. Don't go much farther, please.*

A warning? A caution? A piece of friendly advice?

A poised blond woman has materialized into a stern, dark soldier?

I clasp my knees with my arms, alert and awake, not wishing or needing to rise above my cramped body, my uncomfortable experience. I am freshly aware of the degree to which this is not a pleasant holiday, but the kind of holiday for which I have been peculiarly prepared. The kind of challenges I have been carefully trained to meet in a boot camp much more exacting than the one Jose knew in Cáceres. I feel the shape of my passport in my back pocket. The heavy smell of gasoline seeps through the cold darkness. Warm bodies of strangers press against me. The road runs below, the stars shine above, the night continues.

Just before dawn I huddle beside the road at the southern edge of Tarfaya. The small town lies behind me and the desert stretches ahead. A slight breeze, tinged with salt, stirs the dark, cold air; the road has curved towards the ocean at Tarfaya and now, before me, turns inland again, losing itself in dunes. I draw with a stick in the dust and hum to hear my voice. Through the dimness I see my initials appear beside Jose's within a crude heart. The stick drops and the question of getting back falls unexpectedly, surprisingly, into my mind. I haven't considered the logistics of getting back since I left El Jadida.

I arrived in Tarfaya several hours ago, hungry and tired and cold. The truck from Tan-Tan was pulled over twice more during the night, and in roadside patrol stations I negotiated my way with increasing difficulty through more exhaustive questions concerning who I am, what I am doing, where I am going. From now on, as the war zone draws nearer, there will be more frequent patrol stations, more demanding questions, more severe soldiers. This is only the beginning, this is nothing at all. Going forward will be as difficult as going back.

As my six travelling companions walked swiftly away through the end of the night, at Tarfaya, I listened to echoes interrogate the air around me: Who are you and what are you doing and where are you going? Simple questions once, but there are no easy answers anymore. When the truck reloaded with fresh passengers and turned back towards Tan-Tan, I found myself in an empty, silent street that continued to demand answers, to insist upon information from me. Not a single figure sidled down the street; not one cock crowed an alarm in the distance: it seemed that Tarfaya would fail to waken with dawn, would remain deserted as a ghost town populated by inquisitive, curious spirits. Only a solitary light burned at the end of the street, where an old man slept at the counter of his open-air tea stall. Though he lifted his head, blinked at me, and slowly prepared tea, soup and bread, I suspected that he hadn't really awakened. By the time I began my meal, he was already deep in sleep, now curled on the ground. I ate and drank ravenously, left five dirhams on the counter, walked to the edge of town.

One hundred dirhams left.

One hundred kilometres left until Layounne, then several hundred more to Smara.

How will I go forward? How will I get back?

Will I only disappear?

I can't calculate time anymore, or measure dirhams against distance. Simple questions and simple numbers hurt my head, prick painfully at my mind. How long since I left Sidi Ifni? Since I left Sevilla? Since I considered how I would get back?

No vehicles, not even battered trucks or military transports, pass on the road at the edge of Tarfaya. The single daily CTM bus that leaves Goulimine for the south in afternoon might approach any moment, if it has not already passed. It may, however, be too expensive. It may, in any case, be full.

Who are you? What are you doing? Where are you going?

Before me the desert spreads beneath greying sky. I can't clearly remember the emotion so recently inspired in me by sand and sky. I only remember that at the time I believed that the emotion would last and would sustain me. I wait for another door to open in invitation before me. I hum a tune remembered from the Café Principal in Sidi Ifni.

The heart's station
Is far away
Not in this dungeon
Of dust and damp.

I must find a supply of bread and water, then start walking. Shivering, I draw my brown blanket closer around my shoulders. I both long for and dread the rising of the sun. For an hour it will feel blissfully warm; for the next twelve hours it will burn searingly hot.

Something moves slowly towards me from Tarfaya. From a distance it looks like a crippled animal, perhaps a dog or a cat, crawling beside the road. As it draws nearer, I realize that it is too large to be either animal, yet I can't imagine what else it could be. A kind of desert creature I have never seen before? Gradually, it becomes evident that this is a human being of sorts. It pulls itself through the dust with its arms, legs dragging lifelessly behind. The progress is painfully slow, but steady in a jerky fashion. Its head does not lift to see what lies ahead, but looks at the ground, three inches below, across which it crawls. As the figure approaches, I am surprised that it does not breathe heavily; the motion appears difficult, strenuous. Though I can't tell if beneath its rags this is a man or a woman, it is clear that the figure is accustomed to such crawling. It has crawled this way for a long time, perhaps since birth.

*Bismallah*, I say.

The neck turns and the face looks up at me. Man or woman? Young or old? The face expresses fear that I will kick or spit on it. I wonder where this being can be going? How can it crawl into the desert, where for one hundred kilometres nothing but sand lies ahead. I feel a flash of irritation mixed with fear. I suspect that as I proceed further with this journey I will encounter increasingly grotesque beings – until, by comparison, lepers will seem healthy, until beggars seem blessed. Until I meet corpses dragging

335

their rotting selves across the landscape. Until I stumble upon headless torsos inching towards Mecca.

Still prepared for my foot to crush its skull, the being has frozen in the way animals remain motionless in moments of danger. The sores on its hands do not indicate leprosy, but flesh scraped raw from clawing the ground. One leg is exposed beyond the rags. It is swollen as large as this being's torso, and ends not in a foot but in an even thicker, rounded shape.

Elephantiasis.

I remember a day in Arusha, in 1969. We were at an outdoor celebration; some kind of festivity was taking place. Around us the large, lively crowd laughed and danced in a swirl of bright colour and music. Nearby, head thrown back in laughter, stood an African woman with one leg formed like an elephant's. I couldn't stop staring at the enormous limb and huge, rounded foot extending from her gaudy dress. I didn't want to look, yet I had to look. Where were MJ and Lily? Didn't they see? Was I the only one who saw? Glancing up, I saw that Ardis also stared at this woman. There was a tight, fixed smile on her face. When she turned to me, my mother's expression didn't alter.

*Who are you? What are you doing? Where are you going?*

The figure cowers in the dust. I take out my thin wad of dirham notes, squint at it, then bend down and place half the notes beside the being, who looks at the money and moans. Liquid falls from its mouth and forms a small pool in the dust. Saliva or blood. For a long moment the figure stares at the money, as if frightened of it, as if it were part of a trick. Then its right hand reaches for the notes. More quickly than my eyes can see, they disappear somewhere within the rags.

The sky has reddened to the east, but the desert remains dark and cold. The figure begins to crawl forward again. Its hands reach as far in front as they can, then pull its body forward, like a crippled caterpillar. When it has moved a distance ahead of me, I feel myself drawn forward. In a few steps I have caught up. I walk

336

slowly beside the crawling figure, almost in slow motion. It gives no sign of being aware of my presence; it concentrates completely on moving forward. Its form travels over the ground beside me like my shadow made solid, my shadow made without light. Allah's reflection of my soul. At this speed, it will take us a month to reach Layounne. It will take us all our lives to reach Mecca.

# iii.

Wasn't it in 1971, while we were travelling by boat between Athens and Ios, that Mitch told me about the lost oasis?

His eyes, which had been fixed on me while he spoke, returned to the sea before him in search, perhaps, of Ios now rising before us. They are like the sea, I thought, looking for land myself. Shining and dark and wet, my father's eyes are like the sea at night.

I was confused by his soliloquy. I felt that my father had told me too much or not enough, and that it was too soon or too late for me to hear those words. I didn't understand what they had to do with Ancient Greece, or with water that stretched in every direction around us. Or with my earlier suggestion that Ardis might not get better. Why didn't Mitch wait to tell me about his vision until we strolled one day upon the desert, among the pyramids and the Sphinx? Why didn't he wait until I was perhaps old enough to glimpse what he saw? I wondered, as the wind rose to blow more coldly against our faces.

Did I return to where MJ and Lily curled in sleep upon

the deck, after my father spoke? Or did I remain near him, in silence, with the sense that I should not leave him at this moment because there now existed between us something that had not been there before? Out of respect for this new bridge of knowledge and understanding, and in case he wished to speak further, I should remain close to my father – though he no longer seemed aware of my presence behind him, and, anyway, the rising wind would have rendered further words as inaudible as the cautionary cry of Daedalus before his son began to fall.

We arrived at Ios sometime before dawn. It seems to me that our ship was not able to dock at the island itself; we had to cross to shore in small boats drawn by oars, I believe. People from the island were waiting our arrival. They stood in the shallow water, holding lamps in the dark, their voices growing clearer as we neared. They waited for us as though we had travelled from far away, as though we had been gone and been missed for years. An islander lifted me from the small boat and beneath the stars carried me through the shallows onto shore. It felt like being saved. I felt rescued by those arms. Sometimes, when Jose held me, I would remember that sensation of being carried to land, the safety of the return.

The mystery of what we remember, what we forget. The length of time we stayed on the island, the shape of our days and evenings there, any images of temples and donkeys and white walls, how we finally returned to Africa: all this is shadowy now, and when I returned to Ios, a dozen years later, I would find nothing in the throngs of happy Scandinavian tourists and blaring discothèques to recall the past, and the clear, gleaming light did not dispel its shadows. I would remember Ios later only as a moment that rose from the black, windy sea, as something submerged lifts to sink again, as my father's voice rose from darkness and then fell silent.

For the next twenty years a part of me always waited in suspense for my father to speak again about his private vision.

During our remaining time in Africa, through the wandering years that followed, and after the return to Brale, I knew not to allude to that secret myself: it belonged to my father, to do with as he wished. Sometimes, on those rare occasions when Mitch looked at me with his true face revealed (for example, in the Hotel Carlotta in Mexico City), I felt he was on the verge of continuing where he left off on that windy night between Athens and Ios. At other times, as it became buried beneath years of silence, I wondered if that moment upon the Aegean was in fact without weight, only a casual aside, of no more significance than any of Mitch's verbal flourishes, forgotten as soon as spoken; but always I remembered how, as he spoke, I had a clear understanding that this was something he had thought about for a long time. He had waited precisely for that moment to speak. His tone of voice and choice of words were careful, considered, almost cautious. Only once or twice did I suspect that, though Mitch said my name before he spoke, it could just as easily have been MJ or Lily he was addressing; whoever happened along at the moment would have received his words. I watched my father closely, during the years that followed, for some indication in his eyes that we shared secret knowledge; that he never revealed such a sign made me believe, finally, that the matter was as momentous as I had imagined. And I came to think that my father deliberately chose to speak to me, rather than to my brother or sister; somehow, twenty-one years in advance, he knew that I would be the only one able to follow him, when the time came, to the place he dreamed of.

When Mitch left Brale and did not return, and when later I left Brale myself, I thought perhaps he would send me word of reaching his dream on the back of a picture postcard. *Found it*, I always believed I would read when I tore open one of his envelopes marked *Highly Confidential*. *Letter to follow*, he would scribble beneath a palm, beside a pool of blue.

But, no, he never spoke of his Shangri-La again, not even by code in the black daybook I discovered in Amsterdam, not even in the last postcard I received from El Jadida. He never explained why what he searched for was a miracle of water in the desert – rather than, say, a valley, an island, a mountain's other side.

And I didn't mention its elusory existence to MJ or Lily – neither the next day nor in the future when, finally, we were able to laugh at all our father's dreams and to recall with grimaces all his cryptic terms that for him became the litany of a religion we had never accepted and that in the end revealed itself to be a faith apparently as ethereal as a castle in the air.

But you knew I would never forget, didn't you, Mitch?

You knew that as soon as I received word that you had disappeared into the desert I would remember what you told me that night on the boat between Athens and Ios. I would know that you were finally nearing that beckoning place in earnest. All your wandering until then was only practice, only knowledge accumulated like the sixty lessons of the Koran, essential information needed to prepare your eyes to see the pool of blue reflecting sky, reflecting ourselves, reflecting God.


Through the morning I walk slowly to the left of the figure that crawls beside me. My shadow offers it some protection from the burning sun. Yet I believe that this being does not really require my help; it appears capable of crawling forward endlessly, as though exempt from the limitations of physical energy, and from the forces of heat and thirst and hunger: at the same time that it is painfully hampered by its body's failings, it has managed, I think, to escape that physical plane. As we progress foot by slow foot along the road to Layounne, I become increasingly convinced that this being is helping me forward, as if I were the damaged one. Without it beside me I could not continue to walk hour after hour beneath the sun without food and water. This seems as clear as the air around me. What else could explain why I do not feel hunger or thirst when by every right I should?

Once more there is only sand and sky. The straight, narrow road is empty of traffic, except for the occasional military transport with soldiers crowded into its open back. Sometimes the olive-green trucks slow as they approach us; more often, they roar past as though we were invisible. Now and then I try to speak a few words to my strange companion. I am not certain if its failure to respond means that it cannot hear or speak, or that it is indifferent. It seems completely unaware of me, and I feel more solitary than if I were alone.

It crawls off the road and into the desert. I follow. Our progress becomes slower still. Whenever we encounter a low dune, the crippled body slides down the bank several times before managing to reach the top; then it rolls like an inert object over the other side. Yet there seems a definite purpose for our leaving the road; this is not accident or whim. Perhaps this being knows of blue pools and green palms in the middle of this sea of sand. As we move farther from the road and deeper into the rolling waves of dunes, in fact, I start to glimpse shimmers of blue − dark blue, nearly black − ahead in the distance. I come to believe that this being has the power to lead me to the lost oasis and that I could not find that elusive place alone. Without its assistance I would become as lost as, presumably, my father. When we near where an oasis appears to hover, however, the shimmer of dark blue shifts away with the horizon. I understand that the real devastation of mirage is not the thirst it excites in expectation of being slaked, but the difficulty of carrying on when hope is raised then dashed. It would be easier if the hope were not lifted at all. Better to have nothing than to have the illusion of something.

"Water?" I ask hopefully of the stubborn creature crawling beside me; but once more it does not answer.

Well, I am beginning to see oases, if only the illusion of them.

342

That is something. Even the illusion is better than nothing, I begin to understand. Perhaps it is necessary to envision a thousand mirages before you are permitted to see a single oasis. Perhaps it is necessary to sustain hope and belief even as they are dashed a million times before you are finally rewarded with real water. Is that the test, Mitch? We must offer proof that our belief is something more than fragile, something more than illusion, something more than a mirage of faith.

Or perhaps this fantasy of water simply means I need to drink. I have to drink. I must drink. Though I do not feel thirsty, I will perish if I do not drink soon.

I will not die as long as I am not alone, I think. And even if I do fall upon the sand and fail to rise, my crippled spirit, with a knowledge of the desert far deeper than mine, will continue to inch painfully but steadily forward in the direction of water, in the direction of Mecca, in the direction of God.

By the time I reached Sevilla, in 1989, I nearly stopped expecting a postcard that would inform me that Mitch had found his pool of blue. Only once in a while did the images slip into the clear, sharp focus of a photograph; but before I could study them closely, the evanescent palms and pool evaporated.

For my father, I believe, it was a place he had been exiled from because of his dreams and where they took him, and it was a place he struggled to return to by means of more dreaming. Perhaps it represented an escape into the past, before all the confusion and separation and loss; or it was a place in the future where the damage could be undone. I came to wonder if its importance lay precisely in its elusiveness: it existed as something forever out of reach, the ultimate object of dreams, and its value depended upon it always being yearned for, never found.

"Don't look for anything for me," I never wrote my father,

though he knew about Jose, knew that I didn't need or want what he was still looking for.

"I'll find it for all of us," Mitch told me upon the dark Aegean all those years before.

Maybe he meant that he would discover a place where there would be no crying shame of it all. Where my mother would not hover in a hospital on a hill and my brother would not wince and pale from the pain inside his head and my sister would not swallow pills from a white valise in the back of a dark furnace room. My father hoped to find a place where all of us could be spared what had happened to us and what awaited us. In that place we could start again, from scratch, and this time make no mistakes.

I tried to tell him, in one of our last conversations through the static of a long-distance line, that I was grateful for where my mistakes had led me. I clumsily tried to tell my father that he shouldn't feel bad for not always being able to save us from this, that or the other thing.

"You did the best you could," I said.

My father paused. I could picture him waving my words away with his hand, shaking his head in disagreement as he shifted his weight from one leg to the other. There is a dull pain in his back. He is getting old.

"Stick in the Mud," he accused me, dismissing my happiness; it did not fit into his scheme.

"Now," he continued. "I've got it all under control. It's all worked out. Next month. Three months, tops. First-class tickets for everyone. And don't count out MJ, he'll surprise us all yet. Leave it to the old man, for crying out loud."

As the years passed without MJ reappearing, without Lily descending for good from the hospital on the hill, without your Island girl emerging unscathed from chlopromazine, your search grew more desperate and frantic, I believe. Whatever operations you were involved in, from South Korea to Colombia to Iran, you still believed your connections would help you find what you were looking for. Finally, it may have seemed, the Polisarian rebels south of Dakhla were fighting neither for phosphates nor their own independence. They were fighting for our freedom – though, of course, it would take more than guerrilla warfare to set us free.

It would take more than any bodyguard, more than any Jose, to protect me from you.

When we reach the top of the next dune, the figure suddenly stops, as if sensing danger. Its head turns to our left, in the direction of the distant road, from here a hint of thread upon the sand. I see, from atop this dune, what I did not see before: a patrol station pinpricked beside the road. That is why we entered the desert. We are stealing around the station, circumventing interrogation. Indeed, as we continue forward and the station falls behind us, my wise companion begins to turn our course back towards the road.

Soon after we reach the road, a smudge appears at the farthest point of vision ahead. It seems to remain still, to waver, to blur like mirage; then, at the same moment I am able to hear it, the transport truck appears to move towards us. The crippled being and I shift to the side of the road. I prepare to cover my eyes against the sand that the swiftly passing truck will whip into the air.

However, the truck slows as it approaches. It is heading north, towards Tarfaya. The figure beside me freezes; another moment of danger has arrived. Keep crawling, I say, ridiculously, in English. Keep moving and it will be all right. Act like nothing's wrong. Is anything wrong? Why don't you move forward with me? Why have you frozen in place? Don't stop. Don't.

I shout silently at my shadow as I hear shouting from the truck now just behind me. I move forward very slowly and sense that the figure behind me is still frozen in place. The soldiers' voices are wild, harsh, jeering. Something has excited them. I can't understand what they mean, if it is words. I hear the sound of boredom and cruelty and hate. I know that just behind me a truckload of hot, tired soldiers is travelling from an uneasy cease-fire in the southern desert; against their will, without choice, they have existed in poor conditions, with bad food, uncomfortable housing, no amusement. After a break of a week or ten days in Tarfaya or Tan-Tan, where things are not much better than in the south, they will have to return to Dakhla. Now, in the middle of nowhere, they have happened upon something that will offer relief from what they have suffered. They can make up for what they have been through and what they must face again. Erase it, wipe it out.

All this is clear in my mind. Turning, I see three soldiers in the back of the truck lift their rifles and aim them at the motionless figure in the dust. "Bang, bang," one cries. Remembering the soldiers playing like little boys in Tan-Tan, I feel relieved.

A rifle fires. Perhaps two or three fire at once; I hear only one blast. The first thing I think is how loud the blast sounds, how painfully it slams against my ears. I would have thought such an explosion would be easily swallowed by the empty air, immediately absorbed by the endless space.

The bullet entered the back of the cripple's head. It does not make a clean, neat hole. It rips a large, ragged tear in the rags covering the head. A messy smear of pink and white has splattered through the rip. No blood at all, at first. Blood begins to seep only after several moments.

The lame legs stop jerking as the shot's blast fades into silence. The sound rolls across the dunes; probably it can be heard for miles. Probably, like the loud laughter of the soldiers, it can be heard as far as the last patrol station to the north. The driver and three soldiers in the front of the truck are also laughing. None of them appear to notice me.

Something is thrown upon the road. The truck moves away with a grinding of gears. It seems to take forever to travel out of sight. It hovers endlessly in the distance, a motionless blur on the horizon. I wait for it to turn around.

Now blood has flowed into the sand and stained it black. With its forehead resting on the ground, the cripple appears to kiss the earth it has crawled across. I sit several feet from the body and look into the desert. It is empty and silent. Once in a while my eyes return to the body for a moment; each time, I am surprised to find it there. When my eyes return to the desert, my memory of the body is immediately erased by vacant sand and sky.

Soon flies cover the corpse. This is the first time I have noticed flies in the desert – or away from the towns, at least. They have materialized out of nowhere. I imagine the scent of this body spreading swiftly through the clear air, already common knowledge from Tarfaya to Layounne.

With astonishing speed, the corpse begins to stink. Excrement, for one. I have no inclination to move. I wish to remain here. I can't leave. Though I know how important it is to keep walking when the sun is hottest, I am unable to rise to my feet. I can't convince myself that it was only an illusion that I was helped forward by a being that could not even walk. That I was assisted in my journey by one more fantasy of the desert. That I was saved by one more mirage. That I need the strength of a cripple to continue.

At least its face is not turned to the sky. That seems very important.

My eyes inspect the blank blue heavens. Not one cloud, not the slightest wisp of white. Only unbelievable blue.

I shudder violently, then quickly rise. I drag the corpse off the side of the road without looking at it. The body is surprisingly

347

heavy. I had thought it skeletal, except for the swollen leg. Three feet off the road is far enough. I push sand over the body until, clumsily covered, it resembles a rough, newly created dune. Smoothed by wind, it will soon be indistinguishable from all the other low dunes.

As I begin to walk away, I notice something on the road. It is what the soldiers threw from the truck. A canteen of water. I swallow a warm mouthful, then sling the canteen over my shoulder and softly laugh.

It is late afternoon. The hottest part of the day has passed. The hardest part is behind me. Layounne is still far ahead of me. I am twenty kilometres from Tarfaya, at most; but now I can walk more quickly. Now, to avoid patrol stations and passing trucks, I must walk through the desert, not on the road.

The desert is safer. My body moves into it resistingly. Something has been left behind; I can't remember what. Something important, essential. I avoid looking to my right, where my shadow should fall, where my strong, crippled spirit should crawl across the sand.

No further mirages appear before me. It is probably because of the hour and the light. It has nothing to do with anything else, I tell myself. Once darkness falls and the sand cools, I can take off my shoes and walk barefoot. It will be easier to walk in the sand. It will be simpler beneath the stars.

I remember the fifty dirhams I gave the crippled being. Half my money is buried in the sand. I turn and look behind. A peace offering to the desert. Blood money. Nothing is free.

As dusk turns to evening, I begin to feel lighter. More light than ever before, as if unnecessary weight has been shed. As if I were a shadow on the sand. Only spirit, not flesh.

The moon above, no longer full, has begun to wane.

# iv.

It is hard to find a room in Layounne. All the small hotels are full of soldiers; they seem more like army barracks than hotels. Apparently, there is only one large hotel in Layounne, an expensive place on the hill for the UN brass. It is the middle of morning and I must find a room quickly; I have walked through the desert all night, I have walked for too many days and nights. I wander from one hovel to another, concentrate on each step, keep my eyes fixed as much as possible upon my feet, will myself forward. I can't fall down in these streets filled with coldly staring soldiers, their eyes asking what the hell I'm doing here, this town is not for tourists. I can't fall, not yet, I still haven't reached Smara and we never went on the *Lola*, Jose, I always wanted us to go together on the *Lola*. I need to rest and to gather strength before continuing towards Smara. Careful, don't bump into those soldiers, half the people in these dusty streets are soldiers. The rest are families of soldiers, yes, or people whose work is supported by a military clientele. All the passing trucks belong to the

Moroccan army, look, there are white vans and jeeps with UN printed in black letters on their sides. Keep walking and you'll find a room, I promise, I swear. Notice how large this town is, what a surprise, it sprawls upon a sweeping slope of the desert. There is an upper and a lower town, with dozens of these dusty, poorly paved streets lined with low buildings smeared with dirt. Everything is grey and broken and sad; there is no money for anything else. Even the few palms are stunted, torn, coated with dust. There is a hotel in the next street, see the sign, try that one. The larger buildings are topped with onion-shaped bulbs, how odd, perhaps they are an architectural feature designed for the desert. Perhaps heat rises into the bulbs and preserves the rooms below in comparative coolness. Keep walking and you'll find a comparatively cool room. The entrances of these small hotels seem so dark and foul because you're used to clean Sahara air. Here the air, swirling with desert sand, feels muggy as well as hot. Never mind, keep walking, at least you have no luggage to drag along. The entire population of Layounne appears dull-eyed and defeated by their cheerless surroundings, except for the men who run these small hotels; their eyes are suspicious as they slam doors in my face and shout at me to go away, go fast, infidel, go far, leave. An unbearable place, Mitch, possibly the last town your eyes beheld. How long did you bear it here before striking out towards Smara with a pocketful of almonds and a plastic bottle of Sidi Ali water?

What's this one called? The Hotel de Sahara. Well, that makes sense. It looks similar to the others. I can't see very well, my eyes won't focus, everything is blurred. I can only think of a bed, I am obsessed with the idea of a bed, any kind of bed, I'm not fussy. There is no *fiche* to fill out at this kind of place, of course not. In the bare entrance a man gives me a key, says the room costs fifteen dirhams, points upward, disappears. It's surprising that he doesn't ask for payment in advance, especially since I have no luggage except for one brown blanket. With only fifty dirhams left, I may have to practise leeway at this place. You know how to do that, don't you, you can't say I didn't teach you that.

At the top of the stairs a long, straight hallway is lined on one side with large, open windows which look out on the desert; on the other side, innumerable doors lead to small cubicles, no more than twelve feet by twelve, separated by walls which do not reach the ceiling. There is no window; until I turn on the light, the room is dim. The furniture consists of a cot. A bare, cement space permeated with the smell of a thousand soldiers, with sand and cigarette butts scattered across the floor.

I turn off the light and fall on the bed. I know about cells. After Los Angeles and Mexico, I know about scratching a calendar of days on the wall, and about floating free of your body, floating free of too many empty hours. I know about waiting for the door to open and the sentence to end. Self-imposed or not, it's the same.

Someone coughs nearby. Or is that the sound of praying? Is that the sound of myself praying in the dark? I rise above the surface of the bed, hover for a moment in the air, then am swiftly hurled down into darkness.


Is that you?

The shape stands six steps away, a silhouette slightly blacker than the darkness. I smell clean, strong soap; it is a very particular, familiar scent. A lit cigarette lifts and glows more brightly as it is inhaled upon. Just bright enough for me to see a suggestion of his face for one moment, before his hand lowers the cigarette again. Why does he stand there and watch me? Why doesn't he take six steps and hold me in his arms? I can't go to him myself. I can't lift myself from where I lie. I am buried beneath a low dune of sand; only my face is uncovered. The weight is too heavy to push off; I am not strong enough. I taste almonds in my mouth and see stars swim above. "Help," I say. "Please help." He remains motionless, as if he has not heard my voice, as if he were a thousand miles away. I smell the smoke of black tobacco; it is another very particular, familiar scent. I wait anxiously for the cigarette to lift to his mouth and illuminate his face again. To hint at the shape of his mouth, the slope of his cheekbones, the line of his nose. I struggle beneath the sand. I need to see his eyes. I need to see their expression to understand why he does not come to me and help me. The cigarette burns low. He drops it. I watch the falling glow. It seems to fall for minutes, to fall as far as a star from sky to earth, to fall for a thousand miles before it hits the ground with a spray of sparks. When I look up again, he is gone.

Was that you?


Is that you?

In the evening, having been woken by sharp hunger, I stand in the bathroom down the hall. I would have slept until morning if I weren't so hungry. All my life hunger has woken me, stirred me into motion, saved me from drifting for decades in dreams. I look into the small, cracked mirror nailed above the filthy sink. The face that stares from the speckled glass is darkly tanned and thin. Its features seem to have subtly shifted position. My eyes have narrowed into a fixed squint; they glitter, as though holding too much light. Reaching halfway to my shoulders, my hair appears lighter in colour, and streaked with silver. The same silver as the chain and cross around my neck. I finger the chain. It appears so fragile; it has proven so strong. I am amazed that it hasn't broken during this journey, amazed that the cross it holds hasn't become lost.

I attempt a smile. The face splits in half. No wonder it was hard to find a room, looking like this. I wouldn't recognize me if I passed myself on the street.

I step over a pool of urine and excrement that washes around a hole in the floor. A faucet emerges from halfway up the far wall. I find a scrap of soap on the floor, stand beneath the cold water, try to scrub layers of dirt from my skin. Afterwards, I stand shivering until nearly dry. Reluctantly, I put on my clothes. They should be burned.

Leaving the bathroom, I notice an open doorway across the hall. It leads into an empty room about twice the size of my cubicle. A roughly woven carpet covers the floor. Three walls are blank white. The green silhouette of a mosque is crudely painted on the wall that faces east, towards Mecca. A prayer room. I slip inside and kneel on the carpet, still damp from my ablution. For a moment I don't know who to pray to or what to pray for. I remember waking an hour ago in the darkness, turning on the light, wondering if I only imagined that a scent of strong soap lingered in the air. Crawling amid the cigarette butts scattered on the floor, searching for one with the word *Ducado* written above the filter.

The end of my journey is near, God. I wish to pray that it brings me what I need. Only one more stage remains until I reach the place, somewhere between here and Smara, where my father's passport was discovered near a roadside café. Help me make it there. Help me discover what I need to find, my Father. Help me.

The streets are nearly empty and dark; there are few lights, and the town appears blacked out. The wind moans and dust whips wildly above the ground. The buildings are shuttered tight against the desert night. Spotting a soldier on a corner ahead, I cross the street and pass on the other side. Rats scurry into the blind alleys at my approach. A thin dogs trots by with what appears to be a human hand in its mouth.

My God, what a place. Surely the end of the world. I wonder how you saw this place, Mitch. To your eyes it may not have appeared sinister and secretive. After all the cracks and edges of the world in which you operated for so long, it may have appeared quite ordinary.

I hear music down the block. Something Western, something familiar. Light slopes from a doorway across the street. Café Oasis is spelled in bright-green neon above the door. I pause, surprised and disbelieving, then quickly approach the music and light.

The Café Oasis is clean and brightly lit, with a dozen glass tables and cane chairs scattered across a floor of gleaming tile. Bowls of bright fruit decorate a glass counter, with pastries arranged neatly in the cases below. A fan revolves slowly on the ceiling. Five young Moroccans sprawl around a table littered with glasses of coffee, appearing very much at home.

They stop talking as I enter. A burst of laughter trails into silence. One young man moves behind the counter and smiles as I point to several pastries. He has bright eyes and shining hair; his face gleams in invitation. I sit at a table and eat ravenously, not once looking up from my plate. When my plate is bare, I lift my head and everyone laughs; these boys have been watching me eat, they are amused by my fierce hunger.

"*J'ai beaucoup de faim*," I laugh. "*Comme un cheval.*"

"*Comme un camel*," corrects the boy behind the counter.

We talk while he makes me coffee. His name is Omar. With his brother, Ramedi, one of the boys at the next table, Omar runs this café. The other boys are their friends. After the coffee I have a blended drink made with bananas and milk, then Omar brings *harira* and bread from a room in the back. Tears of gratitude leak from my eyes as I eat and drink. "Sand," I explain, wiping my eyes and laughing until the boys, who have looked concerned at my tears, laugh also.

The room glows with warmth and light and music. I feel very

peaceful, somewhat sleepy. Basking thankfully in the café, I am hardly aware what Omar and Ramedi say, and what I answer. I think they are telling me how much they like Layounne. They used to live in the north, but prefer it here. Things are simpler and easier in the Sahara, they say. What is that song? Ramedi keeps changing the cassette in midsong. He is eager to show me how much Western music he has; he wishes to talk about Michael Jackson and Madonna. The three other boys are shyer; content to laugh like a chorus at Omar's jokes, they scarcely speak. I smile and nod and look around the Café Oasis.

Omar and Ramedi are excited to have me here, anxious that I fully enjoy their hospitality, intent on outdoing each other as attentive hosts. There are never tourists in Layounne, they say. Only UN personnel, unhappy and suspicious and mistrustful, who keep to themselves. Omar and Ramedi want me to return tomorrow to the Café Oasis. I must promise. More of their friends will be here. We can laugh together. We can drink tea together.

Omar becomes offended when I take out my money. "No," he says, suddenly mournful and disappointed. "Please, no." He quickly brightens again. "You can send us a picture of Michael Jackson and Madonna. That will make us happy."

As I leave the Café Oasis, Omar is putting away the pastries for the night, Ramedi is wiping the glass tables, and their three friends bob and weave to the music. Amid promises that tomorrow I will return to drink tea together, I step back into the dark, gusty night.

*Allah-o-Akbar. Allah Lillah. Bismi Allahi.*

I am wakened by the *Fajr* prayer of dawn. I lie in darkness and listen to droning voices in the prayer room down the hall. Nearer, just on the other side of my cell's thin wall, a soldier spits his stomach onto the floor. I hear the retch, then the splatter against cement.

I wonder, God, if I am sufficiently rested to proceed to Smara and to meet what awaits me there. Once again I wearily attempt to sort out the various scenarios which might surround my father's disappearance. Perhaps Mitch deliberately dropped his passport by the road between here and Smara; he wished us to believe that he was irrevocably lost and presumably dead somewhere upon the desert. Perhaps, at the moment his passport dropped upon the sand, he felt free to walk away from his past, unencumbered. Now nothing prevented him from joining up with the Polisarios for one more action, for one more operation. He slipped free from the taint of too many years of failed connections and missed contacts. He liberated himself from the burdensome memory of Ardis and Lily, MJ and myself. With his shadow he stepped away from the role he had played in our lives. And the last thing he wanted, in fact, was to lure me to look for him at the end of the world. The only thing he wanted was to escape for good.

Yet I will try to find the exact place, near a roadside café, where his passport was discovered. At the place and in that moment, with or without solid evidence, I will reach some final understanding about what happened to my father. I am prepared to understand, in the end, that I will never know for certain what happened to him.

After a breakfast of coffee and bread in an especially bleak café, I decide to explore Layounne. I might as well look around while I'm here. You might find something, I vaguely think. And after all this time, Smara can wait one more day. Climbing the dusty streets towards the upper town, I deliberately avoid the Café Oasis. I hope for another kind of small miracle today.

I am startled to discover that Layounne's single large hotel, perched on the upper slope of the desert, is called the Royale. I experience the dizzying sensation of coming full circle. I wonder if this Hotel Royale offers room service and if its menu is written in French but priced in U.S. dollars. If in one of its rooms three children play complex games of cards while waiting for their father to return from searching for contacts and connections. They pick at *salade niçoise* and listen to the air conditioner hum in the hall. From 1973 to 1993 they wait and grow old and refuse to give up hope in the Hotel Royale. "He's not coming back," MJ finally says, after twenty years, while Lily huddles in a corner over a white valise and before the window Richard looks down at vehicles, marked with the letters UN, parked beside the wilted palms.

Holding my breath, I walk past the white UN jeeps and trucks. The air is already muggy and hot. I don't know why it is so humid here, why there are so many flies, why everyone looks so grim. The size of the upper town is surprising. The streets, lined with shops, are wider than those below; they are slightly more lively and modern, slightly less dismal. After wandering for several hours, I gradually realize that my poor sense of direction has let me down. I can't find my way back to the lower town. The streets insist upon remaining flat, the land refuses to slope downward, and I suspect I am walking farther from the lower town instead of closer to it.

The streets with shops trail away and I find myself on a dirt road lined on either side with tents, with only a few shacks made of scraps of tin, set right upon the desert floor. Sprawling, temporary, without design, the city of tents resembles a refugee camp. A long queue waits before what appears to be a single water pump. Barefoot children dressed in rags play listlessly in the dust. Perhaps these are the families of soldiers stationed in Layounne. They look like people who have left everything behind.

Suddenly these camps end, and a different kind of tent city appears on one side of the road. This area looks more permanent and orderly. The tents are much larger, huge bubbles of brown and black material arching over the flat earth, with Moroccan flags stitched to their sides. Many Moroccan soldiers and army vehicles are visible. This is the military camp of Layounne, I realize. The centre of all the forces in the southern Sahara.

The flat, straight road stretches forward, and the military camp extends as far as I can see. There is still no suggestion that the desert may slope downward anywhere soon. I have no idea where I am.

I approach a young soldier standing at slack attention beside the road. When I ask him to point me in the direction of the lower town, he hesitates. It's not a difficult question, I think, irritated by the humidity and dust and heat, annoyed with myself for becoming lost.

"This way." He leads me across the road and into what resembles a makeshift office. A uniformed man sits at a flimsy table littered with papers. Except for a few chairs, and a picture of the king on the wall, the cement room is bare.

The young soldier speaks quickly to the official in Arabic. After the soldier leaves, the official requests my passport. He proceeds to ask the same questions I was asked in the patrol stations in the desert. Where have I come from? Where am I going? What am I doing? Weary of this old routine, I answer automatically. He slowly writes down the information I offer, then asks me to follow him to a similar office next door.

Another official, in precisely the same uniform, asks me exactly the same questions. I have the impression that these men have little to occupy themselves with in their makeshift offices; they are using me to relieve their boredom for half an hour. I just told the other man all this. Don't you have anything better to do with your time? I nearly snap as the second official painstakingly

writes down my mother's name, my father's name, my grandparents' names. I am tired of these questions. I am hungry and
thirsty. All I want is to return to the lower town and drink tea in
the Café Oasis.

This official finally leads me across the road and into the military camp. We enter one of the large tents. It is cool and dim and
neat, and surprisingly comfortable, with carpets and cushions and
cots. Glaring at a portrait of the king nailed to a post, I once more
answer the same questions and try not to reveal how impatient
they make me. This soldier wears more medals and stripes of braid
on his uniform; his air suggests he is important and his questions
seem to go on forever. These questions are beginning to bewilder
me; once straightforward and simple, they seem to grow more
complex with repetition. Who am I? Where have I come from?
Where am I going? I start to hesitate uncertainly; I am no longer
sure of these basic facts. My identity assumes the nebulous,
ambiguous quality of a character in a dream.

When I am led to another tent, the situation takes on the
aspect of a nightmare in which you are brought from one room to
another to another in endless succession, and in each room you
are asked the same questions because you fail to provide the correct answers. But these are the only answers you have, you don't
have the answers which will end this process, you know you will
be once more taken to another room and asked the same questions, you know this will go on forever.

This tent is more imposingly furnished with heavy desks and
numerous filing cabinets. Several soldiers hover near a large, older
officer who sits commandingly at the biggest desk. Though I
can't guess his rank, he is obviously quite important; it is clear that
we are climbing a ladder of command, and the situation assumes
more gravity as it is passed to higher authority. There is no sense
of hurry or urgency as the same questions are once more slowly
posed. I want to ask what is wrong, but decide not to; that would

not improve matters, I somehow know. After being asked if I carry a camera and have been taking photographs, I have an idea what the problem is. I listen to the hovering soldiers confer in rapid-fire Arabic with their superior; I can't make out what they are saying. Presumably, the situation is being debated; several courses of action are proposed and rejected before one is settled upon. At last two of the soldiers motion for me to follow them from the tent. I will be able to go now, I think. My passport will be returned to me and I will be free to walk away.

Instead, I am ordered into the back of a military van. I begin to worry; the situation has become serious. I have no money or luggage, despite saying that both are at the Hotel de Sahara, to back my claim that I am a harmless, ordinary tourist. Through the small window I see that we are travelling towards the lower town. The van bumps down the desert slope. At least I am returning to familiar territory. Stay calm. Nothing has really happened yet. Perhaps I am simply being taken back to the lower town by these two helpful soldiers.

The van stops, the back door opens, I climb out. One of the soldiers firmly holds my arm. Before us rises a large white building with a Moroccan flag flying in front of it. The police station.

"What's wrong?" I ask. Neither soldier answers.

Inside the station I am taken at once into a room cluttered with desks and papers and chairs. After a moment a man in a grey uniform enters and begins to pose the familiar litany of questions.

"I have answered these questions five times," I say. "What is the problem?"

Instead of answering these questions five times, I should ask one of my own. I should ask about my father. For example, I should ask how I might find out if there exists any official record of my father's presence in Layounne last year.

No, don't make a dicey situation more complicated. "What is the problem?" I repeat more tersely.

Ignoring my question, the police officer continues with his own. He focuses upon whether I have a camera and if I have taken photographs.

I try to convey that I was exploring Layounne and became lost. I had no idea where I was. I know nothing about the army and am not interested in the subject. I am simply visiting Layounne for several days. Then I will return north to meet my friends in Agadir.

The officer writes down my replies, then leaves the room. He closes the door behind him and a key turns in the lock.

This is what happens. Once you fall into this kind of situation, it is very difficult to extricate yourself. This is a web with many strands. I am in the hands of too many officials, both military and civilian, with too much time on their hands and too little to do. They have happened upon a case that is somewhat unusual. Their interest is piqued. I could very well spend several weeks answering the same questions without the issue reaching any definite conclusion.

The key turns, the door opens, the police officer re-enters. At once he says that this situation is very serious. I have been in the wrong place. It is forbidden to enter the area of the military camp. There are penalties, there are consequences. I must understand that this is a very serious matter.

Careful. This is the critical moment. I must not protest that there were no signs or guards to warn me that I was stumbling into a highly sensitive area. I must not reveal the slightest sign of impatience or irritation now. It is especially important that I not show how ridiculous the matter seems to me.

Another man, who resembles a clerk, sticks his head in the doorway.

"Telephone," he says.

"Wait," instructs the officer. "One moment."

I stare at the obligatory portrait of the king with my back to the door. In some portraits the king looks pious; in others, he appears paternal or severe. My favourite one shows him as a flashy oil sheik. No matter how much he is despised, the king must look down at his subjects at every possible moment. Omniscient, all powerful, everpresent, he watches us and keeps us in a constant state of fear.

I listen for the door to close and the key to turn in the lock behind me. Silence. Turning, I see that the door stands ajar. My passport lies on the desk beside me. I pick up my passport, walk to the door, and step into the hallway. It is empty. Several doors lead off the hall; I hear voices behind them. The back of a head is visible in the open doorway of the furthest room. I take six steps, turn the corner, see the street before me. No one guards the entrance or the door. Though I expect to see the military van and two soldiers waiting before the station, the street is empty.

I step into the heavy air and walk quickly without glancing behind. I turn the first corner I reach. My heart thumps loudly inside me; beyond, the air seems peculiarly silent and still. Then the *muezzin* calls from a nearby mosque. The *Asr* prayer. It must be the middle of afternoon. I keep walking quickly, expecting to hear shouts and footsteps behind me at any moment. I cross a small square where three soldiers squat and smoke and play cards. They don't look up as I pass.

If I wasn't in serious trouble before, I certainly am now. In this kind of country the police are especially touchy about foreigners. They are particularly anxious to insist that, no matter how wealthy the country you are from, here you are under their authority. Your privilege means nothing to them; in fact, they resent it, and will take pains to assert their resentment.

Obviously I can't return to the Hotel de Sahara. I stated that I was staying there. Never mind. I have nothing except my brown blanket in that room. Mitch, it is time to practise a little leeway. It's time to get out of town. If the bad guys don't get us, the good guys will. Remember? We've done this before. I know how to do this. You taught me this at least.

At a street stall I stop to buy a paper cone filled with almonds and a plastic bottle of Sidi Ali water. I ask the old man where to find the road to Smara. He doesn't understand French. "Smara," I repeat. He points to the upper town. Yes, the road to Smara must begin there, at the eastern edge of Layounne. I swiftly climb the narrowest roads I can find; they are too narrow for trucks to pass through, and are less likely to be patrolled by soldiers or police. Along the way I ask directions to the road to Smara several more times. I can't afford to get lost again. Not at this point. I feel fairly certain that I am heading roughly in the right direction.

Suddenly I reach the edge of Layounne. The desert stretches before me. A little girl in rags plays with a stick in the dirt. Her face is covered with open sores clotted with blood and flies. "Smara?" I ask. She points to a track leading into the desert. I hadn't noticed it because it is so faint, barely distinguishable upon the desert, not a road at all, only sand packed slightly harder than the sand surrounding it.

I didn't mention Smara to the military or the police. I am returning to Agadir to meet my friends, I said. Neither the military nor the police will look for me on this track; this is the last place they would think of finding me. Still, I must be careful. I have no idea how many soldiers may roam this part of the desert, preserving an uneasy peace, looking for anything that might threaten to disturb it.

I am sorry, Omar and Ramedi, but we will not have tea together today.


After an hour I lose any fear of being followed from Layounne, and the adrenalin produced by the excitement of my escape evaporates. I walk dully through the afternoon heat and concentrate upon the difficult task of staying on the track to Smara. It is still only sand packed slightly firmer than the surrounding desert, which in turn remains almost flat, without even low dunes to throw the path into relief. Every several hundred yards or so the track is marked by a large stone placed at its side. Without these guides, I would lose my way a dozen times a mile; as it is, I almost wander off course now and then, however carefully I proceed. I don't know what I will do when darkness falls and limits my vision; tonight the moon will not be full, the sand will not gleam with light. And I do not know how I will survive the cold of desert night without the brown blanket.

As light drains from the landscape, I slowly fill with sadness until the emotion pulls like quicksand at my feet and tries to drag me down. Arriving out of nowhere, inexplicably, the sorrow overwhelms me, and frightens me more than knowledge of approaching darkness and cold.

You feel that you are walking away from the world – forever, for good. You are leaving the world behind without having had the chance to say a proper goodbye. You never knew how much you loved the world; you were not able to value that love sufficiently. You took it for granted, didn't you?

I am exhausted and weak and overwhelmed by an emotion that has no reasonable source. Snap out of it, advises Reyna. You are only walking to the place where your father's passport was found. You are only bringing this search, which you no longer expect to offer significant rewards, to an end. You are fulfilling your part of the bargain so that in the future, when you have settled back into your life, you can say that once your father disappeared and you went to look for him. Out of duty, you did that one last thing for him – and for Ardis and MJ and Lily, and for yourself. You did it to the best of your ability and at some risk, before closing the book on that man and allowing him to occupy only the space we allot for our lost and our dead, and no more.

364

I am not leaving the world at all, I inform myself. In fact, every step I now take brings me closer to the moment when I will be able to return – somehow, with the help of a small miracle – to Jose in Madrid. Perhaps this sorrow is produced by the utter emptiness of the desert; I do not meet a single being as I continue forward, east and slightly north, on this *hejira* where Mecca is Layounne and Medina is Smara, and where a flight from danger is also an honourable escape.

I sit on a marker stone, while the sun lowers below the horizon, and eat the last of the almonds with the remaining bottled water. As the violent, flaming reminder of the sun fades from the sky, and becomes absorbed by darkness, the sadness inside me turns mute and dim, then seeps into the air, drifts away, dissolves.

No, Mitch, I do not want to leave the world. I found the world only shortly before setting out on this journey and I do not wish to lose it again. It is much too soon.

Rising, I look behind. The lights of Layounne lie far beyond my sight. My feet turn to move in that direction. No, I instruct them. Go forward. You are almost there. If you don't continue now, you will always suspect, in the darkest, deepest room of your mind, that only a short distance beyond where you turned around, your father was waiting impatiently beside a roadside café outside of Smara. "What took you?" he would have asked. "Let's get a move on. It's only a hop, skip and a jump from here. Trust me, kiddo. You'll love it there. Where? What the hell do you mean by that? Where do you think?" My father's eyes shine in the darkness; they are all I can see of him. The bones of his fingers grip my shoulder; the scent of lemons curls around us. We move forward through the last door of the desert, the door that closes behind you for good, the door you can never open again.

I walk slowly but steadily through the night, peer closely at the ground, squint to see the indistinct track I must not lose sight of. I have never looked so closely at this earth. At some point during the night, when it seems to have taken an hour to walk from one marking stone to the next, I wonder if it would be faster to crawl. At some point I wonder why I do not feel hungry or thirsty, tired or cold. At some point I believe I have walked into the sky and can see, miles below, a large, dark ball twirling slowly in space. At some point, when I have not seen a marker for a long time, I realize that I have wandered off the track to Smara.

"Don't worry," my father whispers insinuatingly into my ear. "There's no such thing as being lost."

"Shut up," I tell the coaxing voice that falsely promises that I am almost there.


Where are you now? I bitterly ask at dawn.

Daylight offers no illumination or relief. It only reveals flat desert that stretches in all directions. I have no idea where I am. I have no clue where the track to Smara might lie. There seems little point in walking forward when every step might take me further in the wrong direction.

Where are you when I really need you?

The desert has altered during the night. Now it is no longer made of sand; instead, it presents a surface of hard, baked earth spit with numerous cracks. It looks like the dried bed of a lake or sea that has been forsaken by water.

I kneel on the desert floor and pray beneath the rising sun. *Allah-o-Akbar, Alhamdo, Lillah, Bismi Allahi. . . .* I finger the silver cross around my neck and close my eyes until an image of Jose floats before me and lifts me to my feet. Keep going, he urges. It doesn't matter that you don't know what direction to take. At this moment it only matters that you keep moving.

The desert rises before me and hits my face. Please, he begs. Don't stop. I crawl forward. Jose walks slowly beside me. I am the shadow falling by his side, the shape of his soul floating across the ground. Don't stop moving forward, he pleads. Don't stop. Don't.

The sun rises higher and burns hotter. The desert keeps lifting up to hit my face. A promise of water shimmers before me, just out of reach. I inch forward again. A bullet from the sun shoots from the sky, pierces the back of my head, explodes me into liquid darkness.

# V.

"You're back."

Dunes cease rising and falling below me, a bed settles solid and still in their place. My head turns in the direction of the voice. Beside the bed a blurred figure shifts into focus: a woman sitting in a straight-backed chair lowers a copy of *Paris-Match* to her lap. She shakes a tablet from a vial, pours water from a jug on the table beside her, and hands me the glass and pill. She is in her mid-thirties, with short blond hair, pale-blue eyes, and a washed-out complexion. Her tan slacks and blue blouse are neat. Her expression is carefully neutral.

Dagmar or Anke. From Frankfurt or Munich or Berlin.

"Where am I?"

"The Hotel Royale," she says smoothly, startlingly; I thought my question was addressed silently to myself. "In Layounne, I'm afraid. It's not much, but I gather it's a cut above the other places where you've been staying since El Jadida. You were in El Jadida, weren't you? You contacted us from there? Anyway. The Royale was the only place we could put you. There's no decent hospital or clinic down here, of course, and regulations made the UN infirmary out of the question. But Patterson, the CMO there, has been good enough to take your case anyway. He'll be around again later this afternoon."

I hand back the glass. The bitter pill has lodged in my throat. Water has dribbled down my chin onto the front of my white pyjamas. I try and fail to figure out where these pyjamas have come from. Who has bathed me. Who has washed my hair. My heavy head sinks into the soft pillow, sinks down through water, sinks deeper and deeper. Fighting to the surface, I sputter, cough. My fingers grip the sheets. Smooth and rough at once, they smell heavily of bleach. The Royal Hotel. Housekeeping.

"I have to get to Smara."

I try to speak slowly and distinctly, but the words sound like a slurred moan to my ears.

"You were quite lucky, you know," the woman says with a hint of annoyance. "Moroccan patrols found you in the desert just in time. Completely by chance. One in a million odds, as they say. Another hour or two in the sun and it would have been too late, according to Patterson. They contacted us at the Rabat consulate because of your passport. That was three weeks ago. I made the arrangements for you here in the Royale then flew down as soon as I could. It's simply been a question of waiting. I'm sorry. My name is Alice Murrow."

Not German. Canadian. Of course. That flat voice. Those cautious eyes. The chilly air.

"Three weeks? Are you sure it was that long ago?"

"I think I can be sure of the date. Today is March 2. At least this happened before Ramadan. Two weeks later and it would have been impossible. You can't do anything in this country once they start in on starving and abstaining and constant praying. We should get this situation settled in the nick of time. But we weren't sure you would make it until today," Alice Murrow continues. "Fifty-fifty, as they say. You turned the corner this

369

morning when your fever broke. You were quite lucky," she repeats rebukingly, as though I insufficiently appreciate my good fortune.

Alice Murrow picks up her magazine and frowns into it. My head burns, my throat scratches, my bones ache. I am too weak to lift these covers and rise from this bed. I can't walk from this clean, sparsely furnished room in the Hotel Royale in Layounne. There is a reason why I should leave this room. Somewhere I need to go, something I need to do. I can't think what; my mind is heavy and empty. My eyes hurt and I can't see the door from this room. Though the shutters are closed and the room is dim, the light is still too bright. The turning pages of the magazine scrapes my ears. The blades of a ceiling fan whirl directly above the bed. They shift in and out of focus. The woman near me sighs softly and the room slowly spins. The fan blurs. The air around it dims further, then darkens.


"I have to find my father."

Alice Murrow turns from the window. The shutters are open and the sky beyond is dark. I faintly recall the doctor's afternoon visit. A needle sinking into my arm? A scent of mint? A Scottish accent? Now the room glows in lamplight; it is still too bright for my eyes. The woman's face appears more vulnerable and uncertain in this light. I wonder how long she has been stationed in Rabat, what her life there is like, how much she yearns to be posted in Paris or returned to Ottawa.

"Yes, I'm sorry about your father."

"What have you heard?" I try to sit up, then wince as pain shoots through my head.

She looks embarrassed. "We haven't heard anything. I meant that we are well aware of the situation. His file is still very much active. We are continuing to do everything we can. But it doesn't look good. It's been a year now, hasn't it?"

Has it, Alice Murrow? Surely you should know that. Surely you should know something.

A dog barks in the distance. The room is silent except for the faint buzzing of the ceiling fan. A slight breeze carries the scent of the desert through the open window. Closing my eyes, I breathe deeply. Once more I rise and fall over dunes, crawl across sand, float beneath moon and stars. Opening my eyes, I see Alice Murrow press both hands against her temples.

"How do you feel?" The words are as forced as the tone. This situation is disagreeable for Alice Murrow. Flying in a four-seat prop plane down to godforsaken Layounne. Taking care of an irresponsible Canadian who has allowed himself to get into a situation that no Canadian should get into. Waiting around in this hotel, scarcely able to take a step outside – not that anyone would want to, not here, not in this place that makes Rabat seem like Paris. As they say.

I shouldn't be in this position. Alice Murrow, you're right. I shouldn't be lying in the Hotel Royale under your watchful eyes. This is my mistake. My own mistake. I should be in the desert. There is something more I need to do there. Something I didn't finish. Something.

"Did I say anything during the fever?"

Her lips tighten. "Not really," she replies uneasily. "Nothing to speak of." She lights a Dunhill cigarette. "Now it's just a question of time. Plenty of food, liquids, rest. You were seriously malnourished on top of everything else, you know. You can ask Patterson about your treatment if you wish. He says you'll be up and about in a few days. As good as new, as they say. We'll head up to Rabat, then put you on the first plane home."

She turns to the window and looks upon the lower town spread below. "The first plane home," she repeats, closing the shutters, keeping out the perfumed desert air.

Three days pass. My throat no longer scratches, my body no longer aches. Though my head feels less heavy, my eyes remain sensitive to light. I drift in and out of sleep. A hotel waiter knocks and enters with a tray of food. The doctor, calmly efficient, visits each afternoon. Alice Murrow has the room next to mine, I gather. Sometimes I wake to find her sitting in the chair or standing by the window; at other times, the room is empty, and shadows stir in the corners. MJ and Lily whisper. I can't make out what they say. I have forgotten our ancient, secret language.

"I spoke to your mother," Alice says once. She pauses awkwardly. She has not become more comfortable with me; there is something distasteful about me, something that bothers her. "I am sorry she is unable to help you."

What does this mean? Ardis is unable to fly from Canada to take care of her foolish son? Ardis is unable to pay for a ticket to fly me out of Morocco? Ardis was unable to speak coherently when she received this latest call from the Canadian consulate? This latest call was too much for her?

I sense that part of Alice Murrow wants to know how I ended up without luggage or money and near death in the desert. Another part of her really doesn't want to know. She is waiting to ask this until I am stronger or until we are at the Canadian consulate in Rabat, where the correct procedure may be followed. Or perhaps it is not her position to ask. She is, I think, a consular assistant or aide, at most.

During her absences from the room, I remind myself to ask her questions of my own. If any of Mitch's belongings have found their way to the Rabat consulate. What exactly is being done at present to find him. And if the Moroccan authorities have expressed interest in my case. As soon as I see Alice Murrow again, however, her stiff presence suggests that there is nothing she could tell me. Or perhaps part of me really doesn't want to know.

I pick at trays of food and sip liquids and rest. I creep into the bathroom, fall back into bed. I imagine Alice Murrow sighing and flipping pages of old issues of *Paris-Match* in the next room. Or she ventures down to the bar – there would be alcohol for the UN in this hotel – to flirt cautiously or to share North African horror stories with the uniformed brass. You wouldn't believe the case I've got up there, she says, pointing to the ceiling.

Three floors above I dream about the desert. I dream of shadows floating across the sand and buzzards circling in the sky. I dream of drowning in pools of the bluest water while my father, sitting beneath a green palm on the bank, watches with bright eyes and whistles.

On the fourth day I waken to find clothes folded neatly on the chair beside the bed. "They should fit," says Alice Murrow. "More or less. We had to burn your others. By the way, we're set to fly to Rabat tomorrow."

"I'm not going to Canada."

The impatience and irritation hidden behind her careful mask breaks through. "I think," she says, "you are hardly in a position to pick and choose. You should be grateful for any help you get, without trying to dictate its terms. There is a certain procedure to be followed in this case. It is really out of your hands. Your situation calls for you to be repatriated. That means being returned to the country whose passport you carry. That means Canada."

"I'm not going to Canada," I repeat.

"Once you are returned to Canada," she continues in a raised voice, "your passport will be taken from you. When you repay the cost of your ticket to the Department of External Affairs, your passport will be returned. This is not a free ride. This is not pleasant for anyone. Do you think I want to be here looking after someone who lacks the intelligence to look after himself?"

"I live in Spain. I will repay the cost of a ticket to Madrid. You can hold my passport until then."

We stare at each other for a long moment. From the mosque below the *muezzin* calls the *Maghrib* prayer. Alice Murrow finally sighs. "I will have to put a call through to Rabat. I'm not authorized to make this decision, but it's highly unlikely to be approved. I can tell you that."

Turning on her heel, she leaves the room. I close my eyes and listen to the *muezzin's* call fade through the air. I drift with it through the darkening sky, across the desert, beneath bright, cold stars. Waking at night, I am disappointed to find myself still in the Hotel Royale. I try on the clothes folded on the chair, then look in the bathroom mirror. Jose, is that me? A white dress shirt with short sleeves. Grey polyester trousers. Pointed black shoes. Neither clothes nor shoes really fit; the former are too large, the latter too small. I feel stiff, constricted, imprisoned in them. Walking to the window, I look into the night, then at the ground three storeys below. Too far to jump.

I cross to the door. It is locked from the outside. The handle won't turn. Angrily, I try to twist it back and forth, then give up. A faint cough sounds from the hall beyond.


"Madrid it will be," says Alice Murrow early the next morning. Her face is strained and tight in the cold, grey air. I am dressed in my new clothes. Our plane departs for Casablanca in an hour. When I mention that I'd like to thank Dr. Patterson for his care before we leave, Alice Murrow curtly suggests that isn't necessary. "We're doing our jobs," she pointedly remarks.

With a stop to refuel in Agadir, we will arrive in the afternoon at Casablanca, where officials from the Canadian consulate in Rabat will await us. A meeting will take place in the Casablanca airport. A statement will be prepared and a report will be made. I will sign both. My passport will be taken from me; a temporary, one-month passport, along with $100 U.S., will be issued in return. Then I will be put on an evening flight to Madrid, with one brief stopover in Gibraltar.

Alice Murrow has made it clear that these expedited arrangements have been made to get me out of the country and out of the consulate's hands as quickly as possible. I have created an unwelcome problem on top of the already difficult problem of my father's situation. I must not allow this kind of problem to occur again. No one will go out of their way to pick up the pieces if it does. Alice Murrow will be glad to see the last of Layounne and the last of me.

The hotel car waits below. The four-seat prop plane waits at the airfield at the edge of town. I look around this room in the Hotel Royale, then turn my eyes to the sky beyond the window. A door opens in the sky as it changes from grey to blue. Another room appears through that door. It is a room I haven't seen before.

"Are you ready?" asks Alice Murrow. She steps into the hall.

I gaze towards the sky and through its blue door and into its upper room. A sense of loss sweeps over me; swaying, I reach for the bedside table for support. Stabbing loss turns into something gentler, something bearable. I smell the heavy bleach on my clothes and feel the unfamiliar shoes pinch my feet. My fingers touch the cross around my neck.

Am I ready? Of course not.

That doesn't stop me from turning from the window and stepping from the room.

# V

## *The Upper Room*

"There is always one moment . . . when the door
opens and lets the future in."

– Graham Greene

# i.

"We're here."

The taxi pulls up to the curb on Gran Vía. At midnight the wide avenue is gaudy with neon and traffic and noise. A particular kind of light – here glowing diffusely over old stone and iron façades, there sharply illuminating a slice of sidewalk – renders the scene intensely familiar and strange at once. Crowds of Madrileños stroll between cafés and cinemas and bars. *Bocadillos, Coca-Cola, bocadillos,* sing-song Vietnamese hawking plastic bags containing sandwiches and sodas. Women in fur coats step past Moroccans and Sudanese who lean on corners with heroin and hashish for sale. Darker, narrower and less crowded, the Calle Horteleza rises from the avenue. Jose stands in a doorway three blocks up that street, and the new moon floats further above.

"We're here," repeats the driver.

I rub my eyes in the back seat. The scene around me glistens with the light of a hallucination. I have seen versions of it many times before, yet now it appears unknown. Now it shines like a mirage in the dark desert around me. I rub my eyes again. For some reason, they persist in watering almost constantly since my experience in the desert. Something happened to my vision there; after those extremes of blazing light and pure darkness, my eyes no longer tolerate ordinary illumination. I'm not certain what the condition is called (you have to call it something), and if it will linger until I am upon the sweeping sand again.

"Let the meter run for a moment," I say. "I'm not quite ready."

Was it only this morning I left Layounne? Five hours in a small plane with Alice Murrow oozing disapproval and Chanel beside me. An unpleasant meeting in the Casablanca airport with two officials from the Canadian consulate in Rabat. Sign statement, hand over passport, receive temporary document and U.S. cash in return. Pointed silence when I ask if there is any new word about Mitch. The Royal Air Maroc flight to Madrid, with a brief touchdown in Gibraltar. The difficulty of passing through Spanish customs with a temporary passport and the costume of a refugee.

*Who are you? Where have you come from? Where are you going?*

I shiver in the seat, though not with cold; it was this cold in the desert at night. The cab's scent is a familiar mixture of sharp pine disinfectant and the stale smoke of tobacco. A very heavy scent. I want to close my eyes and sink into this strong scent and swoon away from this moment: shivering in the back of a Madrid taxi near the beginning of March 1993.

The driver clears his throat and glances curiously at me in the rear-view mirror. Of course I must look strange in these odd, ill-fitting clothes, with watering eyes, lined and darkened face, long hair streaked with grey. But there's something more than that. I stir on the seat. Something else feels different. Yes. The ancient web of threads — so fine as to be invisible, so strong as to be unbreakable — that has always connected me to Mitch and Ardis, MJ and Lily, even across the greatest distance, has loosened around me. It is still there, the web, but now I can breathe more freely and easily within it.

Wait. Why can't I feel more clearly the newer thread that connects me to the being three blocks away? Isn't it there, strong as a lifeline, after all?

Was it you I failed to find upon the desert?

Of course I'm not ready, Jose.

How could I have thought I would be ready for you – now, so soon, so late?

I pay the driver, step out of the cab, and wind my way through the Gran Vía crowds into Horteleza. The night is cool and fresh; spring will soon be here. I climb past small, bright cafés and stores; then older buildings of three storeys, unlit and silent and apparently abandoned, loom on either side. The street seems much steeper than I know it to be. I feel that I am climbing very high, rising into the sky, nearing the upper room.

The sign appears amid a long block of darkened buildings on my left. Blue neon scrawls the word Ras above a doorway. In the blue pool of light Jose stands with hands in pockets. His face is turned away as he talks to two young men in the doorway. He wears pale-blue Levis and the light-brown shirt he bought for me on Lanzarote. The blue pool, the sand-coloured shirt, the sky above: the sight makes me stop. I rub my eyes. The shirt was too big for me, but fit Jose perfectly; I joked that he knew that all along, that he really bought the present for himself. "Myself? Yourself?" he asked. "What's the difference?" I have forgotten how tall he is, how wide his shoulders are. His light chestnut hair is still short, but longer than when I last saw him at the end of October. Four months ago?

*You've been away too long.*

*Go back.*

His face turns in my direction. His eyes glide over me without a sign of recognition, then return to the two men he is talking to. Jose nods at something they say; he is smiling, I know. The two men turn into Ras; three bars of loud music fall through the opened door before it closes and the street becomes quiet again.

After a moment, Jose turns his face back to me and frowns, puzzled.

I am moving slowly up the narrow street. It is a poorly lit tunnel between the stone buildings pressing closely on either side. The path of pavement draws me forward, commands my attention, pulls me towards the sky at the other end. Jose still stands above me and to my left. As I continue to rise, he suddenly takes half a step in my direction, then stops with the same abruptness. His mouth opens as if he is about to speak. In the corner of my eye, six feet to my left, he freezes at the edge of the blue pool of light. I am near enough to see the pale brown shirt rising and falling with his breath. His mouth closes; his puzzled face clears. His eyes remain unblinking and steady and intent. Then I have moved beyond the figure beside the blue pool. That lies behind and below me now.

Something snaps inside me. A thin chain still rests against my neck and chest. My feet hurt in the shoes, at least one size too small, that were given to me in Layounne. They ache from walking barefoot across the sand. I am aware of every painful step I take. I notice how the thin layer of pavement beneath my feet gives way to expose the old cobblestones below. They fit together roughly, creating an uneven surface which glistens as though wet with rain. I caution myself not to stumble and lift my eyes to the sky that rises above Horteleza. The street seems to lead directly into this space which at its lower levels gleams with the city's light and then ascends into a black expanse, empty except for the new moon and several stars. Jose's face suddenly shines amid the planets. After a moment, it melts away.

Footsteps become audible behind me. The sound grows louder. I turn.

Sloping downward, the street appears empty. In the distance, three blocks away, the last light visible to me glows faintly blue. A smudge of light-brown sand floats upon the pool.

Once there was no such thing as being lost. Once, in a year perhaps, he would have appeared with shining eyes in my doorway. Would have turned, eagerly and agelessly, towards me in a Copenhagen bar five years after that. Walked by on the other side of a wide Vienna street, apparently still no older, another seven years later. Once.

Go back.

You've already found him.

Before me, the magic door opens in the sky.